THEY WERE THE GLAMOROUS SET, WITH ALL THE HIGH LIFE MONEY COULD BUY...

TRUDI GROVES: Born to privilege, she was a fiery beauty who turned heads and broke hearts. When she finally learned what real love was, she would risk her life to save it...

WINSLOW STEVENS: The impeccably dressed playboy was secretly building an empire based on crime and corruption. He was determined to have Trudi at his side, and once he'd set his sights he would stop at nothing...

PHILLIP GATES: The handsome, hard-working lawyer was willing to lose everything in the fight for the woman he loved. But his passion for Trudi was shadowed by the devastating tragedy of his family's past...

LINDA CARTER: Pretty and refined, she was afraid to stand up for the love she believed in. On a self-destructive course, she became a good-time girl—whose fun quickly spiraled out of control...

GARDNER GATES: Phillip's younger brother could win over anyone with his boyish good looks and charm. Tormented by the suffering of his family, he was recklessly bent on revenge...

HIGH SOCIETY

Books by Diane Cory

A Token of Jewels
High Society

Published by POCKET BOOKS

Most Pocket Books are available at special quantity discounts for bulk purchases for sales promotions, premiums or fund raising. Special books or book excerpts can also be created to fit specific needs.

For details write the office of the Vice President of Special Markets, Pocket Books, 1230 Avenue of the Americas, New York, New York 10020.

HIGH SOCIETY

DIANE CORY

POCKET BOOKS
New York London Toronto Sydney Tokyo Singapore

This book is a work of historical fiction. Names, characters, places and incidents relating to non-historical figures are either the product of the author's imagination or are used fictitiously. Any resemblance of such non-historical incidents, places or figures to actual events or locales or persons, living or dead, is entirely coincidental.

An *Original* Publication of POCKET BOOKS

POCKET BOOKS, a division of Simon & Schuster Inc.
1230 Avenue of the Americas, New York, NY 10020

Copyright © 1990 by Diane Cory Grunwaldt
Cover art copyright © 1990 Franco Accornero

All rights reserved, including the right to reproduce this book or portions thereof in any form whatsoever. For information address Pocket Books, 1230 Avenue of the Americas, New York, NY 10020

ISBN: 0-671-64366-5

First Pocket Books printing July 1990

10 9 8 7 6 5 4 3 2 1

POCKET and colophon are registered trademarks of Simon & Schuster Inc.

Printed in the U.S.A.

*Dedicated to
the Quincy High School Class of '57*

HIGH
SOCIETY

CHAPTER 1

The bass player leaned against the wood-paneled wall of the railroad car to steady himself as the train rocked along the track. This wasn't how he wanted to spend his day, playing music for white folks as they traveled to the opening game of the St. Louis Browns. He wanted to be home with his wife and children, for it was his baby girl's first birthday, May 21, 1927. But his jazz trio was a favorite of Mr. Winslow Stevens, who booked them for his private parties at least once a month and always paid them generously. And he needed the money. The family would celebrate tomorrow, maybe take a picnic down to the banks of the Mississippi, and he'd throw a baseball with his two boys.

He smiled, thinking about it, and his mood lifted. He, George Washington Gay, and his friends, Floyd and Ben, made good money playing for these parties on Mr. Stevens's private railroad car, which he had inherited a couple of years ago when his father died. They would be paid for the whole day even if they played only a few hours. They had left the Union Station terminal early this morning to travel north toward Hannibal and Quincy, picking up Mr. Stevens's friends along the way.

He glanced around the car, impressed with its beauty.

HIGH SOCIETY

The walls were paneled halfway up with what he guessed to be cherry-wood, for it glowed with a soft red color. The heavy mohair couches and chairs used during the winter months had been removed; now two dozen white wicker chairs lined both sides of the long car. The burgundy and pink and red colors of the flowered carpet looked even prettier in the daylight than they did at night. He'd like to bring Maude and his mammy to see the car sometime.

He knew that'd be all right with Mr. Stevens. He was a real nice man. Why, Mr. Stevens had said just this morning that he would see to it that George and the boys, including the porter and two bartenders, would get to spend the day at their favorite jazz club on River Street while the other folks were at the game. By the time they had delivered all the young people back to their hometowns, it would be a late night. But he always paid handsome. A real fine gentleman, that Mr. Stevens, real thoughtful. He signaled to the other two musicians to begin "When the Saints Come Marching In," always a popular song, and sure enough, the tempo of the party picked up.

George smiled, watching little Miss Trudi Groves start clapping her hands and kicking up her feet in time with the music. Mr. Stevens always escorted her to his parties, and she was always the center of fun, though she didn't seem to want much attention from Stevens. She was such a tiny thing, too skinny, Mammy would say. She looked so delicate with that pale skin and cap of white-blond curls and those great big blue eyes rimmed with double rows of long black lashes, but she packed a lot of energy into that tiny body. He thought she was the prettiest little thing he had ever seen, a lot like the princesses he'd pictured when his mammy told him fairy tales as he was growing up.

Today she had on one of those thin cotton blouses, what did Mammy call them? Voile? The blouse hung over her pleated skirt but was cinched around the middle by a thin red belt that matched her little red pointed shoes. Even in that full-cut blouse, she looked too skinny. George grinned as she grabbed a champagne glass in each hand and led a line of twenty dancers, all hootin' and hollerin' as they

HIGH SOCIETY

snaked through the crowd toward the other end of the car. Some revelers joined them, some were deep in their own conversations or tucked into a little nook for some light kissing, and some, like Phillip Gates, just stood back and watched.

Gates stood about two-thirds of the way down the car behind a stained-glass partition that separated two sections. Win Stevens had explained earlier that the smaller rear section had been his father's working portion, and that neither he, his mother, nor his sister had been permitted to set foot in that area while his father was on board. The design in the glass was colorful and intricate, really quite beautiful, one that Gates recognized as a copperfoil rendering of the Greek legend of Pegasus, the winged horse. Gates scoffed mentally, thinking of the poetic name of the railroad car, for old man Stevens had been anything but poetic. Ambitious, scheming, ruthless, but not poetic!

Gates's thoughts were interrupted by the advancing line of dancers prancing down the middle of the car. He had an easy view, for at six foot three, a height he sometimes found inconvenient, he could see over the heads of all the partyers. But at this moment he didn't want to look over anyone's head; he only wanted to look at Trudi Groves.

They had gone to Webster Grade School together but he had ignored her, for she was three years younger and big kids never paid attention to little kids. Then she had been sent away to Ferry Hall boarding school as a teenager, and he had lost track of her until this year. He stared at her now, trying to appear uninterested, hoping no one would notice his fascination with her ethereal, fragile beauty. She looked like a porcelain doll, too delicate to touch.

But her actions belied her appearance, for she danced by him singing exuberantly as she plowed through the crowd, not allowing her small body to be intimidated by any obstacles. When the music stopped she stopped, and the line broke up with the participants clapping and whooping. Trudi finished first one glass, then another, gulping champagne like a thirsty child given water. Plunking the empty glasses on the tray of a passing waiter, she headed toward Gates, planted her feet firmly only a foot in front of him, and grinned up at him.

"You're in the middle of a party, Phillip Gates. It's all right to laugh and be silly. Quit standing around like a wooden statue."

Gates smiled, attempting to appear casual. "I enjoy watching the action rather than being part of it."

"From what I hear, you're into a lot of action."

Gates raised his eyebrows quizzically. "I'm afraid to ask what you've heard."

"Only wonderful things. After working your way through Harvard Law School, you return to your hometown of St. Louis"—she lowered her voice dramatically in a comical effort to sound authoritative—"to establish yourself in one short year as a brilliant young star, outstanding in a field of crotchety old geezers . . ."

"Are you making fun of me?" Gates asked seriously.

"No, you fool! I'm flirting with you." She tilted her head and smiled at him, batting her eyelashes with ridiculous exaggeration until he was forced to smile. His full shock of sun-bleached brown hair fell over his thick black eyebrows, and self-consciously he pushed it back into place, ducking his face and combing his fingers over the top of his head in a play for time since he didn't know how to respond to this blatant attention. He stuffed his hands into his pockets and, crossing his legs, leaned back against the wall, studying Trudi out of the corners of his eyes while she stood grinning, staring directly at him.

Trudi gave him her most brilliant smile, deliberately attempting to beguile him, for his reserve was legendary. She had noticed him earlier, propped with a lazy grace against the wall, and her first thought had been of the reluctant majesty with which he held himself, as if he knew and was embarrassed by the fact that he was superior to lesser mortals. She easily dismissed that insight, for she hardly knew him and it was certainly unfair to judge him on his appearance.

She had heard that he never dated, that he worked constantly and came to only half of the parties he was invited to, so she figured it was her job, a duty almost, to help him unwind. Now, as she studied him, she thought it was quite possible that he was unsure of himself, even shy, and she found that endearing because it was so uncommon among this sophisticated crowd.

He could smell her, a faint clean smell of flowered soap with a hint of cinnamon, and he was tempted to bend toward her to sniff her hair, but he would have felt an utter fool. As if reading his thoughts, she stepped even closer—they were practically touching now—and reached up to his neck.

"And another thing, this necktie looks so formal. Do at least loosen it." She began to work at the knot, and he felt a curious rush of pleasure at her intimate gesture. The jazz combo had started a new song, the crowd continued its raucous laughter, but for Phillip Gates the sounds were like a distant echo, so attuned was he to Trudi Groves's closeness. He studied the curve of her lips, the direction of the curls at her temples, the thickness of her long black lashes, as her forehead puckered with the concentrated effort of undoing his tie. He didn't help her. He wanted it to take as long as possible.

The train started around a long curve, jostling the revelers, who swayed and tripped against each other, whooping and laughing. Trudi stumbled, falling against Gates, her arms still upraised so that the length of her fell on him unsupported. Instantly he reached to steady her, not to help her stand but to keep her close. He held her, his arms about her waist, and looked steadily down at her, hoping she wasn't aware of his ploy, hoping she wouldn't move.

Trudi couldn't move. She was paralyzed by a strong surge of heat that immobilized her with surprise. She gasped, for she had never suspected that his touch could have such a powerful effect on her. She, the practiced flirt, the woman who was totally aware of her allure to men, felt an overwhelming flow of energy as her body pressed against Phillip Gates's. The irony of the situation didn't escape her. Here was a studious, reserved man, an innocent in the ways of seduction, who with his first touch had entranced her. His hands moved imperceptibly lower on her hips. Once again a wave of warmth spread through her, and she slumped against him. Their eyes never wavered and the unspoken message between them was so strong, so unmistakable, that Trudi blushed uncharacteristically. She was the first to look away, taking a deep breath and closing her eyes in an effort to break the spell he had cast over her.

She pushed away from him but stood close, her mouth open slightly as she studied his face, trying to find an explanation for the thunderbolt of excitement that had coursed through her, leaving her now feeling weak and defenseless. He stood passively, his face inscrutable, and Trudi was embarrassed by the color she felt in her cheeks. She knew he had felt the same thing, but his face was impossible to read, and she felt at a distinct disadvantage. To flirt now seemed grossly inappropriate, shoddy even, after the depth of her reaction to him. He had felt it too, she was certain, though it wasn't apparent. She found his calm control somewhat irritating, and she narrowed her eyes and tilted her head to study him. Refusing to speak, she clamped her mouth shut, biting her lower lip. Gates noticed the gesture, just as he noticed her every nuance of movement. He would have been amused had he known she was puzzled by him, though he should have guessed, for her face, usually so animated, was quiet and a small frown line showed between her brows.

"This seems to be an interesting conversation," Winslow Stevens said, stepping next to Trudi and putting his arm possessively around her shoulders. He looked at the two silent people, waiting for some comment to match his witticism, but neither one spoke to him or glanced at him or acknowledged his presence in any way. He stood quietly for a brief moment, as if not sure of what to say—unusual, since he was the quintessence of self-assurance.

The two men were a study in contrast: Phillip Gates tall and lanky and slightly unkempt, with hair that looked like it had needed a trim two weeks before and a slightly rumpled suit too formal for the occasion. And then Winslow Stevens, whose white duck trousers held a knife-edge crease even on this sweltering day, whose body was trim and fit, whose hair was always in place, who'd never got soiled even, one suspected, as a child.

"Are you looking forward to the game today?" Win smiled before answering his own question. "It ought to be a good one, but what I really want to do this summer is see the Babe play. The old Sultan of Swat ought to be at the peak of his form." He hugged Trudi's shoulders, attempting to instill his enthusiasm in her, but she remained unimpressed.

"I don't follow baseball closely," Phillip replied, "but I'll take your word that it will be a good game."

Trudi glanced from Gates's face to Stevens's, for she had heard the mocking edge in Phillip's voice. If Win had heard it, he did not acknowledge it. Funny, she thought, where did that sarcasm come from?

"Then why did you accept this invitation?" Stevens seemed genuinely surprised.

"I didn't say I don't enjoy baseball, just that I don't follow it closely." The edge was there again, unmistakable this time. "And I also came, of course, to enjoy the company of the other guests." Gates dipped his head and lifted his glass in a small salute to the rest of the party, which seemed sincere enough to mollify Stevens.

"One more glass of champagne before we arrive," Stevens urged, guiding Trudi into the crowd.

Out of the corners of his eyes, Gates watched them move away, not turning his head, not wanting to be seen watching. He was always cautious that people not know what he was thinking or feeling. That characteristic was one that had helped him become a successful trial attorney.

If they knew how he felt about them, they would be surprised, he thought. He scanned the crowd of bright young men and women, his expression enigmatic but his emotions distinct and strong. Most of the revelers were harmless and would remain so the rest of their lives, living on old family money earned a generation or two before. He scorned them as dilettantes, leading wasted, empty lives with no real substance. But there was one whom he watched closely, studying him surreptitiously, for someday he would destroy him, making sure that the sins of the father were visited on the son. He took a sip of his drink, enjoying the cool, wet taste in his mouth.

The train was slowing noticeably as it approached St. Louis and the piano player struck the beginning chords of "Take Me Out to the Ballgame." Immediately the partygoers, an excellent blend of Win's college friends living along a hundred-mile line outside of the city, began a rousing rendition, singing with great gusto, and Phillip Gates smiled in spite of himself. While he didn't respect many of them, he knew and liked most of them, empty-headed and shallow though they were, and he enjoyed watching them have fun as they bellowed out the lyrics, waving their drinks in the air, calling out crude insults about the team the Browns were to meet that day.

It was only a few minutes now before they entered the city, so he turned to look out the window for one last glimpse of the Mississippi before the cityscape hid it from view. It was low, flat, and brown, wider than a boy's dream, more powerful and beautiful than any song written about it. His favorite view was from high up on the bluffs of Riverview Park, where he would sit on the edge of the low stone wall scanning a twenty-mile stretch of the river bordered with lush trees, thick and full and bountiful, a befittingly rich ribbon of trim for its majestic waters. He loved the river, and had since he was a boy, skipping stones along the surface of a quiet bay, or fishing from the banks with his younger brother. As an adult, he was in awe of its dignified power. He could stand for hours and watch the flow, the only sign of its menacing potential the occasional swirling whirlpool that would briefly surface and disappear, reminding lesser living things not to underestimate its destructive force.

CHAPTER 2

Five hours later, Trudi Groves was appalled by the lassitude of her friends. They sat sprawled and lazy as lizards around the perimeter of the railroad car, sated by a day of hot sun, rich food, and plentiful drink. Disdaining the humble food available at the ballpark, Winslow Stevens had transported individual box lunches, accompanied by iced lemonade and chilled Riesling, to be served to his guests during the fifth inning.

Grimmer, the family butler, had ignored the jeers from the stands and served the food and drink with the same imperturbable nonchalance with which he handled any other responsibility, and well he might act proud since the lunch was a work of art. Opening the lid, Trudi found a baked breast of chicken garnished with a small tomato rose centered on a bed of green romaine and surrounded by fresh fruit in a mosaic of bright colors. Tiny cucumber sandwiches framed the design, which Trudi hesitated to spoil, but spoil it she did, eating every bite and rummaging through Win's box for leftovers.

Now, as they headed back upriver, the day had become muted, with people talking softly or cuddling comfortably while the pianist softly played "Girl of My Dreams." She didn't need to look for him because she knew where Phillip

HIGH SOCIETY

Gates was, seated in the last chair on the right with two young stockbrokers, associates of Win's, seated at his feet. They were talking to him, but he didn't appear to be listening as he gazed out at the river. Only occasionally did he glance in their direction or nod to indicate that he heard what they were saying. Trudi was watching the scene when he looked from the river directly at her as if he knew her eyes had been on him, and he continued to stare in his disconcerting, confrontational way.

Trudi was hardly aware of Stevens at her side until a waiter carrying a tray full of brimming champagne glasses stopped next to them, grinning broadly and alight with joy.

"Mr. Stevens, sir. The wireless just announced the news. Charles Lindbergh made it! He landed safely outside Paris about an hour ago!"

"Hallelujah!" Trudi cried, clapping her hands for attention. "Hey, everybody! Grab a drink." The waiters bustled through the car hurriedly passing out champagne to the questioning guests.

Win raised one hand for silence and, with a glass held high in the other, shouted a toast. "Here's to Lindbergh! He made it safely to Paris in thirty-three and one-half hours!" The party came alive, with jumping bodies, whoops of glee, and glasses raised in salute to the new hero. Win and Trudi led the celebration, jostling from friend to friend, clinking glasses, hugging and laughing. Even Phillip Gates stood to congratulate the daring spirit of Lindbergh, grinning as the three clinked glasses.

"Here's to Lucky Lindy!" Win shouted above the din of the crowd. "Can you imagine the courage of the man? Flying across an ocean! Alone! Hell of a feat."

"An article in the St. Louis paper said yesterday that he's been forced to bail out on four previous occasions," Trudi added. "He really was lucky this time."

"It wasn't luck," Gates announced unequivocally. "He was absolutely, thoroughly prepared." He spoke with a quiet certitude. "He had the best machine available, the skill, the knowledge, and the determination to achieve his goal. I don't call that luck, I call that smart." He spoke in a voice that brooked no argument.

Trudi felt like a child who had just been chastised by a teacher. She set her jaw and turned her back, ignoring the continuing conversation of the two men. More than once during the next ten minutes she shot Gates a dirty look as she moved through the crowd.

The third time, he caught her look, and slowly, almost in apology, raised his glass in a slight salute. She blinked but held his gaze until the train jerked, beginning to slow as it approached Hannibal. That meant it was only fifty minutes before they reached home, and she didn't want to go home. The last place she wanted to be was home.

"Win, stop the train!" She grabbed at his sleeve. "Let's go to the caves. I want to see Becky and Tom's cave!" Win didn't seem surprised by her impetuous request, but it took him a moment to answer.

"I think it might be difficult to get to them at this time of day," he explained patiently. "We may not be able to find a guide."

"Then we'll go alone! If Lindbergh can fly over an ocean, we can go down a hole in the ground. Call your driver in Hannibal and tell him to meet us at the depot. Or we could hike—it can't be more than a mile over to the bluffs. Or have the congressman pick us up. You said he was a close friend," Trudi persisted.

"Give me a minute," he replied before disappearing to the front of the train. Trudi turned quickly and almost ran to the end of the car, yanking open the heavy steel door to step onto the observation deck. The wind hit her body, washing the tension away as she grabbed the railing and leaned over, staring down at the tracks rushing beneath her feet.

Not home, she thought, I just don't want to go home. The huge house seemed empty since Jessica had been gone. I miss Jessie so much. Why did they have to send her away? She turned around to let the wind hit her face, hoping it would take the hurt with it. The scene at home a few months before had been cruel and so senseless. Beautiful young Jessica, at eighteen so much stronger than Trudi'd believed she could be. Trudi hadn't realized how much she loved her little sister until that night . . . and in the three months Jessie had been gone, she had missed her terribly. She remembered the scene vividly, Jessie, with the wide innocent eyes and sweet soul, had had the courage to stand up to her father and admit that she was three months pregnant and intended to marry Alex Badamo. Father had turned red and jumped up from the dinner table. Mother had turned white and slumped in her chair, her correct posture forgotten only in this moment of extreme crisis.

"How could you do this to me?" Madeleine Groves had whimpered.

"Now, Mother. Now, Mother," Father had tried to comfort his wife unsuccessfully before turning to attack his daughter. "And you, young lady, sit there calmly as if nothing is wrong, telling us how you're going to ruin your life!"

"Nothing is wrong, Father. I'm merely pregnant and want to get married."

"The second part is supposed to come before the first, as if you didn't know," he answered sarcastically. "You're an eighteen-year-old child! It's all that boy's fault. He forced you. I'll kill him!"

"No, Father, he didn't. I took part in this willingly. I love him and he loves me." Some of her calm was fading, for at this point Jessie's hands were clasped together in her lap and she twisted them tightly. "We can marry with your permission this week, just a quiet little ceremony. Alex has a good job at the limestone quarry. He wants to be a foreman in one year." She finished with a proud little lift of her head.

"You young fool. I pay more for one of your dresses at Famous-Barr than he earns in a week! What kind of life would that be?"

Jessica looked at him helplessly, knowing that nothing she could say would make him understand that money was not important, that being with Alex was the only thing that mattered.

"Barner, his mother does the ironing for Clare McKenzie. His father works at the limestone quarry. What would people think?" Madeleine moaned.

"He's Catholic! He's Italian!" Her father threw up his arms, glaring at his daughter as if expecting a reply, but she sat wordlessly staring at her hands.

"This all happened because we let her talk us into allowing her to go to the public high school," her mother began to wail again. "I knew we should have insisted she go to Ferry Hall," she cried, wiping at her eyes with a lace handkerchief.

Trudi exchanged quick glances with her brother, Fulton. Neither could believe they were witnessing this scene, nor could they believe their mother's implication that Jessica would have been more protected at the private prep school. They both well knew that more booze, smokes, and sex could be found there than they had ever seen in public schools, mainly because the students at the private schools had so much more money at their disposal and so little close supervision.

"Mother"—Jessica swallowed and spoke in a low voice she was fighting to control—"I have known Alex since we went to Webster Grade School together. I have loved him since I was twelve years old. He is a good, fine, generous person, and I feel honored that he loves me. Nothing you could have done would have prevented this. You are not at fault." Instead of soothing her mother, Jessica's thoughtful words only sent her into another swoon.

"Barner, talk some sense into this child's head!"

"She's not a child, Mother," Fulton bravely interjected. "She's as old as you were when you married Father."

Their father swung an arm around to point at his son threateningly. "You do not speak to your mother disrespectfully, young man. Just keep quiet!"

Fulton shrugged and looked at Jessie as if to say, "I tried."

"Both of you leave the room." Groves swung his arm again, indicating Trudi, Fulton, and the exit all in one gesture. They rose and left with no argument, but not before Trudi gave Jessica a quick hard hug and was rewarded with a weak smile. If she and her brother had only dared, they would have eavesdropped at the door. Maybe then they would have had a warning of what was to happen and might have had the courage to stand up and protest.

None of it mattered now. When Trudi got up the next morning Jessica was gone, and her parents would say only that she was on an extended trip and then refused to allow her name to be spoken. Trudi thought of her sister every day at the most unlikely times. Where was she? Was she healthy? Was she lonely?

She turned at the sound of the train's metal door clanging open, expecting Win, but Phillip Gates stepped out, casually pulling the door closed before leaning against the rail without a word. He didn't say anything to Trudi, didn't even look at her. Instead, he quietly watched the passing scenery. She still smarted from his condescending comments about Lindbergh. She refused to speak first, but stared at him evenly.

Only when he raised a hand to wave at an elderly woman who was pulling sheets off a clothesline did she break her gaze. The woman's meager riverfront home was built on three-foot-high stilts, a puny protection against flooding, but she had a contented look on her face as she waved to the young man, then pulled at the pins that held the clothes on the sagging line. When Gates turned toward Trudi he still had not said a word, and the two stood silently regarding each other. He spoke only after giving his words serious consideration.

"You came out here for more than just a breath of fresh air."

"Why, sir," Trudi said, fluttering her eyelashes in an exaggerated imitation of a southern belle, "whatever makes you think a thing like that?"

A small cloud of disgust passed over Gates's face. "Why do you act like that?" he demanded.

"Like what?" Trudi's eyes opened in mock surprise as she continued her little charade. She wasn't about to let him know what had been on her mind, and he wasn't going to intimidate her with his scowling seriousness. When the door slid open, she was relieved to hear Win announce the next stop as Hannibal. He grinned and gave her a thumbs-up sign.

"It's all set up, but it looks like we have no other takers. It is a crazy idea, you know." He slammed the door shut without becoming aware of Phillip's presence. She smiled smugly.

"I asked him to get us into the caves tonight." She cocked her head. "You want to come?"

"Where?"

"The caves along the bluffs of the river. Popularly known as Mark Twain's cave."

"No."

"Afraid?"

"Hardly."

"Oh, I don't mean you're physically afraid," Trudi hastened to explain. "I think you're afraid to try anything different." She smiled at him sweetly, pulled the door open, and disappeared inside.

CHAPTER 3

The setting sun was casting long shadows as the old man guided his horse into the back drive of the mansion, clucking soft instructions to the old nag. Not many people kept hats on their horses anymore, but Mario Badamo still did. He was sure Nellie wanted it. The only time she balked was when she didn't have the straw bowler sitting square between her ears, so if his old friend wanted her hat on she would have it on, even if the young whippersnappers made fun of her.

Mario grunted as he pushed himself off the seat and jumped to the ground. Well into his sixties, he was still a handsome man; taller than most Lombard Italians at five feet eleven inches, he looked more their height, for he was stooped from thirty-five years of work in the limestone quarries south of town. He was a proud man, though, proud that it had taken him only two years to save enough money to send for his widowed mother and younger brother. They had brought with them a beautiful young girl from a neighboring village close to Milan for him to marry, and he had never questioned his mother's choice, for Appolonia had been a good partner, working equally as hard as he had, bearing six fine children for him. Now they owned their own home and the two oldest children lived close by and were giving them fine grandchildren.

He had come to America in 1895 for there was no work in Milan for an ambitious twenty-eight-year-old. He was thirty-one before his first child was born, but that was the happiest day in those thirty-one years. His children were all grown now with good jobs; only the youngest, Alessandro, still lived at home. He sighed, thinking of Alessandro's broken heart. The boy never spoke of Jessica Groves and her sudden disappearance, but the old man knew that his son brooded about it. The old man thought of her, too, and if he thought of it too much he began to get angry. He was no fool. He had run into prejudice before, and he knew that the Groveses would not be happy to learn that his son and their daughter were keeping company. He knew they would try to stop the courtship, and they had done exactly that. In the beginning, when the girl was first gone, he had hated to see his son suffering, but he no longer had the energy for it. It did no good to be angry.

"Ice," he announced as he raised the tarp cover on the back of the wagon, enjoying the cloud of cool, wet vapors that hit his face. "Ice!"

"I heard you the first time, Mr. Badamo. You just have to give me time to get here. I don't move quite as fast as I used to." Viola Groves laughed as she pushed open the wide screen door.

"You don't fool me, Mrs. Groves, ma'am." Mario touched his hat in greeting as he scoffed. "It's going to take more than a few extra years to slow you down."

The two had been friends for more than ten years, ever since Viola's son had bought the big house and moved her into the city from the family farm after her husband had died. She hadn't wanted to relocate. She had been perfectly content in the little southern Illinois community, but Barner Groves had insisted. She wasn't dumb. She knew her son was very impressed with his position as a wealthy community leader, and didn't want the embarrassment of a widowed mother living on an impoverished farm. Since her son had made all that money twenty years ago, he seemed to think he had all the right answers on how everyone should run their lives. How had she raised such a pompous ass?

"Give me the biggest piece you've got." She pointed to a huge square block of clear ice. "If this spring is any measure, we're in for a scorcher summer." Mario raised the tongs, clamped them on the block's sides, and swung the load over his back in one graceful move. Viola held the door open as he walked through to raise the top of the icebox and drop it in.

"Sure was something about that Lindbergh boy flying across the ocean alone, wasn't it?" she asked as the door banged shut. "The radio says a hundred thousand people greeted him in Paris. Can you just imagine?"

The man shook his head in amazement. "Looks like we got ourselves a new hero." He stood awkwardly for a moment. " 'Scuse me for being late today." He took his hat off and twisted it between his huge, hardened hands. "My wife has not been feeling well. I had extra jobs around house before I start deliveries."

"I'm sorry to hear that." Viola gestured to the kitchen chair. "Is there anything I can do to help? Sit down and have some food." She bustled around the huge room gathering a cool glass of ice tea, cutting thick slabs of homemade bread and spreading them with butter and leaf lettuce, which she set in front of the perspiring man.

He enjoyed this little ritual of rest and talk three times a week. Viola Groves was the only one of the owners of the fancy houses around the north side of Forest Park who ever invited him into her home.

His little house was modest, of course, not comparing to this huge one. The only parts of Mrs. Groves's house he had seen were the first and second kitchens, but those alone were enough to impress him mightily for they had twice the floor space of his entire house. Mrs. Groves said she rattled around the big old place, and the only time she enjoyed it was when her three grandchildren came to visit. In this kitchen alone there were three sinks, and walls of cupboards with glass in them, and a little room called the butler's pantry. Not that she had a butler. Mrs. Groves had a housekeeper and a handyman, both old friends she'd brought with her from the little farm community of Hull. They all seemed to need each other, even though there was a lot of bickering among them. Mario smiled. Hearing them argue was as good as being in the middle of an Italian family's argument.

She pulled out a chair and sat across the table from him. "Now, tell me about your wife. How is she sick? Where? For how long?" She leaned her chin on her fist, ready to listen.

"She's not feeling good two, tree weeks now." His face twisted as he thought about it. "She says she hurts all inside here." He rubbed his lower abdomen. "She's not got a fever, but she looks pale. I wanted to take her to doctor, but she not want to move that much." He rubbed his face with his hand and stared at the floor. "She moans at night when she thinks I am asleep."

Viola sat quietly listening, her concern clearly showing on her face. "Tell me where you live, Mr. Badamo. I can come over and help in some way."

"No, no, no." He held up a hand in protest. "My two daughters come and clean, and Alessandro is good cook. We do just fine."

At the mention of the boy's name, they both blanched. Neither had ever spoken of the heartbreak they felt over the situation of his son and her granddaughter. She thought of the boy and her granddaughter and the baby every day. She wanted that baby, and more important, they wanted that baby! She didn't know if she could ever forgive her son for the cruel, insensitive way he'd handled the situation. That man had them over a barrel as long as no one knew where the girl was. She licked her lips and made a decision.

"Mr. Badamo, I want you to know that I think Alessandro is a good boy. I think about him often."

The man harrumphed. "I got to go now. Three more deliveries to go tonight."

She followed him to the door and waved good-bye, then bustled back through the kitchen into the narrow, dark front hall. Picking up the earpiece, she cranked hard at the handle of the phone and announced, "Edith, get me Dr. Barber's office right away, please."

After she finished worrying about Jessica and Mrs. Badamo, Viola Groves stewed about her two other grandchildren, Fulton and Trudi. Both partying their lives away, neither one knowing what was coming next, and not seeming to care. She stepped up onto the seat of a kitchen chair, took down a strip of used flypaper, put up a fresh one, and harrumphed aloud to herself: "Now, if the family was still back on the farm, the work would be so plentiful there'd be no time for silliness, just good hard work!"

CHAPTER 4

"Drop us off at the end of the arcade, Ingram. I want to walk to the house." Madeleine Groves spoke without consulting her husband, but he seemed oblivious to the nuance. As the car turned into the long drive of the estate and slowed at the far end of the brick-paved colonnade, he got out and turned to assist his wife. Barner Groves was a high-powered executive, community leader, and demanding father—a man always in command, except in the relationship with his wife. It was a charade he played successfully everywhere but with Madeleine, with whom there was no mistake about who was master.

Madeleine stepped into the early evening air and breathed deeply of the fragrance of the trellised arcade, enjoying the brittle euphoria of knowing she had handled herself well at the country club tea dance, fending off prying questions about Jessica's whereabouts with evasive graciousness, using the feat of the young St. Louis flyer to deflect people's curiosity about her own family. She couldn't imagine what all the clamoring celebration was about, since the flight would have so little significance a week from now. She pulled off her wrist-length gloves and tucked them into her small French tapestry bag before moving slowly down the covered walkway, enjoying the movement of her chiffon dress in the evening breeze.

She moved her slender body with the lithe grace of a dancer, holding her shoulders back and her head high. Her sharp features were handsome rather than pretty, as chiseled and distinctive as those of an Aztec princess. Her dark hair was pulled back severely into a chignon, a hairstyle she had worn for fifteen years, impervious to the current rage of short, soft fluff, which so irritated her. Another secret irritation was that none of her three children had inherited her tall, thin body, made to appear even flatter by the binder she wore over her breasts. All of them, even her son, were short and small-boned like their father's side of the family. At least she had been able to instill in them a sense of pride in the heritage her distinguished genealogy provided.

"Why is Gunther still working?" Barner asked, indicating the sturdy young gardener busy in the far corner of the yard. "It's getting rather late in the evening to do gardening."

"I'm sure I haven't the faintest idea," his wife answered with studied indifference.

"You certainly made a good choice when you hired him. He works as hard as all Germans."

"Don't be so stereotypical, Barner. I'm sure there are some lazy Germans. I told you before, I hired him because he speaks both French and German, so he will help me stay current in those languages." She glanced toward the man as he sliced away at the hedge with long, lethal scissors, his heavily muscled back visible through the thin cloth of his shirt. It had taken her weeks to admit to herself that the immigrant from the small village of Sulzburg near the German-French border had gotten the job because his blond physical beauty excited her more than any man had since the first year of her marriage.

Mysteriously, the chauffeur had beaten them to the house, and held the door open as they entered the dark side vestibule. Both nodded their dismissal and started up the steps toward their separate bedrooms. When they'd had the house designed fifteen years before, they had included matching bedrooms joined by twin walk-through baths. When Madeleine realized St. Louisans were amazed by this plan, she'd secretly sneered at their provincialism, for the plan was quite common in Europe. The massive house of imposing Romanesque style, with six turrets and impressive copper trim, was as grand as or grander than any home in the Midwest, and her smile broadened when she thought of the envy of her friends each time they entered. Seeing her secretive smile, Barner took a chance.

At the head of the stairs, he turned to face his wife and almost pleaded. "Let's call today. I do wonder about her health, you know. It's Saturday and the ranch hands will all be in town. She'll be lonely."

"No," she answered resignedly, as if refusing a small child a piece of candy. "She has everything she needs, including a doctor's care. If we called, the operator would know we were placing the call to Colorado and the secret would be out in two days. The Griffiths would let us know if anything was wrong." She patted his hand as if to soften the refusal. He half-opened his mouth to argue, but thought better of it. She had conveniently forgotten that the instructions were very explicit: no calls for any reason until it was all over, then a letter was to be sent stating the details of Jessica's arrival in St. Louis. He nodded and turned toward his room.

Still feeling intense self-satisfaction with her performance at the club, Madeleine turned to her husband and announced, "You may sleep with me tonight." Had she been more sensitive, she might have read the moment's apprehension on his face, but she only heard his reply.

"After my shower at nine, then." He pecked her on the cheek, and they parted company.

He closed his bedroom door and leaned against it, his hands clammy. His wife was a beautiful woman, looking especially bewitching tonight in the finely pleated rose-colored dress with the silk flower at the shoulder. He wanted to please her, but it was becoming increasingly difficult as he aged.

A noise in the hall distracted him and he darted his head out, breathing an audible sigh when he saw Hattie on her hands and knees scrubbing the carpet at the far end of the hall. She ducked her head in an effort to hide, but he motioned for her to come to him. She rose reluctantly, wiping her hands on her apron. She walked silently toward him with her head lowered.

"Why are you here at this hour?"

She swallowed hard before answering. "I didn't have time to finish this chore. I wanted to get it done before laundry time on Monday." She stammered her words, and they didn't sound convincing even to herself. She couldn't tell the truth. Her little girl was sick again, and as soon as she'd seen the Groveses leave for the tea dance, she ran home, ran the whole way from Fourteenth and Maine to Sixth and Spring to check on her. She ran back, too, and was just finishing when she heard them return. Only five more minutes and she could have escaped this scrutiny. Hattie thanked the dear Lord she herself was healthy, because the doctor bills for little April Ray were all she could manage over the last eight years. If Mr. Groves saw the lie in her eyes he didn't mention it, only beckoned for her to follow him into his room. She hesitated and said a silent prayer: O, sweet Jesus, help me.

He didn't say a word after he closed and locked the door, merely stepped in front of her and lifted her heavy breasts with his fingertips, then made a small waving motion, which was her signal to undress. She began unbuttoning her uniform as he stood watching. She folded it neatly and stood in front of him naked. He breathed heavily as he looked at her body, full and voluptuous, with heavy breasts and thick thighs. Her skin was a dark, luscious cocoa-brown, only her palms and nipples a faint pink.

He walked away without touching her and disappeared into the bathroom. She heard the faucet in the tub turned on full force and left to run until he came back and beckoned her into the tiled room. Steam was already filling the air as he began to undress and motioned her to stand in the tub. When they were facing each other, he turned on the shower and began to soap her body with sweet bubbles that were satin on her skin.

She didn't look at his white body kneeling in front of her; she squeezed her eyes shut and pressed her head and hands hard against the wet wall behind her. She tried to concentrate on the money and her little girl, anything but what he was doing to her. Drops of sweat that had nothing to do with the heat formed on her upper lip. She didn't want to respond, but since Clarence had left town two years before she'd had no man to service her and her will was weak.

He knew by now just what made her body move, and he started immediately rolling her nipples between thumb and forefinger before putting one in his mouth, pulling hard, flicking its tip with his tongue. Both of his hands were free to rub her haunches, pulling her hips toward him. He stroked the insides of her thighs, and finally pushed her legs apart. As his tongue traveled down the front of her body, her knees buckled and she protested. But it was too late. When she was finished, he looked at her triumphantly, and stepped out of the tub. Pulling his robe on over his wet body, he left immediately for his wife's boudoir.

Madeleine Groves lay on her bed staring at the ceiling, her arms spread wide across the pillows, her legs together, crossed at the ankles. The first time her husband had seen her thus, positioned in the supplicating pose of a martyr on the cross, he had been startled into inactivity. But this evening he didn't hesitate. He flung his robe aside and crawled on hands and knees to hover above her. She turned her face away from his kiss and spread her legs with a deep sigh as he laid his full weight on her and started pumping his body into hers. Her eyes never closed, her expression never changed. They spoke no words. In less than two minutes, the encounter was complete. Groves broke into a profuse sweat, raised his body from hers, and carefully pulled the skirt of her silk gown down to cover her legs. "Good night, dear," he murmured before grabbing his robe and returning to his own room.

Madeleine Groves reached for the damp towel folded

neatly on a silver tray beside her bed and washed herself. Then she rose and glided to the window to stand looking out over the rear gardens, lovely in the late evening twilight. When the yardman glanced up, she slowly pulled her gown over her head to stand naked in his view. He showed no surprise at the sight of her slender body framed by the lace curtains. His eyes never leaving hers, he dropped the trowel, brushed dirt from his hands, and sauntered across the grass toward the house. He took hold of the rose trellis and began to climb to the second floor, confident it would hold his weight. He had climbed it before.

CHAPTER 5

"I didn't remember the cave being this cold." Trudi shivered and rubbed her arms. She trailed both Winslow Stevens and Phillip Gates, who braced themselves with their hands on the clammy walls as they descended into the huge cave inside the bluffs of the Mississippi. As the small group progressed into the depths of the cavern, the natural light faded, and they were led only by the torch held high over the head of their young guide.

Flickering firelight cast kaleidoscope patterns on the walls, which were already glistening with water seeping patiently through the thick layers of clay. Delicate earth-toned rainbows of beige, yellow, gray, rust, and red streaks colored the sides of the sloping shaft as the explorers slid down the wet, narrow path before stopping to tilt their heads back.

The guide indicated the ceiling as he held the torch high, and they listened attentively as he explained the formation of the vaulted ceiling, created by the groundwater dissolving the limestone inside the bluff. But it was when he lowered the light and they entered the next compartment that Trudi cooed with delight. Graceful folds of stone fell from the roof of the cave, forming undulating walls of draperies, a sight made even more beautiful by the musical sound of dripping water.

"See! I knew it would be worth it!" Trudi gloated. The two men glanced at each other, unconvinced. Stevens had expressed no surprise when Trudi announced that Gates was coming with them, seeming rather pleased to have an extra body along on the expedition. They watched as she bent to dip her hand in the symmetrical pool of white water. "I remember stalactites and stalagmites, huge round pillars, from when I saw the cave as a child. Can you take us to those?" She followed the guide eagerly as he picked his way gingerly through the narrow passages. "Do you remember the pathetic story of the local doctor who brought the dead body of his little girl deep into the cave, hoping that the cold would preserve her until he could bring her back to life?"

"You don't believe that, do you?" said Win, chuckling.

"That he did it or that he believed it might work?" she asked archly. "Faith can move mountains, or so I'm told." She winked at Win. "Have you been here before, Phillip?" she asked without turning around, picking her way carefully along the byzantine path.

"Yes," he answered slowly. "My father brought my brother and me here the summer before he died." He seemed to ponder a little before adding, "All I remember is that my brother ate a minnow he found in the creek outside and then threw up on the ride home. Mother just laughed when she saw the mess."

"Your mother must be a saint," Win observed.

"Close, very close," Phil answered.

"Here, this is the way. This is what I wanted to see." Trudi made a sharp right turn onto a primitive path.

"Don't go that way, miss," the guide called out sharply, swinging around. "That way ain't been roped off . . ." His voice trailed away as they heard a dull thud.

"Damn!" Trudi yelped. "I think I'm stuck."

The torch illuminated a passage six feet wide and twenty feet high with innumerable carrot-shaped stalactites hanging from ceiling to floor. At their bases, Trudi lay in an awkward position, one leg twisted, the foot hidden underneath two parallel stone tables. "My foot's in water, and it's cold." Her face contorted into a comical expression as the three bent to her aid from the top of a slight incline.

"Here, take my hand. I'll pull you up."

"No. Get her under the armpits."

"Shouldn't we see if the rocks will budge?"

"You're hurting my foot."

"Wait a minute, everyone." Phillip's voice rose authoritatively above the confusion. "What's the most pressing problem? Trudi, are you in pain?"

"Only from the cold water. My foot's turning numb." She rubbed her calf and looked up at them sheepishly.

"Can you move it at all?"

"I can wiggle my toes."

"I better go get help." The young guide's voice revealed panic.

"What will we do about light?" Win asked. "There's only one torch."

"We don't need light here. We won't be moving." Phillip stated the obvious. "One of you go get the owner of the cave. He might have had to handle a similar situation. And one of you bring a doctor back, and more torches."

"I don't need any help," Trudi protested, twisting her body, straining her leg in an effort to pull free. "I got myself into this," she grunted, turning onto her stomach, grimacing, and turning back again to lie on her back. "I can get myself out of it." She made another lesser pull, then lay back exhausted.

Gates motioned with his head for the other two to leave. Stevens and the guide scrambled away, leaving

Gates and Trudi in total darkness, an overwhelming black void that pulled at the eyes, creating a frightening sense of vertigo. For a full minute the only sounds were the slow steady drip of water and their own heavy breathing.

"Hold my hand," Trudi whispered.

"You're not in much of a position to be making demands," Phil countered.

"Please, hold my hand," she whispered.

Their first touch was tentative, searching, but once found he gripped her hand securely. Her hand was tiny and delicate, and he felt an unwilling urge to protect her as he rubbed it between his own.

"It's cold."

"I'm cold all over," she answered simply. "And embarrassed."

He held her hand and began to rub her arm brusquely. Her sigh was a heartfelt thanks. He reached for her shoulders and began to massage the muscles at the back of her neck. She responded by moving her body so it was more convenient to his touch.

"That feels wonderful, but I'm still embarrassed." His fingers slid up her neck and touched her hair. He was surprised at the silkiness. The absence of light heightened his other senses. Why else, he asked himself, was he so aware of the softness of her skin, the tautness of her body, the delicateness of her bones? He heard his own breath loud in his ears, and he pulled away.

"Don't stop," she pleaded. "Please stay close. I'm so cold." Her hands reached for him and pulled him close. He lay down beside her, pushing one of his arms underneath her, and pulled her close to the length of his body.

"It might help to get off the damp ground." The explanation sounded hollow, but she didn't protest, merely snuggled against him in an awkward position. Her head rested in the middle of his chest and he could feel her breath through the thin cotton of his shirt.

They lay in silence, their mutual warmth an unspoken succor.

"What's that?" Trudi's head jerked up at an uneven beating sound above them.

"Probably bats."

"I'm not afraid of bats," she answered, her head still rigid. Only when the sound died away did she rest her head against his chest again to resume their silence. The trickle of water flowing nearby was magnified by the quiet, the darkness so complete that Gates finally closed his eyes.

"My foot is numb. I can't feel it at all. If you twist or pull it, you could probably get it loose, and I wouldn't feel the pain." She made the announcement dispassionately, as if talking about a wooden doll.

"It might be better to wait until we have light to see what we're doing. Even if we do get it loose, we couldn't move in this darkness to find our way out."

"I can't wait." A small hint of panic heightened her voice. She let him think it was the cold and the pain that had panicked her. It was neither. She could not control her heart, her pulse that beat strong and loud against his chest. It was too revealing, exposing the weakness she felt when she was close to him, a weakness she was uncomfortable with, a weakness she did not want him to be aware of. "What a clumsy oaf I am," she said flippantly. "The only other time I was this clumsy was when I fell from my tree house. I hung upside down until my brother rescued me fifteen minutes later."

"A tree house?" Gates's interest was piqued. He smiled to himself as he imagined her as a scrawny little girl full of high spirits frisking about in a tree house. "Who built it? Your brother?"

"No, I did!" She sounded irritated by his error. "I was fascinated by Tarzan of the Apes and wanted to live as naturally as he did. So two years ago I gathered everything together and built it in the woods next to our cottage by the river."

Two years ago! He kept his silence but shook his head with annoyance. A grown woman filling her time with such childishness. She needed to channel her abundant energy into something more substantial. His thoughts were interrupted by her chatter.

"I seem to have a lot of accidents." She giggled as she reached down to massage her leg. "I feel like such a fool."

He sat up and slid his hand down her leg until he gripped her ankle. "You *are* a fool," he agreed. "It was a childish, impulsive whim of yours that led us to the cave, and a foolish, careless move to turn into this passage. You *should* be embarrassed."

"You coldhearted son-of-a-bitch!" She kicked at him, effectively loosening his grip on her. "I noticed you were childish enough to take my dare and come with us!"

When the rescue party arrived half an hour later, they found two silent people sitting ten feet apart, hunched up against the cold, two people who did not speak to each other the rest of the hour-long trip back to St. Louis.

> *JOURNAL ENTRY:*
> *What a prophetic man my father was! Everything is working out just the way he predicted seven years ago. I'll never forget the night he called me into the library and revealed his plans, the plans he had been making for a solid year. I was a senior in college, home for the Christmas holidays, and I learned more from him in that evening than I had in all my years of formal schooling. He had married late in life, and by the time I was twenty his voice was losing the timbre of a younger man's. His mind, however, was*

*as sharp as any thirty-year-old's. "Son,"
he said, "I worked hard for three years
for the passage of the Volsted Act. I was
immensely satisfied on January 16, 1919, when
the Eighteenth Amendment to the Constitution
was ratified. Now, in less than a month,
the manufacture, sale, and transportation of
liquor, wine, beer, and other intoxicating
substances will become illegal. Were you
convinced of my sincerity?"* I nodded, and
was nearly jolted out of my chair by the
force of his laughter. He laughed until
tears ran down his cheeks, and I offered
him my handkerchief to wipe them. I could
not imagine what was so funny, until he
explained.

*"Never in the history of our government
has an experiment been so doomed to failure."*
He shifted his weight and took a deep breath,
finally regaining his composure. *"America has
been a drinking nation since Colonial days,
and no Prohibition law is going to change
that. All it's going to do is add to drinking
the excitement of doing something illegal.
I supported the Volsted Act because I saw
in it a way to make money."* When I frowned,
he looked impatient but continued his explanation.
*"The last year, between the ratification and
the enactment of the Volsted, has been a
year of grace for me. It has allowed me
time for buying and converting real estate in
and around St. Louis. It has allowed me time
to develop an elaborate plan for buying and
marketing liquor, so now that the time is
almost here, I have a virtually foolproof way
of working around the law."*

I stared at him, stunned into silence. This
man, my father, was a pillar of the community,
and I had always believed him to have a

strict moral code. He talked to me for the next three hours, and when he finished, I realized he did indeed have a strict moral code, for he saw what he was doing as providing a basic human need. People were going to drink regardless of the law, so he was going into the service industry, providing to the people of the Midwest what the government was going to deny them.

Fortunately, I had five years of tutelage from him before he died. His plan has worked beautifully. What we started together, I am now continuing, and building upon. The only people who know of my secret operations are the ones who need to know—the senator, the mayor, the chief of police—and they are paid well to stay silent and cooperative. The Stevens family name is as prestigious and unblemished as always. When I marry Trudi Groves, the occasion will blend two outstanding families.

Trudi was, as always, entertaining tonight. She is witty, intelligent, and demonstrative, never hiding her emotions. She is as uncomplicated and fresh as a child, without false pride and without ostentation. It will be a challenge for me to make her understand all that I can do for her. She has only to raise a finger to command from me all of her material wants. But she is fresh and unspoiled, never demanding anything except constant excitement. Fortunately, her scrape tonight in the cave will leave no lasting injury.

I am so glad, journal, that I can record my innermost feelings with you, for there is no person I can talk to. Certainly talking to my sister Bonnie would be of no help, since she seems to have no deep thoughts, let alone deep emotions. Her total absorption in sports

HIGH SOCIETY

is a transparent effort to make up for the lack of any love life. Poor Bonnie. Never had a beau, never will have. "Bonnie," such a dreadfully inappropriate name for such a homely woman.

CHAPTER
=6=

The only things Trudi enjoyed about Sunday were singing the hymns in church and the tradition of dinner at Grams's house afterward. Finally ready to go, Madeleine Groves glided slowly down the staircase of her home's central hall, knowing that her husband, daughter, and son had been waiting for her a full five minutes. She wore a thin navy cashmere clutch coat, trimmed with white piping to match her cloche, and merely nodded to acknowledge the compliments she received from her adoring husband.

Trudi's low-waisted, long-sleeved dress was properly demure with its collar and cuffs of thick white scalloped lace. She pulled on short white kidskin gloves to placate her mother further. She had tied a wide white ribbon around her head, adding a perky bow above one ear for a touch of dash, but her mother said nothing about removing it, and Trudi breathed a sigh of relief that she didn't have to recurl her bob. Fulton's outfit was outlandish, as always, his tie much too bright and his striped slacks much too casual for church. Trudi grinned at him, knowing that his choice of clothing was one small way of rebelling against their parents' multitude of strictures; she wanted to lend him moral support with a friendly pinch.

"Fulton, your costume is out of place for church," his

mother commented in passing. "However, we don't have time for you to change now, so you shall just have to suffer the embarrassment of being inappropriately dressed."

"Yes, Mother. So sorry." He ducked his head to cover the giggle he and Trudi shared.

As the family stepped out into the portico, Madeleine Groves turned to her husband. "Dear, I thought we agreed that the Duesenberg was much too flashy to take to church. Please have Ingram bring the Chrysler around instead."

Trudi patted the heads of the two life-size stone lions that guarded the main steps to the Groves mansion. "For all the good they do," she murmured, chuckling. Their best purpose, as closely as she could tell, had been to serve as steeds when she and Jessie and Fulton had played cowboys and Indians as children.

"Don't dirty your gloves, dear," her mother murmured without turning around.

"The woman has eyes in the back of her head," Fulton whispered.

They trundled into the car and drove two blocks to Grandmother Groves's home, past the tall wrought-iron gates that formally set off their neighborhood from hers, past the slender evergreens in huge stone pots and carefully tended flower beds that bordered the stone walls surrounding the largest homes. The wraparound porch on the massive Queen Anne-style house dwarfed Grams as she stood waiting in the same flower-trimmed hat she had worn as long as Trudi could remember. Some things Grams would bend to, but she would not give up her favorite hat, in spite of a closet full of new hats that her daughter-in-law had bought for her. Nor would she give up her chickens.

When Barner insisted that she move into town, she had agreed on the condition that she be allowed to have a chicken coop. The three acres surrounding her house were lush with trees and bushes, which cleverly hid the coop housing twenty chickens. Grams and her grandchildren chuckled to think of what the original owner of the home, a prominent bank president, would think if he could see the chickens scratching in the corner of his yard.

Twelfth and Maine was "church corner," so traffic on Sunday mornings was dense. Episcopalians usually had their drivers drop them off. Methodists parked in the huge lot the church provided. Lutherans took the trolley, and Catholics walked, huge families in tow behind the parents. As Trudi's family settled into their usual pew halfway down the main aisle of the Methodist sanctuary, she ignored the whispered greetings and smiles that meant so much to Grams. She enjoyed the grandiose beauty of the sanctuary with its thick stone support columns, seventy-foot-high arched ceiling, intricately carved altar framed by stiff folds of red damask, and, most of all, the extraordinarily vital colors in the stained-glass windows crammed with biblical symbolism. She wasn't sure old John Wesley, with his severe outlook, would have enjoyed the vivid luxury, but she felt certain he would approve of the pews.

Picking up a palm-leaf fan, Trudi studied the words of comfort offered by Duker Brothers Funeral Home printed on the back. She peeked at her ankle, which was swollen and bruised but basically sound. Still smarting from the sharp words of Phillip Gates the night before, she pondered whether to pray for tolerance or to ask the devil to take him. His air of absolute confidence was so irritating that she was not in the correct mood of sweet patience necessary to absorb Christian teachings.

The processional began, the singing, led by the clear young sopranos of the Reverend McArthur's three daughters, Faith, Hope, and Charity, their white choir robes adding to their air of innocence and grace. She mused about their names. I would wager, Trudi thought, that Phillip Gates harbors none of the above in his despicable heart. She was bored by the monotonous ritual, and the sermon was almost over before Trudi snapped out of her reverie and paid attention.

"Alcohol undermines American industry, the home, the family, the teachings of Jesus, the will of God. Some rant and rave and call it Demon Rum," the reverend intoned, "but I won't go that far. That kind of preaching appeals to the emotions, emotions that can change with the mood of the day. Instead"—he raised a finger into the air and began ranting just as he had promised he would not—"I appeal to your reason, for it is only when you understand intellectually that alcohol is a detriment to a full, God-given life, that you can truly support prohibition. It is alcohol that deludes our young people." Fulton nudged Trudi and pulled back the lapel of his jacket to reveal his silver flask. She only shook her head and scowled at him while at the same time giving him a playful nudge. "Alcohol wastes the money of our working men." The reverend's voice gained power. "Alcohol destroys the homes of innocent women!" The woman in front of Trudi sniffed and dabbed at her eyes with a hankie. "Renew your pledge to avoid, to repudiate, to condemn the use of alcohol!"

The reverend's injunctions were couched in harsh words, but were probably true, Trudi thought. Alcohol, like most things man indulged in, could be consuming and controlling. She glanced at Fulton and pursed her lips, then chose not to think about booze. Bored by the repetition of the message, for she had heard it a hundred times before, Trudi began to fidget.

Three rows ahead of her on the opposite side of the congregation, she glimpsed Linda Carter and William Jefferson, shoulders touching, heads together, sitting as close as decency allowed. They were an incongruous couple, he so earthy and basic, she so intellectual and finely trained. She and Trudi had been friends since childhood, when Linda, an only child, had moved nearby after her father had bought the large corner drugstore, the place they loved to go as children for a frothy sundae, sitting proudly at the marble counter. Mr. Carter had worked hard and within two years he had prospered greatly, buying two more stores. Two years after that, he had died.

The jolt had been hard on Linda, but she was still quite young. It was harder still on her mother, who talked about her husband in reverent tones, his virtues magnified with each passing year since his death, while at the same time the nest egg he'd left dwindled alarmingly. "All I have left is my darling daughter," the widow would repeat. Now that darling daughter was defying her mother by dating Bill Jefferson. "So unsuitable, you know," Mrs. Carter had whispered to Trudi recently, her lips pursed. "No education to speak of. My husband, of course, was almost a doctor."

Trudi craned her neck to look at the couple again as they cuddled together on the church pew. They *were* an odd couple. They had met at a music camp and didn't know each other's friends, though Bill worked hard to fit into Linda's faster, headier crowd. Bill's father had been a policeman, a thin, jovial man who walked his beat with a constant smile. Bill had a technical education, had become an accountant, having withstood his father's pressure to follow the family tradition of serving in "the blues." It would be interesting to see if Linda could withstand her mother's negative attitude about her "unsuitable" friend.

What was it that drew people together in unsuitable matches? Trudi leaned forward to glance at her mother and father at the far end of the pew. She chewed her lip as she thought of Jessica and Alex. She thought of the floozies that Fulton got entangled with. She thought of her own mingled attraction and dislike for Phillip Gates. How foolish men and women were for pairing off as they did. But who was to judge, to know, to try to look into someone's future happiness? Not me, she decided. Maybe Linda and Bill would stay together. She nudged the subject out of her mind as the congregation began a sweet chorus of "Blest Be the Tie That Binds."

Her suspicions were confirmed after church when, as the departing congregation milled around in the bright sunlight, Linda pushed through, hand extended, face radiant with joy, the pleats around the bottom edge of her skirt jouncing in response to her happiness.

"Trudi, look, look, look!" Linda held out her left hand to proudly display a simple silver band topped by a tiny diamond. "We're engaged . . . since last night at ten o'clock! Mother doesn't even know yet, since she was still sleeping this morning."

"Oh, Linda, I'm so happy for you!" Trudi hugged her friend before turning to Bill. "Congratulations!" Bill grinned broadly, shaking hands first with Trudi, then with Fulton.

"She's my Sheba, and—"

"He's my sheik," Linda finished for him, almost jumping with glee. "Gotta run," she added. "I want to tell my auntie."

Trudi watched as they picked their way across the street to the crowd of Lutherans exiting their church, wondering if they had chosen their navy blue outfits to look like identical twins. Her eyes caught Phillip Gates, who was looking straight at her while guiding an older woman gently through the mingling crowd. Neither smiled or nodded; they stood staring at each other, unmoving in the midst of movement. She could pick him out in a crowd, not merely because of his height but because of the unmistakable magnetism he had for her.

Trudi's back straightened and she deliberately looked away.

"There's Winslow, waving at you." Fulton nudged her and pointed toward the Episcopalian church, its ivy-covered walls making it appear older, more substantial than its neighbors. Trudi waved, just a tiny wave, to both Win and his sister, Bonnie, before they entered their waiting Phaeton limousine. She didn't notice Win leaning forward to continue looking at her as the car pulled into traffic.

Behind Trudi and Fulton, Grams silently smiled at Mr. Badamo as he exited the massive Catholic cathedral across the street, but he quickly ducked his head and didn't wave back. Grams knew why. Immediately behind him was one of his daughters with her four small children, followed by Alex, a dark, handsome, brooding boy who seemed not to have gathered any joy from the mass that had just finished.

Grams stared, watching the family walk through the crowd. Alex bent to pick up a curly-haired little girl of about three, who immediately threw her arms around his neck and kissed him, getting a faint smile in return. Then Alex reached for the hand of a little boy who grabbed it willingly, giving his uncle a sunshine smile. The family grew together in a tight clique before disappearing around a corner of the tall cathedral. Grams sighed, then straightened her hat and hustled her own family home.

Settled into the front parlor, the Groveses heard the usual announcement. "Dinner will be in one hour. Why don't you start a game of mah-jongg?" Grams said as she pulled out a lethal-looking hat pin and pressed the waves back into her marcelled hair.

"I'm really not in the mood," Madeleine Groves explained, picking up a copy of the *Saturday Evening Post*.

"I haven't read the Sunday paper yet, Mother." Barner settled into one of the few comfortable chairs in the room. In preparation for the family's arrival, Grams had opened the windows, and a soft spring breeze ruffled the long lace curtains, offering the only freshness in the heavy room filled with ornately carved wooden furniture and oversized, mohair-upholstered chairs. The glass dome over waxed flowers, the fringe on the shades, the dark horsehair covering on the sofa were the original adornments Grams had started her married life with and would no doubt end her earthly life with. To her, a front parlor was a "Sunday only" room, not meant for comfort.

"May I have a Coca-Cola, Grams?" Fulton asked, following Trudi and his grandmother down the long hall into the main kitchen. He sniffed the air, savoring the smell as Grams lit the gas oven and pushed the stuffed chicken in to roast. "Let me guess," he continued playfully. "We're having roast chicken with sage dressing, mashed potatoes with milk gravy, green beans with bacon bits, and baking soda biscuits."

"The very same thing you've had at my house since the beginning of time." Grams grinned. "But with a surprise."

She triumphantly held up a lemon meringue pie, its white crust flecked with brown peaks. "Now, Trudi, you pick up that doily you started crocheting a month ago and work on it while I finish the cooking. Then if you have any trouble with the stitches, I'm right here to help you out."

Fulton opened the bottle of cola, poured it into a glass, then surreptitiously added a slug of rum from his pocket flask before turning back to face the others. "Were you surprised by Linda and Bill's engagement?" he asked, taking a long swallow from the glass.

Trudi thought about her answer before speaking. "I'm not surprised as much as troubled. I don't think it will last."

"Because of Linda or because of Bill?"

"Neither one," Trudi replied. "Because of Linda's mother. She has much more grandiose plans for Linda than marriage to Bill Jefferson."

"You're probably right," Fulton agreed. "Mrs. Carter hasn't put all that time and effort into training Linda for the big time as a concert pianist to allow her to marry an accountant. I give it a week."

"Oh, give Linda a little credit. She'll be able to withstand her mother's pressure longer than that."

"I'll bet on it. Five smackeroos says it's closer to a week than a month."

"You've got it!"

Grams said nothing, pressing her lips together with an effort. She thought the young people were right, but she wished they were wrong. She knew the Carter woman and her daughter from church functions, and had always felt the youngster was leading the life her mother wanted her to lead rather than the one she would choose for herself. Lita Carter had a tendency to put on airs, still trying to live the high life that her husband had provided, but that wasn't sensible, since he had died too young and unexpectedly, leaving her unprepared both financially and emotionally to deal with reality.

Viola couldn't quite put her finger on what was wrong

between mother and daughter, but that child was totally different when her mother wasn't around. She'd come over here with Trudi and pound out ragtime jazz on the old upright, never the classical pieces her mother insisted on. She'd also paint her brows and lips with Trudi's goop, which the old widowed mother would never allow. The girls would listen to the Philco upstairs in the spare bedroom with the volume turned so high that even Viola downstairs would have to shout to be heard. No, that girl just wasn't the same when her mama wasn't around, and if the old biddy didn't give her daughter a little room to live, there was going to be hell to pay. Something was wrong there, and Viola suspected that the old woman's rules were a mite strict for this day and age, and if she didn't let up, Lita Carter would soon be without a daughter a'tal.

CHAPTER 7

"You're the only woman I know who doesn't care if her hair gets blown by the wind." Winslow Stevens grinned at Trudi as they sped down Chouteau in his Hispano-Suiza convertible. Her thin-strapped, filmy dress blew wildly around with the wind; her short blond curls swirled to match. "Do you like my new car? Had it special-ordered just to impress you." He patted the gleaming wooden dash.

"It's the cat's meow," Trudi replied. Win shot a quick glance at her. Something in her voice made him suspect the sincerity of her comment, but he let it drop rather than question her. "Before we hit the party, can we go across the bridge?" She gave him her best smile, then settled back, confident he would do as asked. They sped through the shopping district, turned onto Washington Avenue, and hit a bump with enough velocity to raise them both from their seats. Trudi whooped with glee and raised both hands high over her head as they raced down the steep bluff toward the Eads Bridge linking Missouri and Illinois. "This is as close to flying as I may get!" she yelled to Stevens against the wind. "Go faster," she urged. "Go as fast as Lindbergh!"

Then, as the car picked up speed, she quickly, almost frantically, raised the skirt of her dress, pulled out the tiny sterling flask secured under her ruffled garter, and gulped the burning vodka. She looked across to the checkerboard fields of Illinois bottomlands before squeezing her eyes shut as the tires touched the concrete surface of the bridge.

"Put your hands up!" she yelled to Win. "Put them high or the bridge will fall down on top of us." Stevens hesitated only a second before lifting his hands in the air. "I used to think," Trudi shouted, never taking her eyes from the road, "that if you moved going across the bridge, the whole car would go through the railing and plunge a hundred feet down into the river."

"The car is veering!" Win's grin faded as he grabbed at the steering wheel and pulled the auto back into line. "You win again."

Trudi threw her head back and laughed. "The bridge won't really fall, and we really can move. Right?" She relaxed as he swung the car around on the widest part of the levee and headed back across the bridge. She caught a glimpse of the old courthouse and the trumpeting elephants atop the wall of the Anheuser-Busch brewery, a sight that used to delight her as a child and one she barely registered now. "Look, you can see the lights of the party from here." She pointed north along the west shore past the riverfront wharves and the moored barges to a small bay where six yachts were moored together, snub-nosed motorboats tied like dinghies behind the largest ones. Strings of lights decorated each yacht, bobbing with the current, the water churned by passing barges lumbering against the flow of the river. As they neared the Boat Club, music and laughter floated through the evening air. Cars were parked in disarray, overflowing the lot, squeezed into every nook available.

"It's such a kick going to parties with the older crowd and watching them get bombed." Trudi glanced around as well over a hundred guests picked their way across gangplanks connecting the six luxurious ships. Pretty, expensive clothes, silks, satins, organzas, feather boas rustling in the summer breeze.

Not one low neckline, Trudi mused, but quite a few

flowing scarves wrapped around wrinkled necks. Sequins and bangles dripped from the more daring; ribbons and jewels wrapped around their foreheads held long bangs and short bobs in place. Most of the women under fifty had on short dresses with hemlines above the knee, but a few stalwarts wore skirts to midcalf, many of those dipping even lower in back.

How dreary, how dull, thought Trudi, adjusting the strap of her own revealing middy. It was the diaphanous material of the full skirt that had attracted her to the dress, but after she had tried it on and realized just how sensuous it was, with tiny straps on the shoulders and a tight swatch of material to tie across the hips, she had hesitated for a moment before having it boxed for home delivery. She would do her best to avoid the stuffiness which usually accompanies the conventional.

Moving from each ship to shore, back and forth like trails of busy worker ants, lines of waiters kept the cocktails flowing and the food tables replenished as the partyers slowly filed through the receiving line on the first yacht. Groups swelled and changed with a word here, a word there, light kisses exchanged by women who didn't know each other. Some of the faces were familiar, faces from Ladue, Clayton, and Brentwood, but some, flushed with expectancy, were new and different. Excited women glided among the sea of faces while confident men scrutinized their movements.

"Watch this," Trudi whispered behind her hand to Win. "I'm going to test a theory of mine." She smiled graciously at the first host couple. "Hello, Mrs. Dennis. I'm your husband's mistress."

"How nice of you to come this evening." The matron shook hands and passed Trudi on.

Trudi smiled brilliantly at the next couple. "Good evening, Mr. Wentura. I just helped Sacco and Vanzetti escape."

"Glad you could make it, young lady. Say hello to your parents." Trudi nodded sweetly before moving down the reception line.

"Hello, Mrs. Hulsen. I'm pregnant by your son."

"How delightful you can be with us. Won't you have a cocktail?" Trudi felt Win grab her elbow. He steered her to a quiet corner at the bow of the first cruiser.

Trying to keep his face stern, he implored, "What if one, just one, of those people had paid attention to what you were saying?"

She shrugged and grinned mischievously. "But they didn't, and I knew they wouldn't. Now, let's dance." She pulled him along a narrow plank as the notes of "Baby Face" carried clearly from shore to ship. One woman, forty and stringy-looking, her neck a vertical forest of cording, waved her hands like Frisco as she hopped and spun to the music. She was alone on the dance floor, oblivious to anyone else, bouncing to the tune as her drink sloshed over her hand, well on her way to getting roaring drunk. Aloof for a moment, the crowd finally made its decision and joined her, couples beginning to gyrate in time to the music, long strands of pearls bouncing, feathers bobbing, drinks spilling in a moving tableau of perpetual confusion. Everybody was laughing. Everybody was having fun. Everybody was drinking.

"Why don't the police raid this party? It's right out in the open." Trudi glanced around at the raucous crowd. "It couldn't be more obvious."

Win gave her a wry smile. "Look closer. The hosts are the most successful stockbrokers in town. Let's just say they're protected by their social status." She accepted what he said without comment, but surveyed the scene as they bounced to the music.

"What I'd like to know is, where are all the yachts that belong to the stockbrokers' clients?"

"Trudi. You're being irreverent again." He gave her a warning smile.

Across the water, three ships over, she saw Linda Carter dragging Bill Jefferson from group to group, introducing him to cliques of people he had never met before, and would never have met without Linda's entrée. He looked bewildered and uncomfortable in an ill-fitting suit, but wore a stiff smile and ready handshake. It will be tough for him and Linda to make the adjustment to the differences in their backgrounds, Trudi thought. Worse for Linda, Trudi would guess, for it would take sacrifice on her part, and that she wasn't used to. Win swung her around and she lost sight of them. But her lingering thoughts took the edge off her fun.

She stopped dancing abruptly, using the excuse that her ankle was sore. "Would you get me a sloe gin fizz, please?"

Used to her drastic changes, Win gave her hand a quick squeeze. "This may take a while because I know I'll get stopped a dozen times. Okay?" She nodded, lit a cigarette, and watched as he disappeared into the crowd. She turned to the ship's hatch and stepped down into the hold, climbing ladder-fashion backwards.

"Yipes!" Her ankle, the tender ankle, had been grasped from behind, and she twisted her shoulders to see Phillip Gates standing beneath her, holding her leg firmly.

"That's not a piece of meat, and it's not for sale, so please let go." She glared at him, but truth be told, she was glad to see him.

He was reluctant to release her, surprised that he had touched her at all, knowing the reaction he would have to the warmth of her skin. He didn't let go at her command; instead he inspected the flesh, turning her leg by the calf, forcing her whole body around to face him. She sat on the step, not knowing what to expect from the supremely self-confident man a foot away, but using the opportunity to look at him, to study the heavy eyebrows, the down-dipping corners of his eyes, the narrow bridge of his nose. "Is it still tender?" He didn't take his eyes from her leg.

"Not at all," she lied.

His eyes traveled slowly up her leg, to her hips, her bosom, her neck, and finally stopped at her mouth. He still hadn't met her eyes. She felt the familiar surge of heat, so pronounced it dried her mouth. She swallowed and licked her lips.

"Why aren't you out doing business with the cocktail bunch?" she asked, attempting to break the moment.

He finally lifted his eyes to hers, studying the double row of black lashes outlining the pale blue centers as if he had never seen them before. "That's not my style," he answered softly.

"Won't your date be worried about you?"

"My date"—he almost smiled—"knows me too well to worry about me." There seemed nothing else to say, so Trudi took a deep drag on her cigarette and blew the smoke out in a thin stream above her head.

"A bunch of us are going 'crocodiling' after dark tonight." She looked at him evenly, slowly blinking, daring him to react to her words. "You know"—she tilted her head—"sneaking into private pools and skinny-dipping."

"I have other plans. My date and I are going to watch the moonrise."

"How terribly exciting." She rolled her eyes sarcastically.

"Have you ever watched the moonshine on the river?" he asked equably. "It's a beautiful sight, one that too many take for granted." He hesitated before expanding on his thoughts, and spoke with his head turned away. "At night the Mississippi seems almost peaceful, its churning eddies hidden by the darkness. It is at night that I think about all the untold people who were lured to the heart of our country by these magnificent waters, willing to set themselves adrift in its currents, yearning to start a new life buoyed by its power." He looked into her eyes, his face close, his hands gripping the ladder at her sides. "If you haven't thought about its mysteries and its potential, then you don't know what you're missing."

Without preamble, he leaned forward and kissed her slowly, his lips alone touching hers, holding her, pulling at her with a mysterious force. She felt herself leaning into the swirl of his magnetism, yearning for the kiss not to stop. When he drew away, he continued to peer into her eyes, trying to read her reaction to his words and action. Then he lifted her under the arms, set her in the middle of the stateroom, took two steps, and was gone.

She took a deep breath, dizzy with the effect of his kiss, bewildered by his power to mesmerize her. She slumped onto the divan, made uncomfortable also by the close quarters inside the yacht. She fumbled for another cigarette to steady her nerves. After five minutes, she emerged, back into the gaiety of the party.

Ten feet away, through a tight cluster of laughing men, she saw Win Stevens talking head to head with Senator Kenilworth. Win's sleek silhouette, cool and polished, unruffled by the frantic pace of the party, reassured her and she struggled toward him.

"What topic are you two so deeply engrossed in?" she intruded. The two men stepped smoothly apart to include her.

"Nothing to worry your pretty little head about, Miss Groves," the senator replied, pulling his pipe from his mouth and giving her an election grin, the gleam of his large teeth matching the shine of his bald head.

"I don't worry about anything. You can tell me," Trudi countered. At that, the senator bent his head and knocked the bowl of his pipe clean, avoiding her eyes.

"Trudi," Win explained, "it was just man talk that you would find boring."

"Try me," she persisted, ignoring the senator as he harrumphed aloud and began to fiddle with his pipe more intently.

"Wasn't it exciting news about the Lindbergh boy," the senator put in, moving to another subject with a total lack of subtlety. "Lucky young man," he said, smacking his lips. "Yes, sir. Lucky young man."

"It wasn't luck," Trudi answered, her voice a little more strident than she'd intended. "He was exceptionally well trained and had the best machine available." She held her head haughtily in the air and kept it there while the senator stared at her in surprise.

Win cleared his throat. "Excuse us, Senator." He tugged on Trudi's arm. "I just spied a friend who helped us out of a tight fix last night. Really must say thanks." He pulled her across a gangplank, and extended his hand to grab Phillip Gates's in a hearty shake. "Thanks again for your help, Phil," Win almost shouted above the din of the cocktail crowd.

Phillip Gates was with the loveliest woman Trudi had ever seen. She had the regal bearing of royalty with none of the aloofness. Her smile was as warm and inviting as the autumn sun, her handshake firm and pleasing. She was tall, at least five ten, and her gray hair formed a soft crown of curls around her face, a face that looked remarkably like Phillip's, with a long narrow nose and high forehead. Her dress was topped by a wide cape collar of pristine white that softened the gray of the skirt. Trudi tried to hide the rush of relief she felt when she realized that his date for the evening was his mother.

"My son mentioned your accident." Her look was one of sincere concern. "I hope you are all right."

Trudi gave her a perky smile. "Every day, in every way, I'm getting better and better."

"Ahhh, a devotee of Emile Coué." Evangeline Gates's eyes lit up.

"Well . . ." Trudi hesitated, tilting her head, drawing away from Mrs. Gates's interpretation. "I like his positive outlook, but I think he puts a great deal of weight on the individual's attitude when actually so many other factors influence a person's life."

"How true," Evangeline Gates said, nodding, "like cigarette smoking." Startled, Trudi looked at her cigarette, ensconced in a pearl and ebony holder between her fingers, then back at Evangeline Gates. They smiled at each other, an unspoken message passing between the two. Without another word, Trudi stepped to the side of the ship and flipped the cigarette overboard, watching until it hit the surface of the water and swirled away. She stepped back to Evangeline Gates and gave her a brilliant smile. Both men were astonished by Trudi's unprotesting acquiescence, so out of character for such a thoroughly modern rebel. The women continued their conversation based on newfound intimacy until they were interrupted by the milling guests, and Trudi and Win moved away.

"I can understand why you are so attracted to her," Evangeline Gates whispered to her son, following the young woman with her eyes. "She's vivacious and intelligent. The energy that radiates from her is captivating."

"This time you're wrong, Mother," Phillip protested quietly, turning his back on the glamorous couple to look over the river. "I'm not attracted to her at all. I find her"—he searched for the right word—"excessive."

"My beloved son," she remarked, patting his arm, "I know you better than you think I do. You've always been intrigued by excess, even as a child. You would choose the liveliest puppy in the litter, you would pick the brightest flowers in the garden, you like the loudest jazz. Should I continue?" She looked at him smugly.

Phillip Gates said nothing as he polished off his drink in one gulp.

The midnight moon shone full on the clipped lawns and manicured shrubbery as two groups, women on one side, men on the other, changed into swimming suits behind the cover of a high hedge.

"We'll celebrate for Lindbergh by doing something daring," giggled Jill.

"You call this daring?" challenged Trudi. "We've been doing this since we were teenagers."

"Then maybe we should steal the Civil War cannon from the park and shoot it off," contributed Nancy. "We've talked about it for years and never done it."

"That might be dangerous," warned Linda.

Linda and Bill, Nancy and Chuck, Jill and Henry, all of the usual crowd, snaked their way along the perimeter of the Stilwell mansion, hiding in the shadows, then dashed across the open grass toward the swimming pool. Two by two, they slithered over the side, lowering themselves as noiselessly as possible into the water. Gasps and giggles filled the night air as Trudi brashly climbed the diving board and plunged headfirst into the water.

"Now you've done it. We'll get caught for sure. Let's vamoose!" Win pulled Trudi up and over the edge, and they ran helter-skelter back toward the car, hidden on a side street. Pulling away with a loud roar from the car's engine, the laughing crowd shivered and shouted with glee.

"How about Bonfoeys' pool next?"

"No. Spring Lake!"

"Too far away."

"Bonfoeys' it is."

"I need some hooch." The flask was passed through the crowded car for each to take a swig. Trudi was uncomfortable, pressed up against Win with Bill against her and Linda on his lap. Win grinned as Bill grabbed his fiancée by the neck and planted a long kiss on her mouth. When he stopped the car under the low-hanging branches of a willow, the other revelers piled out and scampered toward the private backyard pool, climbing over the wrought-iron railing surrounding the estate as easily as if it didn't exist. Win jerked on Trudi's hand, spinning her around to face him, and kissed her quickly, taking her by surprise. She pushed away, but he held her shoulders tight and kissed her again.

"Stop it, Win. You'll tear my suit." She adjusted the knit T-top, pulling it down snugly over her hips. She thought of her lie to Gates that the group would be skinny-dipping. Her feeble effort to shock him had not worked.

"You can always take your suit off." Win grinned, as if reading her mind.

"In your dreams!" she scoffed at him before running to catch up to the others, who were already splashing in the pool.

Without warning, a shout came from the house. Lights went on, flooding the yard with stark yellow glare. A manservant in a ridiculous knee-length nightshirt yelled from the back porch, "You young 'uns, git outta here!"

"Run, everyone!" Trudi shouted. The group split up, laughing and running in every direction, to meet back at the car five minutes later, gasping and grinning with excitement.

"Did you hear the watchdog barking at me?" Henry panted. "I thought sure he would get me by the seat of the pants."

"I hid in the bushes at the far end of the drive and the guy ran right past me waving a broom."

They all laughed uproariously as the car careened through the quiet streets. As Win dropped everyone off at their homes, they yelled their happy good-byes, vows of secrecy understood though unspoken. By the time the car passed between the tall brick gateposts of the drive to Trudi's house, she had pulled her dress over her damp suit and fluffed her hair dry.

Win shut off the motor and leaned toward Trudi. She waited for the inevitable good-bye kiss, wondering as his lips pressed hers why his touch was meaningless when the mere thought of being close to Phillip Gates brought a flush to her face. As his kiss grew more ardent, she put her hands on his chest and gently pushed.

"It's late, Win. It's been fun, but it's time to go in." Her words were a gentle dismissal, but he was not having any of it. Instead he leaned farther toward her, pulling her head to him and laying a hand on her breast. She pushed harder.

"See those two lions?" She gestured to the statues. "They aren't really stone. With a snap of my fingers they come alive and attack on command."

"Quit joking, Trudi." Win's voice was husky and serious as he slid his hand down her back and pulled her body close to his, throwing his left leg over her lap, pinning her in place.

"You quit joking." She threw his words back in his face. "Either you let go of me right now, or I scream my bloody head off." He slumped back on his side of the car and threw his hands up.

"All right. All right." He sighed, shaking his head in disgust, before climbing out to walk her to the door.

Five minutes later, Win Stevens's car was parked in the alley behind a tall, narrow brick building on Fourth Street. He trudged up the stairs to a second-floor bedroom. He opened the door without knocking, sure that the woman inside would be alone. They had an understanding. She could direct the activities of the other women in the house, but was to keep herself free for his visits.

Jackie Davis looked up from the careful inspection of her toenails. She wasn't particularly surprised to see him; he usually came after he'd had a date with the Groves girl. She shoved the foot that had been perched on the edge of the chair into the air for his approval.

"You like the new color of polish? The rusty red matches my hair." With one leg held up in the air, the satin gown she had on, skimpy to begin with, now covered even less of her skin. She was older than he by at least ten years, and her body was the round, voluptuous body of a woman in her thirties, but it was still attractive and she knew how to use it to create maximum pleasure. He grabbed her foot and held it high with one hand, running the other hand along the inside of the leg until it could go no farther. He bent his face close to hers. They stared at each other, and she could tell from the cold gleam in his eye that tonight would be wild. Still staring at her, he plunged two fingers deep inside her, and as her lips opened in a gasp, he covered her mouth with his.

JOURNAL ENTRY:
  I watched the shipment arrive last night on
  the docks after midnight. Found a good vantage
  point at Second and Kentucky where I can
  see and not be seen. Bucky has his men well
  trained. They stood quietly in the shadows
  smoking, leaning against the trucks, not talking,
  at least no sound carried to me until the
  engines of the boat could be heard. As soon
  as the freighter got near enough, he flashed
  the signal light three times and received the
  coded response. Then the real work began.
  A dozen men on shore began unloading the
  cases of whiskey from the boat onto the trucks,
  and the whole process was completed within
  an hour. At one point, a police car drove
  within a block of the scene, slowed down,
  and went on by without stopping. When the
  unloading was finished, I followed the trucks
  at a safe distance, and watched until they
  pulled into the distrillery and the doors

there were safely bolted. That is the one location I feel sure is totally secure from detection and invasion.

Leo Elderbrake takes over from there. He's been with me for four years now, and I consider him my most trusted lieutenant. Together we calculated that after the whiskey is emptied into huge vats to be cut precisely with grain alcohol, has coloring added, and is rebottled, we will have more than 3,000 cases to distribute. The initial investment for 1,200 cases was $27 each, or $32,400 total. We will finish with 3,000 cases that will bring up to $400 each for a take of $1,200,000. Even subtracting the shipment, payoffs, rebottling, and distribution costs, there will be a profit of close to a million. An important night!

Jackie was at her best tonight. She learned a new trick from one of her girls who learned it from some Chinaman on an overnight visit from a passing barge. Tiger Jelly, she called it. Nice. She deserve a gift. I'll pick up a dress for her. There is so much I'd like to teach Trudi, if she would only let me.

CHAPTER
=8=

Breakfast was served promptly at eight-thirty, and Barner Groves expected his children to be seated at the table by that time every morning. Holding his gold pocket watch in his hand, he did not snap it shut until his son came rushing in and slid into his chair, pressing his patent leather hair down with both hands in a futile attempt to make it lie flat on each side of the center part.

"You're late, as usual." Groves scowled at his son, who shrugged limply in reply.

"If you would schedule breakfast five minutes later, I wouldn't be."

Trudi suppressed a giggle, which ended abruptly at a warning look from her mother. Trudi swallowed and lowered her head to study the fruit and flower design on the everyday Wedgwood china. She thought it much prettier than the stuffy blue-and-gold-trimmed Limoges china the family used for the evening meals. Her mother and father had made "the compromise so important to be a happy marriage," as her mother was so fond of repeating.

Since Madeleine Groves was made to suffer the country-style meal every Sunday at her mother-in-law's house, Barner had consented to a formal setting for every meal taken at home during the week. Fortunately for Fulton, Jessica, and

HIGH SOCIETY

Trudi, their parents were both very involved with bettering the community, working with committees at the Art Barn, Symphony League, and Rotary Club, so only every other night or so did the entire family sit down together. Except, of course, for Jessica, whose chair had been empty for three months.

Trudi stared at Jessie's chair, wishing she were there, wishing she were home where she should be, wanting to talk to her. She looked at her father as he stuffed a huge bite of scrambled eggs into his mouth, and wondered if he had any idea of the injustice of his actions. Her eyes narrowed in anger, a cold, enduring anger that increased with each mouthful of food that she watched pass his lips. He's a coldhearted monster, and I wish he could suffer the pain that Jessie must be feeling right now, she thought.

"And if you continue to keep such late hours, I will be forced into drastic action," Barner Groves lectured his son between bites of food. "You're slacking off at the office and not really learning anything. I didn't build that company to see it pass into incompetent hands. I expect my son to do more than win a flagpole-sitting contest at college!"

Fulton continued to eat his meal as if he didn't hear a word of the tirade. Trudi looked at her brother in amazement, wondering if their father's lecture really didn't have any effect.

"Maybe, my dear," Madeleine's soothing voice interrupted her husband, "it is time for Fulton to get married and settle down."

Fulton's head snapped up and he stared wide-eyed at his mother. "You can't be serious!"

"But of course I am," she said sincerely. "The best way for a young man to settle down is either to get married or to go into the service, and we certainly wouldn't expect you to go into the army if you weren't going to be an officer, so that leaves marriage."

Fulton dropped his silver and leaned back in his chair. "And I suppose you have someone specific in mind?"

"Not really." His mother took a tiny sip of tea. "There are any number of lovely girls in town."

"Name one, Mother," Fulton demanded.

Trudi watched her mother carefully as she played at giving her son an answer while trying to make it seem spontaneous.

"Well, there is Janet Brenner, who comes from a family of impeccable reputation."

"Not to mention great wealth," Fulton added sarcastically.

"And she's very sweet," Madeleine Groves continued, ignoring her son's remark.

"What makes you say that?" Fulton leaned forward, knotting his napkin beside his plate.

"I've never heard her say a single unkind thing." Their mother tried to sound convincing.

"That is because, Mother, you have never heard her say anything!" Fulton's voice remained low and controlled, but Trudi could see that he was beginning to get upset. "Janet Brenner is the quietest and, therefore, the dullest person that I have ever met. She never has anything to say about *anything*."

"Lucretia Borgia was quiet, Mother," Trudi argued, supporting her brother, "and so was Lizzie Borden. Don't mistake being quiet for being sweet." Trudi glanced at her father, expecting the usual tongue lashing about disrespect, but she realized that he was just as surprised by the conversation as his two children were. Maybe he didn't form all the opinions and make all the rules in this house, as Trudi had always believed. She glanced from her mother to her father, and when she looked at her mother again, it was in a new light.

"Your mother is right," he said finally. "If you don't start shaping up at the office, you can look for a different job this summer." Trudi gave her head a little shake, trying to clear it. That was not what her mother had said at all, but her father continued on the same illogical stream of thought. "I don't have to pay for your senior year at Westminster, you know. It's a damned expensive school. It might do you good to try to earn enough to pay for your own expenses. Nobody ever helped me, you know."

He stopped his lecture as the young black woman entered

the room to begin clearing the dishes. Wiping his face with his napkin, he patted his stomach with satisfaction. "Hattie, tell the cook she did a fine job."

Trudi and Fulton looked at one another with only half-concealed amazement, both thinking the same thing. This man had just dictated his son's immediate future with no regard to Fulton's feelings or desires, and passed it away with the scrambled eggs.

"Right, Hattie. And tell the cook that the toast was done to perfection also," Trudi added with wicked mimicry, wiping her face with her napkin and patting her stomach.

"And the bacon," Fulton added with grave sincerity, wiping his face and patting his stomach. "The bacon was perfect."

Hattie looked out of the corners of her eyes at both the young people, knowing something naughty was going on, knowing enough to keep her mouth closed. Confused and frightened, she hurried through the job at hand and scampered out of the dining room.

"You may be excused from the table," Madeleine Groves pronounced as she rose and left the room.

"Talk to you later," Trudi whispered to her brother before heading after Hattie. Catching up to her in the butler's pantry, Trudi lifted the heavy tray out of the black woman's hands and waited while she picked up the silver tea service, and together they walked into the kitchen. Whispering like little girls, the two women talked as Hattie began scraping the plates.

"You didn't do anything wrong, so you can quit acting like a scared bunny," Trudi tried to reassure Hattie. Many times in the past two years, Trudi had helped Hattie learn the ways of running the house in accordance with Madeleine Groves's exacting demands. "Your job is not in jeopardy," she continued as the woman gave her a skeptical glance. "I just heard Father tell Mother last week that he thought you were our most valuable servant, so just relax, will you?" Her comment only made Hattie tighten her lips and scrub the dishes more thoroughly than before. "How's April Ray?" Trudi asked.

Hattie's countenance relaxed, and she stopped her scrubbing. "She's all right now, but a couple of days ago she weren't feeling real good." She shook her head. "She's the best little girl a mama could hope for." Trudi smiled, watching the proud light in Hattie's eyes. "She'll be taking her first communion this Sunday, don't you know."

"Is that when the little girls get all dressed up in white dresses and crowns and veils?" Trudi wondered, not familiar with Catholic rituals.

"Usually," Hattie answered reluctantly, "but Father Philbert said if we don't got one, then any clean little dress would do. You know, what with doctor's bills and all . . ." Hattie's voice trailed away.

"Let's just see what we can do about that," Trudi announced decisively, shoving a dry towel into Hattie's hands and turning her around to untie her apron strings. Grabbing Hattie's hand, ignoring her protests, she pulled her outside and toward the carriage house.

"Ingram," Trudi told the chauffeur, "if my mother asks, tell her I've gone shopping and took Hattie along to help. We'll be back in about an hour."

"Miss Trudi, you are gonna get us into trouble for sure." Hattie was worried. She scrunched down in the seat of the Chrysler as if afraid to be seen. They left the shaded quiet of the neighborhood and traveled across town, leaving behind the automobiles of the north side and exchanging them for the horse-drawn wagons of the south side. When they pulled up in front of Hattie's tiny brick house at Sixth and Spring, it was Trudi who jumped out and called for the little girl.

"She huntin' coal 'long the tracks," a toothless old lady rocking on the next-door porch informed them. Following Hattie's directions, Trudi headed toward the myriad of railroad tracks that crisscrossed First Street and found April Ray with a gunnysack full of coal shards that had fallen from passing coal cars.

"Let me just wipe your face and hands." Hattie fussed over her little girl as they headed toward the shopping district of downtown St. Louis.

"If I had known about this sooner, we could have planned a shopping trip for the whole afternoon, but I think Stix, Baer will have something nice enough," Trudi explained.

"Oh, we can't go there. We ain't allowed, Miss Trudi." Hattie's eyes were wide with fright.

"You just watch," Trudi answered adamantly, parking beside the department store and pulling on the brake. Taking the child by the hand, she led her companions in through the display area and marched to the back of the store.

"Children's clothing. I think that's the second floor, isn't it?" Trudi was not unaware of the head-turning stares they received, but the most disagreeable look the trio got was from the fat black lady who operated the elevator. Her prim white gloves echoed the tight-lipped disapproval of her face as Trudi called out a sweet thank-you and exited onto the children's floor.

"Here's a rack full of communion dresses!" Trudi was more excited than Hattie and April, pulling out one ruffled frock after another for their inspection. "What size does she wear?"

"I don' know. She's never had a store-bought dress before."

"This looks right. Do you like it, April?"

"Yes, ma'am," the child answered, intimidated by the racks of bright clothing.

"Now for a veil. Do you want a crown or flowers for your head?" The child looked at the cascades of frothy tulle and pointed at the crown. "That one's my favorite, too, April," Trudi said, smiling. On the short walk to the counter, Trudi consulted with the child and mother three more times, and they finished their flurry of shopping with cotton dresses for school and three pairs of boys' pants for play. "Now, just watch that round tube she put my money in," Trudi explained, bending down to the little girl's level. "It's going to be carried up through that long pipe to that woman sitting behind the glass window. See, she's fiddling with it now. Then she'll put the right change in, stick it in another tube, and it will be sent right back down here." A loud popping sound accompanied Trudi's words, and the child watched as the salesclerk opened the canister and counted their change out on the counter.

"It's magic," the little girl breathed, making her mother chuckle. They were still smiling when they walked out the heavy glass doors at the front of the store and bumped into Jolene and John Flanagin, a set of twins seen almost exclusively in each other's company. Both were big, with strapping shoulders and sturdy legs, but John was exceedingly so, towering a full foot above Trudi. Their father, a colorful man who had died two years before of cirrhosis of the liver at the tender age of forty-five, had left them a successful printing company, and since that time the twins had taken full responsibility for the business. They made joint decisions, lived together, and had a habit of finishing each other's sentences. Their closeness went back as far as Trudi could remember. Even as children they had played together and Trudi could still remember the brouhaha when John, much in demand for his athletic prowess, refused to play on a neighborhood baseball team unless Jolene could play, too.

"You've been busy," Jolene said, indicating all the packages April and Hattie carried. "Did you need two helpers to carry your packages?"

"The packages aren't mine," Trudi explained. "They all belong to April Ray."

Both twins frowned. "Did you take them into Stix, Baer?"

"Why, yes," Trudi answered nonchalantly, as Hattie hung her head. The twins exchanged glances and stepped back. "Are you shopping for clothes also?"

"No, no." Jolene recovered first. "We had an appointment—"

"—with our stockbroker." John leaned forward conspiratorially, but Jolene beat him to the news.

"We just sold our RCA stock. It went up from 85 to 495 in the last year, and we only had twenty-five percent down. It's just the berries! Now we're trying to decide—"

"—whether to buy land in Florida for development, really swanky places are going up down there, you know—"

"—or whether to tour Europe for the fall and winter."

Jolene's brow was wrinkled, and she peered at Trudi intently as if expecting help with the decision.

But the depth of their problem eluded Trudi and she shrugged. "If I were you, I'd talk to a lawyer about any land speculation in Florida. I've heard a lot of the state is swampland."

"We're going there next." John turned and pointed to the second floor of the bank building across the street. All three looked at the large plate glass windows that exposed the law offices of New, Keller, Schmutzler, and Hulsen to the street below. As the three gawked, Phillip Gates could be clearly seen loping into his office, wearing the requisite three-piece suit with a stiff-necked collar on his white shirt. As he closed the door behind himself, he pivoted around and jumped spread-eagle into the air, his mouth open in an apparent shout of joy, the papers in his hand flying high. The mouths of all the inadvertent spectators below dropped open.

"Well, I never!" John Flanagin breathed. Trudi laughed uproariously, her irritation at his arrogance melted away. The somber, studious introvert had a human side after all. There were new and fascinating facets to this man that she was discovering by the day.

CHAPTER 9

"Mother," Phillip Gates almost shouted into the mouthpiece of the phone, "get your best dress out. I'm taking you and Gardner to the best restaurant in town, then we'll hear some great ragtime. We're going down to the Tenderloin District. How 'bout it?"

"It sounds delightful," she answered. "But first, you must explain what you are so excited about." Evangeline Gates was surprised to hear the jubilation in her son's voice. For years he had worked at concealing his agitation, both highs and lows, worked at it since an early age until it had become second nature for him to appear controlled. Only the very few who knew him well could read his emotions in his eyes.

"Mr. Keller called me into his office ten minutes ago and asked if I wanted to be a partner in the law firm! I told him yes, of course, as long as they allowed me to take any *pro bono* case I wanted to. I'm really surprised this offer came so soon."

"That's wonderful! Congratulations, dear." She chuckled at the son, usually so somber and quiet. This was the son she had worried about the most, ever since their troubles had begun when he was little more than a child. Always he had been responsible and sensitive, and his father's death had seemed to magnify those qualities, making her worry that her young son was an old man before his time. Now the effervescence in his voice warmed her heart, for she had heard it so seldom in the last ten years.

"Remember," Phillip continued, "I told you I wanted to be a partner in three years or I'd start my own firm? Well, I'm two years ahead of schedule. He said the partners were impressed with the way I handled the Vason lawsuit and by the amount of settlement I got for that young worker injured on the job at Bennett Furniture." His mother laughed and congratulated him. "It's going to cost more than I thought, but a year from now, I can buy you a bigger house."

"Phillip, I don't want a bigger house," she demurred, "but if you're really intent on doing something, I'd love a long screened-in porch on this one."

"You've got it!" he agreed instantly. "Is Gardner at home? I'd like to tell him."

"He's standing right there trying to figure out what the commotion is about. By the way, dear, I put in my fair share of fun time in the bawdy district along Market Street when your father and I were courting." She handed the earpiece to Gard with a satisfied smile.

"Congratulations, big brother! I knew you could do it!" Gates's younger brother's face split in a huge grin as he rammed his fist into the air. "You just soften up those old fogies for me, and when I finish law school at Washington U., I'll come and show all of you how it's done!"

"Sure, sure." Phil endured the good-natured ribbing of his younger brother. The three of them had endured many hardships together in the last ten years, and Gard's infectious sense of humor had carried them through innumerable dark days when all of them were worrying individually about the well-being of the other two. Unspoken among them was the burning desire to recoup the sterling reputation for honesty and integrity that the head of the family, Charles Gates, had established thirty years before as a young stockbroker. Phil grinned, picturing his younger brother, shorter and more powerfully built than he, as he inevitably danced from one foot to the other with excitement. "You think this calls for a camp-out?"

"Good idea," his younger brother readily agreed. "But I think I'll skip the swim. I'm not in top-notch condition." The both laughed aloud at the memory. Years before, when both were in high school, they would get away by themselves on a tiny island, hardly more than a bump off the west shore of the Mississippi, almost in the shadow of the huge bridge. They would pitch a tent for the night, fish, build a rickety raft, fry their catch over a campfire, and tell lies about their physical valor. On a dare, stupid and dangerous as it seemed now in retrospect, Gardner had swum the Mississippi, with Phil rowing a small boat right beside him. They did it in the middle of a hot July night, not wanting to be seen by anyone since it was an achievement earned only for the satisfaction of the two of them. The major danger had come in the form of a huge barge plowing upriver, oblivious to the young scoundrels frantically splashing in its wake. Naturally, when they got home, Evangeline Gates had been able to interpret all the signals: Gard's upset stomach from swallowing so much river water, the whispered giggles, the long afternoon spent sleeping. She had forced the truth out of them. It was the only time Phillip had seen his mother get so angry that she raised her voice, ending her tirade in tears. Nope, no more midnight swims, Gates thought, chuckling to himself, but we'll celebrate just as well.

For some inexplicable reason, he thought of Trudi Groves, wanting her along, wanting to see her bright smile aimed at him. He shook his head quickly to clear the surprising thought from his mind.

Trudi spent the rest of her morning trying to reach her brother. She called him three times, and each time her father's secretary said he was busy and couldn't come to the phone. So she retreated to her room and manicured her nails, doing a much better job than the woman at her mother's favorite salon at the Chase Hotel.

She tried to concentrate on her campaign to fortify

Fulton in a stand against the family Napoleon, but her mind kept skipping back to Phillip Gates. She finished the nails of her left hand and held them out at arm's length to inspect them. Would Gates like such a bright color? No, something more subdued. A soft pink. She erased her work and stared again. The man was so reserved in public, a man like that would prefer soft pink polish. But her certitude wavered. Twice now, when they were alone, he had surprised her, once with the vehemence of his words, once with the heat of his kiss. The single kiss, in a wide, long history of kisses she had received, that she distinctly remembered. She painted a deep rose color on her nails, a thick, rich color with a hint of mystery, a touch of hidden abandon. She decided it was just right.

Finishing the job, she thought again of Fulton. She had to convince him to stand up to their father, difficult as that might be. She felt like a hypocrite, since she herself cringed as much as Fulton did under the old man's domination, but together maybe they could make an impression. Together they should have stood up to him about Jessie. They shouldn't allow him to denigrate and dominate the family so unreasonably. She bit her lip, trying to come up with a solution that would change her father's attitude and Fulton's attitude, a task that would be difficult, if not impossible.

When the bell was rung for lunch, she was dismayed to learn that it would be just she and her mother. There was safety in numbers, a feeling that when the four of them sat down together, the attention was spread around and she was not under her mother's disapproving scrutiny at every moment during the meal. The small table on the glassed-in sun porch was set amidst a forest of ferns, gracefully proportioned, soothing in color, as accepting and agreeable as she longed for her parents to be. Trudi braced herself, spreading the linen napkin on her lap, ready for the first barrage of her mother's criticism.

As instructed, the maid cranked hard at the phonograph and delicately laid the needle on a Caruso recording, carefully turning the scalloped horn in the opposite direction to soften the sound of the music. Trudi was sick of classics, sick of her mother's transparent effort to instill appreciation in her for the "finer things," and made a face in the maid's direction, but Hattie kept her eyes averted while serving the vichyssoise and chicken salad.

"Let me know how everything works out," Trudi said, trying to get her message across about their purchases without revealing too much. "We can always make some changes if we have to." Hattie shot her an alarmed look and scurried out of the room. Why is she always so frightened? Trudi thought, glancing at Hattie's fast-disappearing figure.

"It doesn't do to be too familiar with the help, dear," her mother warned, refraining from any further criticism. One thing at a time. She glanced at her daughter. Her coloring was dramatic. The white-blond curls setting off the huge blue eyes were her best features. The nose, however, was just a little too small and her lips a little too full to be classically beautiful, but Madeleine thought her daughter would mature well. Certainly she was enticing enough to charm men, for she never lacked attention.

"Why is that, Mother? Why can't I be nice to the servants?" Trudi asked with a deadpan expression, looking directly at her, almost wishing for an argument. But it was not to be. Her mother was staring outside with an expression mixing horror, fascination, and embarrassment. Trudi followed her gaze, and burst out laughing.

Gunther, the German gardener, who had been working at the edge of the reflecting pond, obviously had decided on an easier approach to reaching the middle than falling in; he was in the process of carefully removing his clothes. His shoes and shirt lay neatly at his feet, and he was unbuttoning his pants. His back was strongly muscled and already brown from hours in the spring sun. His body was beautifully proportioned, wide and full at the shoulders with narrow waist and hips, but for some inexplicable reason Trudi thought of Phillip Gates as she looked at the nearly nude man. A picture flashed into her brain, a picture of a long, lanky body, hard-muscled but with the elongated slender muscles of a swimmer rather than the full, rounded, short muscles of a laborer. She remembered the feel of his warm body under his clothing, and would have enjoyed the remembering even longer if her mother hadn't distracted her.

Trudi heard her mother draw a quick breath as Gunther stepped out of his trousers and laid them at his feet. He stretched, as if preparing his body for the shock of the cold water, then gracefully stepped in and waded to the pipes in the middle of the small pond. Madeleine Groves still had not taken her eyes from him. Her mother's untouchable poise seemed to be suffering from the sight of the near-naked man, and Trudi was puzzled to see the flush that covered her cheeks.

"This is not acceptable." Her mother's voice sounded hoarse as she rang the crystal bell for Hattie. "Have Ingram tell . . . never mind. I shall do it myself." As her mother left, Trudi spied Hattie peeking around the corner.

"Have you come to see the naked man, too?" she said with a laugh. "Come on out, get a good look." She beckoned to the young woman. But Hattie wasn't paying any attention to the scene outside. Instead, she stood uneasily, her mouth open but no words coming out, an absolutely wretched expression on her face. "What is it, Hattie?" Trudi was perplexed by the servant's bizarre behavior. "What are you trying to say?"

"I . . . I . . . I wanted to thank you again for all the clothes for April Ray." Hattie's hands were clasped tightly over her heart as if the words were being wrenched from her.

"Yes, of course," Trudi said, trying to urge her to continue what seemed to be a painful speech.

"I just thought I ought to tell you about . . ."

Trudi waited impatiently for the woman to continue. "What? You ought to tell me about what?" The doorbell rang, then rang a second time more insistently, and Hattie turned to answer it, running away with such obvious relief that Trudi was more puzzled than ever. When Hattie returned a minute later, her arms were filled with a huge florist's box and the moment of confession had passed.

Trudi opened the box, finding two dozen long-stemmed

yellow roses and a small handwritten card: *Tonight I shall treat you like a delicate rose. My apologies. Love, Winslow.*

Trudi grimaced. I don't want him to treat me like a rose. I don't want him to send me roses, she thought, and sighed. When you get right down to it, I don't want him. She was startled by the thought. Until a week ago, she'd been comfortable with the friendship she had with Win, knowing that it was becoming more time-consuming and would probably end with their eventual engagement and marriage. She hadn't questioned that prospect, in the same way that she had not questioned much about her own life. Father and Mother seemed to have everything under control—at least until Jessie's disappearance.

Now Trudi questioned them, and questioned herself, her own motives, her own weaknesses. And most of all she questioned her feelings about Win Stevens—a likable fellow, but was he really the person she wanted to marry? The thought had never entered her mind until the last few days, until Phillip Gates had stumbled into her life and had filled her thoughts so entirely. And she was in a quandary to understand why! Phillip Gates, by all outward appearances, suffered in comparison to Winslow Stevens. Though both were well educated, Win was wittier and more erudite. Win was more polished and elegant; she chuckled, thinking of Gates's disheveled hair and wrinkled clothes. Win came from old money and would have more time to spend with her and their family, whereas Phillip Gates was a struggling young attorney who would work long, hard hours away from home.

Certainly Win was kind and generous with her, but she felt an attraction to Phillip Gates that couldn't be denied. He had a depth, a strength of character that she found intriguing. He was different. Yes! That was it! He was different enough to stand out in the crowd though he did everything to meld into the background; his efforts to do so made him that much more different. He was a puzzle, an enigma, and that captivated her. He held a mystical appeal for her that she found hypnotizing, and she was determined to seek out the truth about the man before she went any further in her relationship with Winslow Stevens.

She looked down at the roses in her lap and laughed aloud. Listen to me! she thought. Phillip Gates has never shown any overt interest in me, yet I'm spending all this time thinking of him.

Trudi lay in a tub of bubbles, one leg high in the air, thinking through her wasted day and studying the color of the new lacquer on her toenails. The radio played "Yes, Sir, That's My Baby," a tune she was sick, sick, sick of! What had Fulton said the other day? If you turn the radio on and it's not playing "Yes, Sir, That's My Baby," then the radio is broken. The phone rang, and glad of the diversion, she reached for it lazily on the third ring.

"Trudi, I have poison ivy!" Linda Carter shrieked.

"What in the world . . . ?"

"When Bill and I hid in the bushes at Bonfoeys' house after crocodiling, I must have rolled in it, because it's all over my arms and legs." In spite of herself, Trudi laughed. For this to happen to Linda, of all people, Linda who was so sophisticated and intellectual and reserved. "It's not funny," Linda protested. "I itch all over, and I can't get comfortable in any position," she wailed comically.

"Linda, I am sorry." Trudi didn't sound convincing as she continued to chuckle. "I was just thinking of how good Bill is for you. You never would have done anything so wild if he hadn't pulled you along with us. I'm sorry you're suffering now." On the other end of the line, all she could hear was sniffling. "Have you tried calamine lotion?" No answer. "Linda, do you want me to come over?"

"I'm not crying about the poison ivy," Linda finally explained before letting out a pronounced sob. "It's Bill, or rather Mother and Bill. They hate each other, and she practically swooned when I showed her my engagement ring. She hasn't gotten out of bed since, and I've been waiting on her hand and foot, and now I can't move because I hurt so bad . . ." The words came tumbling out before she finished in a long wail.

HIGH SOCIETY

So it begins already, Trudi thought. I really believed Lita Carter might be more subtle with her opposition, but she's pulling out all the stops. Trudi was more than a little disappointed that Linda was buckling under her mother's pressure so soon. Why is everybody so frightened? Trudi wondered. Linda's scared of her mother, Fulton's scared of Father, Hattie's scared of everything! But as she wagged a mental finger at her friend, Trudi thought of her own feeble efforts to stand up to her father, and she softened.

"Linda, have you tried to explain to your mother why you love Bill? Maybe if you could talk to her—"

"Talk to her! Talk to her! She starts moaning and groaning and grabbing her heart whenever I mention his name. She won't listen. Anyway," Linda added soulfully, "how can you explain why you love someone?"

Good point, Trudi thought, as Phillip Gates sprang to mind.

CHAPTER 10

Trudi was in no mood to party, but she made a deliberate effort to smile graciously at Win as they pulled into the long, tree-shaded drive on their way to an anniversary party. The celebrating couple weren't married, but had lived together for one year, and were publicly patting themselves on the back for their achievement.

When she had first learned of the arrangement Trudi had been skeptical, and now she scoffed at the idea of such a party as the height of bad taste. Who did they think they were kidding? A trial marriage? She liked to think of herself as free of hidebound convention, but she was also intelligent enough to know that if you weren't sure to begin with, living together wouldn't provide the answers. In another year, or less, this couple would be parted with justifiable anger, broken hearts, and public ridicule to deal with. "Companionate marriage" was merely another way her generation had to thumb their noses at their parents' Victorian mores, of attempting to heal the festering wounds of the Great War with an ineffective balm.

As they shook hands with their hosts at the door, she refused to offer congratulations to the pseudo-sophisticates for their lifestyle of the last year, but she did accept their liquor, which, understandably, left a bad taste in her mouth.

It was the first really hot day of the summer; humid, heavy heat had settled on the riverbanks of the city as if in punishment for the beautiful spring so quickly ended. The windows were open but no breeze stirred the gauze drapes, and even the overhead fan turned slowly, doing little to move the stagnant air. Everyone was dressed in white or muted pastels, the palest of pinks or blues. The group was not large, the faces familiar, discontented, and vapid. Only a few of the men stood, leaning languidly against the mantel or propped against the wall. Two women reclined, taking the full length of separate couches, lying still and listless. The talk was inconsequential and slow, as if they knew what they were saying was irrelevant.

The notes of Gershwin's "The Man I Love" drifted through the air, and one couple responded. Tucked in a corner, they alone touched, kissing casually. The celebrants stood apart, she fanning herself, looking sorry for ever having invited guests. Trudi knew everyone. It was the same crowd she saw all the time, the same couples who went to the same country club, the same jazz spots, the Muny Opera, always together, no new faces invited. And within the larger group were the small cliques who clustered together, going out to eat together, traveling to parties together, playing golf together. She wondered how they decided who to run with, or even if it was a conscious decision. Was it the family names that drew them together, or the same education? Certainly it couldn't be the individual personalities for there were no individual personalities. They all dressed alike, they all talked alike, they all voted alike.

Maybe that was it. Maybe it was the safety of their sameness that drew them together. The thought surprised her, for she, too, was suffocated by that cloud of sameness. It was the very fact that they were alike that drew them together, for it was unsettling, even a little frightening, to find something different, to step beyond the prescribed limits of convention and think about, talk to, or believe in something or someone not accepted by the majority. To think about a different religious philosophy, to come from a foreign country, to speak a different language would mark a person as different and keep him from the hallowed circle of acceptance. How frightening that they, and I, can be so easily frightened, Trudi thought.

She smiled. That was why Jessica and Alex were so strong and admirable. They, with childlike openness, were willing to look at each other without the prejudices of the sophisticates gathered here. That was also why, Trudi grudgingly admitted, it would be hard for them. As a couple, they would be different in a world that expected sameness. But they could make it together, she was sure, for that openness would keep them from being bored, restless, worn out, sated by too much fun, too many parties, too much *sameness*.

Judy Pike's whining voice drew Trudi out of her thoughts. The woman lay on a couch, one arm dangling to the floor, the other propping her drink on her stomach. Her ebony hair was slicked back against her skull in a tight cap, her eyebrows plucked to oblivion, her perfume too heavy for the hot night air. "But I've been everywhere. I've done everything," she complained. "What's left?" She directed her comments to the room at large, but got no answer.

Trudi surveyed the room, more upset by the lack of response than by the desolate question. "Let's get out of here," she whispered to Win, and turned and left with no good-byes.

The party scene had disgusted her, making her feel all the more disagreeable, but she allowed Win to talk her into dinner. She was worried about Linda, upset because she hadn't had a chance to talk to her brother, and perplexed about the little scene with Hattie. She stopped at the entrance to the dining room of the Cuckoo Clock, allowing her eyes to adjust to the darkness of the nightclub. Win's hand rested possessively on the small of her back. She stepped away from him, but it didn't deter him from leaning close to whisper in her ear.

"You are more beautiful tonight than I have ever seen you look." His eyes swept down her pale aqua dress, cut simply on the bias, which made it cling to her slender figure. The demure lace collar was her only adornment, except for the large aquamarine earrings and pendant, which captured the pale blue of her eyes set off so dramatically by thick black lashes. She shook her head and laughed at his compliment. She had deliberately underdressed tonight to cool his ardor, but it hadn't worked.

Phillip Gates sat at a center table with his mother and brother, but his eyes were riveted on Trudi Groves. Her pale hair, her dress, her skin seemed to create a circle of angelic light around her in the darkness of the room. Only her huge eyes stood out as she smiled in response to a comment made by Win Stevens. Gates sat rigidly, still staring as they began to walk toward their table, stopping to chat with friends along the way.

"They make a handsome couple," Gardner Gates commented, following his brother's gaze.

"Who do you mean?"

"Don't play dumb with me, big brother. I'm trying to figure out who you are so fascinated with, Trudi Groves or Winslow Stevens." Gard was surprised by the sharp nudge under the table that he got from his mother. By the time Win and Trudi reached the Gates's table, Phil's attention was turned to his food, which he began to eat assiduously.

"Mrs. Gates, how nice to see you!" Trudi stopped and smiled brightly. Both Phil and Gardner rose and stood stiffly, their attention on Trudi, avoiding any eye contact with Win Stevens. Not until Trudi mentioned his name did they shake hands nonchalantly, their lack of enthusiasm readily apparent. As Trudi chatted with Evangeline Gates, the strained silence among the three men continued, and when she saw Gardner Gates's eyes flicker from Win's head to his feet and up again without expression, she knew she was not imagining the antipathy. There was a wall of constraint separating the men but, enjoying her conversation, she chose to ignore it.

"Have you read that Edna St. Vincent Millay is writing the book for an opera? She's been commissioned by the Metropolitan, and Deems Taylor is to write the music," Trudi said.

"I think that the production is almost ready," Evangeline Gates added.

When Win coughed, Trudi looked up at him. "Yes, yes, I know. Just a minute." She quickly finished the conversation and was practically dragged away from the table toward a narrow door in the back hall. Innumerable diners dressed in tuxedos and feather boas, dress suits and monkey fur, were packed into the high-backed booths along both walls; they called out and waved to the popular couple, but the only one Win stopped for was a seedy-looking man Trudi had never seen before.

He was short and powerfully built like a boxer, and pulled a fat cigar out of his mouth to whisper into Win's ear. Stevens pulled him away from Trudi and into the dark hallway for a hurried conference before, looking back at Trudi with a brilliant smile, he indicated for her to join him at the Judas window of the speakeasy door. Win knocked once, stood where he could be seen, and entered when the burly man inside unlocked the door and pushed it open, without, Trudi noticed, demanding a password.

"Who owns this place?" Phillip asked his younger brother, after watching the quick exchange out of the corner of his eye.

"I don't know," Gardner said with a shrug, "but it would be easy enough to find out. Just check the courthouse records."

"I believe the Schmidts operate it." Their mother indicated the front desk with her eyes. Her sons glanced in that direction and saw a barrel-bodied woman of about forty dressed in a dramatic caftan who stood talking to one of the waitresses. She lifted both arms above her head and began to shake her hands, her heavy bangle bracelets bouncing from the action. Phillip squinted and stared.

"She says it keeps the hands looking young," his mother said, chuckling, "though I've never been convinced."

"They're only fronts." Phillip shook his head in dismissal and reached for his coffee cup. "Mother," he began casually, "would you have time tomorrow to check the courthouse records? Write down any names you see on the deeds to this property." His mother nodded. "And while you're at it"—he glanced at the speakeasy door—"check out the Rainbow Club and the Sans Souci, also."

He turned back to his food, determined not to let the sight of Trudi Groves escorted by Winslow Stevens upset him. Why should it, after all?

It wasn't until they passed down a narrow basement hall and through a third door that Trudi could hear the music emanating from the speakeasy that occupied the basement area of three adjoining buildings. It was a huge room filled with effervescent partyers. The bar was congested, but none of the drinkers seemed to be bothered by the thick layer of smoke that hung over their heads. The lights were brighter here than in the restaurant upstairs, but not bright enough to diminish the sparkle of the rotating glass ball covered with a mosaic of mirrors that sent shards of light shooting over the room. The dance floor was crowded with people bouncing to the gay sounds of "Yes, We Have No Bananas." The flappers' shingled hair flew up from their heads like wings, gold slave bracelets glittered on their ankles, and long strands of beads bounced on their flat chests.

Shouts of greeting followed Win and Trudi as they settled in at a ringside table, and it was only after Win excused himself for another head-to-head conference with the same seedy-looking man that Trudi spotted Fulton leaning against the bar, a cigarette in one hand, his other hand resting on the shoulder of a blond woman whose body was unstylishly voluptuous. She jumped up and hurried toward him, grabbing his elbow to get his attention.

"Hello, Trudi," he shouted above the din, clapping his arm around her shoulders. "I want you to meet the woman of my dreams, uh . . . uh . . . what did you shay your name ish?" The woman giggled and pushed at his arm. "This"—he indicated Trudi—"is my favorite shister. Acshually, she's my only shister right now." He threw back his head and laughed uproariously at his own witticism.

"Excuse us, please," Trudi said, smiling stiffly at the blonde. "Come on, Fulton, I want to talk to you." She steered him to the quietest corner she could find and leaned him against the wall. "Fulton," she began with a frown, "we have to stand up to Mother and Father. We can't let them keep making all our decisions for us."

Fulton's face fell with disappointment. "I don't want to talk about stuff like that now. It's party time." He waved an arm in a wide arc to take in the crowded room just as half the couples rose to push their way to the dance floor for a jouncing routine of the Black Bottom.

Trudi frowned at him. "Whether you want to or not, we have to get serious about this. Don't you see that we have to stand up to them? They're getting more manipulative all the time."

Fulton held up a single finger in front of her nose. "You mean, big sister, that *I* have to stand up to them. They're not as demanding of you, but as the only son . . ." His voice trailed away as he leaned his head against the wall. "I'm not as dumb as you think I am." He let out a huge sigh. "But Father does have me over a barrel, you know. He does control the money."

Exasperated, Trudi shoved at her brother's chest. "Go out and get a job. You've only got one more year of school. You can earn enough in six months to get through if you scrimp."

"Now, there's where you misjudge me, sister mine." He grinned mischievously. "I don't want to scrimp and save. In fact, I don't even want to work!" He laughed heartily, ignoring her angry glare.

"Aren't you sick of them browbeating us?" Trudi declared. "It's time to quit playing nice-nice and stand up to them. If we just present a united front . . ." Trudi quit talking. Fulton's head was lolling to one side, and he began to slowly slide down the wall, to land in a crumpled heap at her feet. She stood with her hands on her hips looking down at him. "You could at least get a girlfriend who is able to speak a coherent sentence," she snapped, and turned and left him in the corner to sleep it off, disgusted by his excesses.

She gulped down two quick drinks and thought about what he'd said. Hell, it *was* party time. She threw herself into the dances, her arms flying wildly, her knees slapping in a group rendition of the Lindy Hop. Screams of laughter echoed through the air as the other dancers fumbled with the steps of the new dance craze, making her more irritable than ever; she found nothing comic in the clumsy lunges of the crowd. Something, anything, had to help her forget the charming weakling who was her brother, but so far, she didn't know what.

Win shoved his way onto the dance floor, his drink held high over his head, a smile plastered on his face, and was forced to do a quick side step to avoid being knocked over by a stumbling dancer. He was having no more fun than she was in the midst of the mayhem, and followed her willingly as she pushed her way back to the table.

Even there, Win's night seemed to be filled with small business conferences as first the mayor, then two aldermen stopped by their table, gesturing intently, their growling whispers growing more intrusive with each minute that went by.

"Why do those disgusting men keep bothering you?" She jerked her head at the alderman just leaving their table.

Win glanced lazily over his shoulder. "They're not totally without merit. I consider them intelligent and useful." She raised her eyebrows, asking for more of an explanation. He seemed reluctant to give one, but sighed and added, "Useful because they possess the advantage of connections and influence without the impediment of integrity."

Trudi asked no more but made it plain she was bored by the presence of these men and ignored them, sipping her drink and watching for the recovery of her brother. People swarmed in droves to the bar at the end of every song, but only when she was asked to dance by a friend from college did Win leave her side to disappear into a back room. When she returned to the table he was waiting patiently, his facade of cool control as implacable as ever in the midst of the chaos. Her mood didn't improve as the evening progressed, and when Win suggested they leave, she readily agreed. She looked around, trying to be subtle about her search, but the Gates family was nowhere to be seen as they exited through the dining room and into the night air.

"There's something I want to show you before I take you home," Win said as they picked their way through the crowd of parked cars. "I have been planning this acquisition for a long time—" He broke off as they simultaneously stopped walking. They both stood dumbfounded, staring into the backseat of a small convertible that Trudi immediately recognized as Fulton's. Two chunky legs were spread wide apart, one draped over the front seat, the other over the back. A man's bare spine, crisscrossed by a woman's arms, hid the rest of her body from view. As Trudi and Win stood transfixed three feet away, Fulton raised his head from her breast, lifted her hips from the seat, and grunted as he pushed his erect penis into her willing body. They both groaned, and as her legs wrapped around his waist he began pumping rhythmically against her, rocking the whole car with his earnest efforts, urged on by her cries for more.

"Enough," Win managed to say, and pushed Trudi away. She stumbled, her head down, as he prodded her toward his car. She sat red-faced and stone still as he slammed and locked both doors, then pulled her to him. His lips, hot and full, covered hers, denying her efforts to scream. Surprise was his ally, and, inflamed by the scene they had just witnessed, he continued to kiss her, his hand at the back of her neck locking her into position. She twisted and turned, managing a brief moment of freedom.

"I'll scream," she growled at him. "I'll scream and bring everyone from the restaurant out here."

He looked at her, stunned, astonishment widening his eyes as he loosened his grip on her neck. "Scream? You're acting like some kind of stupid virgin. I thought you wanted it—"

"*Wanted* to roll around in a car like a couple of, of, of . . ." She was too furious to finish.

He slapped his forehead. "Just how long do you expect me to put up with your teasing? You're a twenties girl. Quit acting like some naive little tease!" It was the first time he had ever been angry with her, but his anger did not diminish the fury she felt in return.

"I don't tease you!" She lashed out at him with her foot,

but dealt his leg only a glancing blow. It was enough to make him cringe, more from surprise than fear. "If I ever did tease you, you'd know for sure what was on my mind!" She reached behind her and unlocked the door, jumping out of reach of his hand before he could grab her. She ran, not looking back until she had passed four cars lined up like silent soldiers waiting patiently for their commanders to finish the night. She glanced back to see Win struggling with his door, and at the instant his head was turned she fell to her knees, scrambled between two cars and flattened herself onto her stomach, scooting under a low-slung roadster for cover.

"Trudi! Get back here. Trudi!" He ran past her hiding place, his shoes within easy reach if she chose to trip him. But she lay still, her breath coming hard and fast until the crunch of his footsteps died away. Grimacing as a stone cut into her knee, she crawled out from under the car and ran in the opposite direction, and kept running for the next six blocks, ducking into dark doorways at any sound. Finally, in the cover of a narrow alley, she sat down, unbuttoned the single strap of each shoe, rolled down her hose and tucked them into the toes of the empty shoes, and began the long hike home. After a few blocks, she deliberately quit thinking of the scene with Fulton and Winslow, stopped long enough for her breath to catch up with her, and began to enjoy, in a grudging way, the enforced walk home. She'd show Winslow Stevens who was in control of her kisses, and it sure as hell wasn't him.

She looked around, assessing the situation. The quickest way home was up Olive Street and over Vandeventer, and if she walked fast she could make it in half an hour. She had left the business district behind as she passed Tenk Hardware and Brown's Pharmacy, feeling more protected as the huge elms that touched their arms over the street provided an umbrella of dark shadows in which to hide.

She kept glancing over her shoulder, expecting Win's roadster to appear at any moment, but so far only a boxy black Ford had stuttered by, its narrow tires humming over the brick pavement, its passengers unaware of or uninterested in the young girl plastered against the trunk of a massive tree. The perfume of lilac bushes in full bloom floated through the air, and it occurred to her to stop to break off a branch, but she saw a lone man walking purposefully toward her a block away. She ran for cover, ducking into the bushes in front of the Stilwell mansion, and hunkered down hugging her knees, holding her breath until the man passed, his tiny terrier trotting along in front of him. Trudi suppressed a giggle. What if the elderly man had seen her? He would have been frightened out of five years of his life, and she would have had a hell of a time trying to explain why she was hiding in the bushes, barefoot, in a silk dress, after midnight. She blew her breath out and decided to walk through the alleys the last few blocks home.

She felt safe now, as if being able to name all the owners of the mansions gave her automatic protection. She looked into the backyards of all the familiar houses, seeing them from a new perspective, dark on the inside, looming high and impressive over their spacious yards. She leaned against the carriage house at the rear of Judge Graf's drive and bent to slip her shoes back on when the headlights of a car turned, skimming across her before momentarily lighting the length of the alley she was traveling.

The engine of the car continued to rumble as it drew near, but the lights were flicked off. Trudi used the descending darkness to slip inside the carriage house, not bothering to close the small entry door, pressing her back against the inside wall and waiting for the car to lumber past her. Instead, it stopped not ten feet away, and she gulped, trying to think of some excuse in the event that the large double doors were folded back and the car pulled into the spot where she stood. The car's engine puttered evenly, but the lights blinked once, startling Trudi.

When they flicked on and off two more times, she frowned and leaned forward, peeking through the grimy glass of the large door, standing on tiptoe to try to see what was happening. She saw a bulky man who seemed vaguely familiar open the back door of the car to lift out a box of bottles, holding them gingerly to keep them from rattling in the still night air before he set them on the grass edging the alley. "Okay, Judge," the man growled, the lighted end of his cigar bouncing like a tiny beacon in the darkness, "here's da six bottles of scotch you ordered. Two hundred bucks." The judge, wearing a plaid flannel robe over his pajamas, passed the cash into the man's outstretched hand, stooped to pick up his treasure, and scurried up the brick path to his house without a word. The driver stepped back into the car, one foot still on the running board to catch the swinging door before it could close, and pulled slowly out of the alley, not turning on the headlamps until he reached the street. Trudi, her head peeking out of the garage door at waist level, watched the judge hold the screen door open with his fanny, turn the knob of the wood door, then disappear into the dark house. A minute later, a light went on in the cellar; two minutes later, the light went out and the house remained in darkness.

"My, my, my, Judge Graf." Trudi pointed her left index finger at the house, rubbing the top of it with her right finger. "I'd say you interpret the laws of the land very liberally."

JOURNAL ENTRY:
　Trouble in St. Louis and Chicago. From reports
I got tonight from Rats and Bucky, the wars
have started to spread. Because the Sicilian
Gang was losing out to the Irish Gang, Capone
offered to step in to assist the Sicilians.
Tonight six men from the Irish Green Gang
were gunned down in front of St. Patrick's
Church on Dago Hill, each one found with a
nickel in his hand, the trademark of Jake
McGurn, Capone's man. The Irish will take
that as a slap in the face, which is just
as Capone wants it. Capone should know better.
We must have cooperation between the factions
or we will all topple. The Italians manufacture
moonshine and the Irish distribute. Capone must

*be trying to take it all over. It will be a holy
mess if it doesn't stop now. The more the
press gets hold of this, the more hatred will
be stirred up.*

*I remember what my father told me . . . Take
every crisis and turn it into an opportunity.
If I can act as mediator, I come off smelling
like a rose. Tomorrow I talk to both factions
and see what I can do. Omertà, Onore, Fuberia!*

*Trudi Groves won't see me for a while. I
can get my fill with Jackie. Tonight she was
drinking and when she is at just the right
peak, she will do anything. There is nothing
the redhead won't try. When we finished the
first time, I thought we were through for the
night, but she pulled me off the bed to
stand behind her. When she got down on all
fours and arched her back like a cat, I
knew just what she wanted me to do. I dogged
her, and when I started growling, she started
doing the same. I was too tired to listen
to her reports on how the houses are doing.
I told her I'd call her tomorrow and take
down the figures over the phone.*

CHAPTER
== 11 ==

The soft knocking on her door continued until Trudi reluctantly opened her eyes. "Go away, Hattie." She rolled over and pulled the downy satin pillow over her head, but to no avail.

"Mr. Groves will be real mad if you aren't at breakfast on time," Hattie whispered, leaning over her bed.

"I'm not going to get up for breakfast. Tell them I'm sick, that I've got some horrible catching disease and they should leave me alone for the rest of the day. Better yet," she moaned, "for the rest of my life."

"Now, Miss Trudi, you know that don't work. He wants you all at breakfast come hell or high water."

"I'm not going to get up!" Trudi insisted stubbornly, rolling over to bind herself inextricably in her sheets.

"You do look a little peaked this morning." Hattie bent over her and felt her forehead. Sensing Hattie's reluctant support, Trudi flailed at the sheets, freeing herself from the self-imposed trap, and gave rapid instructions.

"First go turn on the hot water tap, then get my rouge, the stuff I use on my knees. It's a little brighter. Then go back and soak a cloth in hot, hot water, as hot as your hands can stand." Hattie was darting around the room, trying to follow all her commands. "Then wring out the cloth and bring it to me, and hurry down and tell my mother I'm sick and will be staying in my room all day." As soon as Hattie left, Trudi began to pat rouge all over her face, dabbing her chin and cheeks thoroughly. She lay back, first fluffing three pillows behind her and sinking back into them in a dramatic position. She folded the hot cloth and spread it across her forehead, waiting until her mother's footsteps had reached her door before pulling the cloth off and flinging it across the room into an obscure corner.

Just as expected, Madeleine Groves crossed the room and laid her hand on her daughter's forehead, peering into her eyes.

She made a quick judgment. "I shall tell your father that you are sick. This means, of course"—she shot Trudi a warning look to let her know it was not going to be all her way—"that you will be expected to stay in bed the whole day." She stopped at the door, her hand on the porcelain knob. Her shoulders seemed to slump before she turned around. "If you wish, I will call Dr. Hildegarde."

Trudi shook her head and gave a weak wave of her hand to signal no, then closed her eyes and let her head fall to the side. As soon as the door closed, her eyes popped open, and she grinned wickedly. A small victory, but sweet in any case. She felt only a brief moment of regret for her minor deception. The illness of one of her children usually solicited tenderness from Madeleine Groves, or more accurately, a deep sense of responsibility. There had been a time ten years before when the sickness of one of her children would have elicited immediate attention, long-lasting, intimate attention, from Madeleine Groves. Until her youngest child died.

Julia Groves had been a delightful, joyous child, the toy of her brother and sisters, and very obviously her mother's favorite. She'd had her mother's dark dramatic face and long slender limbs, and Trudi wanted to believe that was the main reason that her mother had chosen Julia as her favorite, why she spent time and energy and tenderness on her baby. When Julia had contracted chicken pox, it was a cause for concern, and Madeleine Groves rose to the challenge, lavishing sympathy and affection on the feverish child.

But her unstinting devotion hadn't been enough, and even though she spent entire nights next to the child, crooning, swabbing, petting, Julia had died. Madeleine had not cried; even after she'd grasped the fact that Julia was dead, she had not cried. She'd walked through the ritual of the ceremony, the burial, the reception as calmly and coolly as the hostess at a perfect party. Trudi had never seen her cry since. She'd seemed to draw away, for she didn't laugh or run or enjoy life as she had before the little one died. She did everything she had to do with efficiency and élan, but no passion. It was almost as if she had learned a difficult lesson and learned it very well. She came to believe nothing she did was going to make a difference.

Trudi sighed and rolled over onto her stomach, squeezing her eyes shut, determined to go back to sleep. Instead, flashes of the night before lighted her brain. She was disgusted by Fulton, disgusted by Win, but something bothered her even more, something at the base of her memory, down deep, a small something that she was having trouble dredging up. Tossing over onto her back, she stared at the ceiling, trying to pinpoint what was bothering her about the evening.

Her eyes landed on the baroque porcelain chandelier that her parents had found on their first trip to Europe. It was Bavarian, with six curved arms decorated by tiny porcelain flowers and cherubs, each one separately a work of art. Trudi had been entranced with the chandelier when they brought it home, and had used its delicate pastel colors as a guide in decorating the rest of her room. She was still enamored of it, but for a different reason. She wondered now at the artistry that had gone into its design and execution, and wanted to meet the people who were capable of such work.

She glanced around the room at the soft lace tie-back curtains that hung in front of the heavy white damask draperies, the pale blue velvet chaise lounge in one corner, the Staffordshire spaniels that guarded the fireplace, and smiled to think of the contrast between her heavily traditional room and the avant-garde sophistication of the Cuckoo Clock restaurant with its horseshoe-shaped booths covered in black leather, the indirect lighting around the top perimeter of the room, and stark vases of calla lilies for decoration.

The Cuckoo Clock! That's what was gnawing at her. The burly man who'd been whispering so intently to Win at the restaurant was the same one she had seen delivering booze to Judge Graf in the middle of the night. Strange coincidence. She would have to ask Win about that . . . if she ever spoke to him again.

Phillip Gates's lips were pressed together in a thin, tight line that emphasized the bulging muscles of his jaw as he clenched and unclenched his teeth. He glared at his brother, who slouched in the chair in front of his desk. The only movement in the office came from the pendulum on the wall clock and the pencil in Phil's hand as it tapped in time with the clock. In front of him lay the morning edition of the *St. Louis Post-Dispatch* and the unopened envelope that Gardner had thrown there five minutes before. Gardner sat looking for all the world like a rebellious child, sulking after a lecture from the principal. He wore a golf outfit, baggy plus fours and a cardigan over a white shirt and tie. He has Mother's good looks and Father's personality, Gates thought, open and easily read—or so he had thought up until this moment. Now he wasn't so sure.

Gardner leaned forward, his hands on his knees, elbows out, ready to rise. "I'm not going to break the date with Bonnie Stevens, no matter what you say. She's a nice person whose company I enjoy, and the only hesitation I have is that she will probably beat me at golf." He grinned in an inadequate attempt to win over his brother. He stood with his hands in his trouser pockets, trying to look casual, his red sweater the only touch of color in the somber office.

"Of all the women in St. Louis, why did you pick her?" Phillip's question assumed that Gard could have his pick of eligible women, which was true. Not only was he handsome in a healthy, wholesome way, but his brilliant smile had the charm of sunshine. The family had teased him from the time he was six years old, calling him "lover boy" because little girls with long braids or bangs would follow him home from school, giggling and pointing, leaving him notes or sharing their cookies.

Gard shrugged. "I guess I just want to play the country club course, and there's no other way I can do it."

"Don't lie to me." The pencil in Phillip's hand stopped tapping as he glared at his brother. "She's Shrader Stevens's daughter, if you've forgotten, and that's reason enough to stay away from her!"

"I haven't forgotten!" Gardner flared at his brother. "You act like you're the only one who suffered because of that man. You seem to forget that I watched my father die, that I grew up watching my mother sell all her beloved treasures to support us, that I couldn't speak my father's name aloud without cringing—all because of that man! And the whole time, Winslow and Bonita Stevens are living in the lap of luxury, with fancy birthday parties, private schools, and polo ponies." He shook his head and drew a deep breath. "Oh, I haven't forgotten, big brother. I'm planning revenge just like you are. But it will be different from yours. You go ahead and lay for Win. I'm going to go for Bonnie." In three long steps, he was at the door and slammed it behind him.

He was trembling from his tirade, the first he had ever dared against the brother he had always worshiped. To make matters worse, Phillip had sat slouched in his chair looking for all the world like their lanky, laconic father, making it even more difficult to go against him. Phillip had his father's looks and his mother's reserved manner, and Gard had always been a bit afraid of him. But he meant to carry through with his own revenge, and not even the big brother whom he revered so intensely would stop him.

HIGH SOCIETY

In the outer office, the telephone operator pulled the headset off her ears and put down her crossword puzzle, ready to enjoy a brief flirtation, but this time her boss's young brother stormed past her without a word.

Phillip Gates stared for a moment at the door his brother had just slammed, surprised by Gardner's outburst. He wasn't comfortable with Gard's plan. At the same time, Gard was a grown man, or close to it, with his own axe to grind. Phil understood how he felt, so he wouldn't try to stop him. He pinched his lips between two fingers, willing himself not to smile. *The kid's got guts,* he thought. *He'll use his best weapon—his charm. And I'll use my brain. Together we'll do in the remains of the Stevens family. If old Shrader Stevens didn't have to pay for his crimes, we'll see to it that his children do.*

Reluctantly accepting his brother's plans, he turned his attention to the envelope in front of him and skimmed the information his mother had gleaned from courthouse records, as he had requested of her. Leo Elderbrake and Bucky Bathshelder were listed as owners of all three nightspots. He knew those goons didn't have the brains to run a successful operation, and his original suspicions about Win Stevens's involvement grew stronger.

He pondered his next move, then cleared his desk, throwing the unread *Post-Dispatch* in the basket. It didn't matter that he ignored the headlines announcing the gangland slaying of six gangsters on "Dago Hill" in the inner city. He hadn't gotten far enough to make that puzzle part fit.

Trudi continued to loll in her bed, bored by inactivity but determined not to let her mother know. The bright rays of sunlight that lunged through the east window spotlighted a patch of the rose-colored carpet, warming a square where Juliet, the gray tabby cat, slept curled into a ball. Trudi reached for the latest volume of Langston Hughes's work, pulled the embroidered bookmark out, and settled in to read when she heard the ring of the phone echoing in the hall. A few moments later Hattie knocked at the door.

HIGH SOCIETY

"You better hurry, Miss Trudi." Hattie's eyes were wide. "It sounds like Miss Linda, and she's bawling to beat the band."

"Oh, Trudi," Linda sobbed as soon as Trudi picked up the phone, "he stormed out of here. He said he never wants to see me again! All I could do was stand between the two of them and try to calm them down, but it didn't work."

"Wait a minute, wait a minute," Trudi said, trying to calm her. "Do you mean Bill and your mother? Did the two of them have an argument?" She stood in the hall, her shoulders hunched over the mouthpiece, trying to decipher her friend's speech.

"Yes. Mother said she would never allow me to marry anyone who is not T.F.ed, and now our engagement is broken," Linda wailed, a heartbroken cry of misery.

"What does that mean, T.F.ed?"

"Oh, you know, trust-funded." Linda sniffed.

Trudi burst out laughing. "That's the dumbest thing I've ever heard. Surely that's not how your mother gauges someone's worth?" she asked incredulously.

"She says that she has a certain standard of living that she expects me to live up to and that it can't be done without money. She makes it sound so logical," Linda explained defensively.

"But that doesn't mean you have to believe it!" Trudi almost yelled. "Did she say that in front of Bill?"

"Yes," Linda moaned. "And then he took the ring back and said he would always love me but he could never live with me if my mother was going to run my life." She sniffed three times, short little sobs that broke Trudi's heart.

"He doesn't mean it," Trudi said confidently. "He'll be back tomorrow, and you can get it all cleared up."

"No," Linda moaned. "This is the third time we've gone around about this, and he really meant it this time. He said he was leaving town and never coming back."

"Call him. Call him right away and tell him you love him. That you'll marry him tomorrow if you have to."

Trudi's solution was met with silence and faint snuffles.

"Well, you would, wouldn't you?" Trudi asked. No answer. "You would marry him, wouldn't you?"

"How can I, Trudi?" Linda coughed, trying to clear her throat, trying to sound firm. "I can't desert my mother."

"Getting married doesn't mean you'd desert your mother!" Trudi raised her voice for the first time. "Where did you get such an idea—" She stopped, knowing the answer to the question. "I'll be right over."

By the time she parked in the small cul-de-sac in front of Linda's home, Trudi had figured out her tack. She would sing Bill's praises and hope it would help Mrs. Carter see the light.

"He was almost a doctor, you know." Lita Carter sat stiffly on the chair in front of the tea table, her head held high as she gazed in the direction of her husband's photograph, its sepia tones washing pale brown hues over the stolid man's frame. "He was a fine man who contributed his knowledge and skill to the community." She pressed her lips together to keep control as her eyes teared and her voice wavered. "He took good care of me and he adored his little girl." She smiled in Linda's direction, while Linda stared at the floor, her face set from the boredom of the oft-repeated litany.

"Bill Jefferson is a good person, too, Mrs. Carter." Trudi kept her voice low, so low she wasn't sure that Linda's mother heard her, for she did not acknowledge her words. She merely continued to gaze at her husband's picture. "He is a hard worker, but more importantly, he loves Linda."

"There is more to marriage than love." Lita Carter turned her face to Trudi, and she could see the dark circles, the drawn cheeks. She looks years older than my own mother, Trudi thought, though I know they are the same age. Mrs. Carter continued, "He would never make enough money to allow her to play on the concert stage, to dress her in fine clothes, to belong to the country club."

Trudi swallowed her exasperation. How ridiculous it was, how sad, that anyone could care so much for such things! The woman's protests were shallow and without merit. Anger flashed through Trudi. You've never really known your daughter, she thought resentfully. All you've known is what you want for her.

Trudi looked around her at the needlepoint chair covers, now worn and soiled with age, at the single small portrait of an illustrious ancestor with a simple strand of pearls around her neck, at the snapshot of Mr. Carter standing proudly with a mortar and pestle in his hand. Trudi felt a sudden small surge of sympathy for the tidy, narrow-minded woman who all her life had clung to the idea that a female should be protected by a certain standard of life, that a woman received her identity through the status of her husband. It was the only life she could conceive of for herself or her daughter.

"He is a policeman's son." Lita Carter's voice rose out of the silence, its condescension clear. Linda and Trudi both looked at her for an explanation. "Well, everyone knows"—she waved a hand—"everyone knows that policemen are crooked." She arched her neck as if ready to argue.

"Mother, that's not so!" Linda protested. "It's not fair to make a generalization like that."

"Policemen take graft. They help bootleggers by looking the other way."

"Some do," Linda conceded. "But not Mr. Jefferson. He was an honest man who received awards for his bravery. I've seen them."

"No doubt on a table in the parlor."

Linda lowered her head, but not before Trudi saw the color rise in her face.

"And what's more," Mrs. Carter said triumphantly, throwing out her capper, "he's short. Men should be tall and women should be short."

Trudi winced. She felt helpless in the face of such weak reasoning. She met Linda's glance and read the same hopelessness. She rose, motioning Linda to follow her out of the room.

"You know what you need?" She forced her voice to be bright. "You need a shopping run. Let's get all gussied up and do up the town. We'll shop until our feet drop off. We'll go to Stix, Baer, and Fuller, and Famous-Barr, and Scruggs-Barney, and maybe top it off with a bauble from Jaccard's. Then we can get a great Italian dinner at a little place Win took me to on the Hill. Spending money has a wonderful cathartic effect. Let's just do it!"

"Oh, I don't know." Linda hesitated.

"Come on," Trudi urged her. "It will be the best thing in the world for you. I'll pick you up in an hour."

She was pulling off her dress before she got back to her room. Pressing the intercom button, she called Ingram in his quarters in the garage. "In forty-five minutes I want you to have a car, any car, waiting for me at the servants' entrance. I'll need it for the whole day. And don't say anything to my mother." She ran to her dressing room and flung open the closet doors, discarding first one outfit, then another, before settling on a simple one-piece dress in loden green with beige at the stand-up collar and beltline, and three-quarter sleeves, a dress she could wear with a soft cloche pulled low over her forehead.

She didn't want to answer the timid knock at her door, but it was persistent, so she hid behind the door, opening it a crack to talk.

"I have something to talk to you about . . ." Hattie's eyes were downcast and her face was, as always, sagging with worry.

"Oh, Hattie," Trudi pleaded, "can it wait till later? This is really a bad time."

Hattie gulped. "It's kinda important."

"But can it wait?"

"I suppose," Hattie faltered. Trudi closed the door and flew to the bathroom, leaving Hattie still standing in the hall.

* * *

The gas bubbled up in the red pump, the bell dinging with a merry sound, and Trudi's voice chimed over the noise. "I can't believe Ingram didn't take care of getting the car filled up." She twisted around to wind the back windows down. "We are going to have so much fun today!" She grinned convincingly at Linda, whose dark-browed eyes had blue circles under them. She slumped in the seat next to Trudi, her heavy bosom sagging, her thin legs braced straight in front of her, the perfect picture of dejection. She needs more than clothes and a good Italian meal, Trudi thought. She needs some backbone, and I can't give her that. But I can give her a good time. Trudi leaned over to give her a quick hug.

When she turned to face front, Alex Badamo's dark eyes stared back at her as he mechanically scrubbed the windshield, his dark eyes showing no sign of recognition as he rubbed the squeaking cloth across the glass. Trudi's heart lurched, for he looked so different from the last time she had seen him, walking home after school hand in hand with Jessica. He looked so serious now, unsmiling, older than his years. Trudi stepped out of the car and stood silently as he finished the job taking the cash from her hand without comment.

"Hello, Alex," Trudi whispered. He nodded. "I'm surprised to see you. I thought you worked in the limestone quarry."

"I do. The late shift. From nine to three, I work here."

Trudi smiled weakly, and they both stood uncomfortably staring at their feet. "I think about her every day," Trudi said, and looked at him, wanting him to understand she was aware of his pain. "Wherever they are, I'm sure they're safe and healthy."

His head jerked up and he stared into the sky. Finally, he drew a deep breath before looking at Trudi. "They can't keep us apart forever." His voice was quiet, but his eyes burned with a fervid sincerity. "We love each other and we will get married."

"I hope so, Alex." Trudi reached for his hand and held it tightly between her own. "I really hope so."

When she climbed back into the car, she sat for a minute, ignoring Linda's questions, staring ahead and seeing in her mind the two young lovers swinging hands and laughing in the spring sunshine. "I need a drink," she said finally, shaking her head. She raised the hem of her skirt and pulled a small silver flask from her garter. Opening it, she slid down in the seat and took a long drag, handing it to Linda to do the same. "Don't worry about running out." She winked at Linda. "I came prepared." She opened the purse on the seat between them and pulled out another larger flask. They both laughed aloud as the car pulled out onto the highway for the short trip to downtown St. Louis.

CHAPTER 12

By the time they walked through the door of Montaldo's, the two women were giggling incessantly, their need for release and the scintillating effect of alcohol taking effect in equal proportion.

Linda pointed to the massive, three-tiered crystal chandelier that hung in the foyer of the dress shop. "Do you think if you lifted me up on your shoulders, I could swing from that?"

Trudi studied the chandelier, twisting her head from side to side. "I think, if you do, the whole thing will come crumbling down and then you'll be covered with crystal when you should be covered in diamonds." The two laughed uproariously, their silliness echoing through the quiet surroundings. A handsome woman of forty glided toward them, a brittle smile on her face. Her hennaed hair was immaculately coiffed in tidy bangs, and she carried herself with the haughtiness of minor royalty. She openly studied the two young women, mentally tallying the cost of their clothes.

"May I help you?" she murmured after they had passed her inspection.

"You can if you want to sell us a whole bunch of goodies." Trudi cut her down to size with her casual comment, then proceeded to snuggle into a chair and disdainfully wave away one outfit after another as the woman made innumerable trips to the wardrobe room and back. Linda finally chose a bias-cut satin cocktail dress in teal blue, its circular skirt hemmed with the same crystal beading that decorated the short cap sleeves. Trudi tried on a dress of three different contrasting fabrics, its uneven hemline echoed by layers of scarves that formed the draped neckline.

"Red and pink and orange?" She raised a worried brow at Linda. "This may be a touch too wild even for me!"

"Do it!" Linda giggled. "Our crowd has never seen anything like it." Two hours later, both of them left, laden with boxes and bags filled with dresses, shoes, gloves, and hats to match their new outfits.

"We must go to Jaccard's now," Linda insisted, fully absorbed in the spirit of the day. "I need something new to decorate these costumes."

"And how!" Trudi agreed enthusiastically, as they sped down Olive Street toward the jewelry store. A man with carefully brilliantined hair led them through the hushed interior and seated them in plush barrel-backed chairs, laying tray after tray of ornaments in front of them for inspection. Trudi picked out a pair of onyx drop earrings trimmed with tiny seed pearls, and Linda chose dramatic thick gold hoops. "Charge this to Barner Groves, please," Trudi instructed. "We'll take them with us." The man bowed, lacking only white gloves to be the incarnation of a fine English butler. She turned to Linda. "I'm starved! Let's head for Little Italy."

The edge of the shopping district melded into graceful residential neighborhoods, and it wasn't until Trudi spied Evola's Barbershop on one corner and D'Angelo's Meat Market opposite it that she knew she had located the right street.

"I want a hot pepper-steak sandwich and linguini with clam sauce and cannolis for dessert," Trudi said.

Linda ignored Trudi's musings, her head swiveling in an attempt to take in the cacophonous melodies and exuberant colors of the hilltop community of immigrants. The Romanesque walls of St. Ambrose Church threw late-afternoon shadows across the people clustered on Cole Street, visiting, laughing, shouting their greetings to each other. Merchants stood sentinel outside their shops, guarding displays of fresh fruits, silk scarves, and trinkets as people milled around and about. The paperboy bellowed the day's headlines from the corner, while drivers of horse carts and autos jockeyed for headway on the crowded street. The singsong of a hurdy-gurdy was interrupted by the loud boast of a street vendor.

"Fish!" he yelled, holding a shiny specimen high in the air. *"Pesci freschi—the bella insalata!"*

"God! I love this place!" Linda whooped. "How did you find it?"

"Win brought me here about a month ago. Come on, one last swig before dinner," Trudi insisted, offering the last swallow in her flask to Linda before they left the isolation of the car.

"We're the only single women in here," Linda remarked, glancing around the little mom-and-pop restaurant as they pulled their chairs up to the table. A dripping candle, decorated by cascades of melted wax, sat upon a crisp white surface faintly stained from remnants of past meals. Cutting through the thick aroma of garlic, a short, fat man, his white apron tied tightly around his belly, grooming his thick walrus mustache with his fingers, stepped up to take their order.

"We'd also like some booze with dinner, something stronger than Chianti," Trudi added when they had ordered, smiling up at him, but his face turned stony.

"No booze, lady." He waddled away to fill their orders, not offering any more explanation. Two minutes later, a young girl, probably no more than sixteen, with dark liquid eyes and long black curls, put a basket of breadsticks and fresh vegetables in front of them. She smiled sweetly.

"Poppa worries." She waved her hands in a small circle, frustrated by the effort to explain more fully. "Only last month, the *federales* arrested his good friend." She bent close to them, whispering, "Two men, they pretended to be members of a visiting soccer team and came into Louie's saloon across the street, and when he served them whiskey like they asked, they took out their badges and arrested him." She straightened up, satisfied that they understood.

"You mean he thinks we might be government agents checking up on him?" Trudi asked incredulously.

"Sí, yes, yes." She nodded.

Trudi started to laugh but didn't have a chance as Linda grabbed her arm, pointing to the back of the dark cafe. "Look, I think that's Win."

Trudi swung around in time to see four men filing out the back door. Win, or someone who looked just like him, was the second to disappear into the alley. The others, all dark and middle-aged, with bulbous stomachs and bald heads, seemed to be deep in conversation, alert only to the world outside as they glanced carefully in both directions before proceeding.

"No, I don't think so." Trudi's face showed the indecision so apparent in her voice. "I can't imagine what he'd be doing with . . ." She didn't finish, unconsciously protecting herself from any more disturbing thoughts. But the image engraved on her brain created, against her most concerted effort, another nagging doubt to disturb the unsettled balance of her frivolous existence.

After dinner and more drinking, the two young women went to the park on a high bluff overlooking the curve of the river from the Illinois side where they drank more wine, their heads dizzy, their bodies tired. Bill Jefferson's name was never mentioned, though his intractability was responsible for their delirious day. They finished the bottle of wine, bought on a street corner from a fruit juice vendor, and sat looking over the newly installed streetlights of the city below.

"It's pretty, isn't it?" Linda asked.

"Yes, but I don't know if it's bright enough to light our way home." Trudi giggled. They crawled back into the car, edged it through the sinuous curves of the park, and headed back toward the city. The car veered from one side of the narrow highway to the other in such an erratic manner that a farmer, guiding his horses home from late plowing, dove for the ditch in alarm, leaving his horses to fend for themselves.

"It's the funniest thing," Trudi said, bending close to the steering wheel, "but every car we see has two identical sets of headlights right next to each other." Linda slapped Trudi's arm, laughing hysterically. The overhead girders of the bridge leading across the Mississippi formed a lattice work of shadows as they sped up its incline toward St. Louis. The moon stood high in the sky above the opposite bluff, lighting up the sky with a blue, incandescent luster.

"Moonshine, moonshine, moonshine," Trudi sang. "Who was it that was just talking about moonshine?"

"Duke Ellington?" Linda offered, giggling behind her hand.

"No, no, no." Trudi shook her head. "Whoops!" She jerked the wheel to the left at the top of Fourth Street. "We shouldn't go home without saying good night to good ol' Stephen A. Douglas and good ol' Honest Abe, now, should we?" The hard rubber tire in front of Linda bounced up over the curb of the city square, and both women roared with laughter as the car, tilting to the left, traversed all four sides of Washington Park with two tires on the grass, two tires on the street, stopping finally in front of a twelve-foot-high bas-relief sculpture recalling two famous visitors to the city.

"If you grab Lincoln's hand," Trudi grunted as she climbed up the front of the statue, "then take hold of Douglas's nose, you can stand right up here and pretend you're part of the big debate." She let go with one hand and it swung free, as Linda clapped in delight from below.

"I know." Linda's eyes got big in an effort to influence her friend. "Let's take a quick little dip in the fountain to freshen up!"

"Wonderful idea! Great idea!" Trudi jumped from the statue, and the two staggered to the center of the little park, Linda stumbling to her knees only once, Trudi twice. Their shoes went flying, and both squealed as their bare feet sank in the cold water of the fountain.

"It's so pretty," Linda crooned, staring into the morning-glory blossom of water shooting from the center of the fountain.

"Quit mooning. It's water." Trudi splashed her hands toward Linda, drenching her hair and face. "Water, water, water." She laughed with each splash, wincing and turning her head away from Linda's revenge. Their screeches filled the quiet night air as they whooped and hollered with each splash. A lone car with two couples in it slowed down to watch the two cavorting in the water; the spectators laughed with them, tooting their horn and waving in approval as they went past. Only when Trudi started singing "Let a Smile Be Your Umbrella" at the top of her lungs did they meet with disapproval. A policeman stood silently watching, his row of brass buttons gleaming off center on his jacket, his night stick beating time to their music against the side of his leg.

CHAPTER 13

Both women preceded the police officer, who stood back as they stumbled into the station house, Trudi bellowing her protest, Linda weeping pitifully. They clutched at each other's hands and scanned the waiting room with frightened eyes, taking in the bare beige walls and disagreeable smell with wrinkled noses. Like two petulant children, they sat scowling and scared on a hard deacon's bench under a large, somber print of President Coolidge, who seemed to look down on their shenanigans with patient objectivity. What was it Grams had said about Coolidge? That he looked like he had been weaned on a pickle. The thought relieved Trudi, and she shushed Linda, insisting that her friend quiet down and maintain a certain feeble dignity.

"I demand my right to call my lawyer," Trudi announced with more assurance than she felt.

"So call your lawyer, lady. Nobody's keeping you from it," the bored desk sergeant answered, immune to their distress.

"Where's a telephone?" Trudi asked more meekly. He roused himself from his ennui long enough to put the black desk phone on top of the counter for her, then plunked his feet back up on the desktop and returned to his bologna sandwich. "I also need a phone directory," she added, feeling humbled by her repeated requests. He gave her a withering look and passed her the book.

Though her family knew many attorneys who would have been able to help, Trudi didn't even consider calling anyone but Phillip Gates. He answered the late-night call with no surprise or weariness in his voice, and listened patiently while she tried to explain their predicament. "Can you come down here?" she asked, and he agreed without hesitation.

Twenty minutes later, as he pushed through the last set of doors and walked toward them, she felt so relieved and happy to see him that she had to force herself to keep a contrite look on her face. He had a certain air about him, even after having been awakened in the middle of the night, an air of reliability and of patience, and she let loose a huge sigh of relief. He stood in front of the two wet, bedraggled women, his hands in his pockets, his eyebrows up, offering neither consolation nor condemnation but simple support.

"Would you like to tell me how you ended up here?" Both women started to babble at the same time until he held up his hand and indicated for Trudi to speak. She told the story as simply and as truthfully as she could remember, which wasn't too clearly. He listened then to Linda, and between the two of them, he was able to piece together a reasonable facsimile of the evening's events. After a short conference with the officer in charge, Gates sauntered back over to the women, who sat up straighter and nervously smoothed down their damp dresses as if steeling themselves for the worst.

"Come on, you're free to go." He turned around and starting walking down the hall away from them, expecting them to follow. He held the door open and took each one by an elbow, steering them to his Ford. Linda's foot missed the running board, sliding off its edge and back to the brick street. Gates's jaw jutted out and he shook his head.

"I think maybe we'll lay you down in the backseat." He picked Linda up, set her on the seat, and deliberately pushed on her shoulder, standing guard as she tilted sideways in an ungainly heap. "She goes home first," he said, jerking his head at Linda. "You'll have to direct me to her house."

Trudi told him the address on Jersey Street, and after a moment of hesitation added more. "She's not just drunk, you know," she explained.

"Coulda surprised me," he answered without turning his head.

"She's going through a tug-a-war with her mother." Trudi leaned her head against the window of the car, struggling to keep it steady as they cruised through the dark streets, struggling to make herself clear as she tried to explain. "See, Bill Jefferson left town, and she was terribly upset so we went shopping in St. Louis."

"Now I understand clearly." Gates nodded, trying to hide a smile. He reached over with one hand and pulled Trudi out of her slump. "That must have been like the blind leading the blind," he muttered.

"I don't know what you mean." Trudi frowned, trying to focus on his face.

"That doesn't surprise me," he commented, pulling into the alley behind the Carter home. "Let's take her in the back way; it's less conspicuous."

Trudi stumbled ahead of him to ring the bell, waiting nervously for Mrs. Carter to answer. The woman's mew of surprise and anger was quickly quieted by the monologue Gates began to deliver on the care of her daughter, not giving the tremulous woman a chance to become hysterical. "I would suggest that you allow your daughter to sleep as late as possible in the morning, and when she wakes, to remember that a broken heart takes a long time to heal. Your patient will need a great deal of tender attention from you over the next few months. Good night, Mrs. Carter."

Turning to leave, he grabbed Trudi by the hand, practically dragging her out of the house and down the walk to his car. It wasn't until they were back on the main street that Trudi felt free to speak.

"I thought you handled that with a great deal of sensitivity."

"Does that surprise you?" he questioned without turning his head. Trudi twisted her hands uneasily. "I didn't mean to be short with you," he apologized, "but I know the woman, at least my mother does, and she needs to be reminded of someone else's needs other than her own. I doubt if what I said will make any difference." He shrugged. "As bad as Linda feels right now, I'm afraid it's only the beginning of the suffering." It was the longest speech Trudi had ever heard him give, and she was as nonplussed by that as by the insights he offered, with which, nevertheless, she agreed wholeheartedly.

He finally glanced at her. "I'm taking you to get some black coffee. Getting home an extra hour later isn't going to make much difference at this point."

A pool of garish yellow light, conspicuously out of place on the long, dark street, glared from a square of plate glass. Black letters reading "Elder's Diner" arched across the middle of the bright window, the only sign of life on Front Street at three o'clock in the morning. The disk seat on the stool wobbled unsteadily as Trudi sat down and waited for Gates to order. The cook came out of the back room, greeting Gates with easy familiarity.

"All we need, Pops, is two cups of black coffee, in the biggest mugs you've got," Gates ordered. "Then I'd like for you to trust me with them while I take this lady outside. I'll have 'em back to you in twenty minutes."

"Listen, Gates, you can have the damn mugs for all I care, after the way you helped me out. Why, lady"—he leaned into Trudi's face—"this here guy—"

"Come on, Pops, just bring us the coffee, okay?" Gates cut him off. "We're going to watch the Mississippi go by, and if you don't hurry up, it might be gone by the time we get out there."

Trudi was acutely aware as she crossed the street to the waterfront that she would remember everything about this night, every sight and sound and word. She would remember it as clearly a year from now as if it was happening at that very moment. How the bricks in the hundred-year-old street were higher in the middle of the road and sloped toward the gutter, how the boat horn echoed slowly across the water and filled the silence between them, how the coffee mug warmed her hands in the chill of the night as she pressed her fingers around it gratefully, how Gates's coat, still warm from his body, smelled as he wrapped it around her shoulders.

They sat close to each other on top of the low stone retaining wall, shoulders almost touching, taking sips of coffee and listening to the water lapping at their feet.

She looks like a wet kitten, Gates thought, staring out over the river in a deliberate effort to keep his eyes away from her, like a forlorn, wet kitten. He hadn't thought it possible that she was capable of such quietude, and he didn't want her to ruin this moment by saying something inane or stupid. He liked having her next to him, he liked the way she sat, dangling legs over the wall, aimlessly kicking her feet like a child. He felt protective whenever he was around her, an inclination he knew she would rebel against, given her feisty nature. He studied the silver surface of the water, reading the river's currents, enjoying the moonlit ripples that streamed in a broad band before them.

"Sometime," he broke the silence, "I would like to try to scoop up just one cup of moonlight off the surface of the river, just one of those little saucers"—he pointed to the surface—"and put it in a jar, where I could look at it anytime I wanted." Astonished, she turned her head and shoulders to peer up at him. "Why do you look at me like that? Haven't you ever thought of that?" He felt a little silly under her amazed stare.

"Not only have I never thought of that," she said, suppressing a smile, "but I never would have thought that you would." He lowered his head and turned to stare in the opposite direction. She hastened to clarify herself, afraid she had embarrassed him. "I think it's a lovely thought." She paused, and after a minute added, "I've never taken time to study the river—"

"Not just the river," he interrupted, "but everything about it. The moon shining on the river, the eddies along its banks, the sun bouncing off it at sunset. It's fascinating."

"Yes," she agreed quietly. "Yes, it is fascinating." But she was looking at him, not the river.

He turned his head to her. "What do you do?"

"Do? What do I do?"

"Yes. What do you do all day? How do you fill your time?"

"Well," she said with a shrug, "I play tennis at least once a week, and ride my horse a couple of times a week, and visit my grandmother every day, and party, of course." She looked at him sheepishly and laughed, nervous because she had been asking herself the same questions he'd just asked. "Partying is very important, you know." He raised a skeptical eyebrow and she felt forced to explain. "Well, like today. It was a big, long party, and it helped Linda forget her troubles."

"For how long?"

"How long did we party?"

He grimaced in exasperation. "Noooo." He kept his voice patient. "How long will she forget?" She looked at him with such a bewildered expression that he chuckled. "Aren't there better ways to forget a problem? Some way that won't leave you with a hangover in the morning? You may be able to bounce back from partying with ease, but I don't think your friend Linda is as resilient." The fact was, he thought Linda a relatively weak person, one who waited for direction from outside rather than from inside herself, and he was trying to discover whether Trudi Groves was the same sort.

She stared across the water, thinking of what he had said. "I'm not sure about Linda. She has her music"—she jerked her head in a begrudging manner—"or at least, she has the music her mother insists on, but I think she gets some satisfaction from that." She pursed her lips in deep thought. "Hmmmm, what do I do to forget? What helps me forget? I read a lot, all kinds of books, especially autobiographies and poetry, which I find very soothing." She hesitated before adding, "And I write in my journal to my sister every single day."

He heard the melancholy in her voice. "Where is your sister living?" He watched as she seemed to shrink from the question. He saw the way she bit her lower lip, and when she turned to look at him it wasn't a casual glance. She studied him, assessed him for a full minute; finally she must have judged him an ally, for she answered as fully as she could.

"I don't know." Her voice was dull and controlled. "My parents sent her away. She did something they didn't like, so they sent her away and won't tell anyone, not me or Grams or Fulton, where she is." She swallowed hard and blinked back tears. "I worry about her."

This wasn't the answer he had expected, nor the reaction, from the woman he had erroneously judged to be concerned only with herself. He studied her, wondering if she understood how revealing her answer was. What kind of parents could be so coolly manipulative? Why didn't she fight the situation harder? Or was her inveterate partying, her thrill-seeking, the only way she had of tilting at the authority of her parents? She looked up at him, smiling weakly, her eyes brimming, and a great wave of tenderness swept over him. He hesitated only a moment before taking the empty cup out of her hand to put it beside his on the wall.

"Come here, my little friend." He reached over and put his arm around her slender shoulders. She shifted against him, dropping her head onto his chest. She felt snug and comfortable nestled next to him, feeling his strong, steady heartbeat pulsing against her cheek.

Without raising her head, she whispered, "I'd really like for you to kiss me." She heard a deep, low chuckle before his reply.

"Now, that's more like the Trudi Groves I know." He put his hand under her chin, raising her face to his. She smiled at him, her eyes shining with a light that seemed to illumine him, and he fought to keep the kiss light and tender. Her lips were soft and warm, and when she parted them and he felt the tip of her tongue touch his, a rush of excitement washed over him. With one strong movement, he pulled her onto his lap and bent her backward, burying his face in her neck. She wrapped her arms around him, kissing his forehead with sweet, hungry nibbles until their lips met again, rich and full. He rocked her, hugging her to him until her breath was gone. When he finally loosened his hold on her, she continued to lie across his lap as he stroked the hair away from her forehead.

"We're going home now," he said. When she started to protest, he kissed her quickly and admonished, "No arguments. I'm taking you home immediately."

JOURNAL ENTRY:

I've always stayed out of the gangs and acted independently, but I'm being drawn in now whether I like it or not. Negotiations with the gangs didn't go well. The Sicilians don't understand what a massive business we have going. Each one just wants enough profit to buy a better house and a car. The Irish have a better grasp of the immensity of the situation. So I have to concentrate on placating Capone, getting him off the back of the Irish Green Gang, have to make him understand that the Irish have the brains, the organization, and the will to succeed in this business. Let the Sicilians take a backseat. If all they want to do is supply, then so be it. If I get the Green Gang in control of booze, broads and slots in St. Louis and Capone controls Chicago, we've got the whole Midwest wrapped up. The Irish provided Patti Shinn, Danny's daughter, as a "friendly hostage." Capone is sending his nephew, Tony, down to me as an act of faith. I will protect these two kids until negotiations are over.

Bucky reports that a truckers' strike is imminent. I must do what I can to stop it. If I make promises to Capone and the Green Gang to deliver a given quantity of booze to my customers, I can't renege. This is too crucial a time to be bothered with a distribution problem.

Patti Shinn doesn't have a brain in her head. Driving back last night from her father's house, she didn't say a word. I'm probably

HIGH SOCIETY

spoiled because the two women in my life are so sharp. Trudi has a keen wit, and Jackie has the best business mind of anyone I know, man or woman. This kid's young, not more than sixteen, and looks like she just got off the boat from the Old Country, with rosy cheeks and a flowered scarf tied around her head. She refused a drink in the car but was interested in stopping by Jackie's with me. Thought her eyes were going to pop out of her head when she saw Jackie's bedroom, all done up in red and black velvet with mirrors on the ceiling. While Jackie and I went over the account books, she rifled through the closet, pulling out one outfit after another. Jackie seemed to like the kid and gave her a bright blue satin dress that will probably look like hell on her.

CHAPTER
=14=

Lovely, hazy pictures of Phillip Gates floated in the front of Trudi's unconsciousness. Soft, nebulous remembrances of his sound and smell danced in front of her unopened eyes. She tossed onto her side and sighed in her sleep before finally rousing enough to acknowledge the persistent knock at her bedroom door.

Trudi pressed the heels of her hands against her pounding temples. "Don't shout, Hattie. I heard you the first time." It seemed she had gotten only a few minutes' sleep, but the alarm clock next to her bed said it was closer to four hours.

"You have to go down to breakfast. They know you left yesterday and they're both spittin' mad," Hattie hissed, her words still emphatic. "You can't get out of it. Might as well face 'em and git it over with." She handed Trudi an aspirin and a glass of water, along with a reproachful look.

Trudi dressed with little concern for style, yanking a simple dress over her head and hurriedly pulling a brush through her short curls, unruly and still slightly damp from the night before. She tiptoed down the wide, curved staircase and slid into her seat at the table, not looking at either her mother or her father, glancing only at Fulton, who had a fatuous grin on his face since he knew full well that it was her turn to receive the wrath their parents usually reserved for him. Everyone ate in silence, as unhappy families often do, and when Barner Groves pulled out his pocketwatch and snapped it open—the last habit in his early-morning leaving-for-the-office ritual, Trudi thought for a moment that she might escape.

But he looked at her and took a deep breath. "You have been extremely thoughtless, not to mention devious, in the last twenty-four hours." He frowned at her over the top of his glasses, glaring like he expected an answer. Trudi remained silent. "We expect an explanation."

Trudi took a deep breath, thinking of Linda and Bill, seeing again Fulton in the backseat of his car, and remembering Win's hand hard on her neck. She could hear Linda's sobs over the phone; she pictured the police station and Phillip Gates's solemn face. She didn't know where to begin, but she did know that if she tried to explain, they would not understand, would be more upset with her than they were now. She looked at her mother, and felt a fleeting sense of remorse. Madeleine Groves's lips were tight and her eyes were circled with violet. She seemed to be tired, truly suffering. But not enough to understand or listen to Trudi's explanation.

"I left the house hoping to help a friend." Trudi's words were simple and true, exonerating any others involved in the complicated story.

"By buying half of St. Louis?" Her father's voice rose as he indicated the pile of boxes on a side chair. "Those will be returned, needless to say, and you will stay in your room until your mother and I have had a chance to talk about what we will do with you."

Trudi stiffened. This was too familiar. This was the moment to strike her first small blow for independence, feeble and halfhearted as it might be. She held up a hand to stop her father's exit from the table, swallowed with difficulty, then spoke softly, looking him directly in the eyes. "No," she said, her voice casual but definite. "I will not be staying in my room. I have plans today that I will not cancel."

Her father harrumphed in astonishment, as if he had just heard an unexpected declaration of war. His mouth opened and closed wordlessly, making him look for all the world like a fish out of water, and before he could recover, Trudi continued. "I am sorry if I caused you and Mother alarm by not telling you my plans, but I am a grown woman and I refuse to be treated like a child." She rose from the table and walked stiffly from the room, aware that her father's fury was building.

"Now, Barner, calm down," her mother's voice trailed after her as Trudi hurried up the stairs. She locked the door behind her as soon as she ducked into her room. Her heart was pounding and her mouth was dry, but she squared her shoulders with determination, half expecting to hear her father's footsteps clump angrily to her door. She had to act, to get out of the house now that she had made her "declaration of independence." She couldn't stay here when she had stated to her father that she was leaving.

Phillip Gates! I'll call Phillip Gates, she thought. Her hand already on the knob, she cringed at the thought—then swallowed and made up her mind. I'm a thoroughly modern woman, and I can call a man if I want to, she told herself firmly.

She opened the door and crept down the hall to the phone. Cranking it, she murmured into the mouthpiece, "Central, ring 4545, please."

"Funny," he said with a chuckle on hearing her voice. "I was just going to call you."

"Prove it," she replied, and hung up. During the short interim, she realized that once again she had called him in a moment of crisis. It was *his* name, *his* spirit she thought of as refuge, but just why this was so was not clear to her. She recognized that she was rebellious by nature and independent by choice, so she surprised herself by turning to him, by deferring to his reasonable authority. Thirty seconds later the bell rang, and she grabbed it at the first sound.

"How about lunch today?" Gates asked without introduction. "I know a little ribs and biscuits place near the waterfront that is good."

"Manny's?"

"Yes."

"What time?"
"Noon?"
"I'll meet you there."

The air was heavy, made that way by the evaporating waters of the Mississippi, and the sun was hot, but still a haze hung over the city that kept the day from being bright. It was only Trudi's spirits that were light and gay. She tried to tell herself it was because she had, for the first time, openly defied her parents' control, but she knew it was because she was on her way to meet Phillip Gates. For the first time they would be deliberately alone together.

She drove carefully, guiding the car between the confusion of honking trucks, stubborn horse carts, and pedestrians, weaving their way among the slow-moving vehicles with casual disdain. Two small black boys on bicycles made faster headway than the motorcars. Not until she got off Broadway and parked the car on Second Street did she relax.

Here the noises were different. The angry shouts of stevedores wrestling cargo onto huge barges, shrill cries of street urchins begging for booty, and urgent horns of delivery trucks were music to her ears, for she knew she was close to the rendezvous spot. As she walked along Front Street, heads turned, the heads of men and boys, for few women came to this neighborhood alone. She could see him a block away, towering above the bodies that crowded the walk as he scanned the street for her approach. He was leaning against the brick wall of the old building where they were to meet, his hands in his pockets, his feet crossed at the ankles in a casual stance. When he turned his head and saw her, he pushed away from the building and headed toward her, a slow smile growing on his face.

Trudi felt her heart quicken at the sight of him, a sensation she had never experienced before, and it lightened her step until she almost ran. She hoped her grin was not silly-looking, for that was how she felt, silly and light-headed and happy. When he touched her hand, a childhood memory shot through her. When she was little, probably no more than five or six, Father had given her a gift of a huge dollhouse, so big it had to stand on its own table; it had ten rooms, complete with furniture and its own lights, tiny bulbs in the middle of each room. She'd touched an empty socket, and the current had sent a shock through her, not enough to hurt her but enough that she didn't do it again.

His touch gave her the same sensation, an electric thrill starting at her hand and traveling instantaneously up her arm to her heart. No human touch had ever had such an effect on her, and she found herself drawing back imperceptibly, as if to examine him. He didn't seem to notice, guiding her into the darkness of the riverfront diner, thick with the delicious smell of barbecued ribs. A few people, mostly men, turned and looked as they walked in, for their clean clothes, if nothing else, set them apart as different from the usual crowd that ate at Manny's.

Surrounded by the odors of the waterfront and the cafe, Phillip was especially aware of her freshness. She wore a simple dress, sleeveless with a deep V neckline. He could smell her garden scent, so magnificently her own, the same fragrance he had noticed on the train when she'd leaned into him. She conjured images of flowers and spices, an intoxicating mix of lilac and cinnamon never found in a bottle or a box, a combination that he found disarming and mildly dangerous.

She started to speak but stopped, waiting for the bells of the Cathedral of St. Louis to finish tolling the noon hour, and he used the silence between them to inhale deeply, breathing in the smell of her as if to convince himself it was real. By the time the bells stopped chiming, the spell was broken. Manny stood beside the booth, a dead cigar clamped between his teeth, his hands on his hips, his arms framing a round belly.

"You," he said in a deep basso voice, indicating Gates, "should have the special order of ribs, and the little lady should have the blue plate special. Today it's the smoked ham with red gravy and beaten biscuits. You'll get spring greens and corn dodgers with it, to share." He swiped at the table with a damp cloth, and turned to disappear into the kitchen.

Trudi's eyes were huge and amused and she fought her urge to burst out laughing. Gates shrugged. "I should have warned you. He always makes the decisions, and if you argue with him, you're out." He shot a thumb toward the door. "He's the undisputed leader of a jazz band that plays here at night."

"Then I'll keep my mouth shut and enjoy the food without question," Trudi replied.

"Wise decision," Gates murmured, but his eyes traveled over her in a way that made her know he was not thinking of her mental acuity. She never blushed. She was never shocked by fresh words. But she felt a rush of heat to her face as he stared at her, his eyes making a leisurely tour of her face, her mouth, her throat. Uncomfortable, she sat up straighter and crossed her legs at the ankles, folding her hands together on the table.

She took a deep breath and managed to murmur, "Thank you for last night."

"What part of last night?" He continued to look steadily at her, but before she could answer, Manny slid their plates in front of them unceremoniously.

"Ya want any coffee, just yell," he called over his shoulder before trundling back to the kitchen.

"Looks appetizing." Gates's voice was low and his eyes never wavered from her face. His innuendo was unmistakable, but her discomfort was gone. She understood his tactics by now and refused to be surprised by him again.

"Ummm, yes," she agreed, slipping off her shoe, extending her leg, and sliding her toes up the inside of his calf. "Looks good enough to eat." She put a bite of ham in her mouth, keeping her eyes on his face, satisfied to see the pupils of his eyes dilate noticeably. "You want a piece?" She cut a bite of meat and offered it to him, her bare foot hooking the back of his knee and pulling it toward her.

His lips were parted, his eyes blinking slowly, his face blank and a vapid, dazed look in his eyes. He took the food she offered without glancing at it. "Slow," she whispered.

"You'll enjoy it more if you go real slow." She gave him the most seductive sideways look she could muster, massaging his leg with her foot. He swallowed the meat without chewing, dropping his knife as he turned to his own food. Now we're even, she thought smugly.

"Bet you take all your girls here," she said flirtatiously, her eyes traveling the dark interior of the diner. A calendar hung on the wall opposite their booth, while a wood-bladed fan rotated slowly overhead. Five men sat at the counter, their broad shoulders and ham-shaped arms marking them as stevedores. Loud laughter rose from a group of four men sitting around a table in the rear as they played a sluggish game of cards.

"Only the ones I want to impress." He smiled at her. They ate in silence for a few minutes, savoring the simple, delicious food, glancing at each other with an occasional wink and smile. "Do you have time when we're through to walk the riverfront?" he asked finally.

"The question is, do *you* have time? My schedule is not exactly heavy with responsibilities, unless you count shopping, tennis, or riding."

Her self-deprecating remark was not lost on him. "Do I detect a hint of boredom?"

"Not really boredom," she countered. "I've always thought that if a person was bored, it was nobody's fault but his own." She shrugged, not sure how to explain. "But I would admit to some discontent. I look at the people around me, and don't like what I see." She paused, not wanting to talk about anything serious. She crumbled the remains of a biscuit in her fingers, too satiated to eat any more, using the action to avoid further explanation. He finished gnawing at a rib, studying her face in a new way. He rubbed his hands on the cloth napkin, trying to rid them of the tenacious sauce, with little success. Trudi saw her chance.

"Let me help." She reached across the narrow booth and took his hand, drawing his finger into her mouth to lick it. He stared at her, disbelieving; then as she began to cleanse the second finger, licking it all around as her eyes flicked from his hand to his face, he groaned, rolled his eyes, and snatched his hand away. Pulling a bill from his pocket and flinging it onto the table, he grabbed her wrist.

"Let's get out of here." It wasn't a request and she didn't treat it as such, stumbling behind him, grinning broadly. He pushed the door open and dragged her twenty feet to the right, to the first alley he found. Then, pressing her shoulders against the wall and bending to look evenly into her eyes, he hissed at her, "You can't do that!"

"Why not?" She mustered the best wide-eyed, innocent look she could manage.

"Because I can't handle it." His voice was hoarse, and she giggled in triumph at the effect she had on him.

"Then don't 'handle it.' Do what you want to do." To her, the answer was simple.

"I couldn't possibly." He glanced down the deserted alley, then out to the busy street. "Not here."

"Then do what you can do here," she challenged.

He didn't hesitate any longer. Bending to kiss her, he bent her backward so far she was lifted almost off her feet. His mouth covered hers, smothering her, taking the air from her until she was light-headed. But she clung to him, savoring the sensation, matching his fervor with her own. He straightened, but her arms were around his neck and she rose with him, never allowing his lips to leave hers, burning with heat that rushed from her head to her toes and back again. He pushed her against the wall, pressing his body into hers, and she felt again the hardness of him, the lean, sinewy length of him. When he pulled away he was breathless, his face flushed, his lips wet with her kisses. They stared at each other, eyes glistening, but just as he bent to kiss her again, a raucous explosion of applause and laughter rang out. Standing on the sidewalk were three stevedores, their pants dusty from their work, their shirts wet with sweat, watching with approval, clapping and urging on the two young lovers.

"Oh, Christ!" Gates slapped his forehead; then, turning to their audience, he gave a short salute. Pulling Trudi behind him, he made his way through the traffic of horse carts and flatbed trucks, past ten-foot-high stacks of bricks waiting for shipment and into the comparative quiet of the wharves across the street.

"Why is there always trouble wherever you go?" He had stopped at the end of a dock, his feet planted firmly on its wide planks, shaking his head and smiling at her. Trudi stood in front of him, her nose level with the middle of his chest, staring up at him without answer. The water lapped at the thick pilings, the gulls squawked around their heads, and the street noises rattled unabated, but all she noticed was his eyes. Deep-set and serious, with the beginning of a frown line between the brows, they held a hidden message.

He shrugged, implying that his question was unanswerable, and sat on a barrel, stuffing his hands in his pockets. She perched beside him on a stack of bricks, wrapped on a pallet like a Christmas package ready for shipment, and together they studied the riverfront activity, both acutely aware that they were avoiding the intimate contact of words or touch. A coal barge plowed by, guided through the water traffic by two stubby tugs. A freighter finished its final maneuvers before docking, and thick ropes were thrown from its deck to be expertly tied to heavy metal rings embedded in the waiting wharf. Scavenger gulls swooped after the offal of the ships, screaming directions to each other, while Trudi and Phillip laughed at their greedy antics.

"I love coming down here." He didn't turn to her, but the words were soft, meant only for her to hear. "It reminds me of all the business that has gone on along the banks of this river for the last 250 years, all the people who have traveled through here and the exciting, adventurous lives they have led."

She caught a melancholy note in his voice and turned to see his face, but it was expressionless. "Don't you think you lead an exciting life?"

His chuckle was a denial. "Hardly. My life is not exciting. Determined and directed, maybe, but not exciting." He leaned back against the barrels, his hands stuffed casually into his pockets, but his voice was not casual, the hard edge of steel that she had heard before once again very real.

"Determined about what? Directed toward what?" She was interested, but she knew the words sounded prying and she wasn't surprised by the look he gave her, a warning glance that told her she had asked too much.

"Why would you need to know?" he answered simply, and he was right, though she *wanted* to know. She wanted to know what it was that he kept to himself, what it was that created the edge in his voice and the mystery in his eyes.

She had no other answer for him, at least not in words, so instead, she reached for his face, held it gently, and gave him a little kiss. He accepted the first, then warmed considerably to the second, and was deciding on the third when the calliope of a passing riverboat serenaded them with three quick toots.

A double row of sightseers on the top deck of the excursion boat waved as the boat sloshed by, teasing and laughing, pointing in good humor at the embarrassed couple. Men in striped jackets and bow ties tipped their boater hats while the women waved their hankies and children waved little flags in time to the ship's musical wheel. The captain blew the horn one last time on a long soulful note as the boat moved away, leaving a foaming wake and the echo of its laughter.

It was late afternoon, and still hot. Trudi flopped on her bed, still giggling about the episode, exhausted from her lack of sleep the night before, excited about her lunch date with Gates. They had not touched, had worked at not touching, for the rest of the hour together. She'd endured a professorial lecture from him about the sights and sounds and history of the city. She'd listened to him expound on the glories of Shaw's Gardens and the City Art Museum and the Central Library as if he were talking about central Africa or the Left Bank of the Seine. When they'd finally parted, they shook hands, laughing as they did so but with an unspoken agreement that the gesture was the safest they could handle.

She tossed and turned on her bed, remembering his flushed

face, his serious eyes, the hank of brown hair that hung low over the thick brows. When the knock came at the door she didn't hear it, didn't allow it to register because she was so enjoying replaying the last two hours of her day. But when the sound came again, she couldn't ignore it, knowing by its timid nature that it was Hattie.

"Miss Trudi, I been trying to tell you for days," Hattie pleaded. "I know this isn't a good time, but you gotta listen." The maid stepped inside the room and closed the door as Trudi, resigning herself to the intrusion, kicked off her shoes and lay back down on the unmade bed. She stared at the ceiling, still daydreaming, not paying much attention to Hattie's words.

"I been thinking long and hard 'bout whether to say anything or not. I'm so scared about losing this job, with my chil' so sickly an all, I jes can't afford to lose—"

"Hattie, please get to the point." Trudi's voice sounded more impatient than she felt.

Her huge brown eyes pathetically frightened, Hattie gulped and said, "I know where Miss Jessica is."

"You *what?*" Trudi sat bolt upright, all her attention fixed on the woman. "You know where Jessie is?" She jumped off the bed and ran to Hattie, grabbing her arms fiercely. "Where is she? How do you know? Tell me everything!"

"I was working late last week when your mama and papa come home from some party. They didn't know I was around, and they was talkin' 'bout talkin' to her, but your mama said no, the Griffiths takin' good care. Since the Griffiths run your ranch in Colorado, I figure that's where she's gotta be," Hattie finished apprehensively, her eyes still round with fright.

"Hattie, you're wonderful!" Trudi squeezed the woman hard, then clapped her hands in glee. "Of course, that's where she is. Why didn't I think of that?" She slapped her forehead, then practically danced around the room. "I've got to tell Grams." She ran to the bathroom, gulped two aspirin, and splashed her face with water while Hattie stood watching, a relieved grin on her face. Trudi slipped one shoe on and, hopping around in clumsy excitement, trying to stuff the other shoe on, she instructed Hattie, "Tell my parents that I've gone to see Grams, and I'll probably be there the rest of the day." She squeezed the maid one more time and ran out.

Grams cried. They both cried. "She's safe there, at least," Grams decided, "and in the fresh air, and she loves the mountains." They both sniffed.

"Why, she's probably out taking a walk right now, collecting little wildflowers to dry and press for Christmas gifts," Trudi added. They stopped crying and laughing, just sat holding hands across the kitchen table, knowing they were kidding themselves.

"She's miserable, Grams." Trudi invalidated all their musings with the truth. "She loves Alex, she wants that baby, and she misses home. What are we going to do?" The buzz of a circling fly, the cries of children playing outside, the monotonous whirl of the overhead fan were all magnified by the silence of their concentration.

Grams pushed her pressed-back chair away from the table and strode over to the counter, her face tight with the effort of problem solving. She pulled the towel off a huge bowl and flopped a mound of pliable bread dough out on the counter, pushing and shoving it around on the floured surface with little grunts of effort. Trudi knew better than to try to force an answer. Grams did her best thinking when she was cooking, and sure enough, when she put the dough back inside the deep bowl to rest, she turned around and stared at Trudi, her lips pursed.

"First, we're going to talk to Alex Badamo, and if he says yes, we're going to go get her. You and me. We'll get on that big train and just go get her and bring her home. If those two young 'uns want to get married, then they're going to get married. They can live here with me till they can get themselves a place."

"Oh, Grams, yes! Now we're cooking with gas!" Trudi almost shouted as she jumped from her chair. "I'll go talk to Alex." She stopped suddenly, her face clouded. "What about my parents? They'll be furious!"

"We're not going to tell them," Grams announced decisively. "It's about time for the hydrant to pee on the dog for a change."

Trudi was scrupulous about announcing her actions to her mother, without, of course, telling her the truth. She sat on a pillow and peered over the leather-coated wheel of the goliath sedan as together woman and machine set out to get a job done with vigorous purpose. She didn't like driving the big Chrysler around town. Between the heavy curtains, the bud vases next to the windows, and the sheer size of the huge car, she felt like she was driving a hearse. But today she was so elated she didn't think of those objections, and pulled out of the circular drive in front of the house and headed down Lindell Boulevard, hoping to find Alex at the gas station.

"Nope, little lady," the owner said, chewing contentedly on the remnants of a fat stogie. "He works the evening shift this week." She thanked him and sped away before he could lift his hat in good-bye. She raced down Grand, then turned onto Arsenal and headed for Marblehead Road, which led to the limestone quarry south of town. The wind whipped her hair but she ignored it, leaning over the wheel as if her desire would make the car go faster. Thick white dust covered the weeds and trees along the sides of the road in a ghostly tableau, warning her that the gates to the quarry were near. When a small convoy of dump trucks loaded with newly mined white gravel turned onto the highway, she knew she had found the entrance. Squinting against the dust, she turned the corner onto a dirt road, slowing enough to nod to the sentry on duty.

"Hey, lady," he shouted, waving at her, "you can't go in there." She ignored him and didn't stop until she spotted a small office, nothing more than a shack, with three men standing in front, their heads bent over a map.

"I have to find Alex Badamo right away," she explained. "There's an emergency in the family."

"Ah, sweet Jesus." One of the men shook his head sadly. "I bet it's his mom."

"Yes, that's it!" Trudi grabbed the reason he offered. "Please, can I talk to him right away?"

"You wait right here. I'll get him as fast as I can." Trudi walked back to her car, pacing, crossing her arms first one way, then the other, shifting her weight from one foot to the other, until she saw him walking through the huge opening cut into the side of the bluff that served as the entrance to the quarry. His dark hair was dusted with white powder, his eyes outlined by the marks of the goggles he had just removed. She hurried to him and drew him aside, out of earshot of the other men, and whispered in his ear. He stepped away from her, staring as though not believing what he heard, then threw his goggles into the air, and let out a whoop of joy, grabbing Trudi around the waist and twirling her in a dusty circle as they both laughed and laughed.

"Guess his mom didn't die," one of the observers noted.

Trudi, Grams, and Alex weren't the only lighthearted people that day. Nancy Neumann had been startled when her boss, Phillip Gates, had come striding in after lunch with a warm hello and a verve, a springiness to his step that was unusual. If a body didn't know better, one might think that he was in love. Not that he was ever discourteous, just so preoccupied and businesslike that he rarely noticed the office staff. Then, ten minutes later, she got a second surprise when Jolene Flanagin arrived for her appointment alone. It was the first time she had ever been to the office without her brother, and for a moment Nancy didn't recognize her. She held the door to Mr. Gates's office open for Miss Flanagin, and when she'd closed it behind her she snickered. Jolene Flanagin was Irish through and through, but to the secretary she looked like a massive heroine from a Wagnerian opera she had seen at the Muny Opera. All she needed on her blond head was a bowl with cow horns coming out the sides to be perfect for the part.

Phillip Gates's face showed only professional interest in

Jolene Flanagin, but his thoughts were running away with him, and he had to press his lips together and hide his mouth behind his clasped hands to keep his smirk hidden. This woman is so large, so robust and massive, that it would take two, maybe three, Trudi Groves to make one Jolene Flanagin, he mused.

"I'm really worried about the possibility of a strike," she began.

Not "we're worried," but "I'm worried," Gates noticed, wondering how many of the decisions Big John actually made.

"The employees have been grumbling for months now," she continued, "and I'm beginning to think they might really do it." She threw up her hands in a helpless gesture. "We just gave them a dime increase in wages a year ago. I don't know what they expect of us."

"I understand they also want the workday cut to nine hours," Phillip stated bluntly, mainly to let her know he knew more about the issue than she was prepared to tell him. She arched her neck and looked at him from under her lashes, a ridiculously coquettish move from a woman her size. He got the impression that she wasn't used to flirting.

"You've been talking to someone, haven't you?" She wagged a finger at him, the finger of a woman who did not prize herself, for the nails were bitten painfully short.

"I have," he admitted honestly, "and I have to tell you, I believe their request for a half-dollar an hour increase in wages is not out of line."

Her little smile immediately fell away. She sat up straighter and drew back, transformed within seconds into a hard-nosed businesswoman. "And if we do that, we will, of course, be able to afford fewer workers, which would mean a substantial number of layoffs."

Gates had heard the threat before and wasn't impressed. "It's quite possible that the truckers are prepared for that eventuality."

"You sound unsympathetic to our position." Her smile was steely. "You must know that we want you to handle negotiations for us. Is this one of your clever ploys to get a higher retainer?"

Gates's face remained impassive and he did not reply as he tapped his fingertips together, but his mind was racing with the implications of the situation. John and Jolene Flanagin had inherited a successful printing company that would be badly crippled if the truckers actually did strike as they threatened to do. He couldn't be sure whether she spoke only for the two of them or for the management of all the firms that would be hurt by a work stoppage, which would be a considerable number. He thought the latter was possible, that this was a "feeler" call to see where he stood on the issue.

Many businesses in St. Louis still used river transport, but even so their materials had to be off-loaded onto trucks. And if the truckers in St. Louis alone struck, not to mention any sympathy strikes throughout the county, it could have a crippling effect on the local economy. Three men representing the truckers had been in to see him yesterday, their hands rough and leathery, their foreheads white above the eyes, creased by hard work and worry. The case they had presented was compelling, but he had not had time yet to research their chances of winning. At this point, their union was not solid, and they did not have any money or any legal counsel. It seemed hopeless, especially in view of the tight power structure in St. Louis—the same power structure that had so effectively "protected" itself against his father.

When they asked for his help he had put them off, just as he intended to stall Jolene Flanagin. But he knew without hesitation where his heart lay.

Trudi mentally ticked off the list of things to be done as she drove back into town from the quarry. She was still elated by the turn of events, and she grinned as she thought of Alex's joyful reception of her news. She was surprised to realize that life in town was going on without any change in schedules. The milk cart plodded by, the children played marbles in the park, the shoppers exited the grocery market without a hint that today was a monumental day. This was a day when, step by little step, the road to independence was being built. She swung the car into the parking lot near Phillip Gates's law office and pulled on the brake with a newfound surge of power and hope.

"Trudi Groves to see Mr. Gates, please," she said, smiling automatically at the receptionist, who pointed her down the hall toward his office. When she stood in front of his secretary, she met her first block of the day.

"Do you have an appointment?" Miss Neumann asked.

"No, I don't, but it will only take a minute if you could just tell him I'm here."

"He's with someone right now. If you'd like, I could schedule you to see him next Tuesday."

Gates blinked. The frosted glass wall that partitioned his office from the hall distorted figures on the other side, but this was ridiculous. What he was seeing was an angel. An aura of soft light surrounded the tiny figure, glowing even through the oblique cloud of glass. Recognition dawned, and he stood up abruptly, startling Jolene Flanagin.

"Excuse me for just a minute," he apologized to his client, and opened the door to his office to murmur to his secretary, "Nancy, I'll see Miss Groves in three minutes." He closed the door without even glancing at Trudi. True to his word, he extricated himself from his meeting with Jolene and ushered Trudi into his office in record time. They stood grinning at each other, silly secret smiles that said more than any words.

CHAPTER 15

When he reached for her hand, Trudi felt the same current of excitement as the first time he had touched her that noon. She looked up, trying to assess him objectively, trying to fathom the reason for the amazing effect he had on her, but there was no readily apparent answer. He was not a classically handsome man, but the mere sight of him made her catch her breath. His lanky body was angular, its contours long and sharp. But she knew that the muscles beneath the cloth of his suit were lean and hard, and she yearned to pull him close and cushion her head against his chest.

It was his strength, his spiritual as well as physical strength, that magnetized her. Unknowingly, as she gazed up at him, her lips parted, and she let out her breath, her eyes never leaving his face, studying his narrow nose, the thick brows, the hollow cheeks, the shock of sun-bleached hair. She could see herself reflected in his brown eyes, and she watched, fascinated, as his eyes darted over her face in an unconscious effort to take her in more fully.

Gates took a deep breath, inhaling the fragrance of her, the freshness pronounced in the still, muggy air of the office. With a tiny, almost rueful shake of his head, as if resigning himself to the inevitable, he slowly bent to kiss her lips, a long, full kiss that left them both breathless. Wordlessly, he picked her up and carried her away from the glass partition, searching for a private corner in his office. She wrapped her arms around his neck and let him carry her, waiting for the next kiss. She opened her eyes dreamily, then jerked her head up to stare over his shoulder, out the plate glass window overlooking Maine Street.

"Why were you jumping up in the air?" She pulled back from him and frowned into his eyes.

"Trudi," Gates groaned, "this was a romantic moment, in case you didn't know." He dropped her unceremoniously to her feet.

"Last week I was coming out of the store across the street, and I saw you jump up in the air so high you could have touched the ceiling. The papers in your hands went flying all over."

Gates spun away from her and hung his head. When he turned around again, Trudi could see the faint pink flush of embarrassment across his cheeks. He plopped down in his desk chair, slouching like a scolded child, burying his forehead in his hand.

"Oh, Phillip! I didn't mean to embarrass you." She rounded the corner of his desk, frowning with the weight of her faux pas.

"Stay where you are!" he commanded, holding up the palm of his hand. "If you insist on tearing away the last shred of my dignity, I will tell you, but first you have to sit down in the chair on the other side of my desk so I can act like a controlled adult." He waited while she settled herself, not missing the satisfied smirk on her face. Then he stared at her, stared at the huge blue eyes and full lips, but wondering mostly about the peculiar, exasperating fascination she held for him. She raised her eyebrows expectantly, and he finally answered, "I was asked to become a partner of the firm. I was happy." He shrugged. "So I jumped."

She giggled. "I never would have expected you to literally jump for joy."

"I never would have expected you to cry about your sister," he countered. "So we're even."

A stricken look washed across Trudi's face. She blinked, and her hand covered her open mouth. Gates lunged out of his chair to kneel beside her. "Oh, God, Trudi. I'm sorry. I wasn't making light of your feelings."

"That's not it," she whispered, touching his cheek in a gesture of forgiveness. "You haven't done anything wrong. It's me! I came here on my sister's behalf, and look what happens. I forget the world when I'm around you."

"Maybe that's not all bad." He felt silly and flattered, but moved back to his chair in a professional way. "How can I help your sister?"

She related the morning's events as succinctly as she could. "We need to know the legal age for marriage in Missouri."

"Marriage?"

"Jessica and Alex Badamo are only eighteen. Is it legal for them to marry without parental consent?"

He rubbed his hand across his mouth thoughtfully. "That's very young to marry."

She looked directly at him. "They are old beyond their years. They are both mature and giving and totally devoted to each other." She turned her head to gaze wistfully out the window. "I can only hope for a love like theirs." She hesitated momentarily, then looked at him again. "They're going to have a baby in three months."

Understanding dawned, and he answered immediately, "By the time you get back from Colorado, I will have the answer for you."

Jeanne and Hal Mills sat at Grams's kitchen table, their eyes riveted on Viola Groves as she bustled around giving them instructions. They had known her for sixty years, ever since they had all started school together as little whippersnappers in a one-room, drafty old building nestled in the shadow of Mossy Mountain. They had watched her handle one crisis after another in those sixty years, the worst probably the early death of her husband in a farm accident. She had always held up well, but this morning she was as flighty as they had ever seen her.

"After you change all the linens and finish airing out that front bedroom, I want you to start cooking. Do that apple pie you're so good at, Jeanne. Hal, you can help her peel, what with her arthritis an' all." She bustled to the other side of the kitchen and picked up an envelope. "Don't forget to give this to Mr. Badamo when he comes by with the ice, and ask after his wife." She snapped her fingers. "Jeanne, will you call Jewel Frese for me and tell her I can't make the church circle meeting tomorrow afternoon. And Hal . . ."

Hal frowned. He didn't take well to being given orders, but this was special, so he kept his mouth shut. She sure was in a tizzy about this trip, he thought. Trying to keep it secret was frazzling her nerves. He hoped this didn't mean he would miss the weekly card playing at Frank Blackburn's house down in Calftown. The boys had the sweetest setup in the little brick bungalow, having put together their own small still in the bathroom that produced just enough for them to enjoy their once-a-week gathering, where they played poker, scratched, and told lies. Anyone feeling the need for refreshment just helped himself from the fiery liquid in the tub, scratching a mark under his own name written on the bathroom wall. At the end of the evening, the marks were tallied up and the drinks were paid for out of the poker winnings. Why, the firewater they made was getting smoother all the time, downright enticing, and he would hate to miss the fun.

"I wish Trudi would get back," Viola's voice cut into his musings. "We've got so much to get done." She stood with her hands on her hips, looking out the screened door. It wasn't unusual that the three old friends had congregated in the main kitchen. It was massive and cheery, with three overstuffed chairs bunched in front of the huge fireplace, which fifty years before had been used for cooking but now came in handiest for warming old bones. With a floor lamp and the table radio, this room had all they could ask for in comfort. The rest of the house was rarely used, except on Sundays when Viola's family came over, or once a month when the sewing circle met. The Queen Anne-style house was graceful but huge, much too big for a little old farm-lady. When Barner Groves insisted that his mother move into town, she, being stubborn, had done so only on the condition that she could bring her own furniture with her. Some of the bedrooms upstairs were totally bare, and some downstairs only sparsely furnished. The inside of the house looked like it wasn't being enjoyed. But the outside, with Viola's flowers and vegetable garden, was beautiful.

"Thank goodness, here comes Trudi," Viola exclaimed, stepping out to the back porch as her granddaughter drove up. They had a whispered conference that quickly turned ugly—the Millses' signal to disappear.

"Grams, don't ask me to do that! I don't want to have anything to do with him."

"If you don't ask Win if we can use his private car, we lose a whole day of travel. We've missed the Wabash connection, and the CB&Q isn't running that route because of spring flooding. Besides"—Grams played her trump card—"riding in a private car would be so much easier for Jessica in her delicate condition."

Trudi turned up the long drive to Win's home with a knot in the pit of her stomach. Grams didn't know of her treatment at Win's hands, and Trudi didn't intend to tell her or anyone else. It was a situation that was between the two of them alone. She just hoped he wouldn't read too much into her request for his help today, because she had not forgotten his demands.

In St. Louis, a town known for the beautiful homes of its merchant kings and industrialists, the Stevens family mansion was one of the most outstanding. Where most homes had huge lawns, the Stevenses' was surrounded by twenty acres of carefully groomed grounds. At the top of a low rise sat the antebellum house itself, gracious and pristine in the noontime sunlight. The facade was marked by eight massive pillars, two stories high, centered by double doors with gleaming brass fixtures. To the right was the long carriage house, converted fifteen years before to a garage for automobiles. Trudi knew that the back lawn contained the best-kept lawn tennis court and swimming pool in St. Louis. She cringed inwardly as she pulled up to the side of the house, not wanting to be here, not wanting to ask anything of Win Stevens.

She waited in the foyer while the butler went to find Win. She took a huge breath and held it, letting it out noisily between her teeth. She rocked back on her heels and stared down at the tips of her shoes, clicking them together repeatedly. She ran her finger along the edge of a small table. Stupid, she thought. No dust would dare try to rest in these surroundings. She glanced around at the imposing ancestral portraits, the gleaming sterling candelabra on the side table, wondering as she did so why Win had chosen to live here alone since his parents had died and his sister had decided to move into a smaller place closer to the country club golf course.

Before she saw him, she heard his footsteps clicking down the long hall. She put on her perkiest smile to greet him. As usual, he was immaculately groomed. She was almost hoping to find him unprepared and disheveled, for the middle of the day to most people was morning to Win Stevens, since he stayed up most of the night. Instead, he was the perfect picture of casual elegance, wearing a knit shirt and floppy white oxford trousers with a blue cashmere sweater tied around his shoulders. He held out both hands in greeting as if they had parted on the best of terms and, kissing her lightly on both cheeks in the continental manner he so often affected, led her into the library and directed the butler to serve coffee.

"I hope this visit means all is forgiven?" He smiled at her above the rim of his coffee cup. Trudi smiled back indulgently and studied the delicate flower pattern outlining the translucent china dish she held in her hands, thereby avoiding any reply.

"I've come to ask a big favor of you." She peered directly at him, not wanting to prolong the agony. "My grandmother and I need to travel west. The rail connections are inconvenient on public transport . . ."

"You don't need to say another word. The Pegasus will be ready as soon as you need it. Is an hour soon enough?"

Trudi was impressed by how tactfully he came to her aid. "This is really very generous of you," she began gratefully, but he held up his hand to stop her.

"You're not going to get off so easily." He shot her his most ingratiating smile. "If I do this for you, I will insist that you attend a housewarming party in Louisville with me in July."

Appalled by the thought, Trudi fought to conceal her reluctance, hoping he didn't notice the trembling of the cup in her hand. She was trapped. If Win's railroad car was the fastest way to get Jessica home, then she would have to make this concession. She took a deep breath, trying to camouflage her resentment at getting caught in this bind, and then gave a suitable reply.

"That could probably be arranged." She nodded, gritting her teeth behind her smile.

She gave the steering wheel a whack as she drove away from the house; she hated, hated, *hated* asking favors of anyone, most of all Win Stevens. Nevertheless, she was in a better mood an hour later as she watched the Negro porters haul their strapped luggage into the Pegasus with professional skill. As she and Grams nestled in for the first leg of the trip, she had to admit that the accommodations were damned nice. She started whistling "Sweet Georgia Brown" right along with the radio broadcast Win's butler had so thoughtfully dialed in for them.

CHAPTER 16

"Of course, I am upset by the turn of events, Barner." Madeleine Groves sat in her chair on the sun porch looking up at her husband. "But considering the mood she's in, I think that a trip with your mother is a suitable activity for Trudi right now." She was deliberately calm, knowing it was the best way to placate her husband. "After all, what possible harm can she get into with an elderly grandmother for a chaperon?"

Barner Groves kept his mouth shut, but he was amazed, nevertheless, that after twenty-five years of marriage, his wife still did not understand what a little spitfire his mother could be. He had troubling suspicions about this trip, *especially* because his mother was involved, his mother who did not live her life by the same conventions that he and Madeleine followed. Viola Groves scoffed at many things that he held dear, and keeping the relationship between the two women in his life on a cordial but distant level had taken a lot of energy.

He had consciously avoided talking about his humble origins when he and Madeleine met as students at Washington University. He knew she would find them crass and vulgar. He hadn't set out to deliberately mislead her; he just sensed that her refined sensibilities would be offended by his family's rural beginnings. And he had been correct. For she disdained listening to the stories that Grams loved to tell the children, stories of swimming in the hog wallow, climbing trees to shake down pecans, making corncob dolls for play. Madeleine was so embarrassed by the chickens Grams insisted on keeping in a corner of her yard that she would not speak of them, even though Barner had had an elaborate coop built for them, one that looked like a German castle and had cost him $5,000. Still, the problem right now was Trudi. He was irritated by her insubordination that morning, and felt it should be answered without delay.

"Did they say where they were going, at least?" he demanded of his wife. She leaned forward, resting her chin on the back of her hand, staring dimly into the near distance, trying to remember.

"Actually, no, but I do remember she said they would only be gone a few days." She heaved an exasperated sigh. "It was all so sudden. She came in like a whirlwind and was gone again before I could ask many questions. You know how difficult it is for me to deal with her when she gets like that. I so much prefer thinking things through. She confuses me with her vitality." Her husband grunted in disgust, which she knew was directed at Trudi, took a sip of his coffee, and seemed to give up on the inquisition.

He studied his wife, used to her vague detachment. Before the child died, she had had a joie de vivre, a spark, that was difficult to rekindle anymore. Baby Julia had been the most like her, an angelic child, placid and sweet, with the face of a cherub surrounded by soft dark curls. When she had died, his wife's spirit seemed to have died. But he always hoped to spark it again, to make her understand that there were others who needed her. He refused to give up trying. Now he shifted his weight and pulled a small box out of his suit coat pocket, laying it in front of her plate.

"Thank you, Barner," she murmured before opening the gift. Inside was a brooch, centered on a circle of deep blue sapphires and surrounded by small pearls of lustrous beauty.

"I thought it would look nice with the navy blue outfit," he explained. She reached over and touched his hand.

"I hope our children can be as suitably married as we are." She smiled with a brief flash of gratitude in her eyes. He knew it was the only response he would receive, but it was enough.

She straightened her spine, cocked her head, and spoke as if to herself. "Fulton. Yes, Fulton." She seemed to have made up her mind about an important issue. "We must do what we can to assist Fulton. I think it's time for a party, just a small party." Her long fingers played with the fluffy ostrich feathers that edged her satin lounge robe and her face relaxed in a harmony that came from blending her aspirations with her son's needs. She felt so much more confident when life followed a plan.

The music of the jazz band playing in the main ballroom of the country club blared through the open windows, so loud that John Flanagin had to shout to be heard. "It will be a great party." He slapped Gates on the back. "Goose hunting on the north bay is a great excuse for a get-together, away from the irritations of the office."

Gates didn't reply. He leaned forward, his elbows on the arms of the chair, hands hanging free, and his eyes did a slow circle of the table. It was an unlikely group, one that he never would have thought he'd see gathered together, certainly one that he hadn't been expecting when he agreed to have dinner with John and Jolene Flanagin. He had expected that they would be putting more pressure on him to handle the impending strike case for management. Instead, the outing seemed entirely social, and he was impatient, not wanting to be spending his time on the frivolity of dinner at the club.

Behind them, the couples on the dance floor flapped their arms and legs in a raucous rendition of the Charleston, looking sillier than most because of their obvious lack of expertise in executing the intricate steps. Directly across the table from Phillip sat Bonnie Stevens, her round, flat face free of all makeup, her hair unfashionably long, her jacketed dress a tailored style more suitable for a woman three times her age. Her head was bent, her hands clasped in her lap, but she leaned imperceptibly closer to Gardner as he whispered in her ear. It pained Phillip Gates to see his brother with the daughter of Shrader Stevens, but if Gardner's plan worked, they would be one step closer to sweet revenge.

Winslow Stevens seemed oblivious to his sister as he and his young cousin held a drinking contest with Linda Carter. This was the first time Gates had seen Linda since the night he'd taken her home from the police station, and she didn't look good. Her deep-set eyes were lined underneath with violet shadows, and in an effort to hide them, she seemed to have applied an overwhelming amount of makeup to the rest of her face. Her dress was louder than those she usually wore, a dramatic larger flower print in bright colors with a neckline so low that he was sure her conservative mother would have been shocked. Linda's voice, normally wispy and serious, had taken on a loud and grating tenor.

"And I suppose you're going to say," Win scoffed, "that my dream last night was about sex?"

Linda gave him an exasperated look. "But of course, silly man. Freud says everything, but everything, has sexual connotations. Now, if you believe him"—she held her glass in the air for emphasis—"you are a very frustrated man." She took a long swallow from the glass, dripping the corner of her long, flowing sleeve in her plate of food. She sat on Phillip's left, and he had the uncomfortable notion that she was his date for the evening, though he refused to take responsibility for her drinking, which was getting out of hand. Win's young cousin, Patti, who had remained unnaturally quiet the entire evening, leaned forward brightly.

"Frustrated? I happen to know that's not true." Her eyes blinked once, and her rosebud lips parted in an innocent smile. Stevens winced and patted her arm by way of dismissal, hurriedly continuing the conversation with Linda.

"Are you insinuating that Freud is not to be believed?" he said, egging Linda on.

"Now you're catching on." Linda winked at Win. "In Freud's view, women are the lesser sex. He says that they are more masochistic and narcissistic then men, that by the age of thirty they are rigid and unchangeable"—her voice was drenched with sarcasm—"and that they are unable to match the high moral character of the male." She had the attention of the whole table now. "And all this"—she laughed a deep, throaty laugh—"because the infant girl discovered at an early age that she lacked a penis. What a joke!" She sat back and made an exaggerated circle around the table with her eyes. "For thousands of years, women have laid back, eaten grapes, listened to music, spread their legs, and enjoyed life, while men have worked in the fields, fought the wars, gone crazy with brain work, then came home exhausted. Now, you tell me who the dumb ones are." She laughed shrilly, spilling her drink on the tablecloth, while the others chuckled.

Jolene Flanagin stood, with glass held high. "The laugh's on Freud." She reached to clink glasses with Linda. "I've never felt inferior to any man at any time." They laughed like coconspirators. Gates alone remained expressionless, disgusted by the drunken speeches, convinced that Linda Carter was trying hard to shock. He pushed his chair away from the table and walked away without preamble.

He drew in a huge breath of fresh air. He needed it after the glossy pseudo-sophistication of the party inside, the stultifying atmosphere of the club. Linda Carter's looks and behavior matched the brassy edge of the evening, noisy, animated, overdone. The room was filled with flappers, and she was the dippiest of all. He wondered if her actions were deliberately thought through or an unconscious reaction to her mother's restrictive demands. Either way, Linda was at risk of losing her way, for the dramatic difference in her was not a natural evolution but rather a rebellious, unappealing overreaction. Maybe she saw Bill Jefferson's absence as rejection. Maybe Lita Carter had gone too far in manipulating her daughter's life. Either way, Gates was convinced Linda was not handling the situation well, that she was floundering like a child learning to swim. If she was unhappy, did she really think the remedy was in wild parties and loud talk? He only hoped she slowed down soon.

The band stopped for a break, the silence a glaring relief.

HIGH SOCIETY

The evening breeze picked up, ruffling the new leaves of the bushes nearby, adding to Phillip's sense of retreat from the hectic pace of the evening. There were flowers nearby. He could smell their tart freshness, and while it was not the same, lacking the soft spiciness of her fragrance, he thought of Trudi Groves. He wanted her here. He wasn't sure what direction she would have led the conversation, but she was refreshingly iconoclastic, enough so not to have sat idly by and let the drunken statements of her friends go unchallenged. He leaned back against the brick wall and stared up into the bright night sky. It was a brave thing she was doing, going against the will of her parents. He chuckled, thinking of the energy and courage she brought to any endeavor she undertook. He broke off a stem of lilac and held the fragrant blossom to his nose. Trudi, I miss you.

"There you are, big brother," Gardner whispered as the door hissed shut behind him. "Needed a breath of fresh air, huh?" He stood close, leaning toward Phillip's ear. "They're all a bunch of lightweights. They won't know what hit 'em when we get through with 'em."

"Shut up!" Phillip warned. "Don't write them off so easily."

"Oh, testy!" Gardner backed away in mock fear. "Doesn't have anything to do with Trudi Groves leaving in Winslow Stevens's private railroad car today, does it?"

Gates didn't show any reaction to the news. He didn't even wince, but a pain sliced through his chest as if he had been kicked by a horse. He remained immobile as Gardner turned and, with a small salute, disappeared back inside.

She hadn't told him the truth—at least, not the whole truth, only what was expedient for her to reveal. How stupid he had been to misjudge her so completely, and, apparently, her feelings toward him. She was acting in character, actually, he told himself bitterly. She was, after all, the daughter of a millionaire and his hedonistic wife, both of whom had done everything to turn her into an opportunistic brat. It was easy, after all, to understand her. It would take more than he could ever offer to make her turn her back on her own heady world and all of its comforts.

HIGH SOCIETY

He had let his emotions get in the way of reason, and he was more disgusted with himself than with the shallow little Miss Groves. He would control himself in the future.

JOURNAL ENTRY:
Bucky just called. The damned federal agents raided the shop at Tenth and Broadway tonight. Bashed the still in, making it useless, and poured all the booze out in the streets. There will be a lot of drunken pigeons waddling around tomorrow. Neither Bucky nor Leo was on the premises so they can't be implicated, but it will mean a jail term for Zangle and his crew. This is not a major blow, more of an inconvenience, since it's important to keep my small-time moonshiners out in the country in production in case my supply from the city is interrupted. This raid will cost me even more than the forty G's for the still. It means I'll have to promise the boys out in the hills and farms around the Mendon/Mount Sterling area more of a cut because the arrests will scare them. If I could just get the feds on the take like the politicians, I wouldn't have to put up with this kind of nuisance.

Strike talk is building. Flanagin said her session with Gates didn't go well, and she's shrewd about such things. Don't think it did any good trying to wine and dine him at the club tonight, since he doesn't seem to be easily impressed. But if he doesn't take our case, we'll just hire some second-rate attorney and call in outside enforcement to do the dirty work. The other power brokers in town just won't need to know about my underworld resources.

Trudi has to go to Rome's Fourth of July party with me. She has the typical midwestern sense of obligation, which I used to my advantage when she needed the Pegasus. It would be safer to take Jackie, since she knows the situation, but the woman has no class, and I don't wnat to look like a small-town yokel when I meet with the Big Boys.

Tony, Capone's nephew, arrives tomorrow. Then the negotiations can begin in earnest between the Green Gang and Capone in Chicago. My father, as always, was correct. The best move I have made is to stay independent of the gangs. Now, as long as I hold these two kids there will be no bloodshed; makes me nervous as hell to have them, but the risk is worth the additional influence and trust I build up with the two groups. If it works! As part of the deal I have to keep Patti with me at all times, so after the club tonight, she went with me to Jackie's. The houses are doing great, so well in fact that we had to park the car a block away from my protected space. Jackie gave the kid a dozen dresses to play with while we were hard at it. It was Jackie's turn to work on me tonight. She started at my toes and worked up to my ears and by the time she was through, I thought I was going to explode. The second time around was plain old missionary-style, but tonight it had an added twist. The kid was standing at the foot of the bed watching. I don't know how long she had been there, but I'm sure she saw plenty. She had on some skimpy little number of Jackies, and her nips were hard. She didn't say anything and didn't appear to

*be shocked, more like interested. Jackie just
started laughing and so did the kid. We
didn't mention it on the way home, so
I guess it's all right. Maybe the kid's
not as innocent as I thought.*

CHAPTER
=17=

"You're not thinking of Jessica right now, are you?" Grams regarded her over the tops of her glasses, laying her knitting aside.

"What makes you say that?" Trudi avoided giving an answer.

"Because when you think of Jessie there is a little frown on your face and the weight of the world on your shoulders. But just now," Grams teased, "your face was all dreamy and soft with sweet thoughts."

Trudi wasn't surprised by her grandmother's insight. Grams had always been able to read her moods. She'd been thinking of Phillip Gates, picturing his long-legged lope, his flop of brown hair, his sharp, intelligent eyes. Thinking of him made her feel warm all over. She turned her head to stare out the window at the rushing scenery, and smiled, a small, secret smile. She thought of his kisses, and his long hands on her body, and the thought alone thrilled her. He makes me feel sappy, she thought, and blushed.

"Just as I thought." Grams grinned. "You're thinking of a man, and it can't be Winslow Stevens because in all the months you've been seeing him, he's never made you glow."

"Phillip Gates." She enjoyed saying his name. "Phillip Gates. I've known who he was for years but have only recently gotten to know him." Grams sat with an expectant look on her face, ready to hear more. "He's intelligent and gentle and strong." Trudi's forehead wrinkled in a frown. "And mysterious."

"Mysterious? That's an unusual word to use about someone," Grams observed.

"I don't know if it's the correct word." Trudi puzzled, pursing her lips and thinking about it harder. "Maybe melancholy is a better one. Only I don't know what would cause it." She looked directly at her grandmother, hoping the old woman's wisdom would help her understand the elusive quality of Phillip Gates. "He seems to be on the right track. He will soon become a partner in the most prestigious law firm in the city. He's in good health. He's on good terms with his family." She cocked her head. "I can't quite put my finger on it, but something is out of kilter. He's different."

"You've spent a lot of time thinking about him?"

"Yes, I have." Trudi smiled. "You'd enjoy meeting his mother. She's lovely, one of the most gracious, charming women I've ever met." Trudi shifted position, drawing her legs up under her in the commodious lounge chair soft with overstuffed cushions. She stared into the distance, enjoying the gentle rocking motion of the train, enjoying thinking of Evangeline Gates. "She is serene. Yes, that's the perfect word for her. She has such an air of patience and strength and serenity about her, like all the cares of the world have never touched her." Trudi struggled to explain. "Like all the troubles and problems of the world have passed her by."

"No." Grams shook her head slowly but emphatically.

"What do you mean, no?" Trudi quizzed.

"No one escapes the stresses and strains of life," Grams explained. "She's had her share of heartache and pain, I can tell you for sure. No one, but no one, goes through life without trouble. Sounds to me like she's just handled her share with more wisdom and refinement than most people."

Gram's words called for no reply, but Trudi scanned her face and thought about what she had said.

HIGH SOCIETY

Grams was right. Trudi could not think of anyone who did not have problems, some big, some small, some public some private. And, as she thought about it, she realized that different people dealt with their problems in different ways. Lita Carter whined. Linda Carter used booze as an escape. My mother pretends they don't exist. But Grams met her problems head on, considering them a challenge. I like Grams way best, she chuckled, then she leaned back and stared out the window.

The endless plains of Kansas were approaching, and the monotony of the landscape lent itself to introspection. She could see her own blurred reflection in the window, but even more clearly she saw the visage of Phillip Gates. The angles and shadings of his chiseled face were clear to her. Only the mystery behind his eyes was unclear. She knew little about his background, remembering only vaguely that his father had died young, that Phillip and his brother had missed a lot of school one year, and that the teacher had told them all not to speak of it when they returned.

She shook her head and blinked to clear her vision, and looked out across the countryside. The flat grassland was broken by an occasional prairie village, sparse and low, revealed only by a cluster of tall grain elevators and the steeple of a spartan white church. Trudi saw few people, but those she saw were going about their day's duties with determined grace. A woman with a scarf tied tight around her head beat at a carpet hanging on a clothesline, puffs of dust drifting away in the wind. A teenage boy, straps thrown over his shoulder, struggled behind a sway-backed horse and wood-handled plow, careful to create straight lines in the newly turned soil. At the edge of one village, an elderly woman bent to put spring flowers on a new plot in a small graveyard marked by tilting wooden crosses and the leftover weeds of winter. Death on the prairie was as simple and uncomplicated as life.

On the outskirts of another crossroads settlement, two plump children stood in a freshly plowed field, waving as the train sped by. The barefoot boy wore denim overalls and a straw hat, the girl a faded dress that hung over baggy cotton leggings. They jumped up and down, waving both arms, determined to get a response. Grams waved back, watching them until they disappeared from sight. "Bet their mom cuts their hair with a bowl over their heads," she remarked, grinning.

A few more minutes and the train crossed a narrow bridge, the water underneath a muddy brown from recent rains. A whoop of laughter from Grams startled Trudi, and she turned sharply to look out the window in time to catch a glimpse of a battered old car tilted at a precarious angle over the bank of the stream, the farmer next to it scratching his head over the situation.

"Reminds me of the time," Grams began, and Trudi smiled; she adored Grams's memories, "when your grandpa was determined to learn to drive a car. He came home one spring day in 1908 with one of Henry Ford's Model Ts, bright and shiny and sassy as could be. Proud as punch that he was the first farmer thereabouts to have his own automobile. Now, your grandfather, Robert, was one smart farmer, with a back as strong as Sampson, but he was never mechanical, and when I saw that thing I knew it was going to be disastrous. I just didn't know how quick disaster would come." She stopped talking long enough to shake her head and chuckle. "He wanted to show off for me. He was always trying to show off for me. So he insisted I get in the car that very minute and go for a ride. Everything was fine till he had to shift gears, which called for some fancy footwork besides. He got himself all tangled up, and we shot ten yards backwards when we should have been going forwards. We ended up in the pond, me, the car, and Robert. Lucky for us the pond was shallow!"

She waited while Trudi finished laughing. "Lucky, too, that a neighbor was coming by with his team of Clydesdales, and he hitched us out. Robert never drove that thing again. But I did. He'd ride beside me so long as I never mentioned the swim we took with the car. He was as stubborn as the mules he was trying to replace, but always willing to try something new, I'll say that much for him."

"Then you were a good match, weren't you?" Trudi grinned.

"I guess you could say that, girl."

"Do you think that's important, Grams? For two people to be alike?"

"Not necessarily." Grams pondered the question. "I've seen it work the other way, too, where two people not at all alike get along fine. They seem to bring out the best in each other and mesh real nice together." She intertwined her fingers to make one solid fist that couldn't be pulled apart. "It's a mystery how love works, huh, girl?" She smiled and patted Trudi on the arm.

The click of the train's wheels counted off the unending procession of telegraph poles, and Trudi laid her head back on the cushion of the chair, letting the motion of the train gently rock her into an exhausted sleep, the sleep she had lost the night before. Her nap ended abruptly as Grams's voice broke through her dreams.

"Lookee here! Will you just look at this?"

Trudi grudgingly pushed herself up and stumbled to the other end of the car, where Grams stood pointing into the tiny bathroom.

"They even painted the handles and faucet on the lavatory gold to make it prettier."

Trudi chuckled and hugged the tiny woman. "I don't think it's painted, Grams. I think it's the real McCoy."

"Don't that just beat all," Grams replied, rubbing her hands across the surface of the marble basin. Trudi glanced into the galley, noticing Grimmer hard at work helping the steward with the preparation of their meal.

"I don't think you've seen anything yet." She smiled knowingly. "Let's sit down for dinner." The table was ready to receive them, with a fresh bouquet of red roses and crystal finger bowls to the side of each plate.

"This thing"—Grams indicated the length of the car—"is bigger than I thought it was going to be. And did you know that we'll each have our own little bedrooms tonight?"

"Yes." Trudi nodded. "I think Win told me one time that the Pegasus is more than ninety feet long."

"They sure did think of everything." Grams shook her head, obviously impressed, but not so overwhelmed that when Grimmer served dinner she wasn't capable of acting as reserved as anyone born to great wealth. Neither the china with the Stevens family crest emblazoned in the middle, the intricate design of the cut-glass goblets, nor the gourmet meal fazed her. Only when he began to pour the wine did she react, holding her hand over the rim of the glass. "No, thank you." She was polite but firm.

Trudi's eyebrows shot up. "You don't like German white wine? This Riesling is a delicious vintage."

"I don't know if I like it," Grams explained. "But I do know I'd be breaking the law if I drank it, and I'm too old to get thrown in jail."

Trudi threw back her head and laughed, certain that her grandmother was joking, until she looked again and saw the set expression on her face. "You're serious, aren't you?"

"You bet I am."

"But it's such a stupid law," Trudi protested.

"Yes, it is," Grams agreed. "But those legislators who passed it had a good purpose in mind. Who am I to think that I know so much more than they do?"

"Grams, all it does is make drinking more enjoyable because it's forbidden. More people drink now than before prohibition. Already there is a strong movement to repeal it."

"I know there is, and I welcome repeal. But until then I'm not breaking the law." She waggled a finger at her granddaughter. "And just because everybody is doing it doesn't make it right."

It was a mistake to have come. Phillip Gates was aware that the other men in the hunting lodge were going out of their way to make him feel comfortable, but that was part of the problem. Theirs was a false bonhomie. He was an outsider and he knew it. Their motive in having him along on the trip was transparent, and he resented it. He would not represent these owners in the strike because they included him in their inner circle, nor because they paid him a huge retainer.

He looked across to the other side of the massive lodge, to the circle of men playing poker, to his brother, Gardner, who sat enjoying the camaraderie as easily as if he had been coming on the annual outing all his life. If Gard's plan for revenge worked, then so be it, but Gates shunned the deviousness of it. When he paid back Winslow Stevens for the perfidy of his father, it was going to be aboveboard; Win Stevens would know just who had caused him agony and ruin, and he would know why as well.

Phillip watched critically while the men kibitzed as the cards were dealt out, Gard joining in the laughter with grace, seemingly immersed in the good ol' boy network of leading businessmen as if he, too, headed a large corporation. Gates turned back the sleeves of his hunting shirt, a shirt resurrected from the back of a closet, not used for ten long years. He sipped at his glass of scotch, letting the golden liquid work at relaxing him, the rebuke in the front of his brain lying silent. None of these men, all friends, all leading citizens of St. Louis, had come to his father's rescue when he'd desperately needed their help. And he, Phillip Gates, would not help them now. He had decided to accept the invitation to the spring goose hunt on the north bay of the river out of curiosity, and to learn just how high a price tag they were willing to put on his services. This was one of the moments he had worked so hard for, worked through high school and earned a scholarship, worked through college and grad school, skipping the parties, the light times, in order to excel, in order to gain a position of leverage that would lead to Winslow Stevens's downfall.

As always in social situations, Gates sat on the sidelines and observed, learning more by looking and listening than by direct contact. He was enveloped by the massive leather chair, warmed by the low fire at his left, his feet resting disdainfully on the low, thick table carved from a single log that stretched for six feet in front of him. The two-story-high ceiling above him was crisscrossed by huge log rafters and the stone walls of the lodge were decorated with the mounted trophies of past excursions. A colorful green-winged teal shared space with a largemouth bass, both bodies caught as if in mid-motion. Goldeneye and mallard, northerns and walleyes attested to the prowess of the sportsmen gathered in fellowship for the hunt. Membership in the club passed from father to son, a cherished legacy that conferred an automatic acceptance on the holder. Rarely were new members allowed in, this being more hallowed ground than even the country club. A row of guns, their metallic sheen reflecting the firelight, stood quiet, waiting for the dawn hunt.

Out of the corner of his eye, Gates observed the approach of James Hartmann, owner of the local paper mill, as he limped to the circle of chairs around the fire. He was bent like an ancient peasant laborer, though he was not yet fifty and the hardest physical labor he had done was manning his thirty-foot sailboat. His gait had been a distinctive crabwalk for fifteen years, the result of a fall from his diving board that had injured his vertebrae, earning him the compassion that should have been awarded to someone more deserving.

"We have the inside track on the real stuff." He indicated the liquor that swirled in Phillip's glass. "Don't have to worry about rotgut." He chuckled good-naturedly, taking Phillip into the little-kept secret. "Young man, I hear nothing but good things about your work. Followed your last case closely. Thought you really cut your opponent down to size, and a worthy opponent he was, I might add."

Phillip glanced at him and gave a relaxed nod to acknowledge the compliment, but continued to sit wordlessly, waiting for Hartmann to reveal himself. Gates turned his head slowly to look at the man in silent censure. This was a decent man, a man no one thought ill of, but one who, like all the others, had forgotten Phillip's mother's needs after Charles Gates's death. He had, like the courtly gentleman he was, mouthed the usual platitudes—"If there is anything I can do, please call"—at the same time knowing full well that Evangeline Gates was far too proud to ask for anything that could possibly be construed as charity. Instead, she had lived in a downward spiral of genteel poverty, selling her precious family heirlooms to feed and clothe her children, counting on them to do their very best as she was doing her best for them, staying brave and gracious in an ungracious world.

And now he was in a position to start repaying them for their insensitivity. Not if they begged would he help them in the fight against the laborers. Quite the contrary. He had decided to handle the fight for the truckers, even if it meant losing a huge retainer, even if the working men couldn't pay him, even if it cost him the enmity of the community power brokers; he would take the case of the truckers and win.

"Wasn't the meal great tonight?" Hartmann was all good humor. "We can always count on wonderful food at these weekends. That's a fond memory of mine, you know. Great food at your home. Evangeline always prepared the most exquisite meals when she entertained. Always made the other women in our circle jealous that they weren't as accomplished as she. She made light of it, saying if anyone could read, they could cook, but she didn't fool me. My wife slaved over crème brûlée a half dozen times after having it at your home, and she never could get it right. It would curdle or separate every time." He chuckled alone, eliciting no warmth from Phillip. "Your father was a hell of a hunter, a great shot," Hartmann reminisced. "Had a beautiful double-barreled shotgun that he had custom-made by a Czech immigrant. The stock was carved with hunting scenes."

He stopped suddenly, snapping his fingers. "I think the gun is still here. No one thought to return it after . . ." He didn't finish the sentence, but hunched out of the chair and walked to a glass-fronted cabinet in one corner of the great room, unlocking it and reaching in to pull out a long firearm for close inspection. "This is it." He pushed it toward Gates, who rose to receive it. "I would suggest a thorough cleaning. The steward can do that for you, if you'd like him to."

Gates held the gun horizontally, scanning the length of it

as it rested heavily in his hands. "No," he answered slowly. "I'll do it myself."

"He was a damned good man, your dad," Hartmann murmured. "It was a great loss." He quit talking, his gaze hitting the floor after Phillip's eyes nailed him with a cold, accusatory stare. The smoldering look of disdain on the young man's face shamed the older man, and he blanched as he read the look. He knew their conversation was over. "Please give your mother my best wishes." He touched Gates's shoulder and shuffled away in defeat.

CHAPTER 18

Through the pillow, Trudi could hear the muffled clatter of the train wheels in the night as the coach gently rocked its passengers to sleep. The short silk fringe on the bottom edge of the window shade did a dance of its own, matching the excitement she felt. She left the shade open, wanting to see all the little stations come and go, sitting up to watch the passengers board or disembark to receive the hugs and kisses of waiting friends and family. None would be as happy to see each other as her own small clique. A weary baggage handler at one stop pulled a huge wagon down the lonely platform as the night conductor yelled his warning, "Boooard!" swinging his lantern to signal the engineer.

She lay back down and closed her eyes. By this time tomorrow, the Pegasus would have been shunted to a side line and maneuvered into position for the return journey on the Santa Fe line, headed back to St. Louis. Too excited to sleep, she thought of myriad things. She was sorry they had not had a chance to explain to Fulton where they were going and why. He would have been delighted. He also would have been incapable of keeping the secret, in the same way a child cannot, and therefore would have wiped out their advantage of secrecy, so it was just as well he didn't know.

HIGH SOCIETY

She threw off the silk sheet, punched the pillow, and thought of Linda. She would get over Bill, though it would be difficult, and she would, like most people, always remember her first love with a mixture of pain and pleasure. At least, Trudi *assumed* Linda would get over him, since she hadn't cared enough to go after him, to buck her mother's disapproval. But how she got over him was what concerned Trudi.

Linda was angry at her mother, hurt by Bill, and didn't know how to cope with those feelings, both natural under the circumstances. Linda had only her music for diversion, an avocation to her, a way of life to her mother, and therein lay the rub. What her mother wanted for Linda and what Linda wanted for Linda seemed to be very different. Lita was so skillful at manipulating her daughter, at playing on her sense of duty and responsibility, that Linda might never be able to understand what was happening. Without that understanding, she might strike out blindly, going off on one senseless tangent after another. If Linda was not able to define the problem, she would never solve it.

Why did some people have the wisdom, the insight necessary to define their problems and go about solving them? Sweet Jessie had stood up to her parents very calmly and rationally. Her mistake had been in underestimating their power. She had the mature strength to take responsibility for her actions, and no one would allow her to do so!

Linda, on the other hand, didn't seem to be aware of what her true problem was, let alone to have the wisdom to solve it. One weak, one strong. Curious. During the return trip, Trudi would have twenty-four hours to talk to Jessica, to try to understand. She smiled to herself, knowing they would talk themselves hoarse during the trip home.

She deliberately tried not to think of Phillip Gates. Thinking of him, she knew from experience, would not be relaxing. In the past, she would have been irritated by his superior, distant attitude. Tonight she would be agitated by the memories of his passionate kisses, a passion that had surprised her immensely. He had seemed so controlled, so reserved, so removed from the emotions of other mere mortals. It was as if he held himself back with a secret he would not share, a secret mission that put him on a level above other people. When his reserve had broken and he had kissed her, it was with a passion that had taken her breath away, a passion that was the antithesis of his control, a breaking away from his facade. Mysterious man. Intriguing man. She went to sleep thinking about him.

With the first light of dawn, Trudi woke, rolling over to sit up and hug her knees and stare out the window at the clear, rushing water that raced over the boulders in the streambed beside the tracks, a female mule deer and fawn stopping to look back at her. Pressing her face against the windowpane, she saw the brown foothills in the distance, so barren in contrast to the lush greenness of the Mississippi Valley. The craggy peaks of the Rockies rose on the blurred horizon, their majesty only hinted at through the early morning mists. She thought of the stark planes of Phillip Gates's face, the narrow nose and sharp cheekbones; a face that would be at ease in these rugged surroundings.

She bounded out of bed and into Grams's compartment. "Get up! Get up! We have to continue rehearsing what we'll say to Fritz Griffith."

Two hours later, they waited impatiently as the stationmaster rounded up a buckboard for them to use to get to the ranch.

"Too bad the phone lines are out at your place, Miss Groves," he said, delivering his apology in a slow nasal twang, " 'cause I'd sure be mighty glad to call ahead and have Fritz meet you. These spring floods have been a problem in a lotta ways."

"It's perfectly all right, Mr. Harvey," Trudi reassured him. "We prefer to arrive unannounced. If you will just make sure the Pegasus is rerouted, we will be more than satisfied." She smiled at the old acquaintance, known from all the years her family had been coming to their Colorado ranch to spend the month of August.

Even as a child, Trudi had appreciated the beauty of the

ranch, which sat unceremoniously in a broad expanse near the foothills of the mountains just beyond Denver, though then, as now, the immensity of the mountains made her feel uneasy, infinitesimal and unimportant in the face of such magnitude and grandeur. Still, she had always enjoyed the freedom the ranch offered. The time she spent riding, sometimes with the ranch hands, back into the hills and valleys where the cottonwoods and chokeberry bushes and willows provided graceful shade for peaceful picnics, was a relaxing change from city life. But after a week or two, she would be restless, ready for the company of other people. For her father, the ranch time was rejuvenating, and he would return from his hunting and fishing excursions tanned and recharged. Fulton was invariably bored, spending long hours lying on his back watching the clouds scud past in an unending maze of indefinite patterns, while Jessica meandered from one adventure to the next, watching beavers, counting birds, gathering wildflowers, never exhausting her list of things to do and see.

Grams held the reins of the placid team with aplomb, the long-ago-learned skill coming back to her with ease. Trudi clasped her hands tightly in her lap, more nervous with each passing minute. When they topped the next rise, the arched gate of the ranch would come into view, and they could reclaim Jessica.

Fritz Griffith bent his knees to brace the hoof of the old mare and inspect her shoe. He reached for the trimming knife and pried a rock from under the iron band; then, satisfied with the job, he allowed the leg to drop and patted the horse's flank. He loved his life on the ranch and would be forever grateful to his father for having had the courage to emigrate, fleeing the unending wars of Bismarck, and thereby providing a safe, peaceful haven in the United States for his sons. Fritz had been too old to serve in the Great War, and he would never know the agony of sending a son off to fight, since he and his wife had no children. He straightened up slowly and stepped outside the barn to survey the morning sky.

Trudi and Grams spied Griffith as he stepped out of the barn, his lean-legged pants and broad-brimmed hat forming a distinctive silhouette. By the time they reined in next to the gate of the picket fence, he had loped over to grab the reins and tie them securely to the hitching post.

"Sure is a pleasant surprise to see you two." He touched the brim of his hat and moved to help them down from the buckboard. "If you sent a letter saying you were coming, we sure didn't get it." Both Groves women made no comment, having decided the less said the better, but he continued, unaware of their silence, "Hope you've come to stay a spell with Miss Jessie."

"Jessie is the reason we've come." Grams's voice was sweet, and she smiled her most pleasant smile. "If you could tell us where she is?" She turned her head to look questioningly at the house.

"This time of the morning, she'd be down by the creek." He jerked his head to indicate the stream that flushed the pasture behind the homestead. "Guess you're anxious to see her." Their plan of action called for quickness; Grams was to keep the Griffiths talking while Trudi swiftly rounded up Jessie, bag and baggage, at the same time trying to avoid suspicion on the part of Jessie's temporary guardians. Grams pulled a counterfeit letter out of her pocketbook, one she and Trudi had composed after carefully cutting the embossed Stevens family insignia off the letterhead of the paper they had found in the train.

"This will explain our arrival." Grams handed him the bogus letter with the forged signature of her son, Griffith's boss. "And while you're reading that, I'll round up Jessie's belongings and Trudi can run and get her."

With that signal, Trudi walked briskly past the corrals and barns and, once past the last outbuilding, began running as fast as she could, slowing only to scan the meadowland for a sign of her sister. Ponderosa pines banded a small patch of grassland already lush with knee-deep grass and spring wildflowers, and in that patch about a quarter of a mile distant, Trudi caught sight of Jessica. She ran hard, her feet pounding the ground, yelling at the top of her lungs. Jessie was squatting, examining something on the ground, and at first turned only her head. Her soft brown hair fell over her shoulders, the morning light adding a glowing sheen to its surface. Then she rose and turned to face her sister, standing with her arms hanging at her sides, and by the time Trudi reached her, tears were streaming down Jessie's cheeks.

"I don't know about this, Mrs. Groves." Griffith pushed his hat back and scratched his forehead. "Mr. Groves said I shouldn't do anything till I got word from him."

"But this *is* word from him," Grams argued, crossing her fingers behind her back. "The trip to Europe was a last-minute decision. He said something about the market being stabilized now after the war." She scrunched her face up convincingly. "Barner and Madeleine are in New York City now, waiting for us to bring Jessica to them. Then we will spend the next three months traveling. At least, the women will. Barner will have to return to take care of business before then."

"Will you be seeing Ireland a'tal?" Margie Griffith asked, revealing her ready belief in the plan. A small, robust woman of fifty, her red hair twisted in a bun at the back of her neck, the cowhand's wife had had a lifelong wish to see the homeland of her grandparents, and had counted on the extra money they had been promised for taking care of Jessie to take her there.

"I think we will be only on the mainland, but we might change our plans," Grams lied brightly. "And I'm to tell you that you will receive full payment for the responsibility of Jessica's care." A spasm of undisguised joy lit up the woman's face, and Grams knew she had an ally, though Fritz Griffith's face was still clouded with skepticism.

The afternoon sun was gone, the day dark and dreary with rain clouds threatening from the western plains. "Do you have the total, indissoluble support of the men?" Gates's countenance was as gloomy as the weather as he glared at the truckers gathered in his office. They all murmured their assurances, but he continued playing devil's advocate. "What if the walkout drags on for months? How will you feed your families? How will you pay your mortgages?"

"We've been scrimping for months, Mr. Gates," Victor Wellman explained, nervously twisting his cloth cap. "We've got a pool of cash to draw on if we have to, and we've already planted a huge garden out east of town past Baldwin Field. We'll eat vegetables all summer, if need be." The other men chuckled, and Wellman glanced toward them, thankful for the support.

Phillip Gates's face remained stony, his eyes riveted on their faces. He was not convinced that the men were fully aware of the hardships ahead of them. He leaned forward to give his words emphasis. "And if the strike turns violent, what will you do? If they fight with clubs and guns, what will you do?"

The six men, all old beyond their years from long hours of hard work and money worries, shuffled and shifted, hitching up their suspenders and pulling at their shirt collars, and finally nodded to each other in agreement. "We had some hot discussions about that and we decided" —Wellman looked around the room one more time—"we decided we'd fight back. We may not have money and brains, but we got heart and muscle!"

"Hear! Hear!"

"Damned right!"

Gates was not impressed by their bravado, knowing that such enthusiasm was easy to muster now. Three months from now would be the real test. If they wanted more money and fewer hours on the job, they would have to fight for it, and it would be a fight of will as much as brawn. He was prepared to fight to win, and he had to make sure these men were, too.

The group stayed another two hours, talking about their exact demands, what type of opposition they could expect, and what aspects of their demands would be negotiable. By the time they filed out, they were both exhilarated and exhausted. The workmen, humble in their origins, reasonable in their expectations, and energized by their hopes for the future, thanked Gates profusely, shaking hands and nodding their good-byes as he escorted them through the restrained elegance of the law firm's lobby.

He had just seated himself back at his desk, pen in hand to make notes, when Nancy stuck her head in the door. "Mr. New would like to see you as soon as possible."

Gates sighed irritably. Parker New, senior partner in the law firm, was the crusty, capable, cautious focus of the group practice who still wore the stiff collar and cuffs popular in his youth. While Gates respected the old man's acumen, he was invariably annoyed after any conference with him because his mind and tongue worked so slowly. It was difficult to get him to come to the point, and Gates did not have the time and patience to deal with that nuisance at the end of a long day.

"Yes?" Gates stuck his head in the door of New's corner office, not entering completely.

"Come in, come in, my boy." New waved a beefy hand. Gates stepped inside the paneled room, its shelves lined with leather-bound law books, but he deliberately remained standing. New raised his eyebrows in a question. "The group of men who just left your office . . . ?"

"The truckers?" Gates urged him on.

New leaned back and rocked in his high-backed chair, nodding slowly as he tapped his fingertips together, continuing his questioning. "They were here for . . . ?"

"For a preliminary conference before the strike actually begins," Gates explained.

"So you will be their counsel?" New's eyebrows rose.

"That's right." Gates knew what was coming, but remained calm and implacable.

New swung around in his chair and faced the view over Market Street, studying the dark cumulus clouds in the sky, stalling for time before finally speaking. "Do you think that would be prudent?"

"What would be imprudent about it?" Gates was being deliberately obtuse.

New swung back around, unaware that his desk light gleamed off his gold watch chain in a dazzling beam. He raised his face to stare at the ceiling, and thought carefully before answering. "It's going to be a controversial case." He finally looked directly at Phillip.

"I'm aware of that," Gates answered simply and honestly, waiting for the next innuendo, but surprisingly, the attack was direct.

"There might be a conflict of interest. Depending on what companies are struck, of course. If any are clients of ours, you might have to disassociate yourself from the case."

Gates stepped close to the desk and leaned forward on his hands, looking his partner directly in the eye. "No," he said, "I might have to disassociate myself from the firm." He straightened, looked at New for a long, long moment, then strode from the room.

The gathering clouds built to the breaking point, rolled over the city, and broke in a burst of thunder and lightning.

CHAPTER
==19==

Jessica had remained so placid throughout the trip that Trudi was afraid she wasn't feeling well. But as the train tracks paralleled the wide, muddy Mississippi, Jessie's spirits revived, and she walked from window to window searching for the best view.

"Everything is so green and lush," she whispered. "So beautiful." She turned to Grams and Trudi with the most beatific smile imaginable. "I'm so glad to be home." She hugged one, then the other.

Grams was struck once again by the differences between her two granddaughters. They looked like sisters, of course, the same large eyes, full lips, and slight upturn at the ends of their noses. But everything about Jessie was muted, from her tawny brown hair to her full, rounded body to her misty, soft voice. Everything about Trudi was dramatic, from her huge, electric blue eyes to her bouncing milk-white curls to her chiming, bell-like voice. Grams chuckled. Jessie was a moonbeam, while Trudi was a sun's ray.

As the train slowed near the edge of the city, preparing for its stop at Union Station, Jessie grew pensive again, sitting quietly as Grimmer and the two other women prepared to disembark. Her pink cotton dress was still crisp and fresh, her white gloves immaculate. Her expression was thoughtful, her lips pressed together firmly.

"Oh, no," Trudi groaned, peering out the window while pulling her grandmother near to share her view. Barner Groves stood in the center of the platform, his hands clasped behind his back, his feet planted firmly apart, his straw bowler pulled low on his forehead, the frown between his eyes still quite visible as he ignored the jostling crowd that scurried around him. "How did he find out?"

"I imagine Fritz Griffith got ahold of him in some way." Grams heaved a huge sigh. "I never was a very good liar. The old cowpoke isn't dumb, you know. He just didn't believe us."

Trudi stood up, her chin thrust out in resolve. "Just because Father knows doesn't mean we have to change our plans." She peered over at Jessica, who sat unaware of the impending trouble, her spine straight, her hands folded demurely in her lap. Trudi pulled a chair close and grasped her sister's hands. "Father is waiting on the platform."

The train jolted to a stop, its brakes hissing, but Jessica didn't flinch. "Is Alex here?" she asked simply.

Trudi stepped across the width of the car and bent to look out. Alex Badamo stood near the double doors of the platform, clean and neat in his best clothes, a white dress shirt buttoned securely at the neck, his black suspenders tight over his shoulders. His hands were stuffed in his pockets, and he was nervously biting his lower lip as his eyes darted from Barner Groves's broad back to the windows of the train.

Trudi's face broke into a grin. "You bet he is!"

Jessica remained composed, only the tiniest tightness visible around her mouth. She rose slowly, as dignified as any princess, and walked to the exit. Trudi and Grams glanced at each other anxiously, then hurried to follow her down the tiny metal steps.

Barner Groves immediately stepped forward, glowering menacingly. "See here, young lady," he began to bluster.

Jessica ignored him. She remained serene and poised, simply acting as if she were unaware of his presence, walking by him as if he didn't exist. He stopped in his tracks, his mouth hanging open, as his youngest daughter passed him by without a glance, walking directly toward her anxious lover. Trudi and Grams stared at each other incredulously, then back at the monumental scene unfolding in front of them.

Once again Jessie was standing up to her father, and this time her quiet strength would carry her through to victory. Barner Groves took one more step toward Jessica, then stopped, watching helplessly as Alex Badamo hurried toward her and folded his arms around her, holding her close, whispering in her ear as they both cried.

Gardner Gates backed Bonnie Stevens tight against a tree at the edge of the golf course and nuzzled her neck. "Bobby Jones may have a putter he calls Calamity Jane, but I have a golfer I call Bombing Bonnie." She giggled at his twaddle, feeling lighthearted and pretty nevertheless.

She still held a golf club in her right hand, but with her left she pushed against his chest. He took the club away and tossed it farther into the rough; its shaft was barely visible under the thick bushes where it landed.

"I dare you to go after it," he whispered. "I dare you to go anywhere near those bushes." Bonnie blinked three times, her breath short and fast on his cheek. She looked up and down the fairway, deserted at this time of day, and made her decision. She pushed hard and ran away from him, expecting, hoping that he would follow. When she neared the bushes she dropped to her knees, rolling under the low-spread branches of the ancient white oak tree. He growled playfully as he chased her, grabbing her ankle to roll her over on her back, pinning her body flat with his.

They giggled together as he rubbed her nose with his before he grappled with the buttons of her blouse, pulling it open far enough for him to nuzzle her bare breast. She groaned, twisting her body for his easy access. She struggled out of her blouse, the whole time urging him not to stop, wanting him to pull and push and play with her tiny breasts, wanting him to bite and nibble at them until, as always, she would climax in a frenzy of white heat. But he stopped, only long enough to pull off his slacks, then strip her silk panties from under her skirt. When he touched her again, it was with his tongue. He licked at one pointed nipple, then the other, as she panted, her breath ruffling his hair. When he raised himself to kiss her, his tongue entered her mouth at the same moment he penetrated her, and he pumped fiercely in response to the agitation of her pelvis. She squeezed her eyes shut, concentrating on the delicious thickness of him, spreading her legs as she raised her hips from the grass again and again and again, pushing against him, pulling at his back, wanting the sensation to last forever.

He rose to his knees and put his hands underneath her hips, jerking them up, forcing himself as far into her body as possible, closer, harder, three more times, hearing the breath leave her with each thrust, until she cried out in agonized passion. They rolled apart, their chests heaving noisily. Only after they caught their breath did he speak.

"Tennis anyone?"

Nancy Neumann tapped lightly on the door of her boss's office. He had been short-tempered for the last two days, and she didn't want to interrupt him any more often than necessary. Mr. Gates was usually reserved and even-tempered but never unpleasant, and his irritability concerned her. She felt sure the call from Miss Groves would perk him up. She was wrong.

"Tell her I'm busy," he barked, sorry the minute he spoke that he had been so abrupt with his secretary. He leaned back in his chair as she closed the door and ran both hands through his hair, trying to dispel the flush he'd felt when he heard Trudi's name. So she was back in town. Let her wait. He wasn't going to jump at her command like Winslow Stevens did. He wasn't ready to accept her duplicity, and he didn't trust himself to talk to her. He would set the problem aside to deal with it at a later time. When Miss Neumann knocked two minutes later, he was more settled.

"There are three people here to see you, Mr. Gates." When he raised his eyebrows inquisitively, she stepped inside and whispered, "It's the Flanagins and a lady I don't know."

Gates shrugged to show his assistant that he hadn't expected them but also didn't mind. "Show them in," he said as he slipped his suit coat back on, leaving his tie loose at the neck.

Linda Carter preceded Jolene and John Flanagin into the room, giggling and tiptoeing in slyly, her skinny calves and full bust reminding Gates again of a pouter pigeon. She had her short hair slicked back tight against her head in an exaggerated imitation of the newly dead hero Valentino. Her perfume assaulted his nose with its heavy gardenia scent. But the aroma wasn't enough to hide the smell of whiskey. She was drunk, or at the very least tipsy, and she almost fell when she stopped unexpectedly and Jolene bumped into her, giggling equally as hard as Linda.

Gates had not seen Linda often since her break with Bill Jefferson, but each time she had been drunk, and Gardner, who kept current on such things, said she had been seen in the company of four different men in the same number of nights. She had become, almost overnight, a vamp, a user and abuser of men. But what she did, she did openly, more honestly than Trudi Groves. Nevertheless, he was surprised by Linda's actions, surprised that she didn't have more reserves of strength and self-direction that would keep her from such excessive behavior. Gates thought she was acting like a petulant child who hadn't gotten her way and so was going to make her mother pay. He sighed, disgusted with himself for being so judgmental.

Though Phillip Gates was not enjoying the interruption, John Flanagin stood back, entranced with the shenanigans, grinning as though the two women were putting on a show just for him. Linda and Jolene giggled incessantly, whispering behind their hands like schoolgirls. Gates was not amused, but his exasperation was not noticed.

He looked Flanagin in the eye as they shook hands, but even so, he was able to grasp Flanagin's appearance from head to foot. He was large and bulky, already going soft. Gates figured he'd have a potbelly by the time he was thirty. His suit was expensive, a dark brown gabardine with wide lapels and patch pockets set off by the straight, polished oak walking stick he carried.

When Gates indicated the chairs for them to sit down, both Flanagins took heed, but Linda circled the office, wrinkling her nose.

"This place is rather dull. Very impersonal." She spoke to the room, not caring what Phillip Gates felt at her comment. Only when she stood next to him at the desk did he seem to take notice. "Nothing but books, books, books!" She waved her hand in the air.

"This is where I work. Would you prefer I display lace doilies and fresh flowers?" His voice remained equable, but the sarcasm was apparent.

"Silly boy!" Linda laughed. "I just thought you might have pictures of family or a sweetheart around." She smiled at him with head cocked, then walked to John's side and took the cane from him.

I don't have time for this, thought Gates. He was vexed by her coyness, as he was always vexed by coyness in any woman, and because he was tired. He had worked at the office until midnight the night before, and like it or not, he had trouble sleeping because he kept thinking of Trudi. He determined to brush the thoughts aside.

"What can I help you with? I assume this isn't a social call in the middle of the day." He hoped he had gotten his point across without sounding too crusty.

"Yes and no," John Flanagin began.

Jolene finished, "We need your help on a community project . . ."

". . . but wanted to drag you out of here to talk about it over lunch," John explained.

Phillip held up his hand, shaking his head. "I can't take the time off." He was picturing the long, leisurely lunches this crowd was used to.

"See!" Linda interjected smugly. "Didn't I predict he would say that? We have a plan," she hurried on before Gates could object again. "If we go down the block to the Coronado, where they serve pork tenderloin sandwiches in the most delicious bread crust, you can be back here in a half hour." Nonchalantly, she unscrewed the head of the cane and tipped it to her mouth, sloppily swallowing the hidden hooch before passing it on to Jolene.

Gates scowled and glanced at the wall clock, still reluctant, only half listening to what John was saying.

"... in college, so we knew you have great organizational skills, which is what we need to perk this project up."

"What's the project?" Gates inquired.

"Just come with us, and we'll tell you."

The foursome took off down Market Street, walking west toward the library, Gates's long, ambling stride matching the women one step to two. A Salvation Army band stood on the far corner of Washington Park, thumping out a tinny rendition of "Where He Leads Me, I Will Follow." Phillip paid no attention to the band or the flighty conversation of the trio he walked with, concentrating instead on the fountain in the center of the park. The white froth of water that shot like a geyser twenty feet into the air was inviting, and he could just picture Trudi romping in it. He came as close to smiling as he had in days.

Flanagin held the dirty wooden door as the other three entered the dark interior of the grill, hesitating while their eyes adjusted from the bright afternoon sunlight. The place was big, crowded with booths around the outside edges and square linoleum-topped tables nearby. At the far end was a pool table, its hooded light hanging low over the center, spotlighting the bright green felt on the surface. The ceiling was high, hidden from view by darkness, the long wooden bar decorated at the bottom by a thick brass rail. Workingmen, some in uniform, some in street clothes, lounged around, playing pool or standing at the bar in clusters of two or three. Almost all turned to look at the newcomers.

"Don't you just love to come to this kind of place?" Linda whispered as they found a booth and slid in.

"What kind of place?" Gates asked, but Linda giggled and punched his arm without answering. "What is this project?" he asked as soon as they had ordered, wanting to force the discussion along.

"The people involved are supposed to remain anonymous, but it's a poorly kept secret." Jolene gave him a confidential smile.

"Go on," Gates urged.

"The Veiled Prophet Ball . . ." Sharon looked at him seriously.

". . . has been lacking in emphasis the last few years, and it needs new blood." John fished papers out of his pocket to show Gates, but he was stopped before he could really begin. Gates leaned back against the high wooden back of the booth, shaking his head.

"No," he said simply, "I'm not getting involved in the Veiled Prophet Ball. If you want me to work for the orphanage, or—"

He was interrupted by the waiter, a puny guy with ball-bearing eyes, bringing their food. Linda put out her arm, holding her coffee cup for the waiter to refill. The man grinned and flicked his wrist. A narrow rubber hose protruded from his sleeve along the palm of his hand, and with a quick snap, he squirted whiskey into her cup, drawn from the flask he carried in his back pocket through the tube running along the inside of his shirtsleeve.

Gates missed it all. His attention was riveted on the door of an unmarked room along the opposite wall. Six men, too many to fit in a rest room, came walking out, and the burly character he had seen talking to Win Stevens two weeks before was one of them.

"Who's the boxer in that group over there?" He jerked his head, asking the question of the waiter, who didn't even turn his head.

"Why you wanna know?" he countered.

"I know I've met him." Gates tried to sound casual to allay the man's suspicions. "It's either Leo Elderbrake or Bucky Bathshelder. I keep getting the two mixed up." He shrugged, acting dumb.

"Jeez, mister. How can you get those two mixed up?" The waiter shook his head in amazement. "Leo Elderbrake is a pip-squeak compared to Bucky, there." He went away still shaking his head.

Jolene Flanagin ignored the whole exchange and pressed the issue that was of import to her. "We need someone young, someone with standing in the community, to help on the committee." Gates paid no attention to her, watching the door as two men went in and three more came out.

"What's back there that causes so much traffic?" he asked John, not taking his eyes off the door.

"I suppose that's the room where they have the slot machines," he answered. "Every place in town's got them. Never been interested, myself. I prefer the card games at the Cuckoo Clock; much higher stakes. Slots are the workingman's diversion."

Gates could stand no more. He stood up, said his goodbye, and left with no explanation.

"Madeleine, I don't think you understand what I've been saying." Barner Grove's face was livid with frustration. "They've been in Adams for three hours now." He paced the library floor, his footsteps so heavy that the fringe on the lampshade quivered. "I don't think she has any intention of coming home. We can only hope she's staying at my mother's house instead of with that Italian family."

He stopped in front of a narrow panel in the bookcase and slid it sideways for the third time in the last hour. Behind it were four shelves holding bottles of liquor, heavy Baccarat crystal glasses standing with dignified grace on either side of the bottles. He poured himself another scotch, and drank it straight down before sliding the panel closed. He looked at his wife, and took a deep breath.

She was so beautiful, even more so, he realized, when she withdrew into her protective cocoon. She seemed to remove herself from any emotion, any words that would cause her to face harsh reality. She sat in the chair with her relaxed hands falling over the carved wooden arms, her head held high, her face serene, her eyes on the opposite wall.

"You'll be home from the office in time for dinner at eight, won't you?" She spoke for the first time in thirty minutes, still not looking at him. "Tonight is the night we're having the Brenners over."

"Madeleine, I'm concerned about our daughter. I'm worried about what she's doing!"

"And I'm concerned about our son," she answered, rising slowly and crossing the room. She pulled the doors apart and stepped through, turning to close them without looking up at her husband.

The breath left him; his shoulders sagged. He didn't know how to reach her anymore. He didn't want to lose another daughter, but he didn't know how to deal with the situation alone.

In sudden fury, he threw the glass across the room and watched it shatter against the onyx hearth, its shards sparkling in the afternoon sun. He stood for a moment watching a large piece of crystal rock back and forth, until it quieted itself. Then he marched from the library and down the long hall to the basement steps. Not even bothering with the banister, he took the steps two at a time.

Hattie stood beneath the bare bulb, feeding wet clothes into the wringer of the machine. When she turned around and saw him, her heart lurched. He looked angry, his breath coming in deep gulps. Instinctively, drying her hands on her apron, she stepped to put the machine between them. In three paces, he had her by the wrist, pulling her toward the fruit cellar. He didn't speak at all, just started unfastening his clothes, his eyes never leaving her bosom.

She resisted weakly, knowing the futility of it, and finally lay on the floor and squeezed her eyes shut, waiting for his onslaught. When he first touched her, he was rough, pulling at the top button of her uniform, but when he put his mouth to her breast, he was gentle. And by the time he pushed into her, he was as tender as any caring lover, folding her in his arms and rocking her with the rhythms of his own needs.

When it was over she sat propped against the wall, huddled in a ball, her face hidden in her folded arms, while he dressed. When he'd finished, he squatted beside her and forced money into her hand.

"Buy your little daughter a doll. Take good care of that little girl," he whispered, and left.

CHAPTER
20

The Groveses' home had rarely looked so lovely. Fresh white lilies in a huge bouquet cascaded over the top of a three-foot-high trumpet-shaped Ch'ing dynasty vase that decorated the mahogany receiving table in the center of the front hall. The furniture gleamed with lemon oil, the pillows were plumped to perfection, and the silver shone with a soft patina of age. The porcelain chandelier blazed down on the arriving Brenner family, mother, father, and two daughters, one more shy and quiet than the other.

Madeleine Groves considered this one of her most challenging projects, but one that she felt sure would have a positive long-range result. She had chosen her clothes, and even Barner's and Fulton's, with special care, and she felt good about her chiffon dropped-waist dress with crystal beading. Its soft folds flowed, making her appear calmer than she felt. As she led her guests into the dining room, she began to relax. The table was set with a pale yellow damask cloth to complement the centerpiece of fresh yellow jonquils and tulips, which she had arranged herself in her favorite Waterford crystal bowl. The two small candelabra gave off just the exact amount of low romantic light to help even the plain Brenner girls look good. Dinner conversation was stilted at first, but she knew that she could draw the family out by asking about their purebred collies, many of which had won show awards around the Midwest.

"We have always avoided the shows out East, you know," Phyllis Brenner sniffed. "The people are so pushy, so cold, we just don't enjoy the atmosphere as much as in our home territory." She patted at the prim lace Peter Pan collar of her dress, the cameo she wore there as understated as her personality.

"How many dogs do you have right now?" Barner asked politely, making an effort for his wife's sake.

"We have twenty-two, more than usual," Gene Brenner replied. "Had to hire a third groomer to handle them, and good groomers are hard to find. But we'll sell most of the last litter, keep only the two that the trainer says have the most potential."

"You might enjoy coming over to the kennels to see them, Fulton." Phyllis Brenner smiled at the young man who sat directly across from her oldest daughter. "They are beautiful animals. Janet could give you a guided tour. She's becoming quite an expert." Janet blushed and buried her chin in her chest before Fulton could mumble a disinterested reply while studiously avoiding the silent rebuke in his father's eyes.

Dinner was completed with a spectacular chocolate soufflé, and the group retired to the front room for coffee. Madeleine Groves had done her research well, and knew better than to offer the Brenners any liquor. She also knew that her son had excused himself twice already during the evening to secretly swig from his own private cache of liquor. As the Brenners rose to leave, she made a casual suggestion.

"Possibly Janet would like to stay and walk in our garden with Fulton? I have recently begun plantings to simulate the walled garden at the Villa Capponi, which I fell in love with when Barner and I visited Florenza last year."

Fulton rolled his eyes at the ceiling, not as much at the invitation as at his mother's affectation of pronunciation. Janet Brenner cast scared little rabbit eyes at Fulton, who gave her a weak smile while she fidgeted with the tiny pleats on the skirt of her dress. The more drinks he had managed to sneak during the evening, the more inviting Janet Brenner looked. She had not said anything of interest during the entire night, but he had noticed her slender ankles above the pointed satin slippers and her delicate arched neck rising from the loose scarf around her shoulders, little things in a woman that he found enticing. She certainly didn't hold the blatant appeal for him that most of the doxies he picked up did, but still . . . His thoughts stopped there, as the Brenners consented and departed, sans Janet.

When the young couple got to the garden, Fulton chuckled aloud. Good old Mom hadn't left anything to chance. An ice bucket filled with a bottle of champagne and a silver tray with a bottle of scotch and appropriate glasses were resting in the center of the stone table next to the reflecting pool. The night, with its black velvet sky and glistening stars, provided the perfect background for romance. He shrugged himself out of his tux jacket and loosened the bow tie around his neck.

Janet demurred only slightly when he offered her champagne, pretending to be more concerned with the wrinkles she might get in the skirt of her dress. "I really shouldn't," she said, reaching up from the bench where she had settled for the delicate tulip-shaped glass.

"It's better if you drink it quickly before the bubbles are gone," he instructed, watching as the neophyte followed his direction, and then poured himself a generous tumbler of scotch. He refilled the giggling girl's glass, and asked, "How much of the actual work do you do with the dogs?" He was determined to get her to say a complete sentence.

"Quite a lot, really. I spend at least two hours a day with the trainer and pups. We've found that starting before they're at least six months old is wasted effort." The sheen of her dark brown hair was pronounced in the moonlight, and Fulton couldn't tell if her eyes sparkled or if the scotch was playing tricks with his eyes. He sat down next to her, encouraged when she didn't move away from his closeness. "My mouth seems to be dry." Janet's voice revealed her surprise as she gladly accepted more champagne.

Fulton took the last swig of liquor from his glass and set it down before leaning close to the young woman. I wonder if she is a virgin? he thought. I wonder how much she knows? He turned his head and nuzzled her ear, not really surprised when she quickly pulled her head and shoulder together to protect her neck.

She began talking nervously. "Two of our bitches are in heat right now, and we have a stud arriving tomorrow from St. Louis to breed them." That was all the encouragement he needed before making his big move.

The windows were open in the house. From her vantage point a few feet away from the window of her darkened bedroom, Madeleine Groves watched her son lunge for Janet Brenner, just as she knew he would. The girl struggled quietly for a few moments, but as expected, Fulton was able to overpower her. As he lay on top of her, a cloud passed over the moon, spreading darkness over the scene below and smothering the satisfaction Madeleine Groves had felt a minute before. This was no small feat she was engineering, tricky, dangerous, and she wasn't sure it would conclude satisfactorily, but it was worth the risk.

When a small, smothered scream trailed through the night air, she felt her first real apprehension, and moved quickly away from the window. She was ready when the adjoining door to her husband's room opened tentatively. Barner stuck his head in, his hands hurriedly tying the sash of his robe, his voice worried.

"Did you hear a noise just now?" He had his head cocked quizzically. Madeleine Grove's heart was beating with fear, hoping the deed would be over before discovered.

She raised herself on one elbow, her satin gown falling off one shoulder. "It was just a bird, I think. We have to get used to their songs now, dear. It's their season, you know." She smiled seductively, hoping he could see it across the room. "Would you like to sleep with me tonight?" She had to keep his mind off the noises from the garden. He straightened, his surprise apparent from his stance.

"Yes," he answered simply, and began removing his robe before he reached the foot of her bed. He hesitated, looking at the open window. "First, this needs to be closed."

"No!" She tried to stop him, but it was too late. He stood in front of the window with his hands raised on the sash, looking out on the scene in the garden, the silk surface of his pajamas reflecting the return of the bright moonlight.

"Oh, my God! What is he doing to her?"

Grams and Jessica, exhausted by the trip, were already in bed, but Trudi was charged by the thought of seeing Phillip Gates. Her heart pounded as she pulled open the heavy door of the bank building and ran through the outer lobby and up the steps to the second floor. Every office was dark and deserted, except for the faint light that came from deep inside the law office in front of her. She banged on the glass, knocking as hard as she dared, knocking until she saw him coming. When Gates opened the door, she stood with her hands on her hips, glaring up at him.

"Why the hell didn't you call me back? You knew I needed that information."

"What the hell are you doing in pants?" he snapped back. "You look like a boy!"

Trudi was stunned by the anger in his voice, and looked down foolishly at her outfit. The beige pleated trousers were the height of fashion, daring and different, but she didn't expect him to know that. She had chosen the silk blouse with care, its full sleeves and plunging neckline the only differences from the tailoring of a man's shirt.

All Gates saw was the rise of her breasts through the silk, the curve of her hips where the trousers clung to them. He clenched his teeth, determined to remain angry. She had come to him for help and he had given freely, only to find out she used other men in the same way.

Trudi let her hands drop to her sides, her shoulders sagging. His craggy good looks never failed to grab at her heart, his eyes, so serious and angry, still not masking the haunted look deep inside them. She couldn't stay angry.

Instead, she reached for the door and closed it between them, then knocked formally, patiently waiting for him to open it. This time it opened slowly, and Gates looked at her warily.

"Good evening, Phillip." She smiled her sweetest smile. "I do hope I'm not bothering you, but you had mentioned a few days ago that you might be able to get some information for me."

He stood looking down at her and, shaking his head, gave a resigned sigh. He hesitated long enough to rub the stubble on his chin before jerking his head to tell her to follow him, leading her through the darkened outer office to his own, where a single light lit a small circle on the desk. He lowered his long body and slumped unceremoniously into one of the leather barrel-back chairs that circled the table in a corner of the office. Then he stuck his legs out in front of him, crossed his feet at the ankles, and just looked at her, looked steadily without blinking, waiting for her to speak.

"We have Jessica home safely," she began, watching him nod his understanding, "and they're anxious to get married before my parents can create any obstructions." She licked her lips nervously, vaguely aware that he was especially reserved, almost glum. "Depending on what information you can give me, they will make their plans accordingly." She looked him straight in the eyes, trying to convince him how serious she was, but he still did not speak. "I'm sorry I came barging in here. I guess I'm just tense from the last few days traveling."

"Why would that be?" His voice was low and she had to lean forward to hear him. "You had very comfortable accommodations."

So that was it, Trudi thought. He knew they had used Win Stevens's private car. The unshakable, impenetrable Mr. Phillip Gates was jealous! She thought carefully before answering, working hard not to feel smug.

"If you are referring to our use of Win's car," she said, straightening her back as she spoke, "it was strictly convenience. When we could not make immediate connections, my *grandmother* insisted I ask for Win's help, since she felt the element of surprise was very important. We both agreed that Jessica would be more comfortable in the Pegasus." She had said all she was going to say, hoping it didn't sound like an apology. His face remained expressionless, and she could not read any accusation, satisfaction, or censure in response to her explanation.

There was silence in the office while he scrutinized her, and she was aware, as always, of the startling effect his presence had on her. It was hard for her to remain still as he looked at her, his eyes slowly traveling from her hair to her shoes. She couldn't tell if he noticed her shiver.

He sat up, leaning his weight on the elbow of one arm, and cleared his throat. This little blond pixie, so deceptively delicate and fragile-looking, had the ability to unnerve him more than any person, male or female, he had ever met. He deliberately kept his eyes away from the front of her silk blouse, away from her lips, and stared directly into her eyes, trying to stay calm. But once again her fragrance enveloped him, sending him off balance. He gritted his teeth and concentrated. He accepted what she said about the railroad car, but refused to allow her to see his relief. Caution would be needed in dealing with her, more so than with other people since he tended to let his emotions take over when she was near. Caution and control, he reminded himself. He brought the conversation to its business.

"If both participants are eighteen years of age or older, they can marry in the state of Missouri without written parental consent. They will, of course, still have to fulfill all other obligations, such as getting a blood test and buying a license."

"And how long would that take?"

"Shouldn't be more than three or four days." He shrugged.

She stood up quickly and smoothed the front of her trousers, appearing as businesslike as possible. "Thank you for your help." She hesitated, afraid he would be insulted if she mentioned payment, so she walked to the door, aware that his eyes were on her hips.

"I hate pants on women." His voice cut through the darkness of the office. Her hand froze on the doorknob.

Then she slowly turned to face him, and nonchalantly began unbuckling the narrow belt and unzipping the front zipper.

"We certainly can't have that, now, can we?" She stared directly at him, a provocative smirk on her face, as she dropped the slacks to the floor. "Maybe you don't like a man-tailored blouse on a woman either?" she quizzed sarcastically as she unbuttoned her blouse and dropped it to the floor with a flourish. She stood in front of him in satin underwear, the skirted panties edged in lace to match the form-fitting chemise she wore in lieu of a bra. She felt a rush of sheer exultation as she noticed his extreme discomfort.

Phillip Gates had lost his steely composure. His face was red and his mouth slack as he stared, transfixed by her body. When she turned to leave, stepping nonchalantly over her clothes, she did so with studied slowness, relishing her effect on him.

She heard the chair scrape, and she counted six steps before he caught up to her, grabbing her by the wrist, and pulling her back into his office. He snapped the light off over his desk, and they stood in darkness, their heavy breathing the only sound in the room.

"You are the most impulsive creature!" His voice censured her, but he grabbed her shoulders, nearly pulling her up off the floor with the force of his kiss, and his lips belied his displeasure. She opened her mouth, taking his tongue in, pulling at it as she pressed her body into his.

"Ahhh." She curled her arms around his neck, satisfaction purring through her as she whispered into his ear, "Sometimes I get the most rewarding results." She pulled at her chemise and panties, throwing them aside simultaneously, then stood on tiptoe, pressing against him, helping him as he pulled her higher until she could wrap her legs around his waist. She felt his pants drop as she continued to kiss him, licking the corners of his mouth, biting at his neck, until he raised her, setting her on him in one smooth motion. She felt the most exquisite heat deep inside, and she groaned, falling away as he bent his head to kiss her neck. His hands braced her back, traveling low to lift her

HIGH SOCIETY

hips one more time. He took her standing up as she gasped with pleasure.

An hour later, she was still wrapped in his arms and legs. They lay on the carpet of his office, their skin, wet with perspiration, glowing in the moonshine. Trudi wiped the dampness from Phillip's forehead, amazed by the ferocious passion of this most reserved, restrained man. His hands continued to roam up and down her back as he kept her close to his body, relishing the sweet smoothness of her skin, the musty spice of her smell. When they pulled apart, it was only far enough to look into each other's eyes and smile.

Trudi hesitated before speaking, still not sure of the reactions of this fascinating man she held in her arms. But she wanted him to understand, she wanted him to know how she felt. She whispered, "I'm sorry if you were upset because we used Win's train car." He didn't answer, but neither did he draw away. She took a deep breath during the ensuing silence. "Grandmother was insistent about getting out there quickly before my parents figured out what we were up to. She suggested I ask Win for help. I was reluctant, but"—she shrugged—"the advantages seemed to outweigh the disadvantages." She rolled close to him again, putting her hands on his face to kiss him. Beneath her fingertips, she could feel the muscles of his jaw clench and unclench. She was surprised by the obvious intensity of his reaction, but wisely waited for him to speak.

When he finally did speak, it was with revulsion. "The man is a snake in the grass. I despise him, and I despise the memory of his father." His voice was a whisper as he hissed his hatred. Long pauses interrupted each statement.

Stunned, Trudi sat up and stared at Gates. His expression was controlled, his body relaxed, but his voice revealed the depth of his feelings. She waited for an explanation.

"Nearly fifteen years ago, my father committed suicide, driven to it by Shrader Stevens, Win's father." Trudi suppressed a gasp of surprise, listening silently to Phillip's painful revelation. "Win's father was a hugely successful stockbroker. He also controlled one of the leading industries in town, which had been started by his father. As a result, he was a very influential citizen." Gates took a huge breath. Trudi laid a hand on his chest, feeling his heart beating heavily underneath her palm. "My father was a young man, not yet forty, and he worked for Stevens's brokerage firm. For some reason I have yet to discover, Stevens deliberately set my father up for a fall. He fed him false information on stock prices, and then made it appear that my father was deliberately misleading his clients and pocketing the difference. My father's integrity was impugned, so naturally he had to resign in shame from the brokerage company. Why would anyone believe this young upstart over the massively influential Shrader Stevens?" Gates sat up and rubbed his face with his hands, sighing deeply. "Dad was a man of great dignity and pride, and it rotted his insides to try to defend himself everywhere he applied for a job, to see the skepticism in their eyes, to live with the whispered innuendos of people he thought were his friends. Everywhere he went, Stevens had insinuated his power and kept Dad from getting a job. Stevens's influence reached throughout the Midwest. The last job he sought was at a bank 300 miles away, not realizing Stevens was on the board and had already warned them not to hire this 'crook,' as he called him. The humiliation went on for months, until it finally wore him out, and he came home one day and blew his brains out."

All the breath left Trudi, and she could only breathe softly, "Oh, dear Lord, Phillip. I'm so sorry."

He seemed not to hear her. He went on explaining, his voice totally under control. He seemed to have thought about this incessantly, for his words were resolute. "My brother is the only other person who knows what I'm going to do." He took a huge breath. "I intend to ruin Winslow Stevens in the same way that his father ruined my father." He looked directly at her for the first time since he had begun his diatribe, as if to impress upon her the full implications of his words.

Trudi was appalled by his words. Confused and appalled. She had never felt the drive for revenge that he felt. Her heart ached for Phillip Gates. This, then, was the reason for the mystery behind those dark, brooding eyes; this was the reason for his melancholy. It must be a miserable feeling to hate someone.

She drew a sharp breath as a chilling thought shot through her, and instinctively she curled into a ball, hugging her knees. Tears welled in her eyes.

He only wanted me to get back at Win. The thought was so loud in her head she felt certain he could hear it, but he seemed unaware. A hot flush of shame reddened her face as she relived the last hour, relived his misuse of her heart and body. He thinks of me as Winslow Stevens's girlfriend, she thought. He sees me as just another way to get back at Win! Her eyes narrowed in anger as she jumped up and retrieved her clothes, crying fully now.

It took a minute before Gates realized that she was crying, that she was preparing to leave. When he looked at her face, contorted with tears, he didn't understand. "What is it? Why are you leaving?" He tried to grab her, but she darted out of his grasp and continued dressing, tears rolling down her face. "Did I hurt you? Why are you crying?" He was confused, and began dressing, asking for an explanation as he reached for her arm.

"How dumb do you think I am?" she shouted, pushing him away from her. She sobbed, wiping her nose with a swipe of her sleeve. "And to think I almost loved you!"

He stood dumbfounded in the middle of the room, his shirt and tie hanging limply from his hand, and flinched as the door slammed shut behind her.

CHAPTER 21

Alex Badamo's mother was dying of cancer. The doctor had said he didn't know how long she would live, he knew only that it would be a matter of weeks or maybe months. Certainly the time she had left could not be measured in years. Jessie had returned to Grams's from the Badamos' house in tears, the first time she had lost her composure in the week she had been home.

They all sat around the kitchen table, their attention on Jessica as she tried to describe the scene for them, herself looking so young with her soft brown curls falling about her face, the middy blouse she wore barely full enough to cover her swelling middle comfortably. Jeanne and Hal Mills sat next to each other, eyes averted, finding it difficult to talk about the inevitable, neither one realizing that their mere stoic presence was a calming influence. Grams held Jessie's hand, while Trudi, leaning on the knuckles of one fist, stared at Jessie.

"She's so brave," Jessie whispered, "so brave and so sad. She's already bedridden, just lies there with a rosary in her hand and watches her grandchildren play outside. She's been in great pain for some time but didn't want to worry her family, so she waited too long to get help. She doesn't want to die. She said—" Jessie gulped, dabbing at her eyes with a linen hankie. "She said she wants to see her grandchild. She wants to live long enough to see our baby." She smiled faintly, and rested one hand on her rounded tummy. "So I am prepared to do anything to get this wedding over with and settle down to the business of delivering this baby, safe and sound."

This time she looked up and smiled brightly through her tears. "Father Francis at Adams College has agreed to marry us in the chapel and waive the time necessary for me to go through the formal conversion process." She made no mention of the three other priests she and Alex had been to see about getting married, three old men who remembered each word of church dogma but had forgotten what it was like to be young and in love. They had refused to marry the couple unless every letter of church law was followed. Her family and friends all looked at Jessica now, not daring to look at each other, for her voice alone told them she would brook no argument or interference. "He insisted, however, that the banns still be announced, which will take three more weeks."

Both of Trudi's hands slapped the tabletop in alarm. "What about the justice of the peace? You were set to be married by him next week."

Jessie was quick to reassure her. "Mother Badamo wants us to be married by the church, and I intend to honor her wishes. If you're concerned about Mother and Father, don't be. There's nothing to worry about. They cannot stop us." Her voice was so strong and determined that Trudi relaxed halfheartedly, the throb of the headache she had had for the last week beginning to pound again at the back of her head.

Since she had run out of Gates's office that night, she had not slept well, tossing and turning, determined not to think of him, which she found almost impossible. When she went shopping for Jessica, she was determined not to look at the second floor of the bank building. When she left church on Sunday, she was determined not to look across the street toward the Lutheran church. When she went to the club, she was determined not to look for him among the guests. All of her efforts were wearing her out. She had lost weight, and she looked morose, but everyone was so caught up in preparations for Jessie's wedding and baby that no one noticed.

She had seen him late one afternoon a few days ago coming out of Schullian's Grocery, but he hadn't seen her, and she'd quickly turned away so he wouldn't. He wore a white suit, rumpled as usual, reminding her of his single-mindedness, his lack of pretension. She had peeked in his direction and watched him drive away, her heart heavy with love for him but her mind made up not to allow herself to be used for his revenge. She paid no attention now as the conversation continued around her, looking up only as Fulton came through the back door.

Jessie held out her arms and received a hug before Fulton sat in a kitchen chair, tilted on the back two legs, and stuck his hands in the pockets of his sporty plus fours. "All these women keeping you busy with the changes around here, Hal?" Her brother's easy charm didn't fool Trudi. She saw circles under his eyes, and his usual easy grin seemed forced. She watched him intently during the conversation.

"Seen the front parlor, yet?" the handyman asked. "Got it done up real nice for the young folks."

Grams's eyes lit up. "We finally persuaded Jessie and Alex to live here after they're married, at least for a while." Grams was too sensitive to say "until the strike is over and Alex has his job back." "That big old front parlor that is never used will be their sitting room, and the adjoining library, their bedroom. The baby's room is right off that, and the bath is just across the hall. This old house is finally being used proper-like." Grams nodded for emphasis, and grinned at Jessie.

"Come on." Trudi stood up. "I'll show you." She beckoned for her brother, who grimaced and didn't move. "Come on!" She grabbed his hand and jerked him up, dragging him down the hall.

HIGH SOCIETY

They entered the front room, made sunny and distinctive by a five-panel bay window that looked over Maine Street. Trudi pulled the double doors closed and leaned against them, trapping Fulton in the room. "Okay. What's wrong?"

Fulton stood with his back to her, his hand negligently stuffed into his pockets, the folds of his cardigan flaring over his hips. She thought at first that he hadn't heard her, but when he turned, his chin was up defensively, and she knew he was ready to fight. "I can't imagine what could be wrong in this best of all possible worlds." As always, he countered the serious with the facetious, but Trudi refused to be deflected, guessing at his troubles.

"Move out of the house. Get away from Mother and Father. You can't let them manipulate your whole life. Your trust fund will support you until you find a job."

"What in the world makes you think I'd want to find a job?" His eyebrows rose in surprise. "I love being a student. I could be a student forever. I certainly don't want to work for a living."

Trudi gave him a skeptical look. "I don't believe you. I think you just need some—" She almost said "backbone," but caught herself. "Some encouragement." She walked toward him and put her arms around his waist. "Since I've been staying with Grams, we truly are a family. You could move in here with us. There are still two unused bedrooms upstairs."

He sighed and shook her off, turning to look out the window, feigning interest in the trio of mutts that barked angrily at a passing trolley. Somewhere in the near distance a radio played "Yes, Sir, That's My Baby," making Trudi clench her teeth. The summer breeze caught the lace curtains at the window and pushed them toward Fulton, who ignored the material as it billowed around his knees.

A note of pleading entered her voice. "You've just got to break away and become independent from them before it's too late."

His head dropped and his shoulders sagged. She almost didn't hear him say, "It's already too late."

* * *

HIGH SOCIETY

It was a beautiful early summer evening, a faint glow of the setting sun still lighting the horizon, the song of a robin twirling through the air, but the men filing into the Labor Temple took no notice. The hall was packed; rows of pressed-back wooden chairs filled the center of the room, and men pressed shoulder-to-shoulder along the perimeter. The easy summer breeze filtering through the open windows did little to cool the smoky hall. Few men had bothered to change out of work clothes, but a few wore starched white shirts, the collars missing in a nod of recognition toward the sultry air. Men, fanning themselves with pages from the *Herald-Whig*, seemed to be futilely trying to erase the worry wrinkles from their foreheads. The buzz of conversation dulled and died as their leader walked to the podium.

"I can't be too encouraging tonight, men." Victor Wellman leaned forward over the handmade podium, uncomfortable standing on a stage in front of his peers. For all his forty-five years he had lived in this midwestern town, and he knew every man in the hall by name. He was worried that tonight would be the beginning of a long-drawn-out trial that would test the strength of their friendships and tear away at the wall of united needs they had built up. "All I can tell you is that I'm proud of you. Stay strong, and keep calm. Mr. Gates here can fill you in on details of the negotiations, then I'll go over the plans for the march with you. If you have questions, we'll go over them after that."

Phillip Gates had been looking over the crowd as he waited on the sidelines. He recognized three young men he had gone to Adams High with; he recognized the five older men who had first come to his office; and he recognized Alex Badamo, the young man engaged to Trudi's sister. Badamo leaned against a pillar at the back of the room in an inconspicuous corner, but his swarthy good looks set him apart from the rest of the men. The faces of the strikers wore a myriad of expressions from frustrated anger to worried resignation, emotions Gates was all too familiar with.

Trudi Groves had stunned him when she'd stormed out of

his office a week ago. He still hadn't figured out why, and her actions had left him feeling confused and angry. If she was disgusted by his revelations, then she would have to stay that way. He had seen her coming out of church last Sunday, and considered walking across the street to demand an explanation. But he decided that it was she who should make the first move to explain her actions to him. He wasn't going to be deterred from ruining Winslow Stevens because of her. He obviously had misread her feelings and had underestimated her feelings for Winslow Stevens. It was stupid of me to confide in her, he told himself sternly. I won't make a mistake like that again.

He had buried himself in his work, spending long, grueling hours clearing up case after case in order to free his docket for the strike fight ahead. It would be long and frustrating, with two steps forward and three back, but it had to be done. He scanned the drawn faces of the workingmen again, and he could only hope they would all understand. When he heard his name announced, he climbed to the stage in three steps. He shunned the podium, standing boldly in front of them.

"We've got the owners at the table, and they are listening to our demands." He paused for a brief flurry of applause. "So far they haven't granted us anything, but the fact that they are listening is progress. I can only ask you to stand firm. Your demands are reasonable and justified. Demonstrate your solidarity, and stay calm. We will win!" He waved his hand and jumped from the stage, shoving through the crowd of men as he headed for the exit. Some patted him on the back and offered encouragement, some stepped away to let him pass without comment, but as he neared the door, Alex Badamo blocked his way, staring him in the eyes.

"I'm Alex Badamo and I want to do something more." His black eyes bored into Gates's own as he said his piece.

Gates stared back, then pulled him outside, past the stragglers smoking cigars on the stoop, past the wary policeman who stood on the sidewalk, not stopping until he came to the privacy of his car parked under a tall elm tree. The song of crickets buzzing through the air, the smell of the Mississippi drifting up the steep banks, the sounds of the city band practicing a rousing Sousa march were all ignored as he blatantly looked the young man over from head to foot. Alex Badamo had a strong frame and piercing, intelligent eyes. His muscular body was fit and compact, and the picture of a Roman gladiator flashed through Gates's mind. Alex didn't flinch under the inspection, but waited patiently for Gates to speak.

"I may have just the job for you, but it could be dangerous." Gates watched for any sign of hesitation on the young man's face, but saw none.

"I don't care," Alex stated simply. "I want to"—he shook his head—"I *have* to do something to make the world a better place for the workingman. I'll do whatever you ask."

Phillip Gates believed him, though he wondered how long such lofty idealism would last in the nitty-gritty strike battle. Together they climbed into the car and left for a long conversation at Gates's house, a conversation he kept private from both his mother and brother.

Grams had always been patient and understanding when Fulton had gotten himself into fixes as a little boy. But not this time. She was angry, and she let him know it.

"How could you do that with someone you didn't even care about?" Her face, usually so sweet and jovial, was red with anger as she paced the kitchen floor.

"I don't even *know* her, Grams, let alone care about her," Fulton retorted.

"Don't you be smart-mouthing me," Grams yelled, turning to smack him on the top of the head. Trudi and Jessica winced, feeling the blow of Grams's hand as much as her words. The four of them had been sitting in the kitchen for an hour now, discussing Fulton's dilemma. Only Fulton seemed unmoved, disbelieving the situation. Wedding plans for him and Janet Brenner were rapidly progressing, carried out with extreme efficiency by the determined partnership of their mothers. Since Barner Groves had come storming into the garden, catching Fulton in flagrante delicto after the dinner party, the two sets of parents had made all the decisions for the young people. Accusations, tears, and fainting had ceased as it was determined that Fulton would save Janet's honor by marrying her as quickly as possible. Without consulting Janet or Fulton, the four parents had decided on the correct course of action in this unfortunate situation. At this moment, invitations were being engraved, and the wedding dress fitted for the ceremony, which would take place within two weeks.

"Oh, Fully, Fully, Fully," Trudi whispered as she stood behind his chair to lean over and hug him. Jessica sat next to him and squeezed his hand. Both felt the inadequacy of their support. All his cockiness was gone, and in its place was an abject resignation to the steamroller lumbering toward him. At the sweet words of his sisters, Fulton's body slumped, and he stared morosely at the floor as the magnitude of what was happening hit him for the first time.

"Fulton." Grams knelt in front of him and reached up to hold his face in her hands, forcing him to look into her eyes. "I love you now as much as I did the moment I first held you as a tiny baby. I just wish that you would think before you act in the future." Fulton heaved a huge breath as she leaned to kiss him.

"Maybe, Fulton"—Jessie gave him a hopeful little smile—"maybe you will learn to love her." The rays of the setting sun shone through the window, backlighting Jessie's soft brown hair, highlighting the glow of her skin. But it wasn't the sun. It was her love that made her so radiant. Fulton felt sorry for himself as he compared his situation to hers. He was envious of the love that he might not ever experience.

One corner of his mouth went down, and he didn't look at her as he mumbled, "And maybe not."

HIGH SOCIETY

Everyone's anger seemed to have dissipated except Trudi's, but it was not Fulton, weak, pliable, lovable Fulton, she was angry at. It was the manipulations of her parents.

"Come on, kiddos." Win smiled engagingly. "We're going to have a midnight picnic." He pulled the blanket off the backseat of his Belgian-made Minerva-Landaulet to allow Tony and Patty to peer in. They both grinned and jumped into the front seat, in a great mood for fun and games. He had chosen this car precisely because it was solid and dowdy, attracting much less attention on the road than any of his other flashier cars.

Since the truckers had been on strike, Win had had to do some fast, impromptu legwork. All his minions, even the top guys, Leo, Bucky, and Rats, had been putting a lot of miles on their roadsters, making pickups and deliveries of hooch to the outlying districts. Tonight even he was going to help out. With the assistance of the two kids to make the face-to-face contact, he could still remain anonymous and keep the booze flowing with no danger to himself.

He finished folding the canvas car top securely into its well behind the backseat, and the car roared out of his drive as soon as full dark set in. Win pulled the silk ascot off his neck and stuck it under the seat, shoving some bottles out of the way in the process. Every inch of the car was filled with bottles of booze, freshly labeled to look authentic, bottles that in the next three hours would be delivered to the back doors of a half dozen roadhouses in the out districts of Adams County.

The strife between the gangs in St. Louis was winding down, and before long Win's two insurance policies, Patti and Tony, would be returned safely to their respective families. With all his men doing double duty because of the strike, he'd been stuck personally with more than he'd bargained for, and the baby-sitting was wearing him out. Patti's long ringlets blew in the wind and Tony kept pulling out the huge bow she wore over one ear. He'd be relieved to send them home without incident.

"Settle down, kids! There's a Burma-Shave sign coming up. Turn around and read it."

In unison, the two began to chant the words on each small roadside sign as they sped past.

"Ah, that's not the best one," Tony grunted.

Win quieted them down again and concentrated on the job at hand. He'd be glad when he could stop making deliveries himself and get back to the politics of the job. His days had been filled with machinations to get the strike finished quickly, either by legal or illegal means. The absence of trucks on the road made his deliveries too conspicuous, so for the last two weeks he and his men had kept the flow going, but they couldn't keep up with the demand. His first priority was to get the strike settled, and get his trucks, all trucks, back on the road.

"This is a real kick, Mr. Stevens," Patti yelled above the noise of the wind as she bounced on Tony's lap. The two kids hadn't been off the grounds of his estate much in the last couple of weeks, so tonight's adventure would do them good. Patti had dressed up in some fluffy thing with ruffles at the neckline and all over the skirt like she was going to some party. Tony playfully tickled Patti in the ribs, and she squealed and squirmed under his touch.

"When we hit the Rainbow Club near Mendon," he said, starting to give them instructions to settle them down, "I'll drive right up to the back door. Patti, you knock three times, wait, then knock twice more. Tony, you can be getting the case out of the backseat. Just set it inside the door when it opens, and they will give you the money. Don't say anything. Don't look 'em in the eye. Just do as I say. Got it?" Tony nodded seriously, but broke out in a grin when he looked at Patti.

They had traveled ten miles north on the highway toward Hannibal when Win started to get nervous. He glanced in the rearview mirror six times before the girl noticed and began to stare at the car traveling a half mile behind them. "What is it?" Her forehead was puckered in a small frown. "Why do you keep looking?"

"That car has been following us at just the same pace for the last five miles." She still had a dumb look on her face as Tony turned to stare. "It could be the feds following us. Start throwing the bottles out." They didn't understand, so he yelled, "Start throwing the damn bottles in the ditch! If they stop us and we don't have any booze on us, there is nothing they can do. Now, get busy!"

The two scrambled to their knees, reaching into the backseat and tossing bottle after bottle into the ditch along the side of the road as Win glanced from the road ahead to the road behind.

"Mr. Stevens," Tony grunted between throws, "why don't you just pay them off?" Patti had room to crawl into the backseat and throw from there. Her distance was half that of Tony's, but at least the stuff was out of the car.

"Not the feds, kid, not the feds. They can't be had. With anyone else that would work, but not the damned feds. Now, just shut up and listen. There's a big curve in the road about a mile ahead. I'm going to slow down there and roll out of the car. You move behind the wheel and keep going. If they stop you, you're clean, two kids out for a joyride. When you get to Mendon, turn around and come back to pick me up."

When they reached the curve and were momentarily out of the sight of the car behind, Win slowed to a crawl and rolled out, hitting the tarmac harder than he'd expected but managing to keep rolling over and off into the tall weeds in the ditch. He watched his car swerve then straighten, then flattened himself as the second car sped by, not raising his head until it had passed, too late to discern anything except two heads in the front seat. He rolled over on his back and stared up at the black sky, his chest heaving, trying to catch his breath. A full minute passed before he rose to a crouch, looking after the two cars, but they were gone from view. He ran across the road, and began retracing the path of the car. One bottle, then a second he picked up and put near the side of the road. The next three were broken. At the sound of an approaching car, he flattened himself in the ditch again, sticking his head up only enough to get a peek.

Twenty minutes passed before a car came from the direction of Mendon; this time, it was his. He was hugely relieved to see the big Minerva sliding safely to a stop because, at $40,000, it was the most expensive car he had. It had been a calculated risk letting the kid drive it, but anything was better than getting caught. The big car had never looked better, and he jumped behind the wheel as soon as Tony pulled up beside him.

"Everything is copacetic, Mr. Stevens. It was only two old farmers. They were harmless."

"How can you be so sure?" he asked, his hands gripping the wheel tightly as they sped down the highway.

" 'Cause we followed them after they passed us, and they parked in the drive of the Methodist church and went in the back door."

Win laughed. "Sounds safe to me, too. We can give anybody a runaround, can't we?" He gestured toward the deep ditch. "Some hobos are going to think it rained booze from heaven when they wander along here, cause I'm not going to risk picking up any of the hooch we threw out." The trio laughed uproariously.

CHAPTER 22

If at any time in Janet Brenner's life she could have been considered pretty, it was on the day she married Fulton Jewel Groves. The All Saints Episcopal Church glowed in the early evening sunset, the guests shined in their elegant best, the candles in the candelabra blazed from their brass holders, the massive banks of yellow roses shimmered in the summer breeze, but nothing, nothing was as luminous as the smile of the sparkling bride. Any whispered speculations by the guests as to the hurried nature of the ceremony were hushed at the sight of Janet's face. Here was a young woman, unmistakably in love, radiantly eager for the marriage. Anyone paying attention to the groom might have still had questions in his mind.

Trudi stood at the altar with Janet's sister, watching as Janet floated down the aisle on her father's arm. Her gown of silk organza, heavily appliquéd with Alençon lace, was almost hidden by the huge bouquet of white orchids she carried in her gloved hands. Only the egret feather protruding from the middle of her tiara moved as she looked from side to side, greeting friends with a gracious smile. The cathedral-length veil covering her hair streamed behind her, shimmering with sequins and brilliants, and spoke of her joy to the waiting crowd. Trudi glanced at her brother.

He looked scared and pale and drawn. He was sweating profusely, though the summer evening was only moderately warm, and six electric fans had been placed on the floor in front of the pews to keep the wedding party cool.

The look on Fulton's face as the wedding party strode up the aisle after the ceremony was one of utter relief. Trudi shared the exact feeling, for twice during the ceremony, while the soloist sang an excruciatingly slow arrangement of "Oh, Promise Me," she was convinced Fulton would faint, while Janet remained implacably calm. At the back of the church, while the rest of the party gaggled around the beaming bride, Trudi handed her brother a cloth to wipe his sweating face.

"I don't know if I can survive this, Trudi," he confessed in a stage whisper.

"Oh, Fully, you two can duck out of the reception as soon as dinner is finished. Just hang on for a few more hours."

"No, I don't mean the reception. I mean the honeymoon." His face was tight with suffering. "I mean the whole marriage thing."

"Marriage is difficult." Trudi began to commiserate, but he interrupted again.

"No, I mean bed, sex, making love," he whined.

Now Trudi was really confused. "Do you mean you don't know if . . ."

"I don't know if I can keep up to her!" he hissed in frustration. "I'm exhausted. She has been so demanding in the last two weeks, I just don't think I can do it anymore." Trudi's eyes grew wide with disbelief, as she slowly swiveled her head to look at Janet Brenner, meek, quiet, mild little Janet Brenner. Fulton kept whispering as he mopped his forehead. "She thinks she invented sex. She can't get enough of it. Anywhere. Anytime. She wants it three or four times a day. I think I started something I can't finish."

He had such a forlorn, dejected look on his face that Trudi pressed her hand over her mouth to hide her grin. But the irony of the situation won out, and Trudi screamed with laughter, threw her head back and bellowed in glee, joined finally by Fulton, and the two laughed until tears came to their eyes.

The reception was lavish, elegant, and perfect. The six-course dinner was centered on the entree of lobster thermidor, but the individual petit-fours, exquisitely decorated with the bride and groom's interwined initials, took everyone's fancy. Jessica and Alex attended the wedding, arriving purposely late, and sitting at the back of the church in order to leave first, thus avoiding any contact with the senior Groveses. But Grams marched down the aisle in full regalia, finally wearing a new cloche of crushed satin, in honor of her only grandson's wedding, and at the reception she hopped on the dance floor, enjoying the music as much as any twenty-year-old.

Trudi danced with Win, going through the motions of having a good time, mainly for her brother's sake. The guests complimented her on the beauty of her simple lace bridesmaid's dress, but she thought the huge sash around the hips that ended with a huge bow in back was girlish and silly. Her smile was hollow; the laughter of the guests irritated her, for there was no joy in her own heart.

She felt out of place in the midst of the merriment and wondered if she looked as dull and cheerless as she felt. Her bridesmaid's dress, finished only a few days before the wedding, was ill-fitting, baggy, and unflattering. She continued to lose weight and sleep, refusing to admit that her ennui had anything to do with Phillip Gates. Win's hand on the small of her back pulled her a little closer, so she gave him an inadequate smile. He looked especially nice tonight in a midnight-blue tux of the latest cut, and the cologne he wore was nicer than her own. She drew back and looked him full in the face, as if she might find written there the answers to the questions mulling around in her mind.

This wasn't an evil man who was holding her in his arms. He is charming and erudite and generous. He has been patient with me at times when I didn't deserve it. It is wrong, grossly wrong, of Phillip Gates to make Winslow Stevens pay for the sins of his father. Win smiled down at her, a smile of pride, but she felt nothing. I don't love him, but I don't want him to suffer for some wrong for which he is not responsible. This is a fine upstanding man, who would never do anything wrong, never knowingly hurt someone. Just because Phillip Gates is eaten up by feelings of revenge doesn't mean she has to be a part of his plans. Maybe I should tell Win. Maybe I should tell him of Gates's plans for revenge. She opened her mouth to speak but Barner Groves tapped Win on the shoulder.

"My dance," he grinned ludicrously. Trudi rolled her eyes. Her father, with whom she had not exchanged ten words in the last two weeks, was very close to being drunk. She smiled grimly, aware of the satisfaction he must be feeling now that Fulton was safely married. This is as good a time as any to tell him what I think. With a public confrontation he might not be as willing to explode in anger. Win hesitated, looking from father to daughter, then shrugged, ready to release her. Grams stepped in the middle of the threesome.

"Barner, what kind of son have I raised? You haven't asked your own mother to dance yet." The band began a spirited rendition of "Yes, We Have No Bananas." "Good!" Grams almost shouted. "One of my sentimental favorites." She pulled at her son's arm, before doubling back to whisper in Trudi's ear, "I don't like that fire in your eye. Don't you talk to him until I talk to you." Trudi gave her a grudging nod and pulled Win off the dance floor.

"Something gives me the feeling that your grandmother just defused a family spat."

Trudi refused to answer, deflecting his attention by nodding her head toward the clique standing next to them. "Sounds like we arrived in time for one here." Linda Carter stood imperiously in the middle of a small group, weaving unsteadily on her feet but making a noble effort to appear in control of herself. Her dress was an elaborate concoction of chiffon drapings, including one large swatch of material trimmed with a two-foot-long fringe that was to be used for a stole across her shoulders but which kept falling to the ground, slipping off her shoulder, then over her arm to be stepped on by Linda and most of her neighbors. In one hand she held a cocktail glass, in the other, a long cigarette holder from which she took a dramatic drag before waving it under the nose of a neighbor.

The object of her attention, a short round woman, known to Trudi only as Sandi, but whose mouth gave the impression that she played the flute, quavered before Linda's glare.

"I did not say that!" Linda repeated her denial, eliciting uncomfortable smirks from the rest of the group. "I never said you looked like a frog." She put her nose in the air and waved her cigarette dramatically. "I said you looked like a toad. A toad, not a frog!" The object of her scorn blanched, blinked her eyes once and turned to hurry away. The girls in the group snickered behind their hands, while two of the men laughed out loud, stopping only when Linda turned on one of them, stumbling slightly before bending to peer into his face. "Aren't you the one that just told me you are a self-made man?"

He flushed uncomfortably, pulling at his collar before mumbling, "Yes, but . . ."

"What I can't understand," Linda took a long swallow of her drink, "is, if you're a self-made man, why didn't you give yourself more hair?" The whole group burst out laughing as the man blushed, involuntarily sliding his hand over the top of his thinning pate.

Trudi squeezed her eyes shut and groaned. "Let's get her out of here." She could only hope that people understood what lay behind Linda's impulse for savagery, that her nastiness was a pathetic expedient against her own pain by forcing it onto others. The soloist with the dance band began a sorrowful rendition of "The Man I Love" and Linda stopped to sing along until Trudi took one arm and Win the other and together they dragged her off the floor.

On the other side of the dance floor, partially hidden behind eight-foot-tall palm plants, Madeleine Groves was lecturing her husband. "We are going home now. I insist that you wait for me right here. I will send Ingram in for you." Holding her head high, a stiff smile on her face, her shoulders back the better to show off the lines of her original gown by Fabrani, Madeleine Groves said her formal good-byes and stepped outside to signal for the chauffeur.

It took both of them to stuff Barner Groves's body into the backseat where he slumped in an unmoving heap, his posture a direct contrast to the erect immobile silhouette of his wife. "Take him to his room and see that he is put to bed." This was out of the normal range of Ingram's duties, but he daren't protest, though he would have appreciated some assistance getting Mr. Groves up the stairs. He thought of calling for Gunther to come and help, but when he glanced over his shoulder and saw Mrs. Groves walking toward the carriage house that served as the servants' quarters, he knew it would be a futile request.

Madeleine Groves's mouth was dry and her heart was tight in her throat. She had never been so brazen as to seek the German out in his own quarters, but she had never been in such a desperate need of his attentions. When she should have been feeling triumphant over Fulton's wedding, she felt instead a wretched, gnawing emptiness. The children, all four of her children, were gone and she missed them more than anyone would ever suspect. Gunther offered the closest thing to intimacy that she could find, though it was not the spiritual intimacy she so profoundly needed.

No light was on in his room, and none went on in response to her knock, but the door opened wide, as if he had been expecting her. The room was small and plain, a bare bulb hanging from the middle of the low ceiling and a strip of curled flypaper in front of the open window. Even in the dark shadows she could see that it was clean and neat. Spartan, yes, spartan was a good word. Lacking in any personal warmth. Curious, in a man of such passion.

Without a word passing between them, he began to undress her, slipping off the tie from her chiffon wrap-around dress, and pulling it from her shoulders in one easy motion. Standing close, staring into her eyes, he hitched her silk slip over her head and unwound the tight chignon at the nape of her neck. Pressing his fingertips hard against her skull, he fluffed her long thick hair, pulling it forward to fall against her breasts. When he knelt in front of her, she bent her head to watch as he slowly pulled each satin slipper off, carefully putting them aside before gently gripping her thigh between his hands to slowly roll her hose down and off her feet. When he kissed her flat belly, she tensed. Only as his tongue drew small wet circles around her navel did she begin to tremble. He knew now she was ready for anything and he swung her into his arms and onto the bed.

She strained to see him, reaching to touch his hard body, reveling in his beauty. He crouched over her on all fours and she could feel his breath on her face. He didn't kiss her or fondle her; instead he put his hands under her hips and lifted them off the bed, pulling her long legs over his shoulders. He nuzzled the mound between her legs, and she groaned anticipating his next move. When he began, she shuddered, not knowing if she could last, if she could make these moments deliciously long. He raised his head and smiled at her, his white teeth brilliant against his sun-browned face. He murmured something but she didn't hear until they shifted position, and he wrapped her in his arms. She took him inside her, deep and full, wrapping her arms about his neck, clinging to him as they remained still, unmoving, when he whispered again.

"Liebchen, mein leibchen." She burst into tears, and her body responded to his tenderness with a flurry of passion.

"I'm starting to lose patience with Linda." Trudi's voice was cold. "That is the third time in the last month I've had to deliver her to her mother in that state." She slammed her side of the car shut and furiously rolled down the window, hoping the car's movement would create some relief from the sultry summer night heat. She shot a perturbed look into the backseat where Patti Shinn and Tony Billotti sat, more bored by the stuffy reception than she had been. She resented them, feeling like a premature nanny, finding Win's explanations of their presence both doubtful and weak. At least, she sighed, he won't try any funny business while they are around.

"She's just drowning her sorrows," Win chuckled. "Nothing to worry about at this point." He drove with one hand on the wheel, the other thrown across the seat behind Trudi's shoulders.

"Just at what point do we worry about it?" Her question sounded arch, and he ducked his head to glance at her. "She's doing crazy things. She said last week she was going to enter the next dance marathon in St. Louis. She bought a bathing suit that doesn't even have two yards of material in it. It doesn't even cover her thighs!" Trudi ignored Win's smirk and continued. "She acts like she's the only one in the world with a broken heart. I've done everything I can to help her, taken her to lunch, bought her books and gramophone records, took her to see Joan Crawford in 'Spring Fever,' but nothing seems to help. She seems determined to suffer." She stared out the window and heaved a huge exasperated sigh. "I'm tired of helping someone who isn't willing to help herself."

"What would you do if you had a broken heart?" Trudi's head jerked around in surprise. *How did he know? Or did he know? He couldn't know. No one knows but me.*

Aloud she answered, "My heart will never be broken." She jutted her jaw out stubbornly. "Bruised maybe, but never broken. Now let's change the subject." She yanked the wide bandeau off her hair and rubbed her forehead where it had been so tightly bound. "I wish she'd tell her mother to shut up and then I wish she'd swallow her pride and call Bill Jefferson. I wish . . ."

"You sound like a child with all your wishes." *If you only knew,* Trudi thought to herself.

They drove in silence, slowly, almost dawdling through an unfamiliar district of modest frame houses, an area she didn't recognize. When they pulled up to a construction site, marked by a new eight-foot-high brick wall, Win finally spoke.

"I've wanted to show you this for weeks." He walked around and opened the car door, indicating for the two young people to stay in place. "Everything is finished except the landscaping. Come on." He took her hand and led her through the darkness, picking his way carefully through debris until she stopped him. She stood and looked at the house, the most unusual design she had ever seen.

It was white, all on one level, with a flat roof and no ornamentation on the outside except for a rounded semicircle of opaque glass bricks near the front door. The flat wall of stucco that faced the street had only one small porthole window. When he unlocked the front door, the odor of sawdust and new plaster, a fresh inviting smell, greeted them. He let go of her hand long enough to turn the light switch.

The room was surrounded on two sides by glass, large uninterrupted panes of glass, wider than the span of her outstretched arms, larger sheets of glass than she had ever seen in a private home. And the lighting shot up from the rim of the walls to bounce off the ceiling, no fixtures showing, only a soft line of light that indirectly illuminated the huge room. The carpeting covered every inch of floor, from wall to wall, and was all one color, a soft pale purple, the same color as the walls and ceiling. Very few pieces of furniture were in the room, only a twenty-foot-long S-curved sofa and two simple boxy armchairs covered in white leather, smooth and supple to her touch.

The whole room was smooth and supple with a sleek undulating effect Trudi had never seen before. The subdued monochromatic color scheme was relieved by accent pieces of glossy black porcelain; a life-sized peacock perched gracefully on a crystal pedestal, its curved tail dipping to touch the floor, a passive immobile panther reclining in front of the fireplace, itself nothing more than a simple square hole cut into the wall.

"It's stunning," she whispered, her eyes roaming the room, entranced by its simplicity and sophisticated grace. "I've never seen anything like it."

"I built it with you in mind," Win answered from behind her. She spun around and frowned at him, too surprised to react. "It's called Art Deco. I first saw it at a design exposition in Paris two years ago. It's an outgrowth of the Egyptian craze that followed Lord Carneavon's discovery of King Tut's grave. I've been preparing to build this house ever since." His eyes glittered with pride as he pointed toward the glass wall. "Come with me. You haven't seen the best part yet."

He pulled on the glass and it moved, sliding on narrow tracks set into floor and ceiling. When they stepped outside, Trudi caught her breath. All around her, in a thirty-mile stretch from north to south, lay the shining ribbon of river, its mile-wide width reflecting the shimmer of moonlight in a dance of diamonds. The house sat high on a bluff, four hundred feet above the Mississippi, with an unobstructed view of incredible beauty. Now she knew why he had chosen this neighborhood. The site for the house was perfect, secluded, unexpected, with a spectacular view of the river.

Win stood close behind her, and wrapped his arms around her, bending to whisper in her ear. "I hope you like it, because I built it for you."

She stiffened in disbelief. She had never been the recipient of such a magnanimous gift, a gift she had no intention of accepting, but she was overwhelmed by the gesture, a generous gesture from the kindest, most thoughtful person she had ever met.

> *JOURNAL ENTRY:*
>
> *Poisoning industrial alcohol to make it unfit for human consumption has backfired on the federal government, just as I suspected and hoped it would. The booze was inevitably used for private consumption, so thousands of people have been blinded, paralyzed, or killed by it this year. Naturally, all the politicians in my pocket have been roundly denouncing the government's fiendish attempt to enforce Prohibition, which plays right into my hands, since I have built up a reputation of handling only the real McCoy. Those first few years of not diluting my hootch and thereby working with a smaller net profit have paid off. Now*

HIGH SOCIETY

*I routinely cut my imported liquors and pass
it off to the little guys as full strength,
saving the good stuff for preferred customers.
As far as I know, none of my booze has
hurt anyone, but it could never be traced
back to me anyway, so it doesn't concern
me in the least.*

*Trudi seemed impressed by the house and didn't
question me when I said I would have to be
out of town for a while on business. All
the guys in the Midwest will be meeting at
our resort in Boulder Junction, Wisconsin, for
three days of relaxation, followed by three/four/
five/days of negotiations. It's a perfect atmosphere
up there, isolated, beautiful. It has six different
lakes, each stocked with a different kind of fish
to suit any fishing fancy. When the talks begin,
a huge log will be thrown in the fireplace of the
main lodge, and the talks will not stop, no one
will sleep or leave until the fire burns down.
Then we start all over again. We ought to be
able to determine which gang will be in charge
of manufacturing, which will be in charge of
importing, which will take over distribution,
and what each one's territory will be. Our
agreement will be more important and longer
lasting than the League of Nations!!*

CHAPTER
=23=

Trudi winced. She had a pounding headache even after having had nothing to drink at the wedding reception the night before. The bedroom she was using in Grams's house was immaculate but sparsely furnished, and the flowered wallpaper grated on her nerves. She knew she was being cranky and had to force herself to think "nice thoughts," as Grams would say.

Her first thought of the day was of Fulton and Janet, well on their way to a three-month-long honeymoon at an undisclosed location. She wondered if Fulton would actually see any scenery, enjoy any new sights, or if he would be spending all his time in bed with his demanding new wife. She chuckled at the thought.

A teakettle whistled in the kitchen, answered by a banging cabinet door, sounds that traveled freely up the hot-air register, sounds that she found comforting, inviting enough to drag her out of bed and down the steps. Wrapping her robe around her, she clacked down the stairs and into the kitchen, where Grams turned to peer over her glasses at Trudi's slippers.

"Well, I never," she breathed. "I never saw such silly-looking slippers in my life." Trudi looked down at her feet. She's right, she thought as she stared at the pink satin mules trimmed with pink feathers, stared for the first time objectively. What's more, Trudi thought, the stupid-looking things aren't even comfortable. Time to give a little more thought to what I wear. She shrugged.

Snapping open the morning paper, Trudi ignored the local headline, STRIKE VIOLENCE EXPECTED, and began reading instead a report on relief efforts to aid those affected by the flood on the Mississippi the month before. Grams peered over her shoulder.

"Now Secretary Hoover ought to get the Republican nomination for sure this summer; he's done such a good job of organizing help for those people," she commented before returning to the stove. " 'Course, I suppose Charles Curtis still has a chance for the job. But Hoover's proven himself again and again as a great humanitarian and administrator, like after the Great War when he set up the Belgian relief program. He fed Europe, saving any number of lives. Fine man. Then if those Democrats are crazy enough to nominate Governor Smith, we're sure to win, him being a Catholic and a 'wet.' . . ."

She was talking to herself, a fact confirmed when Trudi yawned again. Grams turned on her, appalled and angry. "Listen here, young lady, you pay attention to what's going on in the world! I grew up with the humiliation of not getting to vote, and don't you ever take it for granted!" Trudi snapped to attention, her spine straighter, her eyes wider, and when she did she was able to see through the kitchen window and across the yard.

"Is that Alex feeding the chickens? I thought that was your favorite chore. How long has he been doing that?" The two women stood, shoulders touching, looking out the window above the sink toward the corner of the yard that housed the notorious chicken coop.

" 'Bout a week now," Grams murmured before turning away. "He came and asked if he could do it, and I said yes 'cause I figured he wanted some way to be of help."

Trudi bent forward. "That's Phillip Gates with him! What in the world?" She felt her heart lurch at the sight of him. He leaned against a post, his hands in his pockets, and he appeared to be, if possible, even thinner than when she had last seen him. The two were not looking at each other as they talked. Gates's eyes scanned the row of thick bushes that edged the coop on both sides, while Alex continued to scatter corn to the eager pullets, never looking up from his job. But they were talking to each other, of that she was sure. She grabbed Grams's arm.

"Why is he here?" But the old woman put her palms up and shrugged, her eyebrows high, the corners of her mouth low. When they looked back outside, Gates had disappeared.

Trudi wrapped her robe tightly around her and ran across the grass, the early-morning dew wetting her slippers and chilling her toes. She was out of breath when she reached Alex, and she grabbed at the chicken wire for support, feeling it bite into the pads of her fingers. "Why was Phillip Gates here?"

Alex had seen her coming and hid a small grin. How different these two sisters were, he thought. Jessica would have stood silently, her eyes boring the question into him, until he answered. He threw the last handful of grain to the hens and stepped out of the coop, carefully latching the gate behind him and hanging the empty bucket on a nail. "He's helping the truckers with the strike," he answered simply and as honestly as he could. "Is Jessie up yet? Tell her I'll stop by after my shift at the service station this afternoon." He dusted his hands off and stepped through the bushes, disappearing as effectively as had Gates.

Jessica stood on the seat of a kitchen chair while Mrs. Mills and Grams fussed around her, pinning the hem of her tea-length wedding dress, adjusting the cuffs of the lace jacket, measuring for the length of the short veil. The dress would be a pale, pale pink of dotted swiss, with a bouffant skirt and hip-length jacket, sweet and innocent-looking to befit Jessica's personality.

"Do you think the zinnias and daisies will be in bloom in ten days, Grams?" Jessie asked, trying to peek outside toward Grams's border garden. Grams, pins in her teeth, mumbled a reply.

"Hydrangeas will probably be ready, if you want to use those on the altar," Mrs. Mills offered.

"I'm picturing two great big bouquets of white daisies, purple asters, yellow lemon lilies, orange tiger lilies, and red zinnias, with little pink sweet williams to fill in the gaps," Jessica answered dreamily.

What a difference a month makes, Trudi thought, contentedly watching the preparations.

"When you gettin' married, Trudi?" Mrs. Mills teased. "You're the only one left."

Trudi held her hands up in a defensive gesture. "Oh, no! Oh, no!" Then added smugly, "But Win Stevens *did* build a house for me."

"He what!" Grams shouted as all three women jerked their heads around to stare at her.

Fifteen minutes later all four women were in Grams's black Ford, sputtering down Hampshire Street as Trudi tried to point them in the right direction. "It was dark out, and I'd never been in that neighborhood before," she explained weakly. "Try turning right at the next corner."

Grams did as directed, and suddenly the car was facing the biggest demonstration St. Louis had ever seen. Before them was the Salvation Army band, all gleaming trumpets, booming bass drums, and a chorus of vocalists bellowing "Bringing in the Sheaves" at their loudest. An angry crowd of women, interspersed with young children, carried placards, jeering and pointing at a nondescript, innocent-looking, narrow brick house on the opposite side of the street. Three policemen, two on the sidewalk, one in the street, tried to control the parade of protesters. A short, barrel-chested officer stood in the middle of the street, grim-faced, waving his arms in a distinctive pattern, motioning Grams around and away. Instead she inched the car to the curb and rolled down the window.

"I know what this is about." Her face was flushed with an exuberant, expectant cheer.

"You're not getting out, are you?" Trudi was alarmed, picturing her grandmother in the middle of the melee.

"Good heavens, no!" Grams answered. "But I sure want

to watch the shenanigans for a minute." She grinned and waved to a lady friend, who waved back, a gleam of righteous triumph in her eye. "They're protesting that house of ill repute across the street. Read the signs. They're warning anyone who goes in that their names will be recorded and listed on pamphlets that will be spread all over town."

Trudi and Jessica giggled, but Mrs. Mills was outraged by the sin so widespread in the big city. Trudi glanced at the house, at the lace curtain in the upstairs room that was pulled back to reveal a shapely redheaded woman who lounged against the frame in a vaguely disinterested way. She turned her head to talk to someone in the room behind her, but looked out over the street again and smiled with the patience usually seen on the face of an indulgent mother.

Grams snorted. "Won't work any better than the Volsted Act!"

"At least it doesn't concern any of us," Trudi said with a shrug as the car pulled away, accompanied by a rousing rendition of "Onward, Christian Soldiers."

The afternoon sun was warm on his arm that protruded from the window of the truck, but it wasn't the reason for the sweat that lined Alex Badamo's upper lip. He was scared, and he didn't mind admitting it, even if it was only to himself.

He blew his breath out and reached in his back pocket for a handkerchief to wipe his face. So far Mr. Gates's plan was working, though he hadn't gathered any hard evidence. Following Mr. Gates's instructions, he had telephoned Mr. Stevens and asked for a job, any job, explaining that he was out of work and needed money because he was soon to be married. It didn't make any difference. Stevens was ready to say no, until Alex mentioned Trudi's name, that Trudi Groves was to be his new sister-in-law. Then Stevens had changed his mind, said he might find odd jobs around the house for him and to come over and talk to the butler.

The first two days he reported to the big house on the hill, nothing had turned up. He had spent one afternoon repairing the garage roof, and the next helping clean out the attic. On the third day, he was carrying a load to the basement and caught a quick look at four big galvanized laundry tubs in the furnace room. Nothing unusual about them, except that they were filled with money. The first was full of nickels, so many nickels that they were close to spilling over onto the floor; the second was brimming with dimes, and the third with quarters. The last one was so full of silver dollars that he thought its seams would burst. He only knew he shouldn't have seen them when the butler pushed him along the dark corridor, pulling the wooden furnace-room door shut as he passed it.

When Alex had told Mr. Gates about the money this morning at the chicken coop, he had gotten excited, at least as excited as Gates ever let himself get. Gates told him again that he could stop anytime he wanted, but Alex had been as determined as ever. They had decided to meet every other day at seven o'clock at the coop, and he knew Gates would be anxious to hear about the job he was on now, because he had a feeling that the errand he was carrying out today was definitely not ordinary. When Alex had reported this morning, Mr. Stevens was in a hurry getting ready to leave town himself, and was more impatient than he usually was. Alex had the distinct feeling that Stevens didn't really want him doing this job, but didn't have much choice.

At two o'clock in the afternoon, Alex was bouncing along Highway 24 toward Mount Sterling with specific directions about where he was to be in precisely one-half hour. Mr. Stevens had been adamant: "Memorize the directions. I don't want anything in writing. Empty your pockets of everything, all identification, any pictures, everything!" That's when Alex had realized it wasn't an ordinary job. That's when he got scared.

Maybe he should have been more honest with Jessica, told her what he was doing, but he didn't want to worry her. He also didn't know exactly how to explain, other than to say that he was helping Mr. Gates break the strike, helping in any way he could to assist the truckers. He believed in their cause and felt frustrated just walking around with a sign in front of the quarry office, or hanging out at the Labor Temple listening to the guys complain. He knew the men were getting discouraged, and it made him sad and angry. He had posted a poem on the bulletin board at the Temple when no one was looking, but he didn't think it meant as much to the people who read it there as it did to him. It was a poem by Walt Whitman that confronted all the settled laws and it was a poem that spurred Alex on.

"Jessica, I am going to be a success for you, and for me, and for our baby," he breathed aloud. "I'm not going to break my back all my life and not be able to pay the doctor's bills when I'm old, like my dad. Thinking of Jessie, he smiled. He loved holding her in his arms, loved feeling her sweet lips on his, loved the way she looked when she smiled at him. Soon, in six days to be exact, they would be husband and wife. His dream come true.

Suddenly he quit dreaming, his attention back on the road. Ahead and to the right was the high, arched span of the bridge across the Illinois river. As soon as that came into view, he was to watch for the frontage road that ran between the levee and the banks of the river. He was conscious of everything now, the jarring of the truck's springs, the bugs on the windshield, the knee-high corn in the fields.

He turned hard left and bounced off the road and onto a dirt path, just wide enough for the truck. He thought hard. His next instructions were to measure out a quarter mile and look for a thick clump of willows on the riverbank. He was sweating heavily now, leaning out the window of the truck as if that would make him see better. There it was, and moored next to it, almost hidden by the overhanging trees, was a small tugboat, homely but sturdy, its engines still chugging. He pulled the truck up and jumped out, walking quickly toward the three men on the tug. They stared at him, unfriendly glares, wary and suspicious. He started to say hello but thought better of it, standing foolishly quiet, waiting for them to make the first move. The fat one with the scar over one eye spoke first.

"Where'd you come from, kid?" It wasn't a friendly question, and he swallowed hard before answering, wondering if there was a password he should know.

"From St. Louis." He risked the simple truth.

"Where you taking this shipment?"

"To the Cuckoo Clock in St. Louis."

The three looked at each other slowly, as if weighing the truth of his words. It was enough time for Alex to notice the sawed-off shotgun that rested on the knee of the man who sat in the stern. Then, at no discernible signal, they jumped off the boat, heedless of the mud at the river's edge, and stepped in among the willows.

"Get the hell over here and pull," the fat man yelled, and, heart pounding, Alex did as ordered. Together the four of them tugged out a flexible rolled platform of boards, laying it from the rear end of the truck into the water. It took Alex a minute to understand that it was a portable ramp down which the truck could be backed. With the four working assembly-line fashion, the tug was off-loaded within fifteen minutes, its cargo of top Canadian liquor snug in the rear of the truck. Alex put the truck in first gear, spinning the wheels until they dug into dry earth again, then hopped out to help with the last step of the operation. The boards, lashed together with wire, were flipped over to reveal a surface sodded with grass, eliminating entirely the telltale signs of heavy tire treads along the muddy banks.

"Holy Mary, Mother of God!" Alex whispered as he raced down the highway at top speed. "Am I glad to get out of there." His shirt was soaked with sweat and his mouth was dry. "Wait until I tell Mr. Gates."

"The kid done okay, huh, Rats?" the short one ventured as the tug eased into the main current of the river.

"That's only the first test, stupid," the scarface jeered. "Leo and Bucky will throw a lot more at him before they give him any of the big stuff."

CHAPTER 24

Summer rain, not misty and romantic but a heavy downpour, darkened the sky the day before the wedding. When it broke, Jessie and Trudi ran outside and frantically gathered flowers, cutting and snipping them before the rain could break the blossoms from the stems. Trudi turned her face to the dark sky, squinching her eyes shut, reveling in the feel of the warm rain on her face.

Why did she associate the rain with Phillip Gates? Why did she even think of him? She had seen him only fleetingly in the past few weeks, but he was constantly on her mind. She shook her head, dropping flowers as she tried to dry her eyes, then gave up, throwing blossoms into Jessica's basket with abandon. Grams watched from the kitchen, chuckling, more relaxed than she had been in weeks. The bridal couple had not revealed any reluctance as the big day approached, seeming more sure of their decision than older, long-courting couples. Preparations for the wedding and reception were almost complete, since both Grams and Alex's family had been cooking for the last week.

The rain soaked the strikers outside the quarry offices and their brother workers protesting along the walk in front of the company headquarters on Second Street. Some fortunate ones were secure in their black slickers, long, heavy, rubberized coats that fell to their ankles, but most huddled against the sting of the hard-driving rain in their cotton street clothes.

Alex walked with the strikers, his shirt stuck to his skin, the ends of his black curls dripping rain into his eyes and down the back of his neck. The crowd of men had gathered for a purpose, and the rain, though discouraging, would not dispel them. Today was the march, a mile-long march through the major streets of St. Louis, that would demonstrate their commitment to the cause.

Hundreds of sympathizers from throughout the county were arriving, battered pickups and simple sedans disgorging more men by the minute. There was an air of restrained camaraderie, a renewed feeling of solidarity that had been waning over the last week. The march had been Phillip Gates's idea, and as he was spied loping down the street toward the point where the march would begin, a bevy of hallos greeted him.

"It's going to be a good-sized crowd," Victor Wellman said, feeling optimistic. Gates didn't answer, looking instead at the corps of policemen that had congregated at the end of the street, holding back a cadre of men whose scowls and raised fists marked them as unfriendly to the strikers.

"Are our people ready to withstand abuse?" he asked bluntly.

Wellman shouldn't have looked surprised by the question, but he was, nervously glancing down the street toward the police.

"Maybe you should talk to them one last time," he answered Gates. Both men looked over their shoulders, over the tops of the buildings to the western sky. "Another five minutes, the rain will blow over. I'll gather the men."

Gates vaulted to the top of a car and raised his hands for silence. "Today you put on display your rights as American citizens. You have a right to congregate peacefully and a right to demand better working conditions for yourselves and all those who follow you. You march today to show your solidarity. Remember to keep this gathering dignified and restrained. Let's show the people of St. Louis that you are deserving of respect. Hold your heads up!" The men cheered, waving their arms, patting each other on the back, working themselves up to run the gauntlet that waited for them a block away.

They walked six abreast, without any accompaniment except their own low murmurs and the clicking of their shoes on the wet pavement. Some were dripping wet, good-naturedly taking the ribbing of their fellow workers; some were in their uniforms from the war; most were dressed in the clothes that they worked in. The American flag was carried high at the front of the parade, and behind it only a few placards waved from the midst of the men: "Decent pay for a decent day's labor!" "Forty hours a week is long enough!"

In the first block, little boys in knickers and suspenders chased down the sidewalk, waving and shouting to their dads, jumping in and out of fresh puddles. Women stood proudly nearby, shyly nodding as their husbands passed. As the marchers gained the top of a small incline, the sun broke through with full force, and a few of the younger men cheered the good omen. The street ahead widened as they approached the busy shopping district; here the people along the walk stood grim-faced and unfriendly. Here the police, six of them on prancing bays, joined the marching laborers, forcing them into a longer, narrower column.

"Damned Bolsheviks! Go back to Russia!" The first shout jolted Gates, even though he was expecting it, and involuntarily he swung around to look at the truckers marching behind him. "Anarchists! Reds!" The jeering continued, growing louder, but Gates just shook his head, calming the group with his own cool demeanor.

When the rocks hit, nobody was expecting it. They came from above, from the tops of the tall buildings, and were thrown with great force and accuracy, sheets of rocks that seemed unending.

"What the hell!" "Cut it out!" Men yelled, shielding their heads and faces with upraised arms. Women screamed, grabbing their crying babies and running for cover. The police on horseback charged into the melee, swinging their billy clubs at the fleeing strikers. Gates stood his ground in the middle of the street, watching with a mounting feeling of dismay, as within minutes the humbled workers disappeared into alleys and doorways, running back in the direction from which they'd come, hoping to find relief from the cutting edge of rocks and scorn. Soon only a few people were left, shoppers peering out of store doors, policemen jerking their excited horses, and one bewildered old man clutching a lamppost.

He looked up to the roofs of the bank, the department store, the music shop, looked full-force, trying to recognize the aggressors, but none showed their faces. The worst was over. The only face he saw clearly was that of Mr. New, standing safely behind the plate-glass window of his law firm, grimly watching the scene below.

Trudi was kneeling in front of Jessica, squinting in concentration.

"I feel so silly." Jessica giggled. "I've never had painted toenails before. Alex is going to hoot when he sees them." She held her left foot out for a clear view.

"Hold still," Trudi scolded, "or it will look like you have six toes on this foot." She looked up at her sister. "You don't think he'll be mad, do you? I mean, it's only a pale pink."

"Of course not," Jessica reassured her. "Alex doesn't get mad over silliness like this."

"This is not silliness! You're going to look perfect tomorrow from head to foot."

Grams burst through the door of Jessica's bedroom, her face washed with a look of utter astonishment. "They're all downstairs. I don't know what to do. Help me."

The sisters looked at each other, more confused than their grandmother. When they dashed to the hall and hung over the banister, Jessica was greeted with laughter and shouts of good cheer from the crowd below. Alex's three sisters and their husbands, five members of the Mussolino family, three Bonasingas, and innumerable members of the Billotti family had converged in Grams's front hall.

An ancient lady dressed in black from head to toe, her white hair covered by a scarf tied tight under her chin, her face the texture of old parchment, led the way up the stairs. The others followed patiently, their words a mixture of English and Italian.

"Good evening."

"*Buona sera!*"

"Congratulations!"

Jessica clutched at her robe, stunned into inaction, her eyes frantically searching for an explanation. Only when the happy crowd had found Jessie's bedroom did their mission become clearer. One by one, the well-wishers pinned cash, bills in a variety of denominations, to the bedspread. A blanket full of love and best wishes. Hugs and kisses for Jessie welled over to Trudi and Grams as well. When the crowd moved out of the room on the way to leave, the din finally subsided. The old lady, related to everyone in the group, stopped to pat Jessie's rounded belly, her hand feather-light.

"Happy baby." She grinned. "We cherish this bambino amore." Jessie's eyes brimmed as she clasped the tiny woman in her arms. They left arm in arm as Jessie went to say good-bye to the others clustered in the front hall.

Sonny Billotti bent to whisper in Trudi's ear. "In case she's worried, tell Jessie that Alex was not hurt in the march today."

"Hurt? What march?" Trudi's concern was apparent in her voice, though she managed to keep her expression under control.

"The strikers' march. I thought you knew." He grimaced, upset by his blunder, then hurried on, trying to make amends. "Only two or three were hurt, not too badly. Phillip Gates caught a rock on the back of the head, but he's not in the hospital." Trudi smiled sweetly, thanking him graciously for the news, then turned to the guests, her mouth so dry she could barely speak. By the time the house was clear, her heart was pounding in her ears, but she remained composed.

"Grandmother," she said softly, "I am going out for a short time. I should be home in a half hour." Her back straight, she walked slowly out the front door.

Grams frowned and her eyes narrowed. She looked at the door, then at Jessie, then back at the door. "Something's fishy here. She never does anything calmly and coolly."

Trudi drove recklessly through the quiet evening streets of St. Louis, relentlessly grinding the gears of Grams's old Ford. She almost overshot the Gateses' home in her haste, and arrived breathless at the front door. She stood with frightened eyes and heaving chest as Evangeline Gates opened the door. Through their mysterious bond, the older woman understood, and her first words were soothing.

"He's all right. You needn't worry." She reached out and put her arm around Trudi's shoulders, drawing her into the house. Weak with relief, Trudi sat in a deep chair nestled in the well of the bay window and waited for more information.

Her looks are deceiving, Evangeline Gates observed. So tiny, a miniature china doll, her pale coloring offset only by the huge eyes. But there was nothing small or fragile about the depth of the young woman's feelings, and Evangeline spoke to them now.

"He's at the office, working late again. I'm sure he has a monumental headache. It took three stitches to close the cut." She indicated the back of her head. "But he has taken on the cause of the workers with his usual intensity and would not stay home to rest." She shrugged and gave Trudi a smile that drew them together in a conspiratorial understanding of her oldest son.

"He seems to take on causes with missionary zeal." Trudi's little smile did nothing to hide her feelings. Then, nerving herself with a sip of the tea that Mrs. Gates had offered, she paused and asked, "Do you think his hatred of Winslow Stevens is justified?"

Evangeline Gates, in the process of refilling her cup,

nearly dropped the dish. Her hand shook as she set the cup and saucer on the table beside her. She paused, a long, meaningful pause.

"I understand it." She finally looked up at Trudi. "I wish he could forgive and forget, but it doesn't seem to be happening." She took a huge breath and let it out slowly. Staring out the window into the night, she spoke again, her voice quivering with emotion. "But he is blaming the wrong person. None of it ever would have happened if it weren't for me." Trudi leaned forward, puzzled, intrigued by the woman's words. "Thirty years ago, Shrader Stevens fell in love with me. He was much older than I, but that made no difference to him. He was persistent even after I told him I didn't love him, even months later when I told him I was going to marry Charles Gates. He refused to accept the situation. He was obsessive, pestering me with calls, which I refused to answer, and gifts, all of which I returned. He confronted Charles, too, warning him to stay away from me. I don't think I started to be frightened, though, until the night before my wedding when he showed up at the door of my parents' home."

The memories were painful to her, and she needed time to compose herself. Trudi was heartsick that she had ever brought up the subject, not realizing the cauldron of emotions she was stirring.

"He said that if I married Charles Gates, I would pay for my mistake. That Charles would suffer, that I would suffer." She shook her head as if still not believing what the man had said to her. "It upset me at the time, but not enough to call off the wedding. I never told anyone of his threats, and as we were supremely happy and our lives were unblemished with troubles, I forgot his ravings."

She took another huge breath. "Then when Shrader Stevens got married himself two years later, I thought the whole episode was forgotten." She pressed her lips together, and closed her eyes tightly. "Our respective lives went smoothly for ten years. Then the troubles started for Charles, and I knew almost immediately who was behind it. I called him, begging for understanding, for help."

HIGH SOCIETY

She laughed, an ironic, short laugh. "He said he'd married only to sire heirs. That he still loved me, had always loved me, and would call off the dogs if I would divorce Charles and marry him." Her shoulders sagged. Her face was drained of color, her grief as real as the moment it happened. "Of course, I refused. Within a few months, the pressure became so intense Charles killed himself."

Trudi knelt in front of her, gripping her hands between her own, a look of supreme compassion on her face.

"It was all my fault," Evangeline Gates whispered.

CHAPTER 25

The living room of the Badamos' small house was packed, the air heavy with the odor of garlic and garden flowers and human bodies. From the kitchen, the tinny sounds of an accordion echoed through the house, as the merrymaking after Alex and Jessica's wedding mass reached full tilt.

Rich red wine bubbled from bottle after bottle as the family toasted the newlyweds, the president, the weather, and each other. The party was loud, the happy sounds of laughter and music compacted by the small dimensions of the bungalow. The celebration had started at noon and would probably go on until midnight, but right now, at 6 PM, Trudi's head was pounding, and she was thinking of leaving. She had not slept last night, reliving the story Evangeline Gates had confided, imagining the guilt and pain she and her family had lived with for the last decade.

Only Jessie's joy and Alex's wide grin brought Trudi back to the present, and she laughed out loud when she was grabbed and whirled in a tight circle by the groom's uncle. When he released her, she spun around, bumping into Phillip Gates, who was standing just inside the living room door.

They stood immobilized, staring at each other, oblivious to everything around them. Trudi's vision blurred. The entire room became indistinct except for the circle immediately around him. She backed away, jostled by the dancers, and bumped into a child, who shoved her back. She reached the far wall and stood behind a rocking chair, grasping its spindles for support as her eyes remained on Phillip Gates. Her heart pounded in her throat, and she had trouble drawing breath, but she remained still, frightened by her emotions, frightened by the effect the mere sight of him had on her.

He hesitated, his eyes never leaving hers, his bewilderment growing as he tried to calm the pressure building in his head. He did not understand the effect she had on him. He only knew that he had missed her immeasurably. He had yearned to talk to her. He wanted to touch her, to apologize and try to understand what had kept them apart, for he had never been so miserable and never wanted to be apart from her again. The crowd swirled in front of him, the shouts of greeting lost on him as he stood mesmerized by the sight of her. He took two steps toward her and stopped. She leaned against the wall, her hands flattened against it for support, praying he would come to her, uncertain what she would say or do if he did.

In three more quick strides he was in front of her. He licked his lips and started to speak, but stopped and brushed at the shock of hair that fell over his forehead. In his eyes she saw a trace of uncertainty, which touched her more than any words he could have uttered. She knew then what she would say to him.

"I love you." She said it simply, so softly he could not possibly have heard the sound of her voice, but he knew. His eyes softened, his lips parted, and he shook his head and looked to the ceiling as if giving thanks. He reached for her hand, and they left without a word to anyone.

Twenty minutes later, they were sitting on the riverbank, the expanse in front of them broken only by one small fishing boat anchored 300 yards away. Overhead the sky was cloudless, with only a low, thin rim of stratus clouds lining the horizon. She had directed him to her family's riverfront cottage ten miles south of the city, always one of her favorite getaway spots, removed by distance and heavy foliage from any neighbors. They sat now, only their hands touching, listening to the chirping crickets on the ground, the raucous red-winged blackbirds in the cattails, and the grumping frogs at the water's edge. The protracted silence was broken by Trudi's words.

"I don't belong to Winslow Stevens." She gazed at him almost fearfully. His response was crucial, for he had to know that he could not manipulate and use her for his purposes.

He laughed, which was not the reaction she expected. "I have never thought of you as belonging to anyone but yourself." He reached for her, pulling her into his arms, and kissed her as tentatively as if it were their first kiss. And she believed him.

"I know a more comfortable place," she whispered. She got up, leading him to the edge of the lawn, and pointed silently up into the boughs of a huge weeping willow, toward her tree house. He laughed aloud, a wonderful sound, then bounded up the primitive ladder she had nailed to the trunk and pulled her up behind him. He knelt in front of her, his hands at her waist, and she felt the same wonderful surge of excitement she always felt at his touch. The heat of his hands as they rubbed her haunches sent a tremor of excitement through her body, and she melted to the floor, reaching up for him as he hovered above her.

Within minutes, only the warm summer breeze covered their naked bodies as they tenderly embraced, their apologies spoken through their silent kisses. When he pulled away, it was to look at her body, glowing in the warm light of sunset. He slowly ran his hand from her neck to her thigh and back again; then suddenly, as if unable to control himself another moment, he smothered her mouth with his own, covering her body with his, entering her with an urgent need. Their passions blended and their bodies met in vibrant joy, their hunger for each other not easily or quickly satisfied. Time slowed until it was meaningless, the muted sounds of their lovemaking blending with the soft birds' songs in the moonlight.

While they rested, he kept her close, savoring her nearness. She nestled against him, running her fingertip along the arch of his eyebrow, along the edge of his jaw, and whispered, "I never thought my tree house would be used for this."

He chuckled. "Ah, but what better use?" He pulled her on top of his lean body and wrapped his arms around her.

"We really need to talk," she murmured into his ear.

He heaved a huge sigh. "If you insist." She pushed herself up on one elbow and looked at him earnestly. "This is going to be serious, isn't it?" he groaned, not surprised when she nodded.

She played with a tuft of his hair, tugging and twisting, pushing it up and away from his forehead, stalling for time before finally coming to the question. "Are you still intent upon ruining Win Stevens?" He waited to answer and the silence pounded in her ears, but she would not be intimidated by his reluctance to talk.

He knew the question was not ordinary and that his answer was crucial. He thought carefully. He refused to lie to her and tell her that he had given up his mission. Yet if he told her the truth, he risked losing her, for she had not understood before. He tightened his grip on her. "Yes," he said, his voice strong and sure. "Yes, I am." He felt her wince, but she didn't pull away.

"How do you intend to do it?" Her voice shivered, barely a whisper, but she was willing to listen. He relaxed and sat up, still holding her, to look directly at her.

"Do you understand that the manufacture, distribution, sale, or consumption of alcoholic beverages is illegal?"

"Yes, of course I know it is, but I don't think it should be—"

"That's beside the point," he interrupted. "Anyone who is involved in any of those activities is breaking the law, and is, therefore, a criminal."

"Yes, technically. But it would be ridiculous to think that anyone who enjoys a drink in the privacy of his own home should be thrown in jail," she argued, thinking that was all he had in mind.

"We're not talking about that kind of trivial act. And we're not talking about a gray area. The law is black and white. I have reason to believe that he is intimately involved in every aspect of bootlegging."

She looked at him skeptically. "I can't imagine why he would do that!" He looked at her steadily, the somber look she knew so well, and she began to wilt. "Even if that is true, you wouldn't get much popular support trying to prove it."

"Why would he do it? Big-time bootleggers are making huge fortunes, and he is a greedy man." She thought about that for an instant, and saw that it could be true. He continued, this time addressing her second concern. "I don't need popular support. I only need the support of the courts."

"You may not get even that," she blurted, remembering the late-night scene outside Judge Graf's house. She tried to be honest with him. "If you are pinning your hope on that issue, you may be fighting a losing battle. There is a huge backlash against the Volsted Act already. It may be repealed before you can prove anything."

"True, but what if I told you he was also involved in prostitution and gambling?" She slumped back in surprise. The elegant, upper-crust Win Stevens, involved in the shoddiness of prostitution and gambling? Phillip held up his hand and started ticking off names and events that corroborated his suspicions. She continued to look at him, her skepticism dwindling. "If I could get enough evidence to prove that he was a kingpin in the underworld, would you agree that my revenge would be more than purely personal? That there would be social value in seeing Win Stevens in prison?"

"Yes, of course," she murmured.

"That's my intention." He stated his purpose simply, and she was convinced of his sincerity.

Then a terrific idea came to her, and she straightened her spine as if that would help her think better. She tilted her head and tapped her chin with a finger as she concentrated.

He frowned. "Whatever you are thinking worries me."

"I can help." Her smile was enthusiastic and she wiggled with excitement. "I have access, or can have access, to Stevens's daily life, to his business records; I can get information about him that nobody else can."

"Oh, no!" he almost shouted. "You stay out of this. It could be dangerous, and I don't want you getting hurt. I will do this on my own." He grabbed her shoulders and looked directly into her eyes. "Promise me that you will not do anything stupid."

"I promise." She smiled sweetly at him, the fingers of both hands crossed behind her back, a trick she had learned as a child, a trick that completely negated her words.

JOURNAL ENTRY:
Success! The conference at Boulder Junction went well. All territorial details have been worked out. I will handle the central Midwest, including not only middle Illinois but into Iowa and northern Missouri also. Capone handles Wisconsin, upper Illinois, and Indiana, while the Green Gang takes lower Missouri, Kansas, Kentucky, and Arkansas.

The smartest thing we've done as a group effort in a long time was to buy the resort; the atmosphere of the north woods was conducive to trust and relaxation. When we dont't use the lodge for our meetings, we can send all the punk politicians and their families there for free vacations. The place is huge and can take ten families at a time.

Jackie told me about the churchwomen's rally against prostitution. What a joke! We'll just spread the word that it will be business as usual. But at the Gem City Hotel instead of the Fourth Street house. We may see a drop in business for a few weeks, but those self-righteous bitches will give up their vigil long before our regular customers give up their lifelong habits. This, again, is an opportunity to seize. We'll just convert a couple of more houses around own to divert attention from Jackie's place. She's capable of keeping the books for more than one place. I'll tell her she can attend Rom'es housewarming party, as one payoff. As a joke, I brought her a pair of beaded Indian moccasins from Wisconsin. She wore them, and nothing else, to bed. Kept saying she was a wild woman from the woods and did everything she could to convince me.

Leo and Bucky filled me in on the progress of the strike. The truckers are more stubborn than I ever though they would be; they ran from the kids we hired to pelt them with rocks, but it didn't seem to scare them enough to split their union. So now we bring in the goons from Chicago to get down to the dirty work. I'll talk to the Flanagins and other owners about hiring Pinkertons, ostensibly to protect our business, but they will be my pwans in this game also. Distribution problems are getting worse. I don't like hiring part-timers to fill in, but I refuse to let my customers down on promised deliveries and risk the solid business I have built so carefully.

In three days the kids go back to their families, and they're out of my hair. The Fourth of July party George Rom eis throwing will mark my day of freedom from them, and more importantly, from then on I can pursue Trudi without distraction. I want

*to be engaged by the end of August
so I can have plenty of time to plan
a Christmas wedding, like none that St. Louis
has ever seen.*

*Even if Trudi says yes, I will never give
up my therapeutic sessions with Jackie.*

CHAPTER 26

The evening air was hot and heavy, without a hint of breeze or the promise of cooling off. Win Stevens had all the windows rolled down in the car, not minding if his hair got mussed, enjoying the radio music that wafted through the air from every house he passed. A trio of little boys stopped rolling their hoops to stare in admiration as he passed in his gleaming foreign sports car. He grinned and waved at them. The Hispano-Suiza always got attention, the kind of attention he liked. He was in a great mood. Trudi had called *him* for the first time, and he was encouraged. His patience was paying off.

Maybe she'd missed him while he was in Wisconsin, he mused, but if that was so, she would want to spend time with him alone instead of suggesting that they double-date with his sister, Bonnie, and Gardner Gates, of all people. She threw him off balance with requests like that. If he didn't know her better, he might think she did it deliberately, except that she didn't have a conniving bone in her tiny body.

He pulled up in front of the sprawling Queen Anne-style home that belonged to her grandmother. When he had asked her why she was staying there, she had turned cold; the wall of reserve had been inexplicable but very definite, so he had not pressed for an answer. When she came to the door, though, there was no reserve, for she flashed him a brilliant smile and kissed his cheek. Each time he saw her he believed he had never seen her looking so beautiful, and tonight was no exception. Her dress was sleeveless, a thin silk covered with faint outlines of tiny flowers in pastel colors that fell loosely from her shoulders, clinging to her body as she moved. They walked hand-in-hand to his car, and he explained the plans for the evening.

"We'll meet Bonnie and Gard at a roadhouse south of town for fried catfish. Sometimes they have a good ukulele player, too."

"Sounds great," she agreed, and continued to chat amicably on the short ride. The garish sign announcing "Settle's Foods" could be seen a mile away, and when they stepped inside, Trudi laughed with glee, waving to Bonnie and Gard, who waited at a small table in the middle of the dark, crowded room. "Clever, very clever," she said, laughing again, swiveling her head for a complete view.

The place looked like a small grocery store. Three walls covered with wooden shelves were stacked high with canned goods and boxes of crackers, soaps, and cereals, while a ceiling fan revolved the air overhead. About eight tables were pushed together in the middle of the room, undecorated by cloths or candles. Only the back wall was revealing. It was a fifteen-foot-long bar, its patrons crowded together elbow to elbow, enjoying a variety of beers and cocktails, while the ukulele player, perched high on a stool, plucked away at "Oh! How She Could Yacki, Hacki, Wicki, Wacki, Woo."

Bonnie looked radiant, glowing with happiness, her bright yellow cotton dress shorter and more daring than anything Trudi had ever seen her wear. Her jubilant mood was explained by her first words.

"We're engaged!" Bonnie almost shouted.

Win fell into his chair, his mouth open, looking in amazement from his sister to Gardner and back. Trudi knew what he was thinking, and kicked him under the table before leaning to hug Bonnie in congratulations. When she leaned over to Gard, the hug lasted a tiny bit longer, long enough for her to whisper in his ear, "You aren't fooling me." He blanched, but only momentarily, before recovering his usual cool charm.

"Trudi, we'll have to talk since you've been through two weddings this summer already." Gard smiled brightly as he squeezed Bonnie's hand.

"Oh, yes," she said, smiling back, "we must."

The waitress lugged over four plates laden with food and plunked them down on the table after shifting the catsup bottle and sugar bowl out of the way with the edge of one plate. Each of the four had plunged their forks into the fat white meat of the fried catfish when a loud buzzer sounded behind the bar, bleating its intermittent warning again and again.

"Let's get out of here!" Win yelled above the noise of the panicked patrons. Bewildered, Trudi stood up quickly, then stopped to watch the frantic activities. All of the tables were cleared of food within seconds. The ukulele player disappeared out the back door with everyone else. The tables were neatly stacked in a dark corner. But most surprising, she watched as the bar was rotated, to be transformed into the counter of any ordinary neighborhood grocery, complete with cash register, pickle jar, and candy case. Behind it, shelves, fully stocked with food items, were pulled into place from the side walls. In two minutes, the roadhouse bar had become an innocuous crossroads grocery.

"Come on!" Gardner grabbed Trudi and pulled her out the back door; they were the last two to leave. Win roared up in his car, Bonnie grinning but frightened beside him. "We'll follow you," Gardner shouted and waved them away.

He and Trudi skirted two cars whose spinning tires sent out tails of gravel and dust, and jumped into Gard's little roadster. Trudi craned her neck to look back at the tavern, trying to figure out the cause for alarm, but gave up when Gard pulled away with such speed that she was thrown deep into the seat.

He drove with concentrated effort, but she yelled at him

anyway, "We have the same goal you know." He looked at her dumbly, then turned his attention back to the road, refusing to reveal anything in words or expression. She tried again. "We all—you, me, and Phillip—want to get the goods on Win Stevens." The car swerved for an instant with the impact of her words. She looked at him smugly and kept talking. "I intend to find out everything I can about his personal activities; then I'll record them and give the information to Phillip."

"Does he know about this?"

"Well, sort of," she hedged. "I mean, I told him I was going to do it and he said he didn't want me to, but I didn't promise, so you have to swear you won't tell him because he might be upset."

"That's just what I thought!" Gard frowned at her. "You better stay out of it. This could get brutal."

"You won't tell, will you?" she pleaded.

"I'm not promising anything."

"If you tell Phillip, I'll tell Bonnie."

"Tell her what?" He turned sharply to look at her.

"I'll tell her you don't really love her, that you're just leading her on."

"You wouldn't!"

"Yes, I would." She smiled sweetly but looked him squarely in the eyes to make him understand her determination.

"We're not exactly building a friendship based on trust, are we?" He gave her a rueful glance.

"No, but we could be." She looked at him sorrowfully. "We both want the same thing. Can't we work as allies?"

He looked at her dubiously, his mouth pursed in thought. "Oh, what the hell." He caved in, thrusting his hand toward her, his little finger extended. She crooked her little finger around his, and they pulled hard. "Pals?"

"Pals!" she declared. "Now, tell me. Was Settle's going to get raided? Is that why we cleared out of there so fast?"

"You betcha! Most roadhouses have a warning system set up. Whenever feds or sheriff's men approach, the watchmen stationed a couple of miles away just press the button that rings at the bar. Gives everybody time to clear out.

Settle's has the best system, which is probably why Stevens feels safe going there. It wouldn't do to have one of St. Louis's leading young citizens caught in a roadhouse!"

"Look!" Trudi pointed to Win's car a hundred feet ahead of them. "Where are they going?"

Win had pulled his car onto a grassy field, already filled with a multitude of cars, bikes, even a few horse-drawn wagons, so Gard bumped along behind him, directed into the field by a freckle-faced boy of sixteen who took his responsibilities very heavily, his face set in an unflinching scowl.

Steady streams of people, old and young alike, hurried toward a huge tent, bigger than any circus big top in Trudi's childhood memory, raising a low cloud of dust that refused to settle in the hot summer air. A loud rendition of Sousa's "Washington Post" filled the night, accompanied by the rhythmic clapping of a thousand hands.

"Win, what is this?" Trudi inquired as the two couples met in front of Gard's car.

"Don't ask me." He pointed to Bonnie in a gesture that absolved him of any responsibility for being there.

"It's a revival!" she explained brightly, tugging Gard into the stream of people headed for the tent, and the foursome marched along to the rousing beat of "Stand Up, Stand Up for Jesus." "Haven't you seen all the flyers posted around town?" Bonnie asked. "It's Sister Aimee Semple McPherson and her Foursquare Gospel, all the way from the Angelus Temple in Los Angeles, California."

"I didn't know you were religious." Gard threw the comment to Bonnie as they entered the crowded tent.

"I'm not," she answered honestly. "I'm an agnostic who is moved by hymns."

Win shook his head in wonder, turning to whisper to Trudi, "That's the funniest thing I've ever heard her say."

Inside the tent was packed. Not a seat was vacant, and hundreds of people rimmed the open edge, waving bamboo fans and mopping their flushed faces with hankies. The murmur of expectant voices could be heard above the music of the orchestra as it played a quavering interpretation of "Rock of Ages." A stage was set up, a raised dais on it topped by a heavily carved gold and white throne backed by huge, spreading bouquets of flowers and palm greens.

"Let's stay for a few minutes," Bonnie entreated. "This could be a good show. At least it beats going back to the country club for dinner."

The decision was made for them as a bell rang and instantly the crowd hushed, watching a solemn choir of fifty singers file in from either side of the tent and immediately kneel, facing the throne, on which an electric spotlight had been trained. There was a moment of hushed expectancy. All was in readiness. The audience, workers, orchestra, choir, even microphones—all were waiting. But the throne was still empty, bathed in its soft light.

Suddenly the curtains behind the throne parted, and Aimee McPherson appeared. She was clad in white, with a dark cloak thrown loosely about her shoulders, her rich auburn hair with its flowing waves heaped high on her head. In her left arm she carried a bouquet of red roses and white lilies of the valley; in her right hand she carried a white Bible. Assisted to the throne by an exceedingly handsome young man, she gracefully turned as he removed the cloak, then seated herself, turned to the audience, and smiled, a radiant, expansive smile as the choir began a stupendous, cataclysmic offering of "Rock of Ages."

Trudi's mouth fell open stupidly. She had never seen such a dramatic entrance, and it dumbfounded her just as it did everyone else in the audience. She jumped nervously as Sister Aimee rose, waved her arm, and, with the choir, the trumpets, and an organ behind her, led the congregation in a thunderous rendition of "Jesus, Savior, Pilot Me." When the assault on the eardrums was over, Sister Aimee, standing close to the bulky microphone, raised her hands in prayer, delivered in a shouting shriek to the heavens punctuated liberally by amens from the appreciative audience.

"Let's get out of here," Trudi whispered into Win's ear, and he willingly bent to repeat the message to Gardner. But before they could move, Sister Aimee, smiling, but with the tone of voice used by Napoleon before battle, commanded,

"No one stir. We have a rule that no one shall leave during the sermon, under any circumstances. The ushers will enforce this, please."

Trudi groaned, rolling her eyes toward Win, who grimaced in return. The sermon began, a crude, rambling, self-laudatory talk with the theme "What Think Ye of Christ?" Summoning figures from her memory with a vigorous clap of her hands, Sister talked in turn to a banker, a builder, a politician, a jeweler, and a schoolboy, inquiring of each, "What think ye of Christ?" "He is the wealth of the world," answered the banker. "He is the door to heaven," answered the builder. "He is the Prince of Peace," answered the politician. "He is a pearl of great price," answered the jeweler.

It was hopeless as a sermon, but it was great preaching, artfully executed by a superb actress. Her harsh voice was carefully modulated, used to the fullest, most dramatic effect. With her brightly manicured fingertips, with her poses, her gestures, her facial expressions, her lifted eyebrows, her brilliant smiles and pathetic frowns, she elicited the exact response she wanted from the vulnerable crowd. But the climax did not surge forth until the appearance of her make-believe schoolboy, whose testimony was delivered in a small, childish voice.

"Schoolboy," shouted Aimee, summoning him with a clap of her hands from the recesses of her memory, "what think ye of Christ?"

"Oh, he is the elder brother."

"Yes, he is," shouted Sister. "See the poor little schoolboy going home from school. Behind that tree lurks a big, blustering bully. He pounces on the little boy and pummels him. But down the road comes the elder brother on a bicycle. He leaps on the bully, and has him down; he rubs his face in the dirt. He saves the schoolboy, AMEN!" A chorus of amens echoed through the audience. "Oh, how often I have been that little schoolboy, all alone and defenseless in the world. The big bully, the devil, has me down. He is beating me. But suddenly down the road, on his bicycle of love and grace, comes the Lord Jesus Christ. Praise the Lord! He rescues me!"

Fervent alleluias from her audience filled the air as she sank to the floor of the platform in graceful exhaustion, accompanied by thunderous applause. Instantly she jumped up, totally revived, shouting and banging a tambourine against her hip. "And now the offering, so we can continue the work of the Lord with your help!" A cadre of ushers filed through the audience, quickly and efficiently reaching even the most remote person with long-handled baskets.

"No!" Trudi resolutely held up her hand in refusal when the basket was thrust under her nose. Win and Gardner did the same. But Bonnie, her face flushed by a mysterious, benign expression, opened her purse, digging deep to fish out a handful of bills to pile them on top of the overflowing offertory.

"Now we *are* leaving!" Win growled, grabbing Trudi by one arm and Bonnie by the other. Bonnie struggled, resisting with a righteous might.

"No, I'm staying," she managed to hiss above the noise from the front of the tent.

"All ye who want to be saved, come forth!" Sister Aimee was shouting into the microphone. "Come to the altar of Christ and be saved from the clutches of the devil!" Bonnie raised her hand and moved quickly to the aisle, practically running to the altar while the other three stood watching helplessly.

CHAPTER 27

Nancy Neumann's body listed heavily toward the door of her boss's office as she eavesdropped on the argument, her fingers poised but still over the keyboard of her typewriter.

"And I think you are a stubborn mule!" Trudi's voice was raised but under control, which was more than could be said for her temper. Her nostrils flared and her breath was short, but she wasn't going to back down now. She stood with her feet planted firmly in the middle of his office, her hands on her hips, elbows wide, her anger apparent, but at the same time failing to look intimidating at five foot one and a hundred pounds. "Don't you ever think you can tell me what to do, Phillip Gates!"

He was on his feet, too, glaring down at her from behind his desk. "If you can tell me that you are going to that party in Louisville purely for pleasure, only because you want to, then I'll keep my mouth shut, but not until then."

"I can't tell you that! But I can tell you that it has nothing to do with you and your manhunt for Winslow Stevens!"

"Just as I said before"—he answered calmly now, as if his opinions were vindicated, and slid his body back into his chair—"I don't believe you. I think you consider this a little adventure to add excitement to your boring life." He shot a disgusted look at her. "You are a spoiled, shallow brat, only thinking of what *you* want to do. Otherwise, you would take my feelings into consideration and stay away from that party." He threw his hands out to the side, palms up, as if his logic were assailable.

"Do you know what my grandmother says?"

"I don't care what your grandmother says." Gates picked up some papers on his desk, ignoring her, being deliberately rude.

"She says there are two sides to every coin! I used to think you were wise and strong. Now I know you are just quiet and stubborn!" She wheeled around and jerked the door open, sending Nancy Neumann's fingers flying over the keyboard. "Don't ever think that a roll in the hay gives you the right to order me around!" She slammed the door so hard that Nancy Neumann cringed, certain that the glass inset would shatter.

It was early morning on the Fourth of July, and every street in St. Louis was decorated with yards of red, white, and blue bunting and rows of flags. Periodically, a spat of firecrackers burst in fire, bringing grins to the faces of every little boy who heard. The streets were already full of travelers, ready for a day at Forest Park Zoo or Busch Stadium. The crowd was in a festive mood, unbowed by the heavy picnic baskets and hampers of supplies weighing them down.

Win's party entered the spacious Union Station building, its two-storied ceiling drawing the eye upward with an intricate mosaic design, centered on the three-dimensional figures of four guardian angels gold-leafed into prominence. A forest of potted palms momentarily hid Patti and Tony from view, but they were secondary in Trudi's thoughts for she had caught sight of a fancy lady at the other end of the platform. The red hair looked vaguely familiar, but she thought nothing more of it as Win assisted her into the Pegasus, always the last car on the line. The two teenagers were already on board, and Win seemed relieved and happy.

"I deliver them to their families today, after we get to Louisville," he explained. "In fact, I'm expecting them to be met at the station so we can go directly to the party." Trudi glanced at the two again. It was hard to believe that they were related at all, she with the pale strawberry coloring and he so dark and Mediterranean-looking. Or that they had any connection at all with the polished, elegant Winslow Stevens, since by comparison they appeared to be peasants right off the boat.

"A light lunch has been prepared, if anyone is hungry," Win announced. The faces of the youngsters lit up, and they immediately stepped into the galley, jostling for firm footing as the train lurched ahead. They eagerly inspected the offering while Win settled himself in the chair opposite Trudi.

"I think she's gone wacko." Win spoke without introducing the subject, but she knew full well of whom he spoke. "Bonnie has been captivated by this Sister Aimee." He spoke the woman's name as if he had simultaneously smelled a rotting fish. He had never taken an interest in his sister before, but at this moment the interest seemed heartfelt. He sipped his "breakfast brandy," mulling it around on his tongue as if expecting it to help him demystify the mystery of his sister's conversion. "She's never been religious." He shook his head. "So determined about the use of her body through athletics that she was ignorant of any spirituality. This Sister Aimee merely offers up a sensuous debauch served in the name of religion, you know." His voice was earnest, trying to convince Trudi of something she already believed. She had been there and seen for herself the physical effect of the magic show presented by the ultimate showwoman.

"Her religious message is utterly devoid of sound thinking; it's loose and insubstantial in its construction, preposterously inadequate in its social implications, but"—Win raised a finger for emphasis—"it's amazingly successful in its infallible appeal to the vulnerable."

Trudi could only shrug sympathethically as she murmured a stupid platitude, "Religious convictions have a habit of complicating everyday life." Then her attention shifted, away from Win's droning voice, and onto Jessica's recent observations about her lessons in Catholic catechism.

It had been a lazy day right after the wedding, when Alex was inexplicably gone and the old people in the house were all resting. Trudi and Jessie sat in the backyard, watching the flowers move in the soft summer breeze, chuckling at the mindless chatter of the chickens in the far corner of the yard. Jessica was troubled. Always controlled, she seemed perpetually swaddled in a gentle cocoon of tranquillity, but Trudi was beginning to suspect that Jessie's stillness did not necessarily mean peacefulness. She had confessed to Trudi, a troubled, reluctant confession, that the conversion process was not as she had originally thought it would be.

"It all is so strange to me," she'd murmured, surprised and puzzled by the discovery. "Transubstantiation, transmigration. They seem to have analyzed every aspect of doctrine." She smiled. "You know, the 'how many angels can stand on the head of a pin' syndrome." She heaved a patient, bewildered sigh. "Methodism seems so much simpler, almost purer and more direct. Catholicism is so foreign, the only thing in the world that seems foreign to me. This church comes from a different place in the world, from a different place in the heart and mind. It just is not taking root in my midwestern English soul." She twisted her new wedding band around and around on her finger. "I will go through the formalities, but I'm afraid that way down deep I will always be a Protestant." Trudi stole a glance at her sister, dismayed by the tight look of self-incrimination she saw in Jessie's eyes and by her own inadequate offering of substantial, soothing words of wisdom. After long minutes of silence, Jessie turned to her. "Do you think God knows I'm only pretending for Alex's sake?"

Trudi reached for her hand. "Yes," she answered slowly, "but I think he probably loves you even more for it."

"And it could be Gardner Gates's influence." Trudi concentrated on Win's words again at the mention of Gard's name.

"In what way? I don't understand how you think he

influenced Bonnie. He seemed as disturbed as you by the whole episode."

"I think he has introduced her to"—he hesitated—"to sensuality." His face colored, and he rushed to explain himself. "I think she was a virgin until he came along, and now she is *feeling* so much more." He said the word with distaste.

Trudi couldn't control her giggle. "Why, Winslow Stevens, you sound like an old-fashioned, prudish, protective father."

"She is, after all, my younger sister." He sounded hurt and sanctimonious.

What would he think if he could have seen Phillip Gates and me yesterday on the couch in his new office, before we had the fight? She averted her eyes so that Win could not read her passion and misinterpret it. Gates was a consummate lover, activated, he whispered, by his commitment to her. They moved together passionately, their bodies meeting with no hesitation, with an almost desperate need to reaffirm their love. When they rested, she could not quit touching him, savoring the feel of his lean, tight muscles. Even now, as she sat reliving the feel of his lips on her mouth, her neck, her breasts, she arched her back, and then drew a quick breath, embarrassed that Win might have seen.

The fact that Phillip Gates was a great lover did not erase the fact that he was a domineering, aloof, condescending monster. She was still incensed by his name-calling, and even more certain that she was right in not explaining herself to him. If the two of them were ever going to get along, which didn't look too promising at this point, he was going to have to give her the same amount of free rein he expected for himself.

Union Station in Louisville loomed over them, grand and formal, as they disembarked after a journey so quick it surprised her. The Pegasus was the last car on the train, and they had a long walk into the terminal before finding the car that would be waiting for them. Patti and Tony hurried ahead, stopping only briefly for a quick conversation with the redheaded woman Trudi had noticed earlier. She appeared to be scolding Patti, who stole a furtive look in Trudi's direction before tugging at Tony's elbow and disappearing into the terminal.

"What was that about?" Trudi nudged Win.

"What?" he answered absently, his eyes and his mind ahead of her.

Striding toward them, their expression blank and therefore making them more noticeable, were two men, expensively dressed in a flashy, tasteless way, their hands glittering with diamond rings of a size usually worn by showgirls. They were older than Win by at least a decade, but were deferential as they extended their hands for hearty shakes.

"Trudi Groves," Win made the formal introductions, "this is Duke Cosmano from Chicago and John Coughlin of Cincinnati. My friend, Miss Trudi Groves." Trudi dipped her head, acknowledging the introduction, acknowledging also that the men were shady-looking, a little too brassy to be reputable businessmen. But not until they reached the car did she acknowledge fear.

The car was a huge, heavy Cadillac. In the front seat was a driver, the brim of his homburg pulled low over one eye. Opposite him was a burly man who held a sawed-off shotgun across his lap as casually as if it were a sack of groceries. Neither acknowledged Trudi and Win's entrance into the car as their eyes constantly scanned the street. Behind them in a smaller, faster car rode Patti and Tony, stuffed among four more men of dubious mien. Trudi gave Win a hard stare, demanding an explanation. He held up a hand, pointed ahead through the car window, and gave her a silent nod, making her wait for an answer.

A crowd of people ten-deep lined the street ahead of them, blocking their view, as a Fourth of July parade was in progress. A high school marching band was blaring and drumming its way past the happy crowd. The driver of the car jumped out, corralling a policeman on the curb, who in turn went into action. Waving his baton, shouting some unheard words, he nudged the crowd aside enough for the car to inch forward to the edge of the cleared space, from which Trudi and Win and their sullen companions could see the festivities without leaving the comfort of the car. The driver acknowledged the cop's help with a nod and got a cheery wave back.

After the band passed, a brigade of costumed children pedaled by, their short, fat legs cranking furiously on a variety of trikes and bikes, each ingeniously decorated with red, white, and blue crepe-paper streamers, while the crowd cheered them as obvious favorites. A contingent of straight-backed women, hats firmly on top of their heads, followed with a wide Women's Christian Temperance Union banner held in front of them, braving the good-natured Bronx cheers from groups of men along the sidewalk. A motley drill team of middle-aged men in uniforms from the Great War stretched tightly over their expanded middles stopped long enough to fire a round from their rifles, resulting in loud screams from frightened babies. Trudi chuckled at the sight of the men, but wisely stayed silent.

It was after a group of horses passed, their saddles and bridles more elaborate than the pseudo-western garb their riders wore, that Win expressed his growing irritation. The driver jumped out again, pulled the policeman aside for a short conference, and got back in. Immediately the policeman strode to the middle of the street, held up his hand in the halt signal, and slowed an approaching pack of gamboling clowns to a stop while their car pulled out and crossed the intersection. Trudi slumped down in the car, embarrassed by the unwarranted attention as the crowd of people strained to see who was inside the privileged vehicle. She didn't sit up for six blocks, and gave Win a withering look when she did.

They drove in silence to a thickly green suburb filled with large homes of discriminating pseudo-European architecture. Only when they turned into a paved mile-long drive leading through heavily wooded grounds, beautifully landscaped with flowering plants, did Trudi begin to be impressed. At the entrance to the drive stood two more dark-suited men, lounging casually against the brick columns, not trying to look like anything other than guards.

The house was big, which was the best thing Trudi could say about it. A conglomeration of architectural styles from American Georgian to German baroque were badly blended in the one-hundred-fifty-foot facade. As Trudi, Win, and various other arriving guests stepped out of their Packards, Cadillacs, Pierce-Arrows, and Lincoln Coaches, liveried servants took their satchels and traveling bags and ushered them into the vast living room, grossly overfurnished with carved antiques and featuring a grand piano decorated with gold leaf. Stone statues, the new sort made to look old, stood on marble columns along the sides of the room, grapes trailing from their upstretched hands, gracefully oblivious to the babbling crowd. Heavy baroque mirrors, big enough to reflect a chorus of people at one time, decorated the walls.

"I hope you won't be offended if I say that this is the most grotesque room I have ever seen," Trudi whispered.

"I'm not," Win said, chuckling, "but it might be a mistake to tell our host, George Rome, that. He's an important business associate of mine." How important, and what business? Trudi wondered.

They mingled among the guests, Win merely offering their names in exchange for his own and Trudi's. It was, for Trudi, a confusing amalgam of people. She had suspected that, if there was any truth in what Phillip Gates had said, she would meet underworld activists exclusively, people Win was involved with in his shady deals, and certainly their welcoming committee fit the bill. She wasn't sure what a gangster would look like, but she thought she'd know one when she saw one. But here, at the party itself, was a mixture of people, some polished and erudite, some with the looks and grace of gorillas. Cheesy-looking blondes clung to the arms of squat men twice their age, while expensive-looking women held their noses in the air, aloof from the milieu. Trudi discerned Schiaparelli dresses, Chanel suits, and J.C. Penney sales-rack clothes. A curious assortment.

A receiving line at the far end of the room seemed to be moving fast as the guests did their duties and were ushered into the adjacent dining room, where Trudi spied a huge table laden with food.

"George, Imogene." Win bent to kiss the air beside his hostess's cheek. "I'd like you to meet Trudi Groves." Trudi smiled, shaking hands while giving them a quick once-over. George Rome was short, no more than five feet five inches, the same height as his wife. He was about forty, but already he had the paunch not expected in a man until he reached sixty. His face was soft, his eyes warm and friendly, as he pumped her hand. Imogene grasped Trudi by the shoulders and flagrantly looked her up and down.

"Why, I declare, Win! She is no bigger than a china doll," she remarked with a grin.

Imogene's thick southern accent matched her opulent figure, a figure barely contained in a flamboyant pink chiffon dress trimmed with ostrich feathers, the sort of dress more usually reserved for evening wear than a midday party. A diamond headband wound once around her forehead, echoed by diamond bracelets on each arm and a thick dog collar of diamonds around her neck. Only her hands, decorated by three diamond rings, sparkled more than her eyes, as she assessed Trudi's looks. "She is just the perkiest little thing I've seen in a long time."

Trudi smiled weakly, thinking it could be worse. As they moved beyond the welcoming line, Trudi leaned toward Win. "What makes me think that the Romes have only recently come into money?" Win chuckled and lowered his head, refusing to answer, pointing instead to the table in front of them.

A hilltop of Strasbourg foie gras surmounted by huge fans of peacock feathers centered the table. The glistening carcass of a whole roasted ox filled a special table at one end of the room, while closer to them a fountain of champagne cascaded from a three-tiered silver pool.

"If this is lunch, what in God's name are they serving for dinner?" Trudi asked incredulously. Lunch was served as people moved down the table with their plates in their hands and pointed to each item they wanted, an innovation that Trudi had not experienced before and one that she was not immediately fond of. They filled their plates and moved on to the next room, essentially an indoor swimming pool but transformed for the occasion into a vast dining room. Fifty tables for four, decorated with orchids and gardenias, were set around the huge, sunken pool, itself decorated with a veritable jungle of floating flowers. The room was a vast, marbled-columned, classically proportioned Roman bath, water-centered, with garlands of flowers draped from the glass ceiling and dozens of exotic plants along the perimeters. The guests were duly impressed as they threaded their way to their seats, their laughter matching the cadence of the music played by the orchestra at the far end of the pool.

"May I sit with you?" Trudi turned at the sound of the deepest, softest voice she had ever heard from a man. The owner of the voice stood beside Win's chair, his question directed to Win, his eyes waiting for an answer.

"Of course, Sully. We'd enjoy having your company," Win replied sincerely. "I'd like you to meet my friend, Miss Trudi Groves. Trudi, this is Sully Bozkur."

Bozkur looked deep into Trudi's eyes and lifted her hand, bending to kiss it lightly with elegant old-world élan. He was tall and dark, with the most perfectly proportioned body Trudi had ever noticed on a man. His double-breasted suit was tailored to perfection, showing off his broad shoulders and narrow hips to greatest advantage. His shirt was pale blue, surprising since she had never seen anything other than stark white dress shirts on a man, and it was set off by a blue paisley print tie that matched the silk handkerchief in his pocket. Only his overwhelming masculinity kept him from looking like a dandy. His nose was large, in symmetry with his dark eyes and wide mouth. His hair was sleek and smooth, combed back and away from his high forehead. But it was his skin, smooth, silky, dark and glistening, of unknown ethnic origins, that captured Trudi's attention.

He seemed to know what she was thinking. "You are so

fair, and I am so dark, that together we may appear to be a dalmatian." Trudi and Win laughed at his witticism, and she shifted in her chair, welcoming his company.

"You didn't bring a date?" Win asked.

"No," Bozkur revealed, "but if I may, I will enjoy a dance with Miss Groves after lunch." They all looked toward the dance floor, where couples were already enjoying a spirited fox-trot. Trudi, ignoring her food, peered more closely.

"Isn't that Governor Baker?"

"It is," Win answered, not at all surprised. He took Trudi's hand in a patient, parental way before whispering, "Don't make the mistake of underestimating our hosts."

She kept her eyes and ears open the rest of the afternoon, trying to learn as much as she could without seeming obvious. Twice she excused herself to go to the powder room to surreptitiously write down the names of the guests she had met. But she felt she had not learned anything incriminating about Win, unless she counted the vague reference Sully Bozkur had made while they danced.

"And what is your line of business?" she'd asked him. He cocked his head before answering, looking at her appraisingly.

"I'm a florist," he'd answered simply, a small, enigmatic smile on his face. She was surprised and her expression showed it. "I have a small floral shop adjacent to the Lexington Hotel in Chicago," he explained. "We do a brisk business, especially"—he'd smiled to himself—"in funeral bouquets."

Trudi had censored any more questions, deciding to concentrate on the dance he was so expertly guiding her through. Then, through a break in the crowd, she unexpectedly saw the redhead, and remembered instantly where she had seen her the first time. The window of the brothel in St. Louis on the day of the Salvation Army protest! And Patti Shinn knew her well enough to talk to her at the station, which meant Win must know her, for how else would the young girl from out of town have met her?

Ha! Now if she could just tie Win and the redhead together, this might be something new and interesting for Gates's file.

"Turk! How ya doin'?" A short, fat-lipped man slapped Bozkur on the shoulder so vigorously that Trudi felt the jolt as well. He stood in the middle of the dance floor, impervious to any inconvenience he might be causing the milling dancers, the cigar he held clamped between his teeth radiating smoke up and ashes down onto his suit front. He had not removed his white fedora, and its thick black band matched his heavy brows but did nothing to conceal the scar that ran across his left cheek.

"Hello, Al," Bozkur replied, his voice low and deep but marbled with an unmistakable restraint.

"Did you come down just for the party?" the squat little gnome asked, pumping him for information.

"No, I had some business to take care of first. I've been staying at the Chase."

"Wanna ride back to Chicago with me?"

"No." Bozkur stayed patient. "I go to Kansas City from here."

"Business or pleasure?"

"Business," Bozkur answered with a short warning glance in Trudi's direction that effectively quelled any more questions.

"Talk to ya later." The little man strutted off, followed by two large, bulky companions.

"Who was that little Caesar?" Trudi watched as he pushed his way through the dancers, most of whom greeted him heartily.

"You don't want to know." Bozkur whirled her in another direction, trying to avoid the question.

"Yes, I do," she persisted.

"That was Al Capone. Does that name mean anything to you?"

"No," Trudi answered honestly. "Was he on the business trip to Wisconsin Win went on recently?"

Bozkur looked at her long and hard before bending to murmur in her ear, "If, little one, you are going to hang around Win Stevens very much, you better learn not to ask too many questions. Now, let's watch the show." He led her back to the table where Win waited.

In a circle in the middle of the pool, floating among the rings of fresh flowers, were twenty swimmers, all identically suited, all moving in graceful identical choreography to the music of the orchestra. A team of male divers put on a spectacular display of stunts coordinated with the water ballet. But the end of the show was the biggest surprise.

Their hostess, Imogene Rome, danced onto the diving board, her voluptuous figure daringly revealed in a one-piece bathing suit. Trudi clutched at Win's hand in an effort to keep from bursting out laughing, but when Win squeezed back, hard, her giggling stopped immediately. Imogene bowed, blowing kisses to her audience, then perched on tiptoe at the end of the board and did a perfect swan dive, while her proud husband and guests applauded.

"That's not all, folks," George yelled into the microphone. "At sunset, in about a half hour, we have a fireworks display for you on the back lawn in honor of this great country's birthday. Then the party favors will be distributed." A buzz spread through the crowd, punctuated by happy laughter. And well they should have been happy, for to climax the evening, a waitress placed in front of each man a small box that when opened revealed diamond jewelry, diamond cuff links, diamond tie pins. It wasn't until all the guests were mingling in the foyer at the end of the evening that the women's gifts were announced. The butler threw open the wide double doors to reveal a hundred shiny, regal Buicks lined up in the drive, one for each female guest. Shrieks of surprise and delight filled the room as people jostled to get a better look and hugged their hosts with glee.

"I'm not accepting that." Trudi stood staring at the sedan, standing well back from it, reluctant to claim it even by proximity. "Win, I don't want that car. Win? Win, where are you?" She turned in a complete circle, looking for him. But to her left she found instead the redhead, whose eyes were fastened on the car, an appreciative grin on her face.

"Are you going to accept the car?" Trudi asked, aware of the woman's strong perfume.

"Hell, yes!"

"How will you get it back to St. Louis?"

Immediately the woman's eyes became wary, the grin faded, and she stepped backward. "What makes you think I'm from St. Louis?"

It would be expedient to befriend this woman, so Trudi answered carefully, "I saw you get on the train there."

"That doesn't mean I'm from St. Louis," she replied, abruptly turning to walk away. Trudi watched her disappear into the crowd, knowing full well she had lied, which only validated her theory that the redhead and Win had been deliberately avoiding each other all night and were denying any connection.

"Magnificent gesture of the Romes', isn't it?" Win stood beside her, pointing at the car.

"I think it's gauche." Trudi turned her back on the cars, on the excited women bustling to claim them. "How can the politicians here accept these gifts? Isn't it the same as buying votes?"

"That's for them to worry about, not you." Win put his arm around her and patted her shoulder.

"Well, I'm not accepting it." She turned up her nose.

"Yes, you will," Win answered firmly, a smile fixed on his face.

"I don't know why I should," she shot back testily.

"Because you will not offend George Rome." His smile disappeared, his determined eyes bored into her, and for the first time she was aware of his steeliness.

CHAPTER
=28=

The sky lit up in a cascade of sparks showering down in an umbrella of light. The display turned Phillip Gates's head, the first thing that had distracted him since the Fourth of July parade that morning. He pinched the bridge of his nose, pulled himself from his chair, and ambled to the single window of his small office, stretching his long arms over and behind his head.

I hope Trudi is watching the fireworks display, and I hope she's watching at the club, he thought, chuckling. She would oohh and ahh with the best of them. He was still piqued by her insistence on getting involved with his crusade, a crusade that did not concern her. He hoped she had not gone to the party with Win Stevens. She had no idea of the heavyweights that he was dealing with, and how lethal their tactics could be. This was not a project that could be rushed. It would take patience and perseverance to do it correctly.

A persistent mosquito bumped against the screen, its buzz irritating. Very deliberately he tracked it with the flat of his hand, watching it circle and hop. Then at the right moment he laid his hand flat against the screen and rubbed it out.

Three muffled booms followed by another shower of lights

filled the summer night. He looked up appreciatively, watching the colors fade, before sitting back down to work on more calculations, ignoring the prolonged popping of firecrackers. Since he had left the firm of New, Schmutzler, and Hulsen, he had been more content than he'd thought he was going to be. It had taken some sleepless nights to make the decision, but once it was made, he had felt a huge sense of rightness and relief. Now he was free to make his own decisions, to decide for himself who his clients would be, to set up his own list of priorities. He took a sip of lukewarm coffee, grimaced, and set it down before picking up his fountain pen.

When he first heard the pounding at his door, he dismissed it as another noisy night sound. But with the next rap, he heard his name. Alex Badamo burst through the unlocked door, bent over, panting for breath, his hair and clothes mussed, his shirt torn, his pants dusty. When he raised his head, Gates grabbed for him. His shirtfront was covered with the blood that streamed from his nose.

"Fight on the picket line," he gasped. "Some thugs started it. Police came. Started clubbing people right and left."

"Sit down." Gates led him to a chair and dabbed at his face with a hankie dipped in coffee. "Are you hurt anywhere else?"

Alex shook his head. "Wellman was taken to the hospital. Probably has broken ribs. He was getting kicked a lot." He looked up with frightened eyes. "It was scary, Mr. Gates. The police carted off about twenty of our guys."

Gates's face was grim as he straightened and patted Alex on the shoulder. "I'm sure it was." He sighed heavily. He walked to the other side of the room, and rubbed his chin hard. "What started it? What set it off?"

"The owners brought in scab workers today; probably thought we wouldn't notice 'cause of the holiday. Then some of those new guys called the police and said the trucks had been tampered with. They said that someone had poured sand in the gas tanks. They accused us, but it wasn't!" He stopped for breath, looking up at Gates, beseeching him to believe. "I think those guys did it themselves, to make us look bad. The only trucks damaged were two old run-down flatbeds on their last legs. Maybe they were given permission to do it," he speculated. "But it wasn't any of our guys!"

"It sure as hell better not have been," Gates muttered. "Come on, I'm taking you home, then I'll bail the men out of jail."

Alex pressed his nose with the hankie and looked at the makeshift bandage. "I want to go with you. I can help keep them calm."

Gates turned and studied the young man's face. The circle of light from the desk lamp didn't reach far enough to spotlight his features but gave enough illumination to create deep pockets of dusky shadow on his swarthy features. He looked bruised and battered but calm and controlled. The last few months of this kid's life had been one crisis after another, and each one he had handled with quiet dignity. Gates respected his strength. Alex was right when he said he could calm the men down. The fledgling union had a natural leader here, and Gates intended to foster him.

Two hours later, Gates sat in his car outside Viola Groves's back door, watching until Alex disappeared into the house and a light went on; then he drove slowly home, exhausted from the long day. It was well past midnight, so he was surprised that the light was still on in his mother's kitchen. Before he turned the key in the front door lock, he had a premonition of danger. He went straight to the kitchen.

He saw her, pale and trembling, hunched over the table, her chenille housecoat hanging loose, her eyes huge with fright. Wordlessly she pointed to the back porch. The porch screens had been slashed in perfect Xs, neatly, precisely, professionally. The new mesh curled inward, forming silver petals as mosquitoes and moths danced through the opening toward the light of the kitchen window.

"Are you all right?" He rushed to kneel in front of his mother, grabbing her hands to knead away the cold fright.

She nodded to reassure him, gaining immediate comfort

and confidence from his presence. "It wasn't very long ago. Not more than fifteen minutes. I heard a noise and came downstairs." She gestured toward the porch. "When I looked out the window, the first thing I saw were the knife blades cutting through the screen, the light glinting off the blades. They saw me, too. Two of them, big and mean-looking. They grinned at me before running away."

"Did you call the police?"

She shook her head, the trembling starting anew. "I just don't understand." She rocked back and forth in the kitchen chair, hugging herself. "I just don't understand why anyone would do this."

The phone rang, startling them both, its tinny bell filling the empty hall. Gates grabbed for it.

"Those bastards have been here!" Alex Badamo's voice was furious. "They axed most of Grams's chickens. Jessie's crying. She thought Grams and Mr. Mills would get hurt 'cause they chased them with a shotgun when they heard all the squawking."

"Wait a minute," Gates ordered. "Start again, slower."

Alex took a deep breath. "When I got in the house, all four of them, Jessie, Grams, and the Mills, were huddled in the pantry with the lights out. Hal Mills damned near shot me, they were so scared. Five minutes before, two guys were in the coop killing the chickens. Grams and Hal heard the commotion and went running out there, expecting a coon or a fox or something, but it was two guys."

"Did they see them, recognize them?"

"Oh, they saw 'em real good, but they were strangers, burly guys they'd never seen before. Mills shot at their car, a plain old Ford, but he doesn't think he hit it." Gates was quiet, a multitude of possibilities streaming through his brain. "They know about us, Mr. Gates." Alex's voice was a hoarse whisper. "They know that's our meeting place. They're sending us a message."

"I think you're right," Gates answered. "You're out of this from now on," he ordered the young man. "I don't want you anywhere near the picket line or the Labor Temple or Winslow Stevens's house. Say you broke your leg or have to help take care of your mother; tell him anything. Just don't go near there again. I'd really like to see you leave town till this is over."

"I can't do that, Mr. Gates," Alex argued. "Jessie's due in a few weeks and my mom's not well at all."

"All right, all right," Gates agreed reluctantly, "But don't show your face, don't go out of the house."

"I won't," Alex promised. "I got to admit, seeing all that blood and how scared my family is, I'm scared."

"I know, I know," Gates answered paternally.

"What about you? Aren't you in danger, too?"

"I'll handle it," Gates reassured him before softly hanging up to turn back to his mother.

JOURNAL ENTRY:
All hell has broken out! Just the way I planned. Bucky and Leo were waiting to talk to me when I got home from Louisville tonight. The hired help we brought in from out of town is creating chaos, very creative chaos. Just enough to scare but not hurt at this time. Tomorrow the Pinkertons will arrive. The press conference is called for 10 AM, and the Flanagins have been coached on what to say. The owners, who were reluctant to help pay the cost of the Pinkertons, will agree now that there has been real property damage. Bucky showed me the article in tonight's paper:

> *The continuous operations of St. Louis's industries over a period of fifty years, with a virtual absence of abortive labor disputes and strikes, has frequently been cited as an important contribution to the prosperity of our community. According to statistics prepared last year for the Industrial Committee of the Chamber of Commerce, wage losses due to strikes cost merchants*

of five midwestern cities of comparative size an average of $6,500,000 during the same period. The demands made by the truckers are inflationary and will undoubtedly bring ruin to many families if met, since management would necessarily have to raise prices and lay off many workers to satisfy the strikers' expectations.

George and Imogene Rome outdid themselves on their party. Got a lot of business done while there. Trudi had quite a few questions about the guests, which for the time being, at least, will remain unanswered. I think she was really confused, seeing such a mixture of people, from some really lowlifes to the blue bloods. At some point, after we're married, I will tell her enough to keep her satisfied, but will never tell her everything. I had planned to give her the diamond and emerald engagement ring I bought at Peacock's in Chicago on the way home from Wisconsin, but she was in a testy mood. She was angry because I gave her no choice about accepting the car. It is being shipped up from Louisville, to arrive in the morning. The ring will have to wait.

CHAPTER 29

The high school auditorium was full. It was the biggest crowd for a press conference St. Louis had seen for years. Reporters with press cards stuck in their hatbands, hands full of cameras, pens, and paper, clustered together in the front of the room, speculating about the announcement, while a smattering of wary strikers sat together in the back. Middle-management men draped over rows of seats laughed and joked, cocky about their companies' positions after the drubbing the truckers had taken in the newspaper.

Onstage, Jolene and John Flanagin sat side by side, both dressed in severe, conservative suits, bent toward each other whispering nervously, until Mayor Heinz waddled to the microphone, his stubby thumbs stuck in his suspenders. He liked to brag that he had only a sixth-grade education and was walking proof of the opportunities available in the "good ol'" U.S. of A."

A butcher by trade, Heinz was in over his head as mayor of a growing town, and found it easier, and many times more profitable, to give in to pressures, especially from industrialists, than to fight. He had never taken the time to think through the long-range consequences of his actions, and very probably did not have the capacity to understand them even if they were explained to him. Today was no exception.

"Okay, everybody," he shouted, bending toward the mike. "We got an important announcement today, so I won't waste your time. I'll turn things over to Mr. and Miss Flanagin and let them explain what's going on." Some of the reporters, the ones who considered him a joke, hooted and clapped as Heinz shuffled offstage, waving his hand in naive acknowledgment of the recognition. The Flanagins stepped in tandem to the microphone, fumbled for a moment to adjust it to their considerable height, then spoke loud and clear.

"Because of the growing violence associated with the truckers' strike . . ." John began.

". . . an alliance of business owners have pooled their resources to hire independent agents from the Pinkerton Agency to protect the property of those companies being harassed." Jolene Flanagin finished the first statement, then stepped back to draw a breath, tugging self-consciously at the jacket of her suit. Instantly, from the back of the room, boos and shouts reverberated in the cavernous hall. Some truckers stood, waving their fists in the air.

"Who's going to protect *us*?"

"What about our men in the hospital?"

Reporters turned to snap shots of the demonstrators, their flashbulbs exacerbating the volatile situation, while everyone else turned to watch and babble their own opinions. The angry strikers continued shouting until Phillip Gates stepped into the hall and, with one withering scowl, silenced them, insisting that they remain in exemplary control. He glanced slowly around the room, waiting for the crowd to calm down, then sat close to the strikers, stony-faced and silent.

John Flanagin gulped, collected himself, and began again. "In a labor dispute, we feel it is the duty of local law-enforcement bodies or the government to protect the lives of nonunion employees and the company's property."

"And if, as in St. Louis, they are not able, because of

stringent budget considerations, to handle the additional costs a major strike involves, we feel justified in hiring a private police force to provide adequate protection." Jolene's voice sounded strong and sure; her head was held high and defiantly.

A reporter jumped up, his hand in the air. "Who's paying for this?"

"An alliance of businesspeople," John Flanagin said vaguely, skirting the question.

"How much is it going to cost?" another reporter called out.

"At this time, we have no way of knowing."

"How much ya paying 'em?" the same reporter persisted. The brother and sister glanced at each other uneasily before answering.

"We are not prepared to answer that," Jolene said.

"We're going to find out. You might as well tell us now," the reporter retorted, drawing the first chuckle of the day from the tense onlookers.

"They will be earning ten dollars a day."

Loud mutters growled through the rows of strikers. "That's more than they're paying *us*," one trucker shouted. "It don't make sense!"

Gates turned to fix the man with a steely stare, and he quickly shut up and slouched in his seat.

"These are highly trained professionals," John Flanagin explained. "They will, at the owners' insistence, be sworn in as deputies by the sheriff before setting foot on the premises of any strikebound plant."

Phillip Gates jumped to his feet, finally reaching his breaking point. "I protest! If we allow the owners to bring in the Pinkertons, then what we will have in our community is a private army using the law to protect its activities. This is harassment!" A loud chorus of cheers greeted his statement. He ignored them. "I intend to file a class-action lawsuit against the owners and the Sheriff's Department if that plan is carried through." His voice rose in fury. "This is nothing more than legalized strikebreaking!"

* * *

Gates had calmed down considerably by the time he got back to his office, telling his secretary he would see no reporters until the afternoon, by which time he intended to be well on his way to having a restraining order filed, enjoining the use of the Pinkertons.

For a man who didn't surprise easily, he was startled when Trudi Groves slid through his door, closing it softly behind her. Her appearance here was a conciliatory move, one that he hadn't expected. He was on the phone, his tie loosened, his shirtsleeves rolled up, as rumpled and worried-looking as always, but he managed to look her up and down knowingly as a slow, reluctant smile spread across his face. She noticed and waited impatiently for him to finish the conversation, fanning her face with a magazine and standing directly under the ceiling fan to relieve the heat of the day.

Still, perspiration made her dimity dress stick to her, so she unbuttoned the top two buttons near her neck. Gates immediately frowned and started shaking his head in slow but definite disapproval, feebly attempting to make her stop the disconcerting actions. Fully aware of his discomfort, she grinned flirtatiously, undoing one more button, then moving behind his chair to kiss him on the neck.

"I'm sorry we fought," she whispered in his ear.

"Later," he mouthed, trying to ward her off with a gentle nudge, pointing to the phone. She ignored him, continuing to apologize, kissing his forehead, his ear, his neck.

"I don't like to fight," she whispered, nipping at his earlobe.

He swatted at her playfully, amazed that she was so conciliatory, and when she leaned to kiss him, he grabbed at her, pulling her onto his lap. "I have to go now, Tom. There's someone waiting to talk to me."

With both hands free, he pulled her close and kissed her, a long and passionate kiss that left them both breathless.

"I didn't come just to talk to you," she whispered in his ear. "I came to do this." She pulled her arms from around his neck and began to unbutton the front of his shirt. He protested weakly as she kissed his jaw and neck, her hands inside his shirt. Only when he lifted her and pressed his lips to her breast did she stop her own movements to enjoy the exquisite warmth of his tongue on her body. She moved only enough to straddle him, watching as he feasted on her soft mounds, savoring each flick of his tongue. Finally, her eyes closed and her breath stopped as he spread her legs and reached underneath her skirt, probing her body until she could stand it no longer. Frantically she tore at his suspenders; never allowing their lips to part, she unbuttoned his trousers and reached for him, guiding him inside her, feeling the instantaneous rush of complete pleasure surge upward through her body. He groaned and jerked once, feeling her pulsing response, then gripped her tightly, covering her mouth, pushing his tongue into every crevice, sucking on her lips, crushing her to his breast in a final fury of passion.

"I love you," he whispered, almost reluctantly, pushing wet tendrils of hair away from her face. "Sometimes I wish it wasn't so," he added. "But even in the middle of all this mess, I think about you, worry about you, want to be with you." He held her face in both hands, his expression softening as he studied her features. He closed his eyes and buried his face in her neck, breathing deeply of the fragrance that haunted him, the sweet, seductive smell that she exuded. He sighed, a deep sigh of resignation, as if he was admitting defeat. "I love you like I never believed I could love anyone."

She smiled at him, kissing his swollen lips in a tiny, soft gesture of acknowledgment. "And I love you. I've loved you since that first moment we touched on the train." He raised his eyebrows, surprised by her confession. She wrapped her arms around his neck and lay against him, feeling his heartbeat against her breast. How sweet it was to hear those words. How sweet to be cradled in his arms. She could stay like this forever. She closed her eyes and nuzzled his neck.

"Wait a minute!" She sat up with a chagrined look on her face. "I almost forgot what I came for. I have a gift for you." She got up and, resettling her clothes, searched inside her clutch and brought out a small notebook, flipping the pages until she found what she wanted. "Duke Cosmano, John Coughlin, Sully Bozkur, also known as Turk, Al Capone, George Rome—"

"What is this?" He frowned, grabbing the notebook from her, reading it as he tried to button his shirt with the other hand.

"It's a list of some of the people who were at the party that I went to yesterday in Louisville with Win. Some of them were pretty seedy-looking, too." She made a disgusted face. "If you can give me a few days, I'll get inside Win's house and see what I can find there."

"Damn it, Trudi!" His face clouded over, and he took a deep breath before speaking. "I don't want you doing this. You absolutely can't do this." His voice grew deeper. "I forbid you to do this."

" 'I forbid you to do this,' " she mimicked him. "Surely you know me well enough to know I would regard that as a challenge."

"Trudi, it's just too dangerous. Surely"—his voice was almost pleading—"your family told you what happened last night?"

"You mean, about the chickens? Grams was spitting mad, still stomping around the house this morning." Trudi laughed. "But that was because Alex is involved in the strike. That doesn't have anything to do with Win Stevens, does it?"

"Yes, I'm convinced he's mixed up in that dirty work, too. I don't think you understand how far-reaching his little fiefdom is."

Trudi stared at him stubbornly. "If that's true, then you need my help even more."

Gates threw up his hands helplessly. "I don't want you to help. It's just too dangerous." Then he grabbed his coat and jerked her out of her chair, pulling her out of the office. "Cancel my next appointment," he called over his shoulder to his secretary. "I'll be gone at least an hour." He pushed her in his car and drove off quickly, careening around corners with a determined recklessness very unlike him, while Trudi hung on to the ceiling strap with equal determination.

"See that?" He pointed to an innocuous-looking house, apparently normal in every way except for the heavy padlocks hanging from the doors. "That's one that the feds found. He probably has at least a dozen more houses that are set up inside as stills." He tore off, slowing as he came to a two-story brick home on Fourth Street. "See that? That's the main whorehouse he owns; recently he opened two more in town, and as far as I know he has a dozen more scattered around three counties. They're run for him by Jackie Davis."

"Is she a redhead?" Trudi was almost afraid to ask.

"Yes, why?"

"Just wondering," Trudi answered lamely.

"Now we'll go by the Cuckoo Clock, where big-time gambling goes on upstairs. Not the penny-ante stakes like all the places in the next five counties, not the slots and craps games that go on in most of the taverns in the area. But games where thousands of dollars change hands every day."

Trudi grimaced at his obvious anger, but asked no questions as they sped by the restaurant and headed out Twelfth Street north of town. After two miles, he turned into a rutted dirt road, dusty in the dry summer air and almost overgrown with foliage of a seldom-used path. She winced as a branch hit the windshield, but recovered in time to see a shriveled old woman standing in front of a simple frame cottage that was badly in need of paint. She looked frail, her wrinkled skin hanging loose on her frame, but she held a menacing shotgun in her hands aimed directly at them, and by so doing gave herself great authority. Trudi gasped, but Gates merely waved out the window as he pulled on the brake, and the old woman's sunken cheeks creased in a toothless grin.

"Git out here, boy!" the old woman cackled. "Give Gert a hug."

Gates loped to her side and dwarfed her in a quick squeeze, turning to explain to Trudi, "Gert helped my mother run the house when Gardner and I were growing up. I always felt safe when Gert was around." He grinned at the woman and gave her another quick hug. "She sure did make us work, though."

"This here boy could eat more food than any two other people I ever did see. I used to bring in fresh leaf lettuce from my garden and bake a loaf of bread, spread it with butter, and he would eat the whole thing in one sitting." She punched him in the ribs. "That was just to tide him over until dinner." Trudi grinned, warmed by the love of these two friends, but she wasn't sure why they were here.

"Can I show her the waterfall, Gert?" Phillip took Trudi's hand and led her down a steep path almost hidden by undergrowth. They were walking along a steep, rocky bluff flowered with wood violets and yarrow, and in the distance she caught a glimpse of the silver Mississippi through the trees. She could hear the water before she saw it. It was Gert who pointed her eyes in the right direction, to the prettiest woodland scene she'd ever seen.

A small stream, not more than three feet wide and shallow, spilled over a rocky ledge forty feet above them, cascading from one ledge to the next, down five tiers, creating a shower of water that sparkled in the bright sunlight. Red clover decorated the banks of the upper stream, while yellow marsh marigolds brightened the rushing stream at their feet. But the biggest surprise for Trudi was when Gert led them directly into the spray of water, stepping through a gap in the ten-foot-wide waterfall, and she found herself in a large cave created by the overhanging rock of the bluff.

Shielded from sight by the wall of water was a still, a huge wooden barrel and a copper container very much like a copper teakettle with a rounded lid and an extra-long spout that was connected to a condenser. Trudi moved toward the barrel.

"Don't go breathing it," Gert warned. "It'll knock your socks off!"

"How long you been doing this?" Gates asked Gert for Trudi's benefit.

"All my life." She shrugged. "It's harder now since Jake died, and the blasted revenuers are snooping around the countryside more the last few years."

"How much money do you make on your moonshine?"

The old woman scowled at him. "None of your damned business." Then she relented a little bit. "I make enough to get by, only have to buy the food I can't raise in the garden. Then with the hams and flour you bring to me regular, I don't need too much cash."

The noise of the waterfall made hearing difficult, so the trio climbed gingerly back over the dry rocks jutting through the creek and sat on a grassy bank surrounded by wildflowers in pastel profusion.

"This is getting harder and harder for me to keep going," Gert admitted, nodding toward her still. "Reckon I'll give it up 'fore too much longer." She started waxing sentimental, reminiscing with Trudi about the good old days. "You know, when six men start to make moonshine, they're like six women in a kitchen. No two work exactly the same. Every man has his own recipes for making whiskey, just like every woman has her own recipes for cake. Most of 'em are real old. Go so far back, I couldn't name it. Clear to Ireland, I suppose. And some are dead secret, but that's natural, to keep secrets." She shook her head and cackled with laughter. "When Jake knew he was dying of consumption, he taught me how to make moonshine. The other hill men didn't take kindly to that, and stole my first batch of mash. But they only did that once." She patted her gun. "I was too smart for them after that."

"Who do you sell it to?" Trudi asked.

"Don't know." Gert shook her head. "I leave my jugs near the road 'bout halfway to the highway, and they pick it up in the dead of night and leave my cash in the crotch of a tree."

"What if I told you that people were getting rich on your moonshine? That they take one gallon and cut it with water, glycerin, food coloring, and caustics, which stretches it into four or five gallons?" Gates asked.

"Don't bother me." She shrugged. "I don't want to get rich, just want to get by."

"What if I told you that people got sick from your moonshine? That in the city, wood alcohol was added, and twenty-five people died and a lot more were blinded or paralyzed?"

She struggled to her feet, glaring angrily at Gates. "Not from my stuff, boy! I don't make rotgut. I only make the best corn-mash moonshine and nobody never got sick from my stuff."

The visit was over, the walk back up the hill tense and silent. Only as they climbed back into the car did Gates speak. "Will you let me know if there is anything you need?"

"No, boy, I won't," Gert answered, and waved them off with the barrel of the gun.

Gates was quiet for most of the trip back into town, but he was building steam. "Nobody ever wants to take responsibility for their own actions." He glowered straight ahead. "Nobody wants to believe the immorality of their actions." The speed of the car didn't slow as he reached the city limits, and he kept muttering till they reached Front Street. "Win Stevens runs an evil empire. An empire that stretches from the lowliest, like Gert, to the very top."

Finally they slowed, going by a huge warehouse.

"This is where he stores millions of dollars of liquor that is sold on the black market. And you know how he does it?" His eyes bored into her. "He does it with a lot of help from his friends, big-city friends who are tough and mean, unscrupulous guys who kill people at the drop of a hat. Men like George Rome and Al Capone and John Coughlin." He stopped the car, grabbed her shoulders, and turned her toward him. "Now do you understand why I want you to stay away?"

"I do understand. But if what you say is true"—she held up her hand to stall his protest—"I believe what you say. What I don't understand is why, if it is too dangerous for me to get involved, isn't it too dangerous for you to get involved?"

"It's *my* battle, not yours!" He was exasperated beyond

belief. His shoulders sagged with the effort of trying to make her understand.

"But if these gangsters are as dangerous as you say they are, isn't it everyone's problem? Shouldn't you enlist the help of everyone you can trust?" She frowned, staring at him, waiting for a plausible answer.

"There are very few people who can be trusted," he muttered.

"I don't believe that!" she countered.

"Well, believe this!" He raised a finger and waggled it under her nose. "You are acting like a stubborn child, and if you don't stay out of this, I'll turn you over my knee and spank you."

"You wouldn't dare!" Trudi's back arched and her mouth dropped open at the threat.

"Don't push me," he warned.

The laughter at Grams's dinner table was light and gay. The mood in the house had swung dramatically in the middle of the afternoon when Trudi drove up in the distinctive Buick newly arrived from Louisville, honking and waving, urging everyone to come and see.

"You know that Waterford crystal bowl I gave you for your wedding?" she called to Jessie and Alex, who stood together inside the door, Jessie's maternity blouse tied demurely at the neck, Alex's hand propping her elbow. "Well, that was just to tide you over until the real thing came in." Trudi pointed dramatically to the car. "And here it is!" The young newlyweds were stunned. Alex slapped his head as Jessie first hugged him, then ran to Trudi and hugged her.

"Oh, Trudi," Jessie breathed, "it's just beautiful, but we really can't accept it. I know how much you inherited from Grandfather, and I don't want you spending this much on us."

"Shhhhh." Trudi pressed her fingers to her lips. "I'll tell you the whole story if you promise to keep it a secret." She cupped her hands and whispered in Jessie's ear, pulling back every few seconds to look into her sister's astounded eyes.

Grams and the Millses paced around the outside of the car, rubbing its glassy surface appreciatively while Trudi finished her story. "So now you have to accept it and pretend like I bought it, to make me look good," she said to her sister, giggling.

At the dinner table, Grams clinked her glass for attention. Hal Mills couldn't help but notice the difference in Viola Groves the last few weeks. More like herself since all the family was gathered 'round. Not calmer, 'cause calm was not a word to be used about her. He remembered fifty years ago when Robert Groves had said he was going to marry her, and in the same breath called her a frisky filly, jumpy and spirited. "And what's more," Robert had said with a laugh, "I don't want her no other way." And she never had been. But now with her family around her, she was satisfied and as still as she was capable of being.

"I have a nice surprise that came today, too. Been saving it for dinner." Viola pulled from her pocket a postcard, decorated with a large stamp portraying King Victor Emmanuel III. " 'Greetings from Rome,' " she read. " 'Janet and I are exhausted from sight-seeing—' " She paused as Trudi choked on her coffee, laughing inexplicably before finally calming down and urging Grams to continue. " 'Much time to ponder and think life over. I'm not going back to school. We will breed, show, and sell collies for a living. Will buy place in country as soon as we get back. Hope to have baby cousin for Badamo bambino in nine months' time!' " A spontaneous round of applause, punctuated by joyous laughter, rang through the dining room.

"My, my, my!" Mrs. Mills shook her head. "This family is growing by leaps and bounds."

Grams harrumphed. "I sure hope you all don't expect me to be one of those blubbering grandmas who kitchey-koos over the baby all the time." All the others looked at each other surreptitiously, knowing that to be the biggest lie they'd ever heard, then burst out laughing. "All right, all right," Grams conceded. "I might hold the mite when you insist." Everyone shook their heads in understanding. "Maybe I'll even rock it a bit." Everyone waited for more.

"As a matter of fact, what I'd really enjoy is just sittin' and rocking and patting its backside."

"Now we believe you." Alex grinned, taking Jessie's hand. "We've decided what we're going to name the baby. We're calling it Viola Appolonia Trudi Badamo."

There was a stunned, embarrassed silence. The others at the table avoided each other's eyes.

Finally Trudi said what was on everyone's mind. "That's just awful. You can't do that to a sweet, defenseless baby girl."

"Oh, no," Alex said with a straight face, "that's the name we chose for a boy!" Then he and Jessica screamed with laughter, pulling the others into their joke.

None of them heard the first ring of the bell, but when the doorbell rang again, coupled with an authoritative knock, they all glanced at each other, glanced at Alex's swollen nose and then toward the door before freezing. Silently, Hal Mills slipped from the table, and came back two seconds later with the shotgun in his hand.

"The rest of you stay here," Alex ordered. "I'll take care of it."

CHAPTER 30

Alex slid his feet along the dark front hall, his hand grazing the wall for extra security. Through the etched glass oval of the front door he could see two familiar figures, and he breathed a huge sigh of relief. He unlocked the door, deliberately opening it only halfway.

Barner and Madeleine Groves stood side by side, their faces pale and drawn. Madeleine's gloved hands were clasped tightly in front of her, her beige walking suit hanging as perfectly from her stylish, slender body as it would from a store mannequin. Barner Groves's straw boater was perched squarely in the middle of his head, but his hands were busy fidgeting with a gift wrapped in blue paper tied with a huge pink bow. Alex stood waiting silently, his left hand on the door, his right on the wall, effectively blocking both their entry and their view.

Barner Groves cleared his throat. "We have a gift for the baby."

There was no hesitation in Alex's reply. "Jessica and I don't want any gifts from you."

Groves's face grew red. "You made that clear when you returned the wedding gift we sent to you." His voice was angry, and he stopped himself from saying any more only after his wife put her hand on his forearm. He licked his lips, giving himself time to think more calmly before continuing. "We were hoping you would be broad-minded enough to accept a gift from us for the baby. It is, after all, our first grandchild."

Alex gave considerable thought to his reply. He knew this was a crucial communication. He knew the Groveses had denied a great deal of pride to make this effort; he did not want to sound belligerent, but he did want to establish the independence of his new family from the control of the Groveses. "We will be"—he looked at them squarely—"as broad-minded about your desire to see the baby as you were about our desire to get married."

Barner Groves dropped his head as the breath left him. Madeleine Groves's head flew back with a quick intake of breath. When they recovered, they looked at each other, blinking back tears.

Madeleine Groves spoke for the first time, struggling to keep her voice firm. "Could we at least see Jessica?"

"That's up to Jessie," Alex replied. "I'll ask her." He closed the door and walked back to the dining room, leaving them standing on the porch. Only Jessie remained seated. Trudi was clinging to the doorframe, peeking toward the front door. Grams paced, wringing her hands, while the Millses stood side by side, their eyes downcast. Alex sat down next to Jessie and took one of her hands in both of his.

"Could you hear?" he asked gently. She nodded silently. "Do you want to see them, or talk to them?" Unconsciously, she petted her round belly, then touched Alex's cheek. Everyone in the room kept their eyes averted, waiting anxiously for her answer.

"No," she whispered, "not yet." Alex kissed her cheek, a kiss of understanding, then pulled himself up and walked slowly back to the door.

He couldn't find it in his heart to be blunt. "She said not yet." The hopeful looks dropped from their faces, but they accepted the news without protest.

Barner Groves made one last effort. "Will you at least let us help with the expenses of the baby's birth?"

"No." Alex shook his head firmly, angered finally by their shallowness. "We don't want anything from you." His voice was tight but controlled. "We will make it on our own. When you come to us empty-handed, with nothing, nothing more than love to offer, then maybe we can be friends." He closed the door slowly.

When the telephone rang the next morning, Trudi was in the middle of a deliciously unsettling dream about Phillip. The two of them were languidly floating down a wide river on a primitive raft, with only bright moonshine guiding them. Every few miles, when the raft floated close to brush, Phillip would reach out, grabbing a thick branch or a heavy clump of cattails, and hold on tightly, preventing the smooth sailing of their craft. She could see her own mouth moving, but no sound came out, and after a while, Phillip would tire and let go and the raft would float free again, gently turning in the current. It was so peaceful that the jarring bell of the phone was an unwelcome intrusion, and she pulled the pillow over her ears to block out the sound. But when Grams insisted, she reluctantly slipped on her robe and went to the hall phone.

"Good morning, Trudi," a bright voice bounced over the line, "this is Bonnie Stevens. I'm hoping you will make good on your offer to help Gard and me plan our wedding."

Trudi's heart sank. She was hoping Gardner Gates would abandon his charade of marrying Win's sister. This was a simple, uncomplicated woman who had never played a part in her father's maliciousness. She didn't deserve the heartbreak lying in wait for her. Trudi felt caught in a terrible bind. She didn't want Gard to hurt Bonnie by jilting her. At the same time, she could understand the intense hatred that motivated the Gates brothers, and she didn't feel it was her place to warn Bonnie of Gard's intentions. But she would find it very difficult to avoid revealing the truth of the situation if she was intimately involved in the preparations for their wedding.

"Trudi? Are you there? Do we have a bad connection?"

"No, I heard you," Trudi answered. She struggled to

find the right words. "When are you thinking of getting married?"

"Christmas," Bonnie replied. "We've talked and talked, and finally decided on Christmas because it is such a joyful time of year."

"That's not a very long time to be engaged," Trudi counseled. "Especially if Gard will be away at school all fall."

"Sister Aimee prayed with me about the marriage. She laid her hands on my head and saw a vision saying all would be well. So I'm not worried." Her voice was mellow and confident. "She even said she would come all the way from Los Angeles to perform the ceremony if we wanted."

"For a fee, of course?" Trudi's cynicism went unnoticed.

"For a donation," Bonnie corrected her, "but it all goes to Christ's work, so I believe it to be money well spent."

"I see," Trudi replied, then added in defeat, "Yes, I'll help you. Where will you be married?"

"I'm thinking at Win's place, the old family homestead. If not the ceremony, I would at least like to have the reception there. May I meet you there so we can walk through to see if you think it's suitable?"

A chance to go through Win's house from top to bottom, she thought. Perfect! Maybe she could spot something, some little thing, that could be of help. Then maybe, if she could help Phillip bring Win Stevens up short by quickly exposing his crooked deals, that would be the only revenge necessary. And she dearly wanted to stop Gard from publicly humiliating Bonnie.

When she left Grams's house two hours later, Trudi was feeling twisted, fluctuating between excitement about possibly finding something concrete for Phillip and guilt about misusing Bonnie's trust. This was a situation she was not relishing, and she pulled at the chiffon scarf around her neck as it flapped in the breeze from the car window, its bright colors doing nothing to lighten her mood. Even as she turned up the drive to the mansion, she was biting her lip nervously. She pulled the brake on and got out of the

HIGH SOCIETY

car, straightening her pleated skirt, stalling before turning the polished brass bell in the middle of the huge door.

Bonnie was waiting for her, dressed for the first time, Trudi noticed, in a feminine cotton dress, sleeveless with a flounce of ruffle from midthigh to knee, and a matching ribbon tied around her head.

"How many guests do you think you'll have?" Trudi asked.

"Gard says we should invite the whole town!" Bonnie laughed. "Actually, we'll have about 500."

"Wouldn't a summer wedding be better? Then you could have the reception outside with no worry about space."

"Oh, I could never be ready in time."

"No, I mean next summer," Trudi explained, trying weakly to forestall the inevitable. But Bonnie, babbling with excitement, ignored the hesitation and began the excursion.

They covered the entire downstairs of the huge home, Trudi working hard at remembering the floor plan for future reference. The east wing was fronted by a long, narrow dining room with two crystal chandeliers reflected in the highly polished wood of the thirty-foot-long table beneath. Behind that were a butler's pantry and two kitchens, with servants' rooms at the far end of the wing, which Bonnie dismissed with a wave of her hand. The west wing overlooked the formal flower garden, with the front parlor opening onto the library, lined high with books. The next room was cozier, lacking the huge proportions of the previous rooms, and Bonnie said it was the room she and Win enjoyed the most because of the comfortable overstuffed furniture and small fireplace. The next room, the conservatory, held a wide variety of musical instruments, including a Steinway grand piano, a glowing harp, and innumerable string instruments resting along the shelf on the far wall.

"Neither one of us ever comes in here." Bonnie laughed. "We still remember with horror the hours our parents made us practice." Trudi grimaced with the same memories, but laughed aloud when Bonnie added, "Do you know, after ten years of lessons on every instrument in this room, I can't read a single note!"

Only after an hour did Trudi find the chance to explore on her own. They had stopped to rest and talk in the room that Win used as his office, and the moment Bonnie excused herself to take a phone call, Trudi sat at the desk picking, pulling, lifting, in an attempt to find anything of interest. Her lips were pursed in concentration and her breath came in short, quick bursts. She kept glancing at the door nervously, but did not falter in her search. The drawers were locked, but she found a key in a pen holder and was fumbling with it when the door opened without a knock. Grimmer blinked only once before speaking.

"Excuse me," the butler murmured. "I didn't realize anyone was in here." His expression remained bland, devoid of accusation, but Trudi felt compelled to explain.

"I found this key on the hearth." She pointed to the black marble surface in front of the fireplace. "I thought I'd put it away." She smiled, but her voice sounded reedy and false.

"Thank you, madam. I'll take it." He stepped across the room and held out his hand, waiting patiently while Trudi dropped the tiny key in his open palm. As soon as he turned and left, Trudi dropped into the chair and clutched at her heart.

From the outside, it looked the same as it had always looked, sitting grandly at the base of the triangular parkway shaded by tall elms and thick horse chestnut trees. But the large Queen Anne house that Viola Groves had lived in for ten years was different on the inside. Finally it was filled with people and seemed like a home to her. Hal Mills had brought three more overstuffed chairs into the second kitchen, and one wooden rocker. They had replaced the small table-top radio with a big floor model that looked like an oversized mantel clock. All the windows and both doors were open in an effort to allow any whiff of breeze in. The door to the fruit cellar was open, and sweet, cool air drifted up from below.

The evening air in a river town doesn't cool off; the heat and humidity hung above the Mississippi waters, that moved slowly south to eventually spill into the cool waters of the Gulf. A few strollers walked outside in the shade of the tree-lined streets, men in straw boaters and shirtsleeves, women in their coolest dimities. A few others sat on their porch swings and sipped lemonade. The crowd gathered around the bandstand in the park a block away was smaller than usual, but the players struggled through their numbers, growing redder in the face with each new song.

Grams's group chose to stay inside, keeping Alex company as he avoided being seen. Jessie sat in the rocker hemming cotton into rectangular diapers. Jeanne Mills and Grams both knitted while Hal whittled, carefully keeping the wood shavings contained on the newspaper spread at his feet. Alex lay on a rag rug near Jessie, stretched out on his stomach working on a thick book of crossword puzzles, his tongue curling out of the side of his mouth as he concentrated. Trudi paced restlessly, not taking the same delight that the others did in the "Sam and Henry Show" playing on the radio all the way from Chicago. She plunked herself cross-legged on the floor next to Jessie and leaned her chin on her hands.

"How do you know when you are in love?" She tried to keep her voice low for only Jessie to hear.

"The fact that you asked the question is the first clue," Jessie said, smiling. She pushed the needle into the material and folded it in her lap, thinking about Trudi's question. "To be honest, I fell in love with Alex's family first." She looked off into the distance, remembering. "They all enjoyed each other's company so much."

"But what does that have to do with falling in love?" Trudi was truly puzzled.

"A loving person feels loved by his family first," she answered simply, as if it was the most obvious thing in the world. "Alex is warm and accepting and loving because that's the way his family is. Each one prizes each of the others in some way. So Alex is able to give and receive love freely. That is what I love the most about him." Trudi glanced at Alex, who seemed oblivious to their conversation. He sat up long enough to refill his ink pen, holding the bottle carefully as the fluid rose in the tiny cylinder.

"He is very smart, you know," Jessie added proudly. "I gave him that crossword puzzle book when it first came out a couple of years ago, and just to make it extra difficult, I gave him an ink pen to go with it." Trudi grinned at her sister's bluff. "He's always trying to better himself. I respect that a great deal."

Outside a car backfired, a sound immediately followed by a woman's little scream and a man's curse. "Goldurn things," Hal Mills muttered. "Those motorcars cause more trouble than they're worth. Was a time when people stayed home together instead of gallivanting around in those machines. Read where they're thinking of putting a road in that goes clear across the country from New York to California. Phew!" For Hal Mills, that was a long speech, and all the heads in the room turned to look at him and each other in wonder. But he surprised them even further. "Now, take the radio. It's a real nice invention, and the man that invented it ought to be real proud. It keeps people together. Everybody I know stays in and listens to Paul Whiteman's orchestra together. Real nice dancing music."

"Hal Mills, you never danced a step in your life," his wife accused.

"I know that, woman, but it don't mean I don't like listening to it."

"Loving someone means you adjust to their idiosyncrasies, also," Jessie leaned over to whisper to Trudi, her words covered by the chuckles in the room.

"Does adjustment mean you give in to his wishes?"

"Not give in, exactly." Jessie wrestled with the idea. "But being willing to change, when that change means the best for both of you." She patted her round belly. "We thought we had made our plans, but they didn't include a family so soon. So we shifted, changed, adjusted. We haven't given up anything, just changed the timing a little." She smiled. "After all, this is something we both wanted."

The heat wasn't the only thing that kept Trudi tossing and turning in the sultry midwestern night. Jessie's observations on love also had provoked her restlessness. She loved Phillip Gates, but she wasn't interested in the same life Jessie and Alex planned to lead. She would be bored with the comfortable, repetitive rhythm of family and home. She needed constant challenge, the challenge that the strong heart and keen mind of Phillip Gates would provide.

Phillip Gates filled her thoughts, and she stared at the dark shadows on the ceiling, trying to think of a way to help him, a way he would agree that she could help. She worried that his desire for revenge was poisoning him, and she wanted to rid him of the poison. What Gard was doing to Bonnie was despicable, and she didn't want Phillip involved in a similar plan. She knew him well enough to know that feelings of guilt would gnaw at him the rest of his life if he had to stoop to a dirty underhanded trick to bring Win Stevens down.

She didn't care if helping him involved some risk to herself. She was convinced he had exaggerated the danger. She could be of help to him, if he would only allow her to. She snapped on her bedside lamp and grabbed for a book, as she often did to cut her restlessness, and there on the first page, she found the quote she would use with him.

"To tame the savageness of man and make gentle the life of the world." It was from the ancient Greeks and would appeal to his reason. If she could convince him of the higher good of ridding their community of the scourge of Win Stevens's despicable actions and divert him from his need for revenge, then his actions would be lifted to a higher plane. She read the quote again and again, memorizing it as the book lay on her chest. When she finally dozed off, she knew her thoughts had been centered on Phillip Gates's well-being as much as her own, which was a certain sign of love.

Trudi was surprised and pleased to receive the note in the mail, noting the old-world charm of a written invitation to meet for lunch, when women her own age would have casually called on the phone. Evangeline Gates did everything with class. Trudi hesitated at first, still indignant over Phillip's angry words and continual rebuff of her attempts to help. But after mulling it over, she decided that there was no reason that she and Evangeline Gates could not be friends, in spite of the woman's boorish son. She dressed for the luncheon date with special thought, choosing a simple dress of pink cotton voile with a bateau neckline and butterfly sleeves, its hem echoing the same soft folds.

She was nervous at being alone with Phillip Gates's mother, though she did not intend to even mention the obstinate man's name. She arrived early and sat down at a table to wait. The restaurant was crowded, with diners, mostly women, stuffed into the tables with their shopping bags under their feet, their purses at their sides. Trudi drew her compact out and was fluffing her curls when a familiar voice commented from behind her, "You look lovely, dear." She turned to find Evangline Gates smiling at her.

Trudi was struck again by the woman's classic beauty, a sculptured beauty that knew no time constraints, a beauty that would have been recognized in ancient Greece or Rome, a beauty not only physical but one that radiated from within. Her pale green crepe de chine suit trimmed with a darker shade of silk braid was also a classic design, one that was timeless, but for the length of the hemline.

"I am so glad you could make it today," the older woman said warmly.

"There wasn't any reason not to. I don't have a lot of demands on my time." Hearing her own words, Trudi cringed. "That didn't come out the way I meant for it to," she fumbled. "It's just that my life is rather undemanding right now." Evangeline Gates excused her with a soft chuckle. "My grandmother," Trudi went on, "is trying to teach me to sew, but I can't sit still that long. My horse has a sprained knee, so I can't ride." She shrugged apologetically.

Evangeline Gates was not insulted by Trudi's first words. She knew it to be true that the young woman did not have enough in her life to keep her busy. She lived in a time that demanded little of a refined girl other than to be pretty and decorative.

"Tell me please, if you will, how your sister has been feeling."

"Jessica is fine." Trudi smiled, thinking of her sister. "Considering the strain she's lived through the last eight months, she's remarkably possessed and happy. She and Alex are very much in love." Mrs. Gates nodded with warm understanding. But before Trudi could continue, she felt on odd sensation.

Phillip Gates stood beside the table, his agitation so tightly controlled that it was not visible except to those who knew him well enough to read the signs. His jaw was clenched tight and the hand stuffed into his pocket jiggled the loose change there, while his eyes darted from his mother to Trudi Groves and back.

"What a pleasant surprise." Evangeline reached over to pat her son's arm. "Can you join us?"

"Whose idea was this?" His voice was accusatory, a tone that made his mother sit up and respond much more coolly.

"It was mine, Phillip. Not that I think that is of any importance." She raised both eyebrows with a haughtiness that would brook no arrogance from the man who was her son, a son who still needed to be reminded of his manners. "If you continue in the mood you're in now, I may be forced to rescind my invitation to you."

Trudi kept her head down but managed to peek at him from under her brows, muffling a chuckle at the contrite look on his face. He shuffled from one foot to the other, trying to make up his mind, then pulled out a chair and sat, leaning forward with his elbows on his knees, which lent intensity to his words.

"Excuse me, Mother. I had tried not to let the tension of the last few weeks get to me, but I guess it has." He looked at Trudi and his next words caught her off guard, for she had not realized that he told his mother so much of what was going on inside his head. "Trudi insists on actions that I disapprove of." Evangeline Gates swung toward Trudi, but she listened carefully to her son as he finished his explanation. "I thought she might have set up this luncheon to pry information out of you."

"Phillip! What an awful thing to say. Trudi would never do anything that underhanded! I insist you apologize."

Trudi, a tiny bit embarrassed by the knowledge that she was perfectly capable of such a deed, nevertheless waited patiently for Gates to apologize, smiling sweetly, blinking her eyes in a parody of innocence that made Gates shake his head at her impudence.

His apology accepted, he then insisted, "Mother, would you tell Trudi what happened at our house the other night?"

"You mean the porch?" He nodded, and she demurred somewhat. "Everything?"

"Yes, please."

"First, I should tell you that Phillip recently had a screened-in porch built for me, something I had wanted for years, and I enjoyed it so much." She smiled a thank-you at her son. "I was home alone," Evangeline began, "sleeping less than soundly since neither of my sons was home yet. It was late, well after midnight."

She hesitated, and Trudi glanced at Phillip, wondering why he'd insisted that she tell her story. "I heard a noise, so I went downstairs. I wasn't frightened at this point, more apprehensive than anything. I got frightened, though, when I heard laughing, a rough, guttural laughing outside." She licked her lips, and drew a deep breath. "When I turned on the kitchen light and looked outside, the first thing I saw was the gleam of a knife as it ripped through the new screen." Trudi's gasp made her falter, but she gathered herself and proceeded, her voice so low it was almost a whisper. "The blade sliced very easily through the wire mesh, as easily as if it were cutting through butter. The man holding it was laughing, looking right at me and laughing, like he was really enjoying the maliciousness of his act. Another man was with him, busy cutting open the far side of the porch. They were big men, brawny, muscular. I was paralyzed with fear. I didn't know what their intentions were; I was afraid they were trying to get into the house." She was pale and trembling from reliving the incident, but managed to continue laughing at herself sheepishly—"I hid under the table. I could hear the screen ripping, and I kept picturing the knife blade, the shiny, sharp knife blade. Finally, all the sounds stopped and the men called out obscenities, then left. I stayed under the table until I heard Phillip coming in the front door."

"How horrible for you," Trudi whispered, reaching for Evangeline's hand, but looking at Gates quizzically.

"They were thugs, hoodlums," he explained, "brought in to do dirty work for Win Stevens. I'm convinced they killed the chickens at your house, too." He stared at her. "This was a warning, but the next time will be worse. Now are you convinced that you must stay out of this?"

Trudi swallowed hard, but she was interrupted before she could speak.

"How sweet." Linda Carter's voice was shrill and loud. "This is like a little family reunion." She waved her arms dramatically.

Her costume—it could be called nothing else—was outlandish. The dress was a rumpled red cylinder held up by thin straps. Slung over her shoulders was a fluffy ostrich feather boa that dripped over and around her arms, moving awkwardly with her every gesture. She was thinner than the binder over her chest made her appear, for her eyes were sunken, her elbows bony, her neck stringy. She was decked out in jewelry, a choker of pearls, cuff bracelets on each arm, and a thick ankle chain. It occurred to Trudi that these were probably the same clothes she'd had on all night, and if that was so, Linda was in a faster, steeper decline than Trudi had realized.

"We've been celebrating," John Flanagin explained hastily from behind Linda, aware that Trudi had guessed the truth. "Linda just got her first car." He smiled stupidly, ignoring Trudi's perplexed frown. How could Linda afford a car of her own? The daughter of a widowed mother, no job of her own. It was a puzzle.

"Got a great price on it," Linda added. "It looks a little like a gangster's car, a big black monster. But it's big enough to have a party in, isn't it?" She turned to the Flanagins for confirmation.

A thought gnawed at Trudi. Could she have purchased the redhead's car, the gift of George Rome? "Where did you get it? I mean . . . ?"

"Right here in town," Linda interjected. "Some dumb Dora who had only put a couple hundred miles on it. Let's just call it a gift from John and Jolene."

Trudi shot the twins a dirty look. They were not helping Linda. Far from it. They were adding to Linda's troubles by encouraging her irresponsibility. Trudi continued to frown at them, wondering what it was that they had received in return. The two siblings glanced at each other forlornly, as if sorry for Linda's lack of discretion.

"This is such a cozy little meeting!" Linda stood next to Phillip, but looked at all three, her eyes red and unfocused, her hair disheveled despite its simple cut. The large gold barrette she wore next to her temple to hold back the long sweep of hair across her forehead was falling out of line to sag limply in front of her ear. "Isn't this sweet, Jolene?" Linda's voice was exaggerated as she turned to tug on Flanagin's arm. "Phillip, are you interviewing Trudi? Trying to enlist her help in your fight against the town fathers?" She spoke so loudly that others in the restaurant turned to look, some to stare, some merely to shoot her impatient looks for interrupting their lunch.

She shifted her hip to rub seductively against Gates's shoulder, a move so common and out of place that Jolene and John looked more uncomfortable than the three people at the table. "Maybe you can get some of her daddy's money for your fight"—Linda leaned over to stare into Phillip's face—"since he's one of the few leaders in the community not lined up against you."

Trudi's spine stiffened in outrage. "Bitch," she breathed almost silently. Gates sat stonily, his face registering contempt rather than anger. It was left up to Evangeline Gates to alter the situation.

"Linda"—her voice was soft and gracious as she held out her hand—"it's always a pleasure to see you." Linda stumbled as she reached to shake hands, rescued by John Flanagin from falling onto the tabletop. "Tell me, my dear," Evangeline Gates said, her voice still low but now holding a cutting edge. Trudi saw a glint of ruthlessness in her eyes that surprised her, but then she had not known Evangeline

Gates long enough to know how she handled a situation in which one of her children was being disparaged. "Did your mother pick out your outfit?" Linda was stunned by the mention of her mother, which her peers all knew was a forbidden topic, and Trudi wondered if Mrs. Gates didn't realize it also, for their estrangement was no secret in the community. Evangeline continued, like a canny wolf who has drawn blood, "Maybe Lita is meeting you here for lunch?" She even went so far as to feign looking toward the door, as if expecting the meddling mother to be waiting. "You've always been such an attentive daughter"—her voice was dripping with sarcasm—"that I assume you include your mother in on your merrymaking?"

Linda's face was blank for only an instant before she colored, her neck and face becoming red and blotchy in only seconds. Her mouth opened to blubber a response. It was left up to the most unlikely source, John Flanagin, to rescue the situation. "Come on, come on," he insisted, pulling Linda back in the direction of the exit. He had difficulty hustling the drunk woman away, but he did it, turning her with a determined effort toward the door. Everyone in the small room watched them stumble out except the Gates party.

"Pitiful," Evangeline Gates murmured with a noticeable lack of sincerity as she coolly studied the menu. "Shall we order now? I've heard that the broiled shrimp are very good here."

If nothing else, Trudi had learned from the incident not to underestimate the steely nerves of Evangeline Gates. It was a lesson she would remember and use to everyone's advantage within a matter of a few weeks.

CHAPTER 31

The grandeur of the Catholic mass was at its midpoint when Phillip Gates sneaked in to sit in the last pew at the back of the large, ornate sanctuary. The song of the priest, the same Latin words that had sent millions of souls to their final rest, seemed especially poignant, mixed with the muffled sobs of Appolonia Badamo's loving family and the loud wails of the black-garbed mourners who sat behind them.

Ahead of him, halfway down the middle aisle, Phillip could see the back of Hal Mills's neck, his collar stiff, his hair still showing the rake marks of a wide-mouthed comb. Next to him sat his wife, her white hair tipped by the shades of her blond youth, her straw hat planted firmly on top of her head. Grams sat square-shouldered and inquisitive, the ever-moving tilt of her hat revealing her curiosity. Gates had to shift slightly to see Trudi, her tiny body almost hidden by the assemblage. More visible, at least to him, were Alex's fellow strikers, who stood, respectful but obvious, at various points inside and outside the church keeping a silent vigil of protection over their young friend.

Alex sat next to his father in the front row, leaning over often to offer support to the grieving man. Next to Alex sat Jessica, looking pale and drawn from the week of helping to nurse her mother-in-law through her last days on earth.

With them, around them, surrounding them was a multitude of family and friends, all in black, who had loved the simple, good-hearted woman and who had come to say good-bye. Banks of flowers spread from either side of the casket, their fragrance consumed by the flaming candles behind them.

Alex and Phillip had stayed in close phone contact since Gates had pulled the young man off his assignment of spying on Win Stevens, and in the process Phillip had learned to appreciate Alex's commitment, intelligence, and insight. The young man, a first-generation American, still held to the old-world values of his family origins. Family, loyalty, hard work, and the general sweetness of life formed the core of his beliefs. He rarely failed to mention his wife and the impending birth of their first child when he and Gates talked, his enthusiasm for the momentous step a reminder to Gates of his youth. Maybe it was best to start a family young, before the weight of maturity inexorably pulled a person away from such a responsibility. Gates caught himself; here he was thinking of birth in the midst of a celebration of death, but he felt sure he was not the only one doing so, if only to remember that Mrs. Badamo had not achieved her last hope, that of seeing her baby's baby. But she had instilled in her children the will to better themselves, and that will lived strong in her son, who had willingly jeopardized himself in the cause of the workers.

Both he and Alex, however, were wise enough not to endanger their loved ones, even if the opposition had no such reservations. The National Guard, called in by Governor Sam Baker to calm the strike violence, had instead created more animosity. Gates felt he was finally making progress in his negotiations with the owners, but needed time to win one more important concession on the length of the workday before he was willing to call an end to the strike. He had been able to confide in Victor Wellman about Alex's undercover work, and Wellman had readily agreed to have truckers provide continuous protection for Alex and his family, either at Grams's or at the Badamo house, the only place Alex had visited in the last week. He and Jessie had taken turns sitting at the wake, enduring the cries of shrouded female mourners who gathered in the front parlor around the casket.

Shortly afterward, at the funeral feast, Gates understood the toll of the last few weeks on the young couple. They sat together on the couch in the parlor, refusing to be parted by the tradition still subscribed to by the older people of separating the sexes on such an occasion. All the Italian women, clothed in black from head to foot, were sequestered in the kitchen preparing the food for the dinner, while the men sat scattered throughout the house, drinking heavily, arguing, eating from the mounds of fresh fruit already on the table. But Alex sat next to Jessie, his arm around her, as they slumped wearily together.

Grams and Trudi and Gates stood in a corner. "He's such a good boy," Grams whispered none to subtly. "So attentive and devoted." She put her hand up to cover her words. "He's gonna make a good, long-lasting husband for our little girl. I overheard the men saying how remarkable his father's fidelity to his wife had been. You know, Mario lived here almost three years before he sent for Appolonia. Even during the lonely years, he was loyal to her, never once taking the offers of wealthy American women for, well, you know, stud service."

Trudi gulped, trying hard not to laugh aloud, her efforts cut short by the sound of a huge explosion from the rear of the house. Gates spun around. Shrieks of terror filled the house as the women ran from the kitchen into the surprised pandemonium of the living room, where people screamed and pushed at each other, some cringing on the floor, some crowding out into the front yard, only to be greeted by another explosion from the street. Gates and Alex acted simultaneously, shoving the women to the floor amid the curses of the men and the foul black smoke that filtered in through the open windows. They both tore out the door, bumping into the guards, who waved their shotguns around in confusion.

"That way!" one of them shouted, pointing down the

quiet street at a black car careening out of sight around a corner.

"Bunch of kids!" another man explained. "They threw a glass bottle with a burning rag stuffed in it. Damned thing landed on the porch, but I kicked it off."

Others from the house joined them in an angry mob, the men cursing and making obscene gestures at the retreating car. Phillip hurried to the spot in the yard marked by a browned circle of burned grass and calmly inspected it.

"Scare tactics," he said quietly before turning to the crowd. "Don't worry, folks. They won't be back. It was just a car full of young punks. If they had meant real harm, this thing"—he kicked disdainfully at some broken glass—"would have been a lot bigger." The angry men shouted for more explanation while frightened women clung to them.

Then Gates froze, a separate thought shooting through his mind. "Alex, I'm going to check on my mother," he said sharply. "You handle this, all right?" He ran the few yards to his car and jumped in. Trudi was right behind him, coughing as she waved herself through the acrid smoke. "You stay here," Gates commanded, but she stubbornly shook her head and climbed into his car.

Evangeline Gates was sitting quietly at her rolltop desk writing letters when her son came bursting into the room. She took the news of the vandalism with outward calm, but Trudi detected her alarm, noticeable only in the tremor in her hands and the stillness of her eyes. This woman, who had handled great tension and distress in her life, had not had to deal with physical violence, and it was difficult, if not impossible, to adjust to such an immediate terror at this age. It took very little persuasion to convince Mrs. Gates to bundle up a few necessities and move temporarily to Viola Groves's home, where all the vulnerable people could be easily safeguarded in one place.

As dusk fell, Trudi and Phillip took a reprieve to sit on the back porch swing, holding hands quietly. From inside the house, slow talk and occasional nervous laughter could be heard. The older people sat around the kitchen table, shelling peas and peeling the last of the winter apples, gifts from the strikers to Phillip Gates, gifts that, he was aware, spoke louder than any words. These subtle communications spoke of friendship, said that they trusted him as a friend, not merely as a brash young attorney but as a natural leader of their community who had their best interests in mind. He couldn't have handled the situation as equably if not for the support of the group surrounding him now.

"Never once has any of them asked Alex and me to give up the fight." Phillip spoke softly, indicating the family with a jerk of his head but gazing into a distant corner of the yard where purple martins swooped and dove after their evening meal, oblivious to the tension of their human neighbors. Trudi followed his gaze, watching the graceful swallows go calmly about the business of feeding their young. "I respect all of you for that."

"Don't you have that backwards?" She smiled at him. "We respect you." She leaned over and gave him a soft, sweet kiss, one that lingered and sweetened with each second.

"I didn't know when I fell in love with you that I would be dragging you into danger," he said, coming as close to apologizing as his proud nature would allow. "Are you convinced yet that you must stay away from Stevens?"

She shook her head, explaining, "I don't think those were hired thugs. They were probably just local ruffians out for excitement."

"Trudi," he groaned in exasperation. "Then why did they pick the Badamos' house to harass?"

"Well, Judas priest, Phillip! Half the strikers are standing around outside. You'd think it was a clubhouse for them." She remembered the quote about "taming the savageness of man," but knew he would not be receptive to it after the violence of the day. She said no more.

His jaw set firmly in anger. "I'm asking you again to give up on Stevens. He's certainly not going to admit to anything. There's nothing you can find at his house that will incriminate him, anyway. He's too shrewd to keep any business records around."

"What makes you think that's the only place I'm looking?" Trudi smiled at him flirtatiously before pinching his arm in an effort to lighten his mood. "By the way"—she looked at him with a thoughtful frown on her face—"have you ever made love in the bushes with guards patrolling nearby?"

JOURNAL ENTRY:
The Pinkertons are working out well. As long as we manage to keep them from doing any of the truckers' work, Gates won't have a chance with his lawsuit claiming strikebreaking. The owners are getting restive, too willing to get this strike over with, but through the Flanagins, I think I can control them long enough for one more dramatic incident, which will turn public opinion against the strikers. Then we can get all the laborers we need and break the union's back once and for all.

Ugly scene with Jackie tonight. Attendance at the houses and bars is off, revenue from craps and slots is down, and deliveries are late, all because of the damned strike. Then to make matters even worse, the idiot do-gooders were praying outside the house so loud we could hardly hear each other, and that probably set me on edge, but what really infuriated me were her lies. She told me she thinks something is fishy about Trudi Groves. Then she tried to tell me that Trudi Groves called her today, and almost came right out and asked for a job! That's ludicrous! I told Jackie she wasn't good enough to speak Trudi's name and if she ever did again, it would be the last word she ever spoke. She tried to hit me, but I got her first. The violence continued right into sex, the most passionate sex we've ever had. If she thinks for one minute that her petty jealousy would make

*me believe such outrageous slander about Trudi,
she better think again.*

*I presented baseball uniforms for all the
boys at Chaddock School today, and got good
coverage in the* Post-Dispatch. *Babe Ruth is
having such a great season that it was a stroke
of genius for me to think of this publicity
ploy. By Christmas time, it will be Winslow
and Trudi Stevens giving to the Woodlawn
Home for Children.*

CHAPTER 32

The morning headline screamed at Gates: "PINKERTON FOUND DEAD." He snatched up the paper and scanned the first few paragraphs to learn the essentials:

> The body of Gene Stickler of St. Louis, 38, was dragged from the river this morning by two fishermen who immediately called police. Foul play is certain, since the man's feet were roped and weighted with a cement block. Winslow Stevens, at whose manufacturing plant Stickler had been working as a guard, offered the opinion that truckers would be the most likely suspects. The police have arrested two truckers and are holding them in protective custody since a surly mob gathered on the steps of the jailhouse.

"That scum!" Gates muttered, slamming his coffee cup down on the desk and rushing immediately to the courthouse.

By midafternoon, he was exhausted from his efforts to bail out the two strikers who had been taken in as suspects, from trying to calm the near-riotous truckers, and from containing his fury at the devious machinations of Win Stevens. When he stormed back into his office, the first person he called was Alex Badamo. They conferred for twenty minutes before Gates asked to speak to Trudi.

Alex hesitated. "That's something else I'm worried about. She's going out with Stevens tonight. She doesn't know that I know, but I heard her on the phone. I wish I could tie her to the kitchen table, but you know how headstrong she is."

Gates's heart sank at the news. With Alex's words, he made a decision that wrenched at his guts, but one he knew he could not put off any longer.

"Trudi," he said firmly when she came to the phone, "meet me at the Indian mounds in South Park in fifteen minutes. Make sure you're not followed."

"Well, of course, my lord and master." She tried to make light of his command, but the tone of his voice worried her. She grew even more concerned a little later as she hurried to him along the narrow dirt path leading through the timber of oak and elm and maple that surrounded the burial grounds of ancient Plains Indians. It was a beautiful location, high on a bluff overlooking the Mississippi, removed from the traffic and noise of the city. But he clearly wasn't here to enjoy the view; he was grim, with dark circles under his eyes, and he leaned wearily against a tree trunk, his hands sunk deep in his pockets, watching her run toward him with a sunny smile. His heart was swollen with love for her and pain for the hurt he had to cause her. She stopped in front of him and reached for his face, her eyes swimming with emotion.

"I love you so much, my darling," she whispered. "I want to wash all your cares away." She stood on tiptoe and pressed her soft lips against his, sweeping his mouth gently with her sweet tongue. He resisted, keeping his hands in his pockets, willing himself not to give in. But when she leaned into him, maneuvering her leg between his, he groaned.

"Trudi, stop," he croaked, his voice barely audible. She paid no attention to his request, using her hand to rub his growing bulge while she clung with her other hand to his neck, kissing him with an almost desperate passion, murmuring his name over and over. "Oh, dear God, forgive me," he whispered before taking her into his arms, crushing her to him, pulling her with him down to the soft grass.

Wildly they shed their clothes, their hands searching all the perfect spots on each other's bodies, their mouths locked in a heated kiss. She arched beneath him as his lips reached her tingling breasts, licking them greedily with a hunger that inflamed her. She wrapped her legs around his back as he plunged into her, his body hot with longing, his muscles taut with desperate desire. Wildly they moved to the music of their love dance, shifting and rolling in the hot summer air as their passion exploded in a flurry of white heat. Trudi moaned with pleasure, her body pulsing with the culmination of her love for him. He stroked her wet back, turning her to cover her flushed face with kisses before pulling away to lie beside her, taking long, exquisite breaths to steady his pounding heart.

After long minutes of rest, she reached over to touch him, but he pulled away. "Get dressed," he said, and moved to do the same. He sounded angry.

Trudi didn't understand. She looked at him, but he wouldn't look back, continuing to pull on his clothes with a speediness that surprised her. She did as he said, still puzzled by his tone of voice.

"Are you going out with Win Stevens tonight?" Now he looked at her, his eyes boring into her. So that was it, she thought. He's still on that jag.

"No," she answered flippantly, brushing at her hair, avoiding his eyes.

"Don't lie to me!" he shouted at her, and her mouth flew open in surprise. "You're so damned simple you don't understand the danger, and you're so damned devious that you lie to me." He turned his back on her and walked a few paces away. When he wheeled around, he swept his hands apart in a final angry gesture. "I'm through with you. No more. I don't want to have anything to do with you ever again."

Trudi was stunned by the vehemence of his words, and she blanched, not sure whether to believe him. "All right, I admit it." She tried to explain, and only with effort was she able to keep a pleading quality from her voice. "I think I can find evidence against him that you wouldn't have access to any other way." Her eyes searched his face. "If we can 'tame the savageness of man and make gentle the life of the world,' then I want to be a part of that. If he is responsible for what you say he is, then let me help you. I am in a unique situation—I could find evidence against him that will hold up in court. If I lied to you, it's only because I love you and think I can help you."

Gates's heart lurched at her words, and for a moment, a very brief moment, his determination faltered. Over the last few months his love for her had brightened and dimmed like the sunlight on a cloudy day, but the heat, the light of it, had always burned within him, and never more strongly than at this moment. He swallowed hard before whispering, "Well, I don't love you, and I don't want to be bothered by you anymore. You're a self-indulgent, spoiled, impetuous child. Understand?" He turned quickly to stride away, but not before he saw hurt tears well up in her eyes. By the time he reached his car, his own eyes were burning with tears of agony.

Trudi lay spread-eagled on her bed, staring at the ceiling, her tears spent after two hours of crying. She had called his office twice, only to be told by his secretary that he was not taking any calls. She could hear the house bustling around her, could hear the voice of Evangeline Gates in the kitchen below, but she was too ashamed to talk to her. She vacillated between being hurt, humiliated, and angry. Half the time she didn't believe him; she knew in her heart, as only a woman can know, that he loved her. Then she would crumple into tears. If he loved her, why would he have said those horrible words? If he didn't love her, he had misused her terribly, embarrassingly, by making love to her and then telling her afterward how he felt! Her face felt dry and drawn and she could still smell their lovemaking on her body. She rose with an effort to bathe, her mind and body aching along with her heart. She was bending to wash her swollen face when someone knocked at her door.

"I don't want to see anyone," she called out rudely. "I'll be down later."

"It's your sister. It's Jessica." Evangeline Gates's soft voice carried through the closed door.

"What is it? What's wrong?" Trudi said, her own woes instantly forgotten, grabbing a robe and running to open the door.

"There's nothing really wrong, dear. It's just that she has gone into labor, and I thought you'd want to know."

"But it's too soon!" Trudi's voice was filled with anxiety.

"Not by much, and with all the strain she's been under the last few weeks . . ."

Trudi ran down the steps, followed more slowly by Mrs. Gates. They found a tight little clique in the hall. Hal Mills stood with his beat-up work hat in his hand, twisting and turning it beyond recognition. Grams stood in the kitchen doorway twisting her apron and Jeanne Mills sat on the deacon's bench along one wall, while Alex paced, first to the front door to look without seeing out into the bright August sunlight, then back the full length of the hall to the kitchen, where he would turn and start again.

"Who's with her?" Trudi was surprised by the calm.

"Dr. Hildegarde," Grams replied, "and Hattie. She wanted Hattie, so I called your parents' house, and she came right over." Trudi stared at the closed door of Jessie's bedroom, amazed that she heard no cries, only soft footsteps and low murmurs.

All other eyes were on Alex, who continued his restless pacing. After an hour, Hal Mills could stand no more and left through the kitchen, but the others sat or stood or walked, waiting for news from the inner sanctum. At one point, Hattie came to the door.

"We need a couple more sheets, sun-dried." She was possessed and calm, her simple face sweet and dignified. "She's doing a good job." She smiled at Alex. "This is just going to take a while, this being the first and her so tiny and all."

After another hour, Mr. Badamo arrived, carrying a huge basket of fresh fruit. With him was one of his dark-eyed, dark-haired daughters, who carried a one-year-old toddler, a beautiful child with soft black ringlets covering her head, and luminous, light blue eyes as big as silver dollars, a lovely blue surprise considering the child's dark coloring.

"This is Maria," her proud mother introduced the child. "She's a freak of nature." She grinned, rubbing the little girl's mess of curls, making everyone chuckle, helping to relieve the tension. The adults watched the antics of the child, but their ears were still riveted on the muffled sounds from the quiet room. Mrs. Gates brought glasses of lemonade on a tray, and when she came back a while later with a stack of sandwiches, Trudi realized that it was almost dinnertime.

Mr. Badamo's presence calmed Alex, whose face relaxed only when the old man spoke to him in Italian, patting his son's hand.

When Win Stevens knocked on the front screen door, Trudi was startled. She had totally forgotten about their evening date. He stood framed by the bright sunset, unwittingly in full view of the people in the hall. Trudi heard a growl from Alex, and a wall of silence descended behind her. She looked down at her wrinkled robe self-consciously, but stepped outside to speak with him anyway.

"I'm sorry I didn't let you know, but I have to break our date for tonight," she apologized.

"Is something wrong?" He was surprised by her unkempt appearance and peered inside, but he couldn't see down the dark hallway.

"No." She refused to let him know what was happening. She wanted to get him out of here quickly. Pushing at his chest, she whispered, "I'll call you tomorrow. Go on out and have some fun for me." He was puzzled but turned to walk out to his car.

As he drove away, Trudi was jolted by the sight of the next arrivals. Her mother and father got out of their car, looked toward the house tentatively, then hurried up the walk, empty-handed. She stood with her hand on the door, uncertain of what to do until she glanced inside at Alex, who slowly gave an affirmative nod. She opened the door and ushered them in.

"How is your wife?" Barner Groves asked the young man, who smiled gravely, holding out his hand to shake.

HIGH SOCIETY

Trudi had not seen her mother for weeks and was struck again by her harsh, haughty beauty as Madeleine Groves moved to whisper with her mother-in-law. Alex formally introduced his father to his in-laws, and the old man pulled himself up straight and tall, all eyes upon him, as Viola Groves stood protectively beside her old friend.

"This is a happy day for all of us," he murmured.

"Ah, yes," Barner Groves agreed, "but you have the advantage over us. You have at least been through this before."

Everyone chuckled, and Trudi sighed in relief, glad of her father's charm.

Then, as if on cue, little Maria toddled in from the kitchen, a graham cracker clutched in her chubby hand, a bright smile of welcome lighting her tiny face. Madeleine Groves gasped loudly, clutching her husband's arm, as she stared at the child. Everyone stiffened, not sure of the cause of Madeleine Groves's reaction, and looked at Maria then at Madeleine, then back at Maria. The woman was mesmerized, staring at the child.

She moved slowly, stepping toward the child cautiously as if afraid she might disappear, then knelt in front of her and reached out to touch her cheek. Trudi was dumbfounded. She turned to her father for some visual explanation, but she caught her grandmother's eye first. Viola Groves had a look of complete sorrow on her face; her whole body sagged before she sank to the bench, her eyes on the woman and child.

"Julia, sweet Julia," Madeleine Groves whispered. "Darling, look." She glanced brightly up at her husband. "It's our baby." She scooped the child into her arms and laughed as Maria offered her the wet edge of the cookie. She kissed the child's velvety cheek, holding her close to her bosom.

"No, Maddy, no." Barner Groves stepped to his wife's side, huge tears welling in his eyes. "She looks like our baby, but she is not." He put his arm around his wife's shoulders and led her to a chair in the living room; the baby's mother followed them, hovering in alarm near her daughter, not understanding. Trudi's heart melted, and she felt more sympathy for her mother than ever before, realizing for the first time what a stunning blow her little sister's death had been. Madeleine continued to stroke the child's hair, cooing sweet words in her ear, while her husband looked around at the others, his eyes begging for their understanding and patience.

Alex took his sister's hand, and together they backed away, allowing Barner to talk to his wife. She looked up at him in a daze, not wanting to comprehend, not wanting to release the child; but he continued whispering to her, until at last her eyes became clear and she shuddered. She sighed, an anguished sigh of resignation, before kissing the child's head and rising to hand her to her mother. Turning to her husband, she put her arms around him and sobbed, deep, groaning sobs so long pent up, and her husband cried with her.

From beyond the melancholy room, a tiny cry, really nothing more than a pathetic little squeal, pierced the silence. Mario Badamo smiled broadly and hugged his son, electrifying everyone with his joy. With Alex leading the way, they formed a rough semicircle around Jessica's closed bedroom door and waited for more. The second cry was louder, a healthy protest at the new environment, and everyone laughed and hugged each other with excitement.

When the door opened, Hattie held an impossibly tiny bundle, swaddled loosely except for the arms and face. Alex took one look, touched one tight fist, then pushed past to be at Jessie's side, where Dr. Hildegarde still worked. Hattie grinned hard and held the baby high for inspection. A soft bubble escaped the baby's red lips, and everyone laughed, their hearts captivated. Thick black curls lay wet against the angelic face.

"This little baby girl Badamo is going to break a lotta hearts," Hattie cooed.

CHAPTER
==33==

Gates dropped into bed, exhausted, feeling he couldn't raise his arms if he had to. The night air was close and warm, adding to his fatigue. His mind reeled with the events of the day. But he put off thinking of Trudi. He forced himself to picture his office, the face of a police officer, recall the voice of one of the arrested truckers' wives, anything to keep from thinking of Trudi.

The evidence against the two strikers pulled in for questioning about the death of the Pinkerton was so weak and circumstantial that he felt they could not possibly be found guilty if the case went to trial, but he was bringing in outside assistance for added assurance. It had been shrewd of Stevens to set up the death and make it look like the truckers were the perpetrators; Phillip had no doubt that Stevens was behind it. Winslow Stevens, with his Machiavellian mind, had been a step ahead of Gates, but soon, very soon, he would take action against the bastard. Little by little, he was gathering evidence, but only when he was certain, dead certain, that a conviction could be obtained would he move against the scum.

A cat yowled outside. He heard a garbage can tip over, then a dog bark. Gard wasn't home yet. He hadn't seen him in days. Phillip missed having his mother at home to talk to at the end of the day, but felt much more secure with her under guard at Viola Groves's house. He wondered if Trudi had talked to her. He was glad he hadn't told his mother what he was planning to do. At least, if Trudi did tell her, she could be sincerely shocked.

He tossed irritably in the bed, his long leg hitting the foot rail. He cursed. If Trudi weren't so damned stubborn, if he could only trust her to stay away from Win, he wouldn't have been forced into such a drastic measure to keep her out of danger. She might never forgive him, but he'd known that risk when he made the decision to push her away from him.

He swallowed hard, picturing Trudi with the morning sun filtering through the trees illuminating her white-blond hair, exaggerating her large, dark-lashed eyes, her face flushed and soft-looking after their lovemaking, sitting on the grass like a delicate wood nymph. The greatest pain he had ever felt was when the tears welled up in her loving eyes. He flopped over on his stomach, and punched the pillow. Damned headstrong woman!

He didn't feel rested when he woke five hours later, but he did have a plan that would assure Trudi's anger. If she didn't believe his words, then she would believe his actions. It was too early now to call, but as soon as he got to the office, he would set up a date with Linda Carter.

She was still tortured by Phillip's words. They echoed in her mind when she woke. A stabbing pain shot through her chest and a hot flush washed across her face as she remembered them. He didn't mean it. He couldn't mean it. What was it Grams always said? Actions speak louder than words, and his actions proved the lie of his words. He was only saying it to keep her away from Win, away from harm.

Trudi made up her mind to keep the postponed date with Win Stevens. No sooner had she made that determination, however, than she lowered her head, chagrined by her selfishness. Jessie had been through a physical ordeal yesterday. She was in pain and needed her. Trudi jumped out of bed and pulled at the shades, determined to make this a productive day. But the sunshine didn't grab at her aching heart, and tears of self-pity welled in her eyes. She blinked them away and ran to her bathroom for a soaking bath brimming with bubbles and perfume.

When she ran downstairs to offer her help, she saw something she had never seen before. Jessie lay on the bed nuzzling her daughter; but at the foot of the bed, on her hands and knees, was Madeleine Groves with her skirt hiked high, her hair held in place by a bandanna, scrubbing the floor, pushing a foot-long bristle brush in small, hard circles. Trudi's eyes grew wide with surprise, but when Jessie smiled and shrugged, she refrained from making any flippant comment.

Jessica's calm acceptance of the inevitable quirks of those around her was her greatest strength. She was aware of the differences between individuals, but those differences only added to their appeal for her. She seemed to have been born old, an accepting, benevolent old woman in a young person's body. Nothing surprised her. Nothing upset her—nothing except cruelty in others.

"Come see our beautiful baby." Jessie shifted, her face pale but happy. Trudi was awed by the delicacy of the child who lay peacefully in her mother's arms, but she never got a chance to comment. Grams bustled in, barking commands.

"Come on, Madeleine, come on, Trudi. Have some breakfast." She bent to touch her daughter-in-law's shoulder. "Quit your working for a few minutes and come nourish yourself."

Madeleine sat back on her haunches and sighed. "Isn't she beautiful?" she said to no one in particular as she smiled in the direction of her new granddaughter, then rose to leave the room.

Grams looked after her and shook her head sadly. "Doing penance, she is," Grams grunted to Jessie and Trudi, "penance for the way she's treated you kids. She's going to have to scrub a lot of floors to cleanse herself."

"Grams," Jessie said slowly, a warning note in her voice, and Grams shut up but only after a parting shot.

"Let her suffer a bit. Maybe she won't be so damned uppity."

"This house is getting crowded," Trudi remarked, sitting down with the others. She hadn't eaten all day yesterday, and still the huge breakfast Grams and Mrs. Mills had prepared held no temptation for her. She followed the conversation with little interest, and when the phone rang, she bolted for the hall, her heart racing with the hope that she would hear Phillip's voice.

"Trudi, I just can't do it," a voice so familiar that it made her catch her breath wailed over the phone.

"What, can't do what?" she whispered.

"I just can't betray Bonnie," Gardner Gates explained. "I don't love her, but I don't hate her. I just can't humiliate her by standing her up at the altar. She's not responsible for her father's actions, and I just can't carry out my revenge on her."

After a long pause, Trudi answered, "I understand. And I agree with your decision."

"She's living at the big house now, and it makes me feel so guilty to watch her bustle around with plans for the wedding." He heaved a huge sigh. "I kept my promise not to tell Phil about your plans, so now will you help me?"

"Help you what?"

"Help me tell Bonnie. I really should tell her before I leave for college."

"Gardner! I can't do that," she exclaimed. "You have to do it yourself."

"I'm afraid I'll turn coward if I face her alone."

"Then take your brother."

"Are you kidding? He's so busy I never see him; then, when I did see him this morning, he about bit my head off." Trudi got some small satisfaction from those words, hoping that Phillip was suffering. "He wouldn't go near that house or that family in the best of times."

"Then ask your mother."

"She doesn't know the whole story," he explained sheepishly. "She'd be pretty disgusted with me if she knew I was planning to deliberately jilt Bonnie." He laughed uneasily. "I can just hear her now—'I'm disappointed in you, Gardner.'"

"Well," Trudi thought out loud, "why don't you write it all down? People always make more sense when they write what they are feeling." She chewed on her lip and thought hard before continuing. "Then I'll go . . ."

"Swell! Oh, swell." Gard breathed a huge sigh of relief.

"Wait a minute," Trudi said. "I'll go *if* you help me." She glanced nervously toward the dining room, making sure no one could hear her. "You have to find out when Win is not going to be home so I can do some quick snooping on my own."

"That's almost as bad!" Gardner protested.

"No, it's not," Trudi rationalized. "I'm trying to get hard evidence on him, not her!"

There was a long pause before Gard replied. "He's gone today. He's out of town on business until this evening."

"Then pick me up at one o'clock."

"You're looking very dapper, considering you're on your way to break a woman's heart." Gard wore a navy blazer with white slacks and white buckskin shoes, but his face was grim and his mood was worse.

"I'm not taking this lightly, Trudi," he snapped, so she let it rest.

"If I were you, I wouldn't tell her your original plan," she cautioned. "Just tell her you've had a change of heart, that you think you are too young, or that you want to wait until you are out of college." For answer, he handed her a three-page note that outlined almost exactly what she had just said. "When we get there, I want time to get the library desk drawer open," she explained as they drove up the long drive. He grimaced but didn't answer as they knocked at the door.

The butler nodded agreeably when they asked to wait in the library, and Trudi began her task before he shut the door. She overturned the pen holder and, her hands shaking, stuck the small brass key in the center drawer. Gard stood near the door, his ear pressed to the wood, his eyes on Trudi. She gulped hard, then gasped with satisfaction as the key turned and the drawer slid smoothly open. Her eyes lit up with excitement when she saw the official-looking leather-bound book, but when she lifted it out, her heart sank. It was huge, the size she pictured Bob Cratchit doing Scrooge's ledgers in, much too big to slip into the handbag she had brought along for just that purpose.

"Can it!" Gard hissed, frantically waving his hand. She shoved the book back into the drawer and snapped it shut, dropping the key in place as Gardner took Bonnie by the shoulders and kissed her lightly. Trudi stepped away from the desk to stare out the French doors, open for the breeze, and didn't see the look of puzzled surprise on Bonnie's face at finding them together.

Gardner hemmed and hawed, walked in a small circle with both hands in his pockets, glancing at Bonnie and then Trudi, then stopped to stare at the ceiling.

"Gard is here to tell you something very difficult," Trudi began when she realized that he could not. Bonnie's face grew concerned, and she clutched her hands together in front of her, staring at Gardner. Her hair hung long and close to the sides of her face, and she fidgeted with it, pushing one strand behind her ear.

"Bonnie, I . . . Bonnie, I . . ." he stammered gracelessly. Bonnie's eyes were downcast, and she bit her lower lip as she clutched at a silver cross that hung at the neck of her simple dress.

"You don't want to marry me," she whispered. Gard's startled eyes fixed on Bonnie, then held Trudi's as Trudi hastily walked toward the door.

"I'll wait in the hall until you finish," she murmured, closing the door softly behind her.

Five minutes later, he came out, his face tight and pale.

"How is she?" Trudi felt her own heart aching for the young woman. "Should I talk to her?"

"No." Gard shook his head. "She's quite calm. She said she knew it was too good to be true." He slammed the door of the car as he got in, and they drove away in silence.

CHAPTER 34

The smoke in the cocktail lounge burned Gates's eyes, and the music, even though it was the jazz he loved, merely grated on his nerves tonight. He was drinking even though he didn't want to, in order to create the right scenario when Trudi walked by, as he hoped would happen. He had to make her understand that he meant it when he said he did not want her involved, that he was serious enough about it to destroy their relationship if it would keep her from the danger of tracking down evidence on Win Stevens.

Linda Carter, already in her cups, sat cuddled at his side babbling away inconsequentially, and he paid her little attention, keeping his eye on the front door. Win and Trudi had not arrived yet, nor had they been at the country club for dinner, and he was beginning to think the evening would be a waste. He wasn't sure how long he could tolerate Linda Carter, but he knew one thing for sure. He would date her long enough and publicly enough for the news to get to Trudi.

"I made an important phone call," Linda said with a giggle, raising her eyebrow and leaning toward him.

He ignored her comment. "Do you know the password for downstairs?" he asked abruptly.

"But of course, silly boy." Linda grinned, pulling a long

drag on her cigarette, then posing with the gold-plated holder high in the air.

"Come on, let's go down there." His words were not a request.

"Just a minute," Linda protested, digging for a large, square compact in her purse. She spit on her fingers to flatten the curls in front of each ear, then spread another layer of bright red gloss over her lips. Her getup was embarrassing, not to him, for he did not feel identified through her, but embarrassing for Linda because it was so obviously devised to shock. The dress was purple satin, cut on the bias. The material was gathered at the shoulders and pulled apart to form a deep V neckline that plunged halfway to her waist, revealing all but the ends of her breasts. Her forehead was bound by a tight band that held a pink feather over one ear, and her hands were covered by pink gloves in a latticework design. If Linda was determined to repudiate her mother's strictures, then her immodest costume tonight was a giant step in the right direction. When she bent to reroll her hose, Gates glanced toward the door and saw them enter.

Trudi preceded Win into the dining room, looking, if possible, more fragile and delicate than usual in a soft, mint green, sleeveless dress of silk organza that fell from her shoulders in thin folds but still did nothing to camouflage her soft curves. This was going to be harder than he had expected, but Gates took a deep breath and began his planned routine.

He leaned over and ran his hand up the same leg that Linda was working on, and she squealed, just as he had counted on her doing. When she leaned toward him flirtatiously, he kissed her lightly and handed her a small giftwrapped box. She tore at the box with childlike glee and he smiled, sure the timing would be perfect. Just as Win and Trudi neared the table, Linda screamed and threw her arms around Gates, smacking him with a wet kiss.

"How precious! How truly precious!" She held the pin close to the candle. About four inches long, the sterling and marcasite pin gleamed with two ruby eyes.

"A lounge lizard." Win's smooth voice cut through the noise of the room. "How appropriate, don't you think, Trudi?"

Trudi's eyes narrowed as Linda held up the pin for inspection. She colored, then blanched as her lips grew straight and hard. She looked directly at Gates, who lounged back in his chair, a smug, self-satisfied smile pulling down one corner of his mouth. "A lovely gift," she murmured. "To cement your long-standing friendship, I assume?" Patting Linda on the top of the head, she slid her arm through Win's and walked gracefully through the room, never once looking back.

Gates leaned forward, his elbows on the table, and buried his face in his hands. Without even looking at Linda, he pushed his chair back and growled, "Let's get out of here. I feel sick."

Win guided Trudi down the long, dark hall at the back of the restaurant in silence. Trudi stopped at the entrance to the basement speakeasy and leaned against the wall, a surge of pressure building in her chest, her head echoing the painful pounding of her heart. "Win, take me home. I feel sick."

She stayed in bed for three days, no fever, no vomiting, but pale and drawn with a general malaise. Winslow Stevens sent a dozen yellow tulips the first day, two dozen red roses the second day, and three dozen pink carnations the third day. She ignored them all, just as she refused his phone calls, all phone calls, especially one from Linda Carter.

"It's not the symptoms of the grippe," Grams muttered.

"It's not consumption," Jeanne Mills noted. "That always starts with a fever."

"Did you check her for sore spots like the cancer?" Mario Badamo offered when he stopped to visit his grandchild.

"Does this have anything to do with my son?" Evangeline Gates was perceptive enough to ask her directly.

Trudi wouldn't answer. She wouldn't speak. She hadn't spoken for the entire three days, but when her eyes filled

HIGH SOCIETY

with tears at Mrs. Gates's words, the light dawned. A conference was held at the kitchen table.

"She should fight for him," Grams announced.

"She's done that," Evangeline Gates answered.

"Couldn't she simply tell him she loves him?" Jessica asked.

"I'm afraid she's done that, too." Mrs. Gates hung her head and wrung her hands.

"If you are worried about me"—Trudi stood leaning against the doorframe—"you needn't be. I am just fine and getting better all the time." The others were frozen with surprise to see her. She didn't look fine. She looked pale and peaked and stale, her face gray and tired, her hair matted and dull.

But it was her eyes that told the true story. Grams looked at her and gave an imperceptible nod, knowing she would be all right. For Trudi's eyes sparkled with the devilish glint of old, a strong, unmistakably vengeful gleam.

Trudi walked across the wooden platform of the train depot with her back straight and her head held high. This trip marked the beginning of a new attitude for her. Instead of being the willing dupe for some man, she would start calling the shots. If Phillip Gates intended to humiliate her, she certainly wasn't going to let anyone else know he had hit the mark, least of all him. She intended to enjoy life without him, probably even better without him, she thought, her chin jutting defiantly in the air. She had spent the last few days in a blue cloud of self-pity, confused beyond reason by the turn of events, but her final, lingering feeling was anger, an anger that motivated her to move on and out! If Phillip Gates thought she was spoiled and self-indulgent, he hadn't seen anything yet!

Earlier in the day, she had called Win and used her most charming voice. "Thank you so much for the lovely flowers, Win. It does make a woman feel so good to be pampered."

Win was ecstatic. "Anything you want, my dear. I've told you that time and again."

"How sweet," she cooed as he played right into her hands. "I was thinking of going shopping. Spending money has such a cathartic effect on me. It just works all the poison out of my system."

"Use my name, Trudi. I insist."

"You're so generous." She'd finished the conversation and immediately left the house. Her first stop was the Busy Bee, an emporium frequented by the working class of St. Louis that would stock everything she had in mind.

"Could you show me your children's clothes, please? And then I want to see women's dresses and men's work clothes." The salesman hustled around, calling for extra help, and by the time she left an hour later their stock was depleted.

Her next stop was Bonasinga's Fruit Distributing Company, a large brick building that sat on the corner of Third and York. She parked her car, pulling at the brake with gusto, and made her way carefully across the brick pavement, entering the front office only to find no one about. She hit a domed silver bell, and within a minute a rotund man, a white apron wrapped around his belly, pushed his way through a swinging door to greet her with a sunshine smile.

"I would like to order some fruit baskets, your largest ones, please." She smiled back.

"One problem, ma'am. We usually only sell wholesale."

"I think the order will be big enough that it will be worth your time. I want 400 baskets delivered to the Labor Temple as soon as possible."

The man blew out his breath and raised his eyebrows. "It may take us till tomorrow to put 'em together."

"Perfectly all right," Trudi assured him. "Another purchase I made this morning won't be delivered until tomorrow either." She turned to go, then stopped. "Please charge that to Winslow Stevens." She turned and walked out before she could see the man's eyebrows rise in surprise.

She was so immune to her surroundings that she had passed by the sleek black Buick before she recognized it. Linda Carter was driving and it was, without a doubt, the same car that George Rome had presented to his guests. Craning her neck to stare in the rearview mirror, she could make out the distinctive mark of the dealer on the back bumper, one that the redhead had not deemed necessary to remove. It didn't surprise her that the redhead had sold her gift. She had spent her life giving gifts in exchange for money.

But Trudi was not above getting a perverse satisfaction from knowing that Linda Carter was driving the car of a whore.

Trudi stood on the railroad platform and raised her face to the sunshine, smiling smugly to herself, wondering if Win would finally feel she had gone too far when he got the bills from her morning shopping spree. Hal Mills stood beside her, ready to assist her onto the train as soon as it stopped. He glanced at her, noticing the mysterious smile.

The women of the house might be fooled into thinking the little mite was feeling better, but he didn't believe it. She'd been acting mysterious all morning. Whatever had been wrong for all those days she lay in bed looking like death warmed over hadn't suddenly disappeared. She was working it out inside herself, he felt sure. He'd never had any kids of his own but if he did, he would want his daughter to have this one's spunk. Should be bigger, though, a little hardier-looking. She was so tiny she looked like a strong wind would knock her over.

When the sleek silver train pulled in to receive passengers, Trudi was eager to get on the train, get on with the trip, get on with the next step of her recovery. She settled herself in the lounge car and pulled out a copy of *The Sun Also Rises*, by a young author named Hemingway, which she'd been meaning to read for months. She waved to Hal as the train pulled away, and he waggled a finger at her. She frowned. It was a warning finger.

The train moved slowly until it reached the edge of the city. The Mississippi slumbered along the right bank of the rails, and to the left the bluff rose, the same bluff that hid the creek where old Gert did her moonshining. The falls would have made a beautiful place to make love, the noise of the rushing water masking their inevitable unabashed cries of passion. For a moment, gazing at the river, she pictured Gates's lean body, his brooding face, his finely etched lips. Then Trudi shook her head, shook the thought away, determined not to think of him. But her own reflection in the window mocked her. Her face looked ghostly. No matter how brightly she had smiled, no matter how chipper her voice had been, she had felt hollow and disconnected all day long. Most people had been fooled, but not Hal. He said little but thought much, and she was sure he had seen through her false bravado.

She was glad she hadn't told anyone what had happened. She knew Gates was tight-lipped and gentlemanly enough not to say anything either, so the humiliation burned in her heart alone. When she had seen Gates and Linda together at the Cuckoo Clock, a knife had gone through her heart, to be twisted even harder when Linda shoved Gates's gift under her nose. The feeling of nausea that swept over her had been so overwhelming, she didn't think she could make it back to Win's car. When he had put his arms around her to kiss her good night, she had not resisted, and only when Win's embrace became more demanding was she able to rally enough to convince him she truly was not well. She had run from the car and straight to bed. The anguish she had suffered the next few days had left her drained and weak. Phillip Gates was the man she loved, the man she would do anything for, and he had abused and betrayed her outrageously. His words had hurt her, but it was his actions which spoke loud and clear.

She lifted her chin and blinked her eyes, refusing to allow the burning to turn to tears. So now I recoup, she told herself. I start a plan of pleasuring myself and forgetting him. She took a huge breath, knowing it would be easier said than done, for thoughts of him were inescapable. She leaned her head on the high-backed cushion of the chair and tried to let the rhythm of the train lull her to sleep.

CHAPTER 35

Four hours later, Trudi hailed a cab outside Union Station in Chicago. "The Drake Hotel," she announced, while the cabbie stuffed her case in the trunk. Dusk was settling over the city and the traffic was horribly congested, but Trudi settled back to enjoy the delay, relishing the noise of the overhead commuter train, the blaring of the horns, the insults shouted back and forth between the cabbies. Double-decker buses carried double numbers of bodies out of the heart of the shopping district, while closed sedans and open coupes fought for forward rights. On the grass verge next to the busy roadway, horseback riders and bicyclists jostled for position along the lakefront, ignoring the city noises, enjoying the cool breezes off Lake Michigan.

"Worst traffic in the world," the cab driver muttered, shaking his head with impatient bewilderment. "And the new double-deck on Wacker Drive is gonna make it worse, carrying twice as many cars into the Loop." He gave a dismissive wave of his hand. "I ask you, what are we gonna do with all the cars now?" Trudi shrugged, not really interested in his chatter, until his next pronouncement. "This is my last week here." He shook his head with finality. "Yep, next week Monday, me and my wife and two kids are taking off for Russia. They're putting together a perfect society over there. Everybody will share and share alike. Even a little man like me can have a real go at a good life." He threw his right arm over the back of the seat and glanced around at her. "Ever read Karl Marx or Lenin?" Trudi gave her head a quick shake. "Well, they got some real good ideas. Now that the Bolsheviks are in control, they're gonna set up a utopia."

"That's a big decision," Trudi murmured, impressed by the firmness of the man's opinions.

"Not so big, lady." He put both hands on the wheel and swerved into a hole in the traffic. "They promised us a plot of land all our own. I can get my kids out of the walk-up we're in now and into the free air."

"I hope you're not expecting too much," Trudi said, smiling weakly, and grabbed for the hand strap as they swerved around a corner.

"If you don't expect much, you don't get much!" He gave her a quick, engaging grin. "Here you are, lady." The cabbie jumped out and opened the door, then pulled her suitcase out and set it on the curb. She tipped him, then stood watching as he touched his hat, a confident smile on his face, jumped into the car, and plowed back into the traffic. She was struck by his words, amazed by his indomitable spirit, humbled by the comparison of her own feeble efforts to effect a change in her life with the risk he was taking.

"Best of luck, Mr. Cab Driver." She waved, but he didn't see.

The Drake stood solidly on a corner at the north end of the Magnificent Mile, looking more imposing than Trudi remembered with its huge fireplace in the center of the lobby and its thickly carpeted serenity. The bellhop ushered her down the Avenue of Palms, its double row of fat, octagonal columns hidden behind fifteen-foot-high potted palms and high-backed Jacobean chairs.

As they stood together in the elevator, Trudi studied the young man, who whistled softly as he swung the key chain at his waist in a noisy circle, stopping long enough to tease the operator about who had the whitest gloves. The double row of brass buttons on his tight jacket gleamed, his pillbox hat perched at a precarious angle on his head, and his carefree smile all conspired to make her feel depressed and puzzled. How could this man be so jovial and lighthearted when she was so miserable?

"Do you enjoy your job?" She gave up waiting for his answer as he ushered her into her suite, deposited her suitcase in the huge closet, opened the curtains to a sweeping lake view, plumping the pillows with a showman's flourish.

"I love it, ma'am. It's the berries." He grinned infectiously. "Get to meet lots of interesting people. Just this week that writer, H. L. Mencken, and Red Grange, the football player, were in. Not together, of course." He laughed at his own joke. "And Valentino was here just before he died. Caused quite a stir, I can tell you. But the best part of the job is that I can help people in a lot of different ways." He bowed theatrically and handed her a formally printed business card. "Jake Gurn, Interior Decorating," she read, glancing up to his sly grin.

"I can get anything for you, ma'am. Unlimited supply."

"Bring me a bottle of Canadian whiskey, please. The best you've got. And I want it within the next half hour. And two packs of Lucky Strikes, also." He gave her a jaunty thumbs-up sign and scooted away.

She sat quietly by the window, waiting as the maid ran her bath and turned down the bed, watching as the waves broke like ocean surf on the breakwater beneath her room, echoing the turbulence in her heart. Phillip Gates, she thought with a snort, would have a screaming fit, if he knew how easy it was to get booze, how pervasive the illegal liquor network was, how deliberately she paid her money into it. He might be able to strike a blow against the kingpin in their community, but nothing could touch the impervious, entrenched forces of corruption of Chicago life. Elliot Ness and his invincible army of federal agents were fighting a losing battle, in spite of the highly publicized raids and arrests she read about in the newspapers. She enjoyed scoffing at Gates's puny efforts, feeling comfort in her cynicism, at least momentarily.

She paid the bellhop for the liquor, delivered in a brown paper bag, and poured her first drink. As the smooth warmth spread through her midsection, it erased her earlier contempt for Gates's efforts, forcing her to admit to herself the importance of his mission, and in the process of that admission making her feel contrite, puzzled, even more hurt by his rejection. She grew more morose with each sip, wondering if she was doomed to carry a torch for the bastard all her life. She stood up, holding the window ledge to steady herself and decided on action as the best escape from her mood.

The Silver Forest Room was vast, running the entire length of the north side of the Drake. Hundreds of diners filled the round tables edging the central dance floor, cigarette holders held high, glasses raised in toasts, laughter drowning out the clatter of the dishes served by a battalion of waiters. The easy dance music of Phil Spitalny's all-girl orchestra drew people onto the floor, and Trudi leaned back, watching the fancy footwork at they spun through fox-trots and tangos, girls in sleeveless dresses with sparkling trim smiling up at their dates flirtatiously.

Couples, all couples, paired off in happy parties of four or six, and Trudi felt left out and conspicuous. She ignored the food in front of her and fidgeted. When Evelyn Waugh stood in front of the mike with her "magic violin" and began sentimental renditions of maudlin love songs, Trudi's mouth turned down and she slumped in her chair, finally fleeing the room in the middle of "I Can't Give You Anything but Love, Baby."

Her head felt fuzzy the next morning, but no worse than she had felt for the last few days even without liquor to blame. She had had no trouble falling asleep the night before, but her heart and mind kept up a sporadic review of Gates. She relived their laughter and lovemaking, until finally she rose before dawn to force the beginning of the new day. She showered quickly but lingered afterward polishing her body with the silky lotions and creams she had brought along. Phillip had always loved to stroke her bare skin, humming his pleasure at the touch.

She stood up straight and threw back her head. Do not think about him, she commanded, marching into the dressing room and pulling out her finest daytime clothes and most comfortable shoes. She chose a white pleated skirt with a hip-length jacket of navy blue trimmed with crisp white braid. She pulled a navy blue cloche down over her brows in a determined effort. She had some hard and fast shopping to get done today, at least enough to get her to New York, where she intended to do even more. When she got back to St. Louis, she would knock people's eyes out!

Her first stop was at Maurice's Beauty Salon, where she surrendered to the complete beauty routine of facial, leg wax, body rub, eyebrow plucking, and hair trim with pomade before purchasing the complete line of La Dorine face powder and rouge compacts, "recently imported direct from Paris."

She was waiting at the door of Peacock's Jewelry Store when it opened, and was ushered in ceremoniously by the floorwalker, the pristine carnation in his buttonhole matching the spotless decor. He guided her to a low barrel-backed leather chair, where she settled in to make her selections from the glass cases running the length of the narrow room.

"I would like to see emeralds and pearls, please," Trudi announced prissily, pulling Win's letter of credit out to lay it discreetly on the counter.

"May I suggest the emerald earrings?" the man said. "They complement your hair beautifully." Trudi tried them on, savoring her reflection in the mirror.

"I'll take them, and the third ring on the left." She pointed nonchalantly to the tray in front of her.

"Now may I show you these new diamond ropes? Much less ostentatious than the popular dog-collar style."

"Both," Trudi said casually. "I'll take both. Please box them up. I'll take them with me." Five minutes later she rose to leave, but hesitated at a display case near the door when a whimsical pin caught her eye. It was a gold filigreed truck with diamond circles for tires, a band of rubies for a roof and dark sapphires forming the body. How appropriate, she thought. This strike is going to cost Win in more ways than he ever thought. "I'll take that, too." She pointed to the pin.

"If I may say so"—the clerk looked down his nose—"it is not the same quality as your other acquisitions." Trudi shot him the most withering look she could muster, silencing him. "I'll box it up immediately," he murmured by way of apology.

The wind had picked up when she stepped into the street, and she pulled her cloche tighter around her head before stepping into a cab. The ride was a short one, and when she arrived at Evans Furriers she stood on the street for a moment trying to remember her mother's lectures about various furs. She tugged nervously at her wrist-length gloves, threw her shoulders back, and walked in.

"This raccoon is quite collegiate-looking, but may have a tendency to overpower you," the saleslady offered her opinion. "Now, this sealskin and this Persian lamb are both shorter furs and might be more to your liking." She pulled them both out, twirling them in a circle for Trudi's perusal.

"No." Trudi frowned. "I want to see a full-length Russian sable." The almost imperceptible rise of the woman's brows told Trudi she had remembered her mother's words well. "We have only one in stock, and I'm afraid it may be too big for you." The woman smiled in a sickly way wringing her hands, hating to lose the sale.

"How long to have it cut down to size?" Half an hour later, Trudi left, a smug smile on her face, with the promise that the coat would be delivered before the fall chill hit the air.

The innovative architecture of Chicago had always refreshed Trudi, just as it did today. She stood back for a moment to enjoy the magnificent facade Louis Sullivan had designed for the Marshall Field store, thinking how much Phillip would enjoy the craftsmanship that had gone into it when a strong gust of wind funneled down Randolph Street practically blowing her off her feet, rescuing her from her own thoughts. She leaned forward and stumbled into the sanctuary of the revolving doors, and immediately headed for the designer dress shop.

Two hours later, she was exhausted, and readily agreed when the clerk offered to find taxis to deliver all her purchases to the Drake within the hour. She had two tailored suits by Coco Chanel, three cocktail dresses with varying hem lengths by the House of Worth, and half a dozen sweaters by Schiaparelli with innovative trompe l'oeil designs on them. She'd found five pairs of shoes and a dozen pairs of silk stockings in six flesh-colored shades. Three new hats, large and small, and four purses from satin to alligator completed her spree. Back at the Drake, she fell on the bed fully clothed and slept through the evening and into the next morning.

When she arrived at the La Salle Street Station at noon, the taxi driver hustled to find a porter with a cart large enough to transport three new gladstone bags and four Louis Vuitton trunks. Crowds pushed into the terminal, horns honked out on the street, porters shouted at each other as they trundled trunks through the doors. A brassy woman holding a bejeweled poodle swept past, followed by a cluster of reporters. A film star, no doubt, though her face was unfamiliar to Trudi.

Even in the cavernous depot, the click of Trudi's heels echoed behind her, comforting her with the thought that she was moving, advancing, making progress against the heartache that idleness in St. Louis would have brought. Passengers and their friends crisscrossed each other's paths. Shop tenders called attention to their wares while paperboys hawked the latest news, each group ignoring the other. Businessmen in three-piece seersucker suits and carrying leather briefcases, and elegant women, a few with pampered pets on leashes, stood on the imperial crimson carpet lined with huge potted palms that marked the path to Trains No. 25 and 26 of the New York Central's Twentieth Century Limited.

Newspaper reporters with cameramen in tow jostled each other mercilessly, pestering the more famous and infamous passengers for pictures and interviews as they waited to board the train. The line moved slowly, due to an unavoidable delay at the gate where they surrendered their tickets to the conductor. Trudi shifted her weight, enjoying the chance to study the other passengers from the vantage point of her own anonymity. Ahead of her, only one clump of passengers separating them, were two imperious-looking men trying to ignore the reporters, turning their backs to the flashes of the cameras.

"Mr. Morgan! Mr. Morgan!"

"Herr Von Clous!"

The reporters persisted until the two men, by mutual agreement, turned to answer a few questions. The older man, his penetrating eyes shaded by bushy black brows, his portly middle covered by an artfully tailored suit, stepped forward. Trudi could hear only the reporters' questions as they waved their press cards over their heads to get attention.

"Sir! When will the work of the War Reparations Commission be completed?"

"Is that what you were in Chicago for?"

"How do you feel about traveling on the same train as John Barrymore?" The last question got a round of chuckles, as did Morgan's response.

"I've always enjoyed his paintings." The financier waved and turned his back on the reporters to bend in quiet conversation again with his traveling companion.

The man called Von Clous was tall and broad-shouldered, younger than Morgan by twenty years, but when he talked the older man listened intently. Von Clous held himself erect but with the casual elegance that comes from relaxed self-confidence. His full head of hair was a gunmetal gray with uneven shading, which intrigued Trudi. She didn't realize she was staring until the man looked her way and stared back. She blushed and turned her head quickly, aware that he continued to look.

"Ticket, madam." The conductor's request startled Trudi, and she opened her bag to fumble for it as he stood patiently waiting.

"Could you give me the exact spelling of your name, please, and your compartment number?" The train secretary stood next to the conductor, his pen poised expectantly over the tablet he held firmly in his left hand. "This is for future records, and," he answered Trudi's question, "in case our passengers receive any messages during the night."

"More likely for Mr. Morgan than for Miss Groves." Trudi gave them a subtle, skeptical shrug, which brought a suitable chuckle from the two men before they motioned her down the line. A steward, his jacket whiter than the brightest white, escorted her to her compartment, explained the small conveniences of the room, and bid her a pleasant trip before pulling the windowed door shut.

Trudi sat on the banquette for a moment, then realized she hadn't eaten all day and was hungry. She pulled open the door to catch the steward, but came face to face with Von Clous. Recognition lit his eyes as he clicked his heels and gave the slightest of bows.

"Miss Groves, good day." He touched his forehead. Trudi's surprise showed on her face. "I overheard your name as you gave it to the secretary," he explained with a small smile. "Actually, I strained to hear it, since the train crew will never make introductions between passengers." His candor charmed Trudi, and she could not restrain a pleased smile. "My name is Barend Von Clous. We have adjoining compartments"—he nodded toward the neighboring room—"which bodes well for us. I was hoping you would agree to be my dinner guest."

"Aren't you traveling with Mr. Morgan?" Trudi asked. He raised his eyebrows, and Trudi realized immediately that her words revealed her previous interest in him, but he was gallant enough not to point out that fact.

"I am, but as an exceedingly important financier, he has brought along his personal stenographer and attorney, and they will be working far into the night on unrelated business." He stood confidently with his square shoulders thrown back, looking down at her with gentle, inquiring eyes, waiting patiently for her answer. His air of calm unobtrusiveness reassured Trudi, and she agreed to his offer with a quiet nod. "Good." He smiled. "When would you prefer?"

"As soon as possible. I'm starving. Shall we say half an hour?"

The dining car was as plush as any private club Trudi had ever seen, with mellow brass fixtures, a thick carpet, fresh white roses on each table, and a strolling violinist. She had changed into a dinner dress with a soft, flowing neckline and tiny green print pattern, specifically in order to wear her new emeralds. At first she had felt she looked ostentatious as she glanced repeatedly into the wall mirror, twisting her head, putting them on and pulling them off, and deciding finally to wear them. One look at the other women in the dining car, though, and she felt underdressed, for they lounged in their seats with diamonds and pearls dripping from every appendage.

"May I recommend the Century's hallmark dish?" Von Clous offered. "The Maine lobster Newburg served on toasted cornbread is excellent. There is a particularly succulent brand of watermelon relish made in Cambridge, Massachusetts, which I intend to order also."

"You seem to know the menu well."

"I have traveled this route innumerable times," he said, nodding. "This nonstop train is still faster, more comfortable, and far more reliable than air travel to New York."

"Do you come to the Midwest often?" She wasn't merely making polite conversation. He was distinctly foreign, so polished as to be out of place even in the midst of the obviously affluent passengers, and she was curious about his background.

"Yes, I am here about every six weeks. I travel a great deal between New York City and Geneva, with frequent side trips to Chicago." She listened with an open, expectant expression until he continued. "I am with the International War Reparations Commission."

She frowned with surprise. "Is that still active? That was formed when I was in school. Isn't the work finished?"

He chuckled. "Everyone asks the same questions." He leaned back in his chair. "The recommendations were made in '22 but the work continues—arranging loans, setting up payment schedules, arbitrating disputes." He heaved a patient sigh. "I think it is endless."

"You are German?" Trudi was oblivious to the innuendo

of her question, for many Americans still harbored strong anti-German feelings, but he glossed over it.

"My father was German, but my mother is Dutch and so I hold dual citizenship. I consider myself Dutch, since I was raised in the Netherlands and attended university there."

"I have heard that the inflation is terrible in Germany right now."

"Yes, it has been for some time. But it is not just the economy that is unstable. Emotions run high. The desire for revenge for the perceived injustices of the Armistice is very strong, fueling outrageous prejudices. I worry about another war."

Trudi was shocked. "But we just fought the 'war to end all wars!' "

"I hope that is true, but I believe it is not. It is not just German desire for revenge that is a threat to peace. When Russia comes to full power and settles down after its revolution, it, too, will be a force to be reckoned with. I foresee another war within the next decade."

They were quiet for a minute, thinking somber thoughts, both aware for the first time of the thunderous speed of the train as it rocketed across the plains of northern Indiana. Trudi cocked her head and studied him blatantly.

He was an impressive man, intelligent and powerful, without the superior arrogance often found in young men who had reached heady stature early in life. He was large, with square shoulders and a deep chest, confirming Trudi's suspicion that he actively kept his body trim. His skin had a soft, peachy quality, with a natural rosiness on his cheeks, curious in such a powerfully masculine person. He looked back at her, nothing more than interest apparent in his soft brown eyes.

Von Clous leaned forward, his hands on the table's edge. "Now, why don't you tell me what is it that you are running away from?"

CHAPTER 36

Trudi drew back in her chair, looking at him for five full heartbeats before her jaw jutted in anger. "I can't imagine why you would ask that!" Her eyes flashed, and her chin lifted defensively. "Even if it were true, it's certainly none of your business."

She pushed her chair back and rose from the table, her rapid exit causing more than a few turned heads. She tried to maintain some dignity as she hurried down the aisle and into her Pullman. She didn't look back once, fumbling quickly for her key and slamming the door to her compartment with a satisfying bang.

She pulled a small gladstone from the top ledge, yanked her jewelry off, and threw it in. Grabbing the whiskey stashed there, she poured a healthy dollop into a glass. Before she could gulp it down, there was a tap at the door. She snapped the shade down and ignored it.

"I don't intend to leave until you accept my apology," Von Clous announced firmly. She pictured him standing in the corridor, solid, impassive, immovable, and knew she should listen. She opened the door.

He stepped inside and immediately took the glass from her hand, setting it aside and leading her to the couch. He sat down opposite her and leaned forward, his elbows on his knees. "I was too blunt. But when I see a beautiful young woman with dark circles under her eyes and no smile on her lips, it sincerely concerns me." Trudi kept her eyes downcast, but his soft voice cut through her anger and registered in her brain.

"When I first glimpsed you, I thought Botticelli's *Birth of Venus* had come alive, but as I continued to study you, I saw a sadness in your face that is missing in the painting." She looked up at him now and saw that he was speaking sincerely. She saw only benevolence, a soft, sincere amity being offered, and she was sorry for her outburst. He radiated goodness and wisdom, and when he reached to grasp her hand in his, she felt the warmth of his kindness and did not resist. "I hope you will accept my apology. I was concerned."

Trudi felt her eyes burning. She pressed her lips together, refusing to cry, but her heart ached. Was her pain so obvious? She swallowed hard. "I thank you for your concern," she said, her voice strained, "but I assure you, my trouble is nothing that I can't handle." She raised her head and looked at him steadily.

A small smile tilted the corners of his mouth, and he patted her hand. "Good," he said, not believing her. He leaned back and crossed his legs. "You're still hungry. May I suggest that we continue dinner in here?" She nodded her assent, and he rose quietly. Five minutes later, a steward entered to set the table more elaborately than those in the dining car, with white cloth and fan-folded napkins, fine china and crystal stemware and a lush bouquet of white roses and baby's breath. When the food was rolled in, the aroma made Trudi's mouth water, but Von Clous held up his hand to signal a toast. Ceremoniously he uncorked a bottle of white wine retrieved from his own quarters, poured, and held his glass aloft.

" 'I cannot rest from travel; I will drink life to the lees. All times I have enjoyed greatly, have suffered greatly, both with those that loved me and alone,' " he said.

Trudi smiled in recognition of Tennyson's poem. " 'I am part of all that I have met!' "

Von Clous touched his glass to hers. " ' 'Tis not too late to seek a newer world.' "

Stumbling only a little, they continued together, " 'Though much is taken, much abides; and though we are not now that strength which in old days moved earth and heaven, that which we are, we are— One equal temper of heroic hearts, made weak by time and fate, but strong in will to strive, to seek, to find, and not to yield.' "

They both grinned, proud of their accomplishment and of the newfound intimacy of kindred hearts.

Two hours later, they lingered over still more wine, pausing in their talk to enjoy the brilliant sunset over the Pennsylvania landscape. A rainbow painted the horizon, bright oranges and yellows at the lowest levels, with purples and blues fading into the dark color of the cupping sky.

"Would you like some music?" He indicated the face of a small radio framed in the wall next to the door.

"If it's all the same to you, I would prefer not." She gazed back out the window, watching the sun disappear quickly behind the horizon. "I don't trust myself with music. It has such a powerful effect on me that I don't feel in control, so I avoid it." His interest registered on his face, so she continued, "A joyful song lifts my spirits so readily that I want to sing or dance. But conversely, a melancholy song makes me sad, morose." To her it was simple.

He smiled benignly. "Wouldn't it be possible to choose to listen only to joyful music rather than to deny yourself all the pleasure it can bring? After all, life is nothing more than an endless series of choices." He watched her closely to see if his arrow hit the mark.

"And have you always made the right choices?" she asked him archly.

"Most of the time." He shrugged. "But then, I do not take chances. I am basically a dull person, while that is not in your nature. I admire the risks you have taken. You, at least, will experience the full range of emotions that life has to offer, while I lead a rather pedestrian life."

Slightly affronted by his words, Trudi tried to deny them.

"You can't possibly know me well enough to categorize me as a risk-taker."

"You are right again, and I apologize." He nodded, raising his wineglass in a salute. "What I thought I saw was a beautiful young woman of wit and intelligence, who feels things so deeply that she guards herself against those feelings and yet is suffering now because she let that guard down and fell in love. Possibly with some fool who is not worthy of that love. So rather than brood, she throws herself headlong into a trip of such hedonistic nature."

Trudi gaped, stunned by the accuracy of his words, but still able to absorb his next comments.

"You have heard, no doubt, of America's young poet Edna St. Vincent Millay?" Trudi nodded. "She has a poem that reminds me of you. It's called 'My Candle Burns At Both Ends.'" Once again he smiled benevolently on her, then recited the poem.

She was silent for long minutes, brooding about what he had said, appreciative that he did not press her for a reply, before he bowed gracefully and bid her good night.

When the train arrived at Grand Central Station the next morning, Trudi was still unsettled, but ready to take on the challenges of city life, a city boisterous and crowded and gay, impervious to the troubles of one insignificant soul.

She and Barend Von Clous had both decided to stay at the Waldorf-Astoria, he because he always did when in the city, she because of the romance surrounding the place. Ever since a huge reception had been held there for the visit of the dashing David, Prince of Wales, she had been curious about it. She fell instantly in love with Central Park. The huge park was astonishing, for here amid the protective, bushy arms of towering trees and flowering bushes could be found peaceful walking trails and busy bridle paths, nannies pushing prams and old people sunning themselves in a tranquil oasis in the middle of the biggest and most bustling city in the world.

The hotel room itself was grander than she had expected, with pale pink walls and damask draperies trimmed in the same satin as the bedspread. Fresh fruit and flowers awaited her enjoyment, and the RCA radiola was tuned to the relaxed music of the Vincent Lopez orchestra. She took the time to place a long-distance call, waiting patiently until the operator called back.

"I have your party on the line. Go ahead, please."

The crackle of static rushed into her ear and she shouted her greetings. "Grams? I'm at the Waldorf-Astoria Hotel in New York City. Can you hear me?" Faintly, she could hear a voice but was unable to make out the words. "The Waldorf-Astoria, Grams," she repeated loud and slow. "I'm all right, but I don't know when I'm coming back." Once again she heard only indiscriminate sounds. "I'll send a note." She gave up, putting the receiver down in its cradle, still wondering if she had been heard.

She set out shopping, telling herself that new clothes were always cathartic, choosing to walk from store to store in the compact district of central Manhattan, distracted from her foul mood by the vitality and vivre of the noisy city. She bought her lunch from a street vendor on the corner of Fifty-seventh Street and Fourth Avenue, standing awkwardly as people bumped past. By the end of the afternoon, she had more clothes, including a green velvet cape by Phillipe and Gaston and a royal blue wraparound mantle that reached from neck to ankle trimmed along the entire hem in black fox.

That evening began a series of activities that left her head spinning. She and Von Clous went to a Greenwich Village brownstone on Washington Square converted to the posh Club Gallant, where access was easy after Von Clous flashed his membership card. This was not the typical rowdy speakeasy that Trudi was used to. Instead, it was dimly lit and only an occasional soft laugh broke the quiet.

"Many of the Bright Young Things congregate here when they are in New York," Von Clous explained. He didn't need to say more. Trudi was aware of the fast-paced life of the ultra-wealthy of British society, including the Guinness women, Barbara Cartland, Brian Howard, and, on occasion, Winston Churchill and David, Prince of Wales, who partied outrageously and endlessly. She glanced around, trying to be subtle, but he caught her. "No, they won't be here now. If they were, you'd know because of the increased decibel level. In summer, they refresh themselves on the north coast of France."

After a dinner of caviar and oysters and a triad of cocktails, Manhattans, Bronxes, and Sidecars, they attended *Abie's Irish Rose,* agreeing it was the worst play they had ever seen in spite of its long run on Broadway. They escaped to Harlem, leaving the taxi to thread their way through a long line of limousines to descend the steps of Connie's Inn at Seventh Avenue and 132nd Street into a room so low-ceilinged as to be cavelike. The women's cloakroom was crowded with half-clothed girls shrugging out of their corsets, checking their undies with the attendant as they sped out to the dance floor to dance with less restriction, jiggling their way through the shimmy and the black bottom with abandon.

But it was the jazz, the exotic and colorful jazz, that the white patrons came to hear, and the music blared obligingly to the rowdy audience as they ignored the bad booze and concentrated on the nervous pep of the trumpet of Louis Armstrong, a dipper-mouthed black man in a boiled shirt, who grinned at them slyly between songs, his gravelly voice announcing each piece with boyish glee. A thick layer of blue hung a foot below the ceiling, growing thicker by the minute as trails of cigar and cigarette smoke lofted upward. People milled around, their conversations nothing more than short repeated shouts above the din of the music, while the cigarette girl conducted her transactions in sign language, deftly fighting off the pinches of drunken men.

A woman with pomaded hair and magnolia white skin sat to Trudi's left in a trancelike state, unmoving, glazed eyes fixed on the distance. At the same table, a woman jiggled in constant motion, her shoulders and fingers keeping time to the music, her lips moving incessantly, stopping only long enough to pull at her cigarillo or swallow her drink. Noticing the difference between these two, Trudi leisurely studied the room full of people, and saw that they could roughly be divided into the same segments. Either they were still, with vacant eyes and bored faces, or they were overheated, jerking around in spastic motion with zealous eyes and flushed faces. Neither extreme appealed to her.

Von Clous, in contrast, sat at Trudi's elbow, the tiny table between them big enough to hold only an ashtray and two drinks, letting the blast of music pour over him with the same effect as if he were listening to Beethoven's fifth piano concerto. He sat still and relaxed like the calm at the middle of a storm while the gray noise of the room swirled around him unnoticed. It was that quality that had led to their new friendship. The steady calmness he exuded promoted trust, and on that basis they had begun exchanging opinions, which led to confidences and, the mark of true friendship, the survival of disagreement.

But the frenzy of the drinkers and the relentless beat of the jazz was more than his serenity could override and more than she could endure, and she winced as a dull headache pounded at her temples. "Enough!" Trudi nudged Von Clous and they left, thankful for the relative freshness of the New York night air.

Before parting, Von Clous recommended certain sights for her to see during the next day, including the Metropolitan Museum of Art and the Lower East Side, a crowded old-world bazaar of sights and sounds she had never experienced before. Their second evening in the city was a repeat of the night before, with a different nightclub and play. The Ziegfeld Follies, a lavish revue of spectacular costumes poured over gorgeous women, was capped by the comedy of W. C. Fields, whose cynical humor Trudi could identify with. The grandly dressed spectators gleamed in their lounge suits and sparkling dresses, talking at intermission with such unrelenting clatter that their conversation created a dull din that steadily rose in power. Heavily made-up women, their mouths painted in dark red cupid's bows, their eyebrows plucked to invisibility, leaned toward each other intently. Men in narrow-lapeled tuxedos clamped thick cigars in their mouths and turned their backs briefly to swig from silver pocket flasks before resuming their loud conversation. Everybody was talking and nobody was listening and the spectacle mesmerized Trudi.

But it wasn't until Von Clous guided her into the huge Roman Ballroom that the evening lost its luster. In front of them, hundreds of dancers milled to the tinny music, their hair mussed, their clothes bedraggled, their arms slung across each other's shoulders for support as they entered the fourth night of a dance marathon. In one corner, a white-uniformed nurse, the wings of her cap incongruously crisp, massaged the feet of a contestant, whose disappointment at her withdrawal lined her face. Spectators, held back by a slim wood railing, rimmed the dance floor, calling encouragement to their favorites, who staggered in near-exhaustion to the tune of fox-trots played by a meager three-piece combo.

"My girl's gonna win!" A barrel-shaped woman next to them poked Trudi, who stared at the lady's jowls, which wiggled as she bobbed her head in time to the music. "Gonna win $3,500 so they can get married." The old woman cackled with glee, so sure was she of her prediction.

Trudi's nose wrinkled at the smell of sweat and the taste of swill, the harsh booze sold in small paper cups by young boys who hawked it as lemonade. She drew away from the woman and close to Von Clous, leaning into him as if for protection from the desperate scene. Three couples plodded in front of them, dragging aching feet that seemed glued to the floor in one agonizing step after another. A tall, hawk-nosed man tugged at the arms of his partner, who hung from his hands in defeat. He pinched her breasts, getting no reaction, and called her name again and again, before allowing her to slip to the floor, collapsing with her.

"One more down!" the fat lady whooped. "They're going to start dropping like flies now." She put her hand up to her face to keep secret the information she passed on to Trudi and Von Clous. "You know what their secret is? They pickle their feet." She nodded smugly. "Soak 'em in saltwater for three days before the contest, then they don't feel no pain."

Von Clous led Trudi away and back to the hotel without a word exchanged between them.

* * *

HIGH SOCIETY

After only three days, the city had turned stale and brash, and the revengeful fulfillment Trudi had expected to find in nightclubbing, theatergoing, and shopping had lost its appeal. These were, after all, activities that kept only the body busy, doing little to heal any wounds deeply felt inside the soul. They were stopgap at best, a stopgap solution that paled when she thought of her life as a whole, thoughts that Von Clous had planted in her brain.

She was drained of emotion. The anger she had felt a week ago had dulled to resignation; the need for revenge had receded into apathy. She was conscious now of a lingering sensation of inertia and drabness, a hollowness that echoed between her mind and her heart.

She needed time to think about what she wanted to do with herself, for it was herself alone that would be the key to her happiness. She would have to find her direction, discover where she wanted to live her life and with whom, and, more importantly, why and how. What motivation would add weight to her life?

Jessica, no doubt, would find complete satisfaction in the simple complexities of rearing a brood of children with the man she loved. Grams had had a fruitful life working the land in partnership with her husband. Bonnie Stevens was invigorated by her newfound faith in the Lord. Phillip Gates was motivated by the urge to fight for the underdog, a path he would follow all his life. Even Win Stevens's drive for power and money, greedy as it was, still constituted a guiding force in his life.

She had to find a spark, a fire to guide her on her way, one that would not burn her out but would sustain her with the soft glow of satisfaction in a life well led. It had to be something more than the jejune, self-indulgent parties that had lured her and so many of her friends into an extravagant pattern of lost lives. The frenetic pace of the largest city in the world held no appeal for her.

She knew what she wanted. She wanted to be with Phillip Gates, and the acknowledgment added to the burden of her discontent.

* * *

"Could we have a quiet dinner in the hotel tonight?" she suggested. Von Clous agreed, and they went down to the dining room. She had chosen one of her new outfits, a regal and sophisticated gold lamé tube dress that made her look and feel years older. She waited while the maître d' seated them, then accosted Von Clous with her words.

"You have deliberately kept me so busy that my head is spinning. Am I right?"

"I have only suggested, my dear. You have kept yourself busy. You have experienced quite fully what the fast-paced life would bring."

"And the slow!" She laughed.

"Then you are ready to make a wise decision about which side of the fence you will jump down on. You have been walking a narrow, tight line lately. Now you have explored both sides. You will make a better choice." He shrugged.

Trudi raised her wineglass in silent salute to him. "You said something on the train from Chicago that I have not forgotten."

"Only one thing?" He chuckled.

"Why do you consider yourself dull and pedestrian? Have you never taken risks?"

"Certainly," he admitted. "Some have worked well, some have not." He shrugged. "I can admit to my mistakes. Do we not all make them? I think it is *how* each one of us admits to his mistakes, to his problems, admits them to oneself or to others and then goes about actively solving them, that distinguishes the thoughtless from the wise person." His face, open and full, seemed to watch as she took in his words.

"And what if we all do not have the resources"—she waved her hand indecisively—"you know, the brains, or the education, or the training to make good decisions?"

"It takes none of those things." He gave his head a little shake. "It takes, how do you say, the spirit, the courage, the determination in here." He pointed to his heart. Then his forehead wrinkled in thought. "It takes . . ." He waved his hands in a small circle in front of him. "Pluck! Yes, that is the word. Pluck!"

Trudi grinned and looked out the window toward the street traffic without seeing. "But what about with your heart? Did you ever take chances with your heart?"

Now it was his turn to think about her words. "Not when it really mattered," he murmured mysteriously. She waited, looking at him steadily, expecting more. "When I was young, I was very much in love. She was all good things: bright and witty and lighthearted." He smiled wistfully, remembering. "She made me laugh." The sky outside the dining room darkened; only a thin line of light was left behind the skyscrapers. Shades of shadow softened the room, adding to its intimacy.

He continued, his voice low and slow, his eyes unfocused. "She had thick blond curls, and when she let her hair down, it reached to the middle of her back. Her eyes were blue, a rich turquoise. I was devoted to her, and made an easy decision that I would remain dedicated to her. I went away to school and became engrossed in my studies. I wrote. She wrote more often—toward the end I would receive a letter almost every day, each one of which I treasured. I continued in my obsessive work habits, determined to do well so she would be proud and so that I could support her and the family I wanted to have with her. And then the letters stopped." He paused.

"By the time I became alarmed, I found out she had married. Her letters had been a cry for attention, a signal that she needed reassurance of my love, but I was too obtuse to understand that. I was so sure of my love for her that I thought she was equally as sure." He took a huge breath and let it out. "I was shattered. I tortured myself with thoughts of all I should have done. I should have taken the risk of marrying her before I left. I did not understand the risk of leaving her unattended."

They were both quiet for a long time, staring out the window, lost in their own thoughts.

"You never married?"

"No, I never risked falling in love again."

"Do you still love her?"

"Yes," he answered simply, without hesitation. He took a last sip of wine, then looked at her intently. "Do you still love him?"

"Yes, but—"

Von Clous held up a hand, protesting, "No 'yes, buts.' Either you love him or you don't. There can be no reservation."

"He doesn't love me!" Trudi spat out.

Von Clous mulled that over. He looked at the floor. He looked outside. Finally he looked at her. "I don't believe that," he announced. "He may have decided that you cannot marry, or that you don't love him, or that . . ." He waved his hand in the air. "There could be any number of stumbling blocks, but don't ever believe that he doesn't love you!"

She looked at him stupidly. "How can you be so sure of someone you have never met?"

"I am not sure of him. I am sure of you! You would never have given your love to someone who did not love you back."

"Nor would you!" she argued back. "And look what happened to you." Her words stung him, and she was immediately sorry. She reached across the table and took his hand, stroking it by way of apology. "Where is she now?"

"She is in London. Her husband was killed in the last battle of the war. She has two children, a ten-year-old son and an eight-year-old daughter who looks just like her."

"You've seen them?" Trudi's surprise made her voice rise.

"Yes," he answered slowly. "Six months ago on my last trip over there."

Trudi pushed away from the table and jumped up, her mouth hanging open. "You really make me angry!" She pointed an accusatory finger at him. "You lecture me on love and risk and problem solving, and yet you continue to sit on your fanny when all you say you hold dear is yours for the taking." She held up her hands in the universal gesture of bewilderment. "Why aren't you with her now? Why haven't you married her?"

He looked at her dumbfounded, astonished by his inability to give her a legitimate answer.

A bellboy stepped up to the table, looked back and forth between the two as they stared at each other, biting his lip in hesitation. Finally he cleared his throat and asked, "Miss Groves? Miss Trudi Groves? Telegram, ma'am."

It took a moment for her to respond, but when she did, she grabbed at the envelope and ripped it open, reading it as Von Clous tipped the young man.

> COME HOME IMMEDIATELY STOP
> PHILLIP GATES IN HOSPITAL STOP GRAMS

CHAPTER
=37=

Trudi was exhausted. Unable to sleep the entire night, harassed by her speculations about Gates's injuries, she had sat stone-still and silent for almost twenty-four hours, not speaking until she woke the slumbering taxi driver at the St. Louis station. When she entered St. Mary's Hospital, the deathly quiet of the empty halls heightened her fright, and when she stopped at the central desk, the nun, clothed in her stark white headdress and somber black habit, looked up at her with a severe frown.

"Mr. Phillip Gates's room number, please," Trudi requested without hesitation, knowing full well the best defense against a visit in the middle of the night was an ever-ready offense. Force of habit made the woman look at her entry chart, but she caught herself.

"I'm sorry, miss, but visiting hours don't begin until nine o'clock in the morning. You can't—"

Trudi lunged across the counter and grabbed the list. "I'm his wife," she lied without compunction. "Family can visit at any time." She was off and running for the stairway before the startled woman could protest. Trudi ran up the steps, pulling herself around the corners of the metal banisters with determined effort. She stopped, leaning against the cold plaster wall of the third floor landing, and gulped for air before peeking through the door to determine her direction. She slid noiselessly along the dimly lit hall, decorated by one large crucifix, and finally found Room 303.

"Let him be all right," she prayed, then slipped, wide-eyed and fearful, into the dark room.

He lay on his back in the white bed, shrouded in a white gown, with thin white sheets covering his long body. A glass jar of clear liquid stood near the headboard, a tube dangling from it to the midpoint of his arm. Her breath caught. She had never seen him looking so vulnerable, his gaunt features softened only by the glow of bright moonlight from the double windows next to the bed. She tiptoed across the floor and bent over him, looking for telltale signs of injury.

He jerked, sensing her presence, his right arm coming up in a protective move, and his eyes opened wide, staring at her. She squeaked and stepped back, then bent to him again, touching his dry lips with her own in the briefest of kisses. "Oh, Trudi," he whispered, his voice awestruck, and grabbed for her with his free arm, pulling her close, breathing in her fragrance, kissing her neck and mouth with anxious, eager kisses, until finally he shifted and pulled her onto his chest, kissing her with the strong, succulent sweetness she had been longing for. "I thought I was dreaming," he whispered, moving his hands over her face and shoulders, holding her fast in front of his eyes.

"I've missed you," she whispered, softly kissing his eyelids, tracing the ridges of his brows and cheekbones with her fingertip. He hugged her fiercely, burying his face in her hair, then winced, and she heard the small, involuntary groan.

"I've hurt you!" She pulled away, horrified at her insensitivity, but he grabbed her wrist and pulled her close again.

"It's worth it." He smiled, though his face remained yellow and drawn.

"What is it? Where did they hurt you? I've been so worried." She looked him over quickly from head to foot.

"The same place they always hurt you for an appendectomy." He rubbed his right side inside his pelvic bone.

"A what?" She jumped back. "An appendectomy!" She slapped her forehead. "I've been had!"

"I'm sorry it wasn't something more glamorous." He gave her a wide-eyed, chagrined shrug. "What did you think it was?"

"Well, I . . ." she huffed. "Naturally, I assumed—"

"Mr. Gates!" The head nurse stood in the doorway, backlit by the hall lights, her disapproval apparent by the stance of her body. "This young woman will have to leave. Your records indicate you are not married."

"I never said I was," he tried to explain feebly.

"She did." The woman pointed a fat finger at Trudi, who waved her fingers at Gates and slipped out the door.

By nine o'clock in the morning, she had her forces assembled around the table in Grams's big kitchen. Hal Mills clicked off the radio as they all sat staring at Trudi.

"It will work," she repeated. "It's the best way I can think of to get what we need and get this whole thing over with so our town can go back to normal."

Grams jumped in enthusiastically. "I'll do the chickens. This will be the most fun I've had in ages."

"I'll take care of the junk car in the river." Gardner Gates raised his hand.

"I'll do the pig, then, but only if it's one"—Jeanne Mills held up a lone finger—"and only if it's a young 'un."

"I got real strong doubts about this," Hal Mills said, running his hand through his hair, "but I'll handle the bonfire. That'd be too much for you women." Grams snorted and his wife shot him a dirty look, but Trudi chose to ignore him, for she was too certain of her own abilities to argue with him.

Victor Wellman raised a hand. "Me and my boys can

stage a couple of collisions around town. Two motorcars, or a car and a buggy." Trudi gave him the thumbs-up sign.

Evangeline Gates sat with her chin on her hand, tapping one finger on her lips. "I have something that might help, too," she mused. "When my dressmaker's mannequin is robed and hatted, it looks just like a person. If we could hang it from the trusses of the bridge, that ought to be quite distracting as well."

"Great idea, Mom." Gard patted her on the shoulder. "I didn't think you had it in you."

"Well, this is, after all, for the good of the community." She smiled primly, and everyone burst out laughing.

"Okay, troops, we'll spend the rest of the day collecting supplies. We clear up the details at dinner and plan on leaving here right after it gets dark, say, nine o'clock?" Trudi looked around the table for approval.

"I would like to help," Jessie announced from the rocking chair on the far side of the room where she sat feeding the baby. "You talked about two places for the chickens. I could do the second one."

"Who'd take care of the baby?" Alex said, frowning.

"I think Grandmother and Grandfather Groves would love to take Julia for an hour or two." She smiled down at the suckling child.

"Then my dad could be the driver, to round up the ones who won't have their own cars," Alex added. "God, this is going to be great! Just great!"

"And secret, remember, it must stay secret," Trudi stressed. "When you call for supplies, don't breathe a word of what is happening. It will work only if we surprise everybody." *And if Alex and I can be successful thieves.* But Trudi kept that thought to herself.

"Oh, and Grams"—she stepped next to the little woman, put her arm around her shoulders, and whispered in her ear—"we have to talk about that telegram." Grams looked up at her and grinned idiotically, all wide-eyed and innocent.

* * *

Gates thought it was strange that no one called him all day. The only human contact he had was with the hospital staff, and then only sporadically. He could hear the clatter of equipment and the voices of other patients' visitors, but they were hollow sounds that he didn't enjoy.

His first thought when he woke had been of Trudi. He was sure for a minute that her visit had been a dream, so much did he want to see her. But remembering the feel of her, the smell of her, the taste of her, he began to doubt and hope hard that she had been real.

"Do you always cause a ruckus wherever you go? Even in a hospital?" The morning nurse was not unfriendly, just brusque. "I know who you are, you know. I read the newspapers." She gave him the same look a teacher would give a naughty student. "Always causing a stir."

"But what have I done since I've been here?" Gates gave her a look of hurt surprise. "All I can do is lie here, listen to the radio, and eat tapioca."

"That little blonde who came sneaking in in the middle of the night? She wasn't here to see you?"

Gates found himself grinning. So it was true! But the smile disappeared soon enough. Glad as he was to see her, the situation still was too volatile to have her involved. She shouldn't have come back. It wasn't safe. The fight wasn't over yet, and he didn't trust her not to get back into the midst of it.

He felt sure there would be a settlement soon in the strike, surely within the next two weeks. But bitterness from the strike would linger, and the whole community would have to pull together again, and that could take months, maybe even longer. This wasn't going to be a pleasant place to live for a while. Especially since he would concentrate on Winslow Stevens as soon as the strike was settled.

Phillip could have sworn he had made the right decision a week ago, the decision to trick Trudi into believing he had betrayed her, but after seeing her, touching her last night, his resolve wavered. Only when he remembered the recent murder, the ruthlessness of professional gangsters such as Win Stevens and his ilk, did he know again that he was correct.

His fight against Stevens would get ugly, worse possibly than the strike violence, his only hope being that Win would keep his fury directed narrowly at him. Still, it was too great a risk and he didn't want Trudi around. As much as he had missed her, he had to get rid of her again. He thought he had convinced her he didn't care for her, but she wasn't as gullible as he'd thought.

He called Viola Groves's house a half dozen times, but strangely Trudi was never "available." Even his own mother was evasive with him, taking only long enough to ask about his health before hanging up, obviously preoccupied.

Dinner had been served ridiculously early, and the sun was still in the afternoon sky when Phillip heard a light knock at his door. He was expecting Nancy Neumann, his secretary, with preliminary news about the hearings of the two truckers arrested for the Pinkerton murder. "Come on in," he called. "I've been waiting for you." He shifted to a more comfortable position, and turned toward the door.

Jackie Davis stepped inside and let the door swing slowly shut behind her. Gates was immediately alert, sensing trouble. The woman was dressed in a prim outfit, a navy blue voile dress trimmed at the neck with white lace. Her thick red hair was tussled up under a white toque, and she carried a large white straw purse. But even in a Sunday school teacher's outfit, she could not disguise her voluptuous body. She stood with her back to the wall, her hands protecting the purse. The look on her face made Gates hesitate. It wasn't threatening or angry, but resolute nevertheless.

"Do you know who I am?" she asked. He nodded in a simple gesture, leaving the talking to her. "I need some answers from you, and I would appreciate the truth." She looked him directly in the eye as she stepped forward to sit in the chair beside his bed. He didn't answer her, not knowing what her questions might be, and he refused to answer falsely.

"Winslow Stevens and Trudi Groves"—she licked her lips and swallowed hard—"do they see each other?" The question took him by surprise, but his training stood him in good stead and his expression remained immobile. He took his time answering, and during that time her eyes never left his face. "I mean, do they see each other regularly?" She leaned forward, a poignant need to know visible in her whole body.

"Yes." He nodded slowly.

"Are they engaged?" Her questions were coming faster. He shook his head. "Does he love her?"

"Yes," he whispered, "I think he does."

She slumped back in the chair and the breath left her fast, as if she had been kicked in the chest, as if her worst suspicions had been confirmed. Her face sagged as she stared at the floor, her eyelids batting repeatedly. The left hand clutched the purse to her bosom, and her right began patting it in a curious maternal gesture.

Gates was aware that she had a very precarious hold on her emotions. But she rallied. She took a deep breath, swallowed, and looked up, her decision made, her eyes rekindled with a blue spark of anger.

"I have something for you, something that will nail him to the wall." All the sadness had drained from her voice, to be replaced by a grating edge of sharpness. She stood up slowly and gently laid the purse on his lap, waiting patiently for him to open it. He pulled out the records for the red-brick house on Second Street, all the entries in neat, legible accountant's script. He didn't need to ask why she was relinquishing the accounts.

"How will this help? There's nothing here that incriminates him," he said after glancing through the material.

"There is if you compare it with the deposits made in this account at the Mercantile Bank. They correspond perfectly. I think the Internal Revenue Service would like to see that." She pointed needlessly to the ledger. "The account is in Bucky Bathshelder's name. All of Stevens's various businesses are kept in separate accounts, so it will be hard to get him on everything, but this material ought to send him up for a few years, at least." She spoke with no hesitation or regret. "The deed to the house is in my name. You'll find it in the back pocket of the book, along with my personal deposition. I'm not sure that will hold up in court, since it wasn't done legally, but there's enough fat to keep 'em chewing for a while."

"Won't you be in danger for having given me this?"

She shrugged nonchalantly, the tough woman of the streets back in charge. "Yeah, but I'm leaving town as soon as I walk out of the hospital, and nobody will know if I'm in Saskatchewan or Singapore. Stevens thinks I'm going to do a favor for him, and by the time he catches on that I'm not there, I'll be out of his reach." Phillip's doubt must have showed, because she threw one hip out and rested her hand on it in a provocative gesture. "Listen, Gates, I've taken care of myself for close to forty years, and I can manage another forty real easy." He smiled at her for the first time, and she flashed him a brilliant smile in return. "Consider this my good deed to the community." She turned and strutted out, hips swaying, stopping at the door to give him a cocky wave before disappearing.

He lifted the book in both hands high over his head in a jubilant gesture, then brought it to his lips for a loud smack.

"Nurse," he called out to a white-clad figure passing in the hall. "Bring me a cup of coffee, please. No, better yet, bring me a whole pot. I have a lot of reading here." He settled in, putting a pillow over his stomach to serve as an impromptu support, then began reading Jackie's testimony.

An hour later he called his house, anxious to share his good news. The phone rang and rang, but Gard didn't answer. He called Viola Groves's house. The phone rang and rang, and finally, after the sixth ring, Jeanne Mills answered.

HIGH SOCIETY

"Could I speak to Trudi, please. This is Phillip Gates calling."

There was a long moment's pause before the woman spoke. "Well, I'll tell her, but I don't know if she can come to the phone." There was silence for a couple of minutes, then a clatter as the receiver was picked up.

"Phillip, I love you, but I can't talk now." Trudi's voice was rushed and breathless.

"But I have something really great I want to tell you about," he explained weakly.

"Couldn't it wait, sweetheart? Just a few hours?"

"How about my mother? Could I talk to her?"

"No, she's busier than I am." Trudi talked so fast, he could barely understand her. "Really have to run now. Kiss." She smacked the phone with her lips.

"Trudi! Trudi, wait!" Gates yelled into the dead mouthpiece. "Why do I get such an uneasy feeling," he muttered, staring at the silent telephone as if expecting it to answer.

CHAPTER
38

Trudi's heart was pounding so hard it echoed in her ears. She huddled against the south wall of Win Stevens's house, watching the light in the upstairs bathroom and listening for any footsteps on the first floor. The sky was black overhead, but the stars shone with a clarity she had never known possible and the moon smiled down with irritating brilliance. That afternoon she and Alex had compared notes and had been able to come up with a detailed drawing of Win Stevens's house and grounds. She was waiting for the right moment, reviewing the information in her head and fingering the bulky camera clutched in her hands. She had chosen the outfit she wore specifically because it was dark and had pockets, deep, numerous pockets in the skirt and jacket. She took a deep breath in an effort to calm her nerves until the assigned moment came. She had prepared as thoroughly as she could. The rest was luck.

Alex Badamo pressed his body hard against the stone retaining wall, watching the guard warily as he lackadaisically patrolled the street side of the riverfront warehouse. When the man disappeared in the black shadow of the building, he was still easy to follow since the end of his fat cigar glowed like a tiny tracer beacon. This was a local thug, unfamiliar to Alex except by his manner of dress and the typical hunting rifle he held casually in his hands. Alex and his father had driven around the building three times that afternoon, as slowly as they could without attracting attention. The best way to get inside, they had decided, was through the transom over a small door, seldom used if the weeds that grew in front of it were any indication. The thick rope and repelling hook Alex carried would allow him to scale the eight-foot height.

The low moan of an approaching freight train sounded from the south, and Alex dropped to the ground, careful not to jar the camera he held, confident that his black garb and the overhanging brush of the bluff would hide him from the sweeping headlight of the engine. From this vantage point, the girders of the bridge seemed even more menacing. The dust of the road tickled his nose uncomfortably, and he wiggled his arm until he could see his watch, gauging how many minutes until the assigned time.

Since the Belasco Theater and the Cuckoo Clock were only a block apart, Jessica and Grams waited together, hidden in a dark pocket of a short alley halfway between the two. Each woman was dressed plainly in dark clothes with a scarf tied tightly under her chin. Jessica's eyes were huge, and Grams chewed on her cheek, as they continually peeked around the corner of the building, peering through the darkness at the large, illuminated hands of the clock outside the Missouri State Bank. When they had driven through the downtown district that afternoon with Hal Mills to decide on the most expedient drop-off and pickup points, their plan had seemed easier, more fun. But now their breath came in short gulps, and their arms ached. The chickens they carried in gunnysacks were not cooperating, and lay quiet for only brief moments before kicking and squawking in protest. Grams didn't want them wearing themselves out before they were dumped in the Belasco and the restaurant, or else they wouldn't make a loud enough ruckus. Please God, Grams thought, let nine-thirty come fast!

* * *

HIGH SOCIETY

The junker car chugged laboriously along Third Street and wheezed to a stop in the middle of the intersection, its wheels turned sharply to the right, pointed downhill toward the river. Two blocks down the steep street was the boat ramp, a final gentle slope that led directly into the river in the shadow of the huge Memorial Bridge. Gardner Gates, dressed in overalls and a dark cotton shirt, slowly got out of the car and raised the hood, feigning car trouble in the event a passerby wandered along the deserted street. He glanced up toward the bridge, but saw only two cars, one going in each direction, and no foot traffic at all. His mouth was dry with fear, which embarrassed him, since he figured he had the easiest job of all. At least, his was the most plausible activity, if he was stopped and questioned. All he had to do was pretend to be disgusted by the faulty engine; then, when the assigned time came, he could give the car a huge heave and guide it on its way into the river.

Evangeline Gates had one of the most difficult assignments, since she had to lug the bulky, unwieldy mannequin along with her. She had visited the Salvation Army store that day and purchased old clothes not traceable to her. As soon as dark came, Mario Badamo had loaded the newly attired wooden body into the back of his wagon, and together they had taken back streets all the way to the bridge, where he had helped her unload it in the shadow of the fifteen-foot-high decorative stone pediments that stood sentinel at each end of the bridge. She waited now, uncomfortable only when car lights coming from the Illinois side briefly illuminated both figures at the end of the bridge, one alive, one fake. She had the twenty-foot length of rope coiled neatly at her feet, out of view, ready to be wrapped around the mannequin's neck and tied to the rail of the walkway at precisely the correct moment. As soon as no cars were in view from either direction, she would walk fifty feet out on the bridge, tie the knot, throw the body over the side, and hurry back to the shadows, where Mario would pick her up. She strained to see up the bluff over her left shoulder to Third Street. She grinned when she saw

Gard bend over the old junker, and a surge of excitement raced through her body. Then she peered the other direction, where she knew Alex was hiding in the shadow of the warehouse. Her heart dropped again, for he and Trudi were the only ones in real danger of bodily harm. She licked her lips, dry from anxiety, and waited for the time to arrive.

Jeanne Mills sat in the cab of the truck, dividing her attention between the entrance of the police station a block away and the rooting pig in the back end. The station was quiet, with little foot traffic at this time of night. The animal had finally quieted down when Hal gave it a bucket of slop, but periodically it squealed, protesting the tight quarters. Three-quarters of the truck was filled with boxes, wooden crates, and twisted bunches of paper. She grunted in response to a noise from the pig and her husband chuckled. "I should have known Viola Groves would get us into something crazy like this," she remarked.

"Can't blame her," Hal corrected. "It was the young 'un's idea." He lifted his hat and ran his fingers through his hair. "But there's nothing that said we had to do it. You just shove the pig in the lobby of the station house and run back out to that big tree. I'll pick you up as soon as I finish my chore." He nudged his wife affectionately. "Don't think I've had this much fun since our honeymoon."

Jeanne gave him a sideways glance, then stepped out and closed the door quietly. She got a firm grip on the piglet and, looking both ways, scurried across the street, turning back to give him a quick, hurrying gesture with her hand.

Hal Mills drove slowly away, chugging cautiously along Fourth Street, checking his pocket watch as he steered. Everyone ought to be in place by now, waiting to do his job, waiting for the inevitable bedlam it would create. He stopped the truck at the intersection of Fourth and Maine, and nervously glanced down the bluff toward the bridge, but he couldn't see Evangeline Gates, though he knew she was there waiting for his signal. He got out of the cab and walked to the rear of the truck, opened the five-gallon can of kerosene, and poured it over the stack of wood and paper. He stopped and leaned casually against the side of the truck as a car whizzed by, the driver not giving him a moment's notice. He finished his job, studied his surroundings thoroughly, then hastily pushed the stack out of the pickup and into the intersection, making sure the truck was a healthy distance from the pile. He didn't think he was nervous until he struck the first match and saw his hand shaking. Finally, the third match took, and he tossed it on the pile and ran. Behind him, a loud whoosh and burst of light filled the air. Jamming his foot on the accelerator, he chanced a backward look. A huge bonfire lit the intersection, and already people were bursting out of the Cuckoo Clock and the bars and the theater to see what was happening.

The moment Trudi heard the wail of the first police siren, she knew it had started. She rose halfway, staying bent, rubbing her cramped thigh muscles, then headed for the service entrance. Quickly jamming the screwdriver into the padlock, she broke it on the first try and scurried up the four steps toward the kitchen. Pausing inside the hall to get her bearings, she backtracked and started down the basement steps. She wiped the walls with her empty hand, hoping to find a light switch, continuing her forward path in the dark, counting the doors as Alex had told her. At the third one, she turned the knob and pushed the door open.

She could faintly make out the form of the round furnace and the coal room beyond, but little else. She fumbled with the camera clumsily; raising it to her eye, she aimed to the right and snapped. A flash responded, and she gingerly pulled out the used bulb and dropped it, still hot, into her pocket and hurriedly replaced it with another. She aimed blindly to the left and took another picture. Only partially satisfied, she started back up the steps toward the faint light of the first floor.

Feeling her way through the kitchen and the butler's pantry, she didn't emerge into the main hall until she knew she was close to the library. She cocked her head. More sirens could be heard in the distance, signaling trouble in half a dozen different places, enough trouble and enough places to distract the police for at least the next hour. She muttered a swift prayer that no one would be caught, then slipped into the dark library, allowing herself only five minutes to find and retrieve the interesting book she had seen earlier.

The aroma of fresh flowers filled the air of the closed room, and she pictured the huge bouquet that was always on the mantel. She tiptoed to the French doors and very slowly pulled the draperies apart to allow enough moonlight into the room to make her job easier. Turning quickly, she stubbed her toe on the corner of the desk and gasped in pain, biting her lip to keep from yelling out loud. Grimacing silently, she laid the camera on the carpet and fumbled for the pen holder, tipping it until she found the tiny brass key. Her heart raced excitedly as she turned it in the lock of the center drawer and carefully pulled the drawer open, holding her breath. There it was!

She laid the book carefully on the desktop and opened it. Win's handwriting! A private journal! She ran her finger down the first page, and when she found Jackie Davis's name, she knew she had what she had come for. Tucking the book under one arm, she closed the drawer, stooped to pick up the camera, and began tiptoeing toward the French doors.

"Trudi?" Bonnie's soft voice questioned as a bright square of light filled the room from the hall door.

Trudi stopped in her tracks, shifting the journal, trying to make it inconspicuous.

"Did you take the journal?" Bonnie asked simply. Trudi's shoulders sagged, and she held her breath as she turned around to face Win's sister.

"You knew about it?" Trudi looked her friend in the eye. Bonnie simply nodded slowly and sadly. "Are you going to tell on me?"

"What are you going to do with it?" Bonnie wanted to know.

Trudi looked long and hard at the young woman, a woman who only recently had had to endure the heartbreak of a lost love. She wasn't sure how much more shock Bonnie could stand, but at the same time, she felt the woman didn't deserve to be lied to. "I am taking it to Phillip Gates. He will decide what to do with it."

Bonnie remained silent and still for what seemed an eternity, then stepped inside the library and closed the door. "Do you love Phillip Gates?"

Trudi's heart sank, and she hated, absolutely hated to answer, knowing the pain it would cause. "Yes, I do," she finally responded honestly.

"I loved Gardner, too." Bonnie's voice was barely audible and her words made Trudi wonder what direction their conversation was going. She swallowed hard and broke out in a chilling sweat, feeling the dampness under her armpits. One raised word from Bonnie would bring the servants running, and quite possibly even Win. It would be impossible for Trudi to explain her presence. The room was dark again and Trudi could not see her expression, but she saw Bonnie walk to a chair and sit down, her soft white lawn nightgown billowing out around her. She folded her hands in her lap and bowed her head for the briefest of moments, then took a huge breath.

"I believe you are doing the Lord's work. No one will ever know from me that you were here." Her voice was almost a whisper. Tears of gratitude sprang to Trudi's eyes, and she hurried to Bonnie's side, bending to kiss her cheek.

"I know that was a hard decision for you," Trudi replied, softly stroking Bonnie's hand.

"Many times it is hard to do what you know in your heart is right." She waved her hand toward the door. "Now, you better hurry and leave before someone else finds you here."

CHAPTER 39

Alex's ears told him it was time. The strains of police sirens filled the downtown area of St. Louis. He watched as the warehouse guard turned at the sound, his interest piqued as a black and white patrol car sped by on the street at the far end of the warehouse. The man shouldered his rifle and walked in the direction of the commotion, finally breaking into a gallop as the orange-yellow glow of a fire could be seen over the top of the bordering building.

Alex sprinted across the brick pavement and scooted around to the river side of the warehouse. He planted both feet and threw the hook to the top of the building, watching it arc slowly upward. It bounced off a foot from the top, and he had to duck to keep from being hit as it fell with a thud to the ground near his feet. Again he heaved, and this time it caught, with more noise than he wanted. His broad shoulders and compact physique stood him in good stead as he pulled himself hand over hand to the transom. Wrapping the rope around his leg three times, he steadied himself and tried to jimmy the catch of the window. It wouldn't give, cemented by years of paint into a tight seal. He paused, listening to his surroundings. Above and beyond him, he could see the lights of a police car and an ambulance on the street surface of the bridge. A small crowd of people had jumped from their cars, curiously watching as the police attempted to retrieve what seemed to be a suicide. He took a chance. He turned his head, squeezed his eyes shut, and rammed his elbow into the glass, breaking it with the first try. Only one big shard of glass fell to the floor of the warehouse, tinkling with a merry sound as it broke again into smaller pieces. Alex cursed, hoping there was no one inside the building, then began pulling at the triangles of broken glass that remained in the frame. One by one he yanked them out and threw them over his shoulder to fall in the weeds at his feet.

Then he noticed the smell, not unlike sauerkraut cooking. A still! They hadn't expected this, thinking instead that the warehouse was used only for storing smuggled liquor. I've got to get a picture of this, he thought. Positioning himself with care, he grunted his body halfway through the window, then stopped to survey.

The perimeter of the building was lined with legitimate manufactured goods, crates from the Stevens family cast-iron stove company. But they were only a flimsy front, for lining the inside of the square were thousands of crates of imported liquor, and inside that was a massive still, the size of a blast furnace. Only a faint light glowed from three bare bulbs hanging from long cords, and Alex worried that the flash of his camera would be too meager for the film to pick up any image. But he had to hurry. Everyone was to get his job done in five minutes and move away, and precious minutes had already been wasted. He didn't have time to jump inside, so he leaned as far forward as possible and took the first picture. The pop of the camera and its pathetic light upset him, but he continued, taking as many pictures as he dared.

"What the hell!" An angry voice echoed up from below. Startled, Alex drew back, hitting his head on the window's edge, jerking the bulky camera out of sight. He felt a burning sensation on the inside of his arm, but ignored it, letting his body slide down the rope until he hit the ground with a thud. He hesitated, wondering for a second if he should take the time to retrieve the telltale rope. He decided against it, and ran full force, his head down, toward the brush-covered bluff where he had originally hidden. He jumped to the top of the wall and dove into the thick brush just as a bullet ricocheted off the stones, and he heard the blast of the gun. Scrambling frantically, he emerged on Second Street only feet from his father's idling car, the back door standing open, waiting for him.

"Blood!" Evangeline Gates gasped. "You're hurt!"

Phillip Gates had rarely had such a hard time containing himself. He was overjoyed by the gift of the account book Jackie had brought in, and he had to tell someone. The four plain walls of the hospital room were restraining him almost beyond endurance. He had tried calling everyone with whom he could share the news.

What were they all so busy with? Gardner didn't answer. Nancy Neumann didn't answer. He was running his hands through his hair impatiently when the door swung open, and Linda Carter came sweeping in, her peculiar pigeon-toed gait lost in the dramatic movement. Behind her she pulled Jolene and John Flanagin, whose compressed lips and downcast eyes revealed their extreme reluctance at being in his presence.

"So sorry to hear of your surgery." Linda smacked the air near his cheek, her whiskey breath making him cringe. She still held Jolene's hand, pulling her to stand next to the bed. The large, imposing woman seemed uncharacteristically docile as she stood, her head turned away from his eyes, her shoulders sagging. "We've come to say goodbye." Linda smiled her most charming smile. "And Jolene and John want to shake hands and make up before we go, don't you, darlings?" Jolene's jaw jutted sideways, and she gave Gates a pained look, hoping he would understand her reluctance. John was the first to offer his hand.

"We've been on opposite sides of the fence with the strike," Jolene said, offering her hand for a shake, "but I wanted you to know I admire your integrity and commitment." Gates took her hand in a brief, firm connection, but said nothing. She looked down at her feet before continuing, "And I want you to know that it was Winslow Stevens's idea to bring in the Pinkertons, and he's the one paying their salaries."

That piece of news heartened Gates, and he sat up straighter. "Would you be willing to testify to that in court?" He stared at both of the Flanagins, making them squirm beneath his penetrating glare. But they shook their heads in a definite, unhesitating refusal. "What if he can be linked to the murder of the Pinkerton?" he asked bluntly.

"*Especially* if he can be linked to the murder." Jolene looked back at him steadily now, and he realized she knew more than she would ever say. "It all got more violent than I ever thought it would. I'm sorry, really sorry."

The sounds of a police car's siren and the lights of an ambulance on the street below didn't draw a second glance from any of the four in the room. Linda broke in, "I came to tell you, also, that you didn't fool me with the gifts and the dates and dinner and all that silly stuff." Gates remained silent but lifted his eyebrows questioningly. "Oh, I know how you feel about Trudi Groves. No one who is in the same room with you two can miss it. You two are just so . . ." She flitted her hand through the air. "So magnetic. The sparks just fly." Gates shrugged, a chagrined smile on his face. "But now my really big news. Bill, my Bill, is arriving back in town tomorrow morning!"

Gates cocked his head, not knowing what to say, not knowing if this was good news or bad. Linda grinned at him, a lopsided drinking grin. "I know what you're thinking. I called him and we talked for thirty minutes. He said he loved me"—she toed the floor like an embarrassed child—"he said together we could handle anything, even Lita!" Everyone chuckled at that remark. "I have you and Trudi to thank for giving me the courage to call him. If you two can make it work, so can Bill and I. You made us realize how much we love each other."

Before she could say any more, Jolene peeked through a crack in the door, then signaled to John, who pulled champagne glasses from the bulky pockets of his coat while Linda opened the wine bottle with practiced ease. "On last toast," she said, offering a glass to Gates. "We leave in one week for Florida to start a new life."

Gates's eyebrows rose in surprise.

"This strike business has been dirtier than we ever imagined," John explained. "We've got the company up for sale and we're going to the Miami area. It's *the* hot boomtown right now. We'll all start new and fresh. Whatever business we get into, Bill Jefferson will be our top accountant."

Gates's eyes darted from one to the other and rested on Linda Carter. Her smile was radiant, expectant, and hopeful. This had to be a tough move for her to make, one that called for real determination. He was happy for her, and sincerely wished her the best.

When three more police cars sped by, their sirens whining, all four in the hospital room totally ignored them, so overwhelmed were they with their newfound camaraderie as they touched glasses in a hearty salute to each other.

Trudi jumped out of her car and pulled the garage doors open, grunting with the effort. "Gunther! Ingram! Get down here," she yelled up to the servants' quarters, clapping her hands for added emphasis. When the two men came clamoring down the steps, she pointed to the family cars. "Move 'em out. Park them in the drive. Leave the garage clear for others that will be here soon." The two men looked at each other, but did her bidding, then stood sentinel along with Trudi until first Mario Badamo's old truck, then Hal Mills's pickup, and finally Grams's Ford chugged into the berths, and the double doors were pulled shut behind them. Trudi did a quick head count, then led the excited crew in the servants' entrance of her parents' home.

Barner Groves poked his head into the hall, his glasses on the tip of his nose, the newspaper crumpled under one arm. "What in the world—?" he started before being cut off by his daughter.

"Daddy, I'll explain later. Would you just call Dr. Hildearde to come over? Alex needs some stitches for a cut on his arm." Groves's mouth worked open and closed wordlessly he stood watching his mother and daughter pull off their scarves and comb their hair in the hall mirror. Evangeline Gates smoothed her dress down and regained her regal poise before his eyes. Hal and Jeanne Mills disappeared into the kitchen to wash clean of pig slop and kerosene.

"Barner, if she said she will explain, then she will." Trudi's mother stood behind her husband, implacably calm in the midst of the mayhem. She cradled baby Julia comfortably in one arm as she reached for the bellpull with the other. "Jessica, go upstairs with Alex and wait for the doctor. The rest of you, come with me." She led the way into the parlor, making sure everyone was comfortable before turning to her daughter.

"We have been gathering evidence that we think will end the strike." Trudi tried to be succinct as she glanced around the room, drawing support from the nods of the others. "Some of the things we did were a little . . ." Her voice trailed off.

"Illegal," Grams finished for her, ignoring her son's groan.

"But necessary," Evangeline Gates added.

"Now we need a place to rest for a few minutes. It may not be wise to go to Grams's house just yet." She smiled sweetly at her parents.

"Does this have anything to do with all the police sirens we've been hearing for the last half hour?" her father asked, controlling himself with effort. The culprits all shook their heads, tiny, incriminating little shakes.

"Hattie," Madeleine Groves spoke to the maid, who stood wide-eyed in the doorway, "bring glasses of lemonade, iced tea, cups of coffee, anything that's ready. And cookies or cake, too. Quickly!" She seemed to sense the immediacy of the situation before her husband. "Oh, and call Dr. Hildegarde back and tell her to come to the side entrance." Trudi grinned broadly at her mother, grateful for her unquestioning support.

Madeleine Groves indicated the piano. "Do you play, Evangeline?" When Mrs. Gates said yes, Madeleine indicated that she should begin, then motioned Jeanne Mills, who'd returned from the kitchen, to stand beside her and sing as she played a pleasant little hymn. Practically gra bing the refreshments out of Hattie's hands when the maid returned, she commanded, "Now, eat, everyone. Fast!"

When the police car pulled to a stop in front of the house, the two officers respectfully took off their hats, intimidated by the lions, if not by the sheer size of the home. The door was answered by Madeleine Groves, a cool look of irritation clear on her face, but she graciously invited them into the imposing entrance hall.

"Excuse me, ma'am." The man rolled his hat in his hand. "But I wonder if you could tell me the whereabouts of a Mrs. Viola Groves, and a Mr. Hal Mills?"

"I certainly can, officer," she responded calmly, "but first I have to ask why you would want to know."

"Well, it seems there was a disturbance downtown tonight, and their cars were seen in the vicinity." He craned his neck in the direction of the parlor, where the piano music grew louder and the conversation more animated.

"What's going on here?" Barner Groves strode into the hall, puffing his chest out in indignation.

"Something about your mother's car, dear. It seems she was seen downtown tonight."

"That's impossible!" Groves huffed, throwing the doors to the parlor completely open to reveal a warm, comfortable family tableau. "These are my guests, and they've been here since before dinner. I can attest to that personally." The policemen's eyes traveled the full circuit of the room; then they looked at each other helplessly.

"Seems to have been some mistake," the first one muttered as they backed out of the house.

The Groveses' guests just managed to contain themselves until the police car pulled slowly away before they began laughing and slapping each other, with a few hugs thrown in for good measure. Trudi hugged her mother and father especially hard.

"Good evening, Mrs. Carter." Lita Carter's face paled and she put a hand protectively over her heart. William Jefferson stood squarely under the porch light, when she had thought for months that he was out of her life for good.

365

"May I come in? I want to speak to you alone, before Linda arrives."

He stepped into the room confidently, removed his cloth cap, and sat down without invitation. "Linda doesn't know I'm here and if you cooperate, she will never know I've been here, because I won't tell her." The woman stared at him wordlessly, trying to regain her composure as he spoke. "You know my father was a policeman?" She nodded mutely. "I understand that you have questioned his honesty."

Lita Carter thought she would swoon. She gripped the arms of the chair as the blood drained from her head. She had never had to face up to her silly or malicious words before.

"It might interest you to know that I have found out that my father *was* on the take." Jefferson's eyes never wavered from hers and he noticed the small recovery of her confidence as her eyes narrowed and a smug smile played at the corners of her mouth, but he dashed it immediately. "Among others who paid him to keep quiet about their activities was your husband."

The breath left Lita Carter so forcibly that it could be heard across the room. Jefferson continued his attack. "Your husband sold liquor in his stores quite legally for 'medicinal purposes,' but he sold such vast quantities that it caught my father's eye. Your husband was making a small fortune from his illegal sales. How do you think he was able to expand to three stores in only two years? Irving Carter paid my father $100 every week not to report him." He was silent for a moment, allowing his news to soak into her narrow skull. Only when she began to open her mouth to protest did he speak again. "If you doubt me, I can bring in my father's records—which, of course, can also be made public."

He took a deep breath before continuing in a low voice. "I am here to pick up Linda. We will be leaving town to begin a new life. We hope to do it with your blessings, but we will do it without them if we have to." He stood up, put his hat back on, and walked to the door. "Good night." He closed the door softly behind himself.

* * *

Bonnie Stevens was on her knees at her bedside, praying for God's guidance, when she heard Winslow's car roar up the drive and slide to a stop. She hurried downstairs and found him in the library, his clothes mussed, his hair windblown, his face frantic as he rifled through his desk drawers.

"It's gone! I can't believe it! They got the warehouse! They got the journal!" He was shouting, not even aware of her presence as he turned in desperate circles like a wild animal.

"Winslow?" she whispered. He jumped, startled by the sound.

"Get out of here!" he ranted, waving his arms. "Just get the hell out of here!" She turned and ran into the hall and up the stairs to her bedroom, pressing her body against the door, waiting for her pounding heart to calm down.

Then she heard a second car coming slowly, confidently up the drive. She scurried to the window and pulled back the drapes, trying to see, but it was already out of view. She ran to the closet and pulled out a robe, pushing her arms into the sleeves, and rushed back to the door. In the hall she slowed down, tiptoeing slowly to the railing of the curved staircase. The bell hadn't rung, but the front door stood wide open. Unsure, frightened, she held the railing with both hands and slowly started down the steps. Halfway down she heard a pop, a loud cracking sound not unlike a firecracker. But her breath caught. She knew better, and when the tall, swarthily handsome man stepped out of the library, her heart stopped.

Sully Bozkur didn't blink an eye when he saw her. He walked slowly, and the gun, still smoking, was in his gloved hand held low against his side. He didn't look around, merely strode past the terrified butler, through the open door, and into the waiting car.

The Green Gang's retribution had begun.

Only one other crime of consequence occurred that night, and it was not discovered until the next morning. The police, harried to distraction by Trudi's harmless planned chaos, could have done nothing to prevent it, since they

HIGH SOCIETY

were up against a cool professional killer, so good at his job that he lived to a comfortable old age basking in the sun of the new mecca of the rich and infamous, Miami, Florida.

Sully Bozkur had instructions to wipe out Winslow Stevens and any of his cohorts who might profit by his demise. Bozkur had three people in mind besides Stevens, but found only one before he cut short his plans, pestered beyond endurance by the ubiquitous police. He was more than a little unsettled, for he had been led to believe that St. Louis was a sleepy river town with a passive patrol force that made a habit of looking the other way. But tonight the cops were everywhere, running on foot, careening around in their patrol cars, frantically answering one call after another at a variety of landmarks all over town.

After doing his job at Stevens's house, he had located the car as expected outside the Cuckoo Clock, and had restlessly staked it out until the woman came out, said her good-byes to two friends, and got in to drive away, none too steadily. He waited until the car turned onto a deserted industrial street before he had his driver pull immediately next to its driver. He saw the usual surprised look on the face of his victim as he poked the machine gun's barrel out his window and let fire.

Linda Carter's first thought as she saw the barrel of the gun was her last: I'm going to die. Mother will be so embarrassed.

It was the car that misled him, the big black Buick with the license plate issued to Jackie Davis. He knew the car, not the woman, so when he took aim and fired, he did so with smug satisfaction that he had at least gotten half the job done before he wisely decided to flee St. Louis, whose police had the town blanketed. Instead, he headed back to the safe anonymity of Chicago.

Leo Elderbrake and Bucky Bathshelder unknowingly had Trudi Gates and her plan of controlled mayhem to thank for their lives.

By midnight, the jubilant group of conspirators gathered at the Groves mansion had calmed down, convinced they had enough evidence to pin Winslow Stevens.

"There is just one more place I have to go tonight," Trudi announced. Heads swiveled, but everyone knew better than to try to keep her away from Phillip Gates.

She felt confident sneaking in the service entrance of St. Mary's Hospital, and when she tiptoed into his darkened room and slid under the sheets beside him, Phillip Gates only grinned, immune to any more surprises from her. They wrapped their arms around each other and kissed, a long, patient kiss that healed many wounds. He buried his head in her neck and held her close, breathing the fragrance that was so definitely her own. She held his face in her hands and kissed him again, then sighed deeply. This was where she wanted to be. As close to him as she could get.

"You're never going to believe what I did tonight," she whispered.

"Yes, I will." He smiled before smothering her with another kiss.

EPILOGUE

Trudi trudged through the snow up the sidewalk to her little bungalow. She stopped and turned full circle, savoring the beauty of the day. Wet, heavy snow still clung to the trees and bushes, their branches glistening low with the weight of a thick coat of crystalline ice. It was a magical moment before the warm sunshine melted the scene away. It was a wonderland, she thought, a gloriously beautiful wonderland. It ought to be a good Christmas for the family, for the whole town, especially since the strike had been settled two months before to everyone's satisfaction. Alex hadn't gone back to work for the quarry. He was in school at Washington University, studying prelaw. Neither he nor Jessica would say where they'd gotten the money, but Trudi suspected it was from Phillip Gates. That man would never get rich if he kept giving it away, Trudi thought with a chuckle, walking again toward the house.

She wondered if Grams, Mario, and the Millses' dancing class would be called off tonight because of the slippery streets. Their rendition of the Castle Walk last week had had everyone in stitches. Grams had been puffed up like a pigeon ever since Mario had proposed to her. "Old man," she'd said, "I wouldn't make a good wife for you. But I'd sure make a good friend." Trudi smiled, wondering what the next few months would bring.

Other than a new baby, that is. Janet and Fulton were happy as clams, painting the bedroom next to theirs in the huge farmhouse a neutral yellow to receive a boy or girl baby with equal grace, busy every other minute of the day with the ever-increasing brood of collie pups they bred for show and sale. Evangeline Gates's porch had been repaired before the first snowfall, in time to show it off to the book review club she had chartered.

Trudi stamped her boots on the porch and opened the door, setting the groceries down on the hall table. She wiped her dripping nose on the back of her glove before shrugging off her coat. The house was quiet, which she welcomed. She'd start a fire and get some mulled wine warming, then have a few peaceful moments to herself before starting her gift-wrapping. She was tired, having spent the majority of the day with city and county officials making sure everything conformed to regulations for the old folks' home she was establishing.

Win Stevens had been true to his word on one thing, at least. The deed to the rambling art deco home overlooking the river had been in Trudi's name, as well as a substantial portion of his cash estate. She didn't want either, and was vociferous about not accepting them. Evangeline Gates had come up with the idea for the home for the elderly. The very first beneficiary to move into the home had been Lita Carter, her dreams of being supported by Linda's rich husband, as well as other, more noble dreams for her daughter, dashed at the time of Linda's death. Win's cash would be used to endow the home, and Trudi had agreed to sit on its board of directors, a move that she hadn't yet realized, was the beginning of her active participation in sanctioned community activities.

She smiled when she picked up the mail. In it was the handwritten note she had been expecting for weeks now. Bonnie Stevens and Bill Jefferson had married quietly over Thanksgiving weekend. They had been an immense comfort to each other in the months after the double tragedy of the deaths of her brother and his fiancée, drawing solace from each other's strength. Only those closest to them knew how fond they had grown of one another, and most of the town would be surprised by their announcement.

A muffled knock made her turn, and she took the telegram from the Western Union messenger with a smile. "Merry Christmas," she yelled after him.

I RISKED IT STOP MARRIED DEC 1 STOP NEVER HAPPIER STOP THANK YOU STOP LOVE BAREND VON CLOUS

Trudi clasped the paper to her chest and turned in a circle of joy. Then she pulled her coat back on, stuffed her gloves and boots back on, and ran six blocks to the nearest Western Union office, her fingers numb as she wrote out the message for the clerk to send.

ME TOO STOP TRUDI GROVES-GATES